"It is kind of you to show concern, Detective King."

"Please, call me Samuel."

"Samuel." Her soft voice drew his attention. "Who are you, Samuel? You dress like an Amish man. Our men are not detectives." Her eyes studied him.

"I assure you, Sarah, I am a detective. I was raised Amish. I left my home in Ohio and joined the police force about fifteen years ago."

"You are very far from home, aren't you?" she asked.

"I wanted to get as far away as I could." Sam shrugged. "Memories aren't always good."

Her eyes shimmered, and he fought not to lose himself in their beauty.

"I wish I had some memories," she whispered.

"Memories aren't all they're cracked up to be, Sarah. I have memories, but no one to love me. You don't have memories, but you have people who love you very much."

Her beauty spoke to him, stirring feelings better left dormant. Stepping back, he reminded himself of his own rules.

D0324716

Diane Burke is an award-winning author who has had seven books published with Love Inspired Suspense. She won first place in the Daphne du Maurier Award for Excellence in Mystery and Suspense and finaled in the ACFW Carol Award for book of the year. When she isn't writing, she enjoys taking walks with her dog, reading, and spending time with friends and family. She loves to hear from readers and can be reached at diane@dianeburkeauthor.com. She can also be found on Twitter and Facebook.

Debby Giusti is an award-winning Christian author who met and married her military husband at Fort Knox, Kentucky. Together they traveled the world, raised three wonderful children and have now settled in Atlanta, Georgia, where Debby spins tales of mystery and suspense that touch the heart and soul. Visit Debby online at debbygiusti.com, blog with her at seekerville.blogspot.com and craftieladiesofromance.blogspot.com, and email her at Debby@DebbyGiusti.com.

DIANE BURKE

&

USA TODAY Bestselling Author

DEBBY GIUSTI

Dangerous Amish Memories

2 Thrilling Stories

Hidden in Plain View and
Her Forgotten Amish Past

LOVE INSPIRED
INSPIRATIONAL ROMANCE

If you purchased this book without a cover you should be aware that this book is stolen property. It was reported as "unsold and destroyed" to the publisher, and neither the author nor the publisher has received any payment for this "stripped book."

LOVE INSPIRED®
INSPIRATIONAL ROMANCE

ISBN-13: 978-1-335-47327-1

Dangerous Amish Memories

Copyright © 2022 by Harlequin Enterprises ULC

Hidden in Plain View
First published in 2013. This edition published in 2022.
Copyright © 2013 by Diane Burke

Her Forgotten Amish Past
First published in 2019. This edition published in 2022.
Copyright © 2019 by Deborah W. Giusti

All rights reserved. No part of this book may be used or reproduced in any manner whatsoever without written permission except in the case of brief quotations embodied in critical articles and reviews.

This is a work of fiction. Names, characters, places and incidents are either the product of the author's imagination or are used fictitiously. Any resemblance to actual persons, living or dead, businesses, companies, events or locales is entirely coincidental.

For questions and comments about the quality of this book, please contact us at CustomerService@Harlequin.com.

Harlequin Enterprises ULC
22 Adelaide St. West, 41st Floor
Toronto, Ontario M5H 4E3, Canada
www.LoveInspired.com

Printed in U.S.A.

Recycling programs for this product may not exist in your area.

CONTENTS

HIDDEN IN PLAIN VIEW

Diane Burke

This book is dedicated to the family and friends who offered nothing but love and open arms to both my son and me during our long-overdue reunion.

I also wish to thank Rachel Burkot, my new editor, for jumping in midstream and doing a phenomenal job of helping me make this book the best it could be.

Don't be afraid, for I am with you.
Don't be discouraged, for I am your God.
I will strengthen you and help you.
I will hold you up with my victorious right hand.
—*Isaiah* 41:10

Prologue

Mount Hope, Lancaster County, PA

Sarah Lapp wasn't thinking about guns or violence or murder on this unseasonably warm fall day. She was thinking about getting her basket of apples and cheese to the schoolhouse.

Pedaling her bicycle down the dirt road, she spotted the silhouettes of her in-laws, Rebecca and Jacob, standing close together in the distant field.

Sarah knew when she'd married their son, Peter, that she had been fortunate to have married her best friend.

But sometimes…

She glanced at them again.

Sometimes she couldn't help but wonder what true love felt like.

Chiding herself for her foolish notions, she turned her attention back to the road. A sense of unease taunted her as she approached the school. The children should be out in the yard on their first break of the day, but the ball field was empty.

She hit the kickstand on her bike and looked around the yard.

Peter's horse and wagon were tethered to the rail, a water bucket beside them. Children's bicycles haphazardly dotted the lawn. The bats for the morning ball game rested against the bottom of the steps.

Everything appeared normal.

But it didn't *feel* normal.

Sarah climbed the steps and moved cautiously across the small landing, noting the open windows and the curtains fluttering in the breeze.

Silence.

Her pulse pounded. *When was a room full of children ever silent?*

She'd barely turned the knob when the door was pulled wide with such force that Sarah was propelled forward and sprawled across the floor.

Peter started in her direction.

"Stop right there, Peter, unless you want to see your wife hurt." The speaker was John Zook, a cousin who had recently returned to the Amish way of life. He pulled Sarah roughly to her feet.

"John?" Sarah gasped when she saw a gun peeking out from the folds of the carpentry apron tied around his waist.

Immediately Peter and the teacher, Hannah, gathered the children together and took a protective stance in front of them, shielding their view of the room.

Sarah stood alone in the middle of the room and faced the gunman. She saw fear in his hooded eyes— fear and something else. Something hard and cold.

"John, why are you doing this terrible thing?" she asked.

"Is he out there? Did you see him?"

"Who, John? Who do you think is out there?" Sarah tried to understand what was frightening him.

"What do you want?" Peter's voice commanded from the back of the room.

"I want you to shut up," John snapped in return.

Sarah glanced at the children and marveled at how well behaved and silent they were. John had made sure the adults had seen his weapon, but Sarah was fairly certain the children had not. They seemed more confused and curious than frightened.

John lifted the curtain. "He's out there. I know it."

"John, I did not pass anyone on the road. It was just me." Sarah kept her voice calm and friendly. "We will help you if you will tell us what it is that frightens you so."

When John looked at them, Sarah was taken aback by the absolute terror she saw in his eyes. "He's going to kill me," he whispered. "There will be no place I can hide."

Peter, his patience running thin, yelled at the man. "You are starting to scare the children. I am going to let them out the back door and send them home."

"Nobody moves," John ordered.

Feeling the tension escalate, Sarah tried to find words to defuse the situation. "Peter is right. Whatever's wrong, we will help you. But you must let the children leave."

John shot a furtive glance at the group huddled in the corner and then nodded. "All right. Get them out of here, but make it quick."

Peter ushered the children outside, with whispers to each child to run straight home. When the teacher came up behind the last child, Peter ignored her protests and shoved her to safety, too.

John shoved a felt pouch at Sarah. "Hide this and don't give it to anyone but me. Understand?"

The heavy and cumbersome bag felt like rocks or marbles were nestled inside. She used several straight pins to bind it to her waistband.

Suddenly the sound of boots pounding against the wooden steps filled the air.

"Shut up. Don't make a sound!" John ordered. With trembling hands, he aimed his gun and waited for the door to open. But it didn't.

Instead, bullets slammed *through* the door.

"Sarah, get down!" Peter yelled from across the room.

Pieces of wood from the walls and desks, as well as chunks of chalkboard, splintered as each bullet reached a target.

John Zook grabbed his shoulder. Then doubled over and clutched his stomach, groaning in pain.

The door banged open and slammed against the wall. A stranger entered, this one much taller, with darkness in his eyes that cemented Sarah's feet to the floor in fear.

"Hello, John. Didn't expect to see me, did you?"

The slighter man's body shook. "I was gonna call and let you know where I was, Jimmy. Just as soon as I found a safe place for us to hide out."

"Is that so? Well, I saved you the trouble. Give me my diamonds."

Diamonds?

Instantly, Sarah's fingers flew to the pouch hidden in the folds of her skirt.

"You've got until the count of three. One."

"I don't have them. I have to go get them."

"Two."

"I don't have them!" John's voice came out in an almost hysterical pitch.

"Please, Jimmy, honest." John pulled Sarah in front of him. "She has them. I gave them to her."

Sarah looked into the stranger's face, and evil looked back.

"Three."

The sudden burst of gunfire shook Sarah to her core.

A small, round hole appeared in John's forehead. His expression registered surprise and his hand, which had been painfully gripping Sarah's arm, opened. He fell to the floor.

The loud, piercing sound of a metal triangle rent the air. The children had reached their homes. Help was on the way.

The shooter leered at Sarah. "Let's take a look and see what you're hiding in that skirt, shall we?"

"No!" Peter yelled, and ran toward her.

The intruder fired.

Her husband's body jerked not once but twice as he grabbed his chest and collapsed in a heap on the floor.

"Peter!"

Sarah's heart refused to accept what her mind knew was fact. Peter was dead.

Before she could drop to his side, something slammed into the left side of her head. Another blow to her arm. To her back. Pain seized her breath. Weakened her knees. Crumpled her to the floor.

She stretched her right arm out toward Peter, their fingers almost touching as she slid into blessed oblivion.

Chapter One

Where am I?

Sarah Lapp lay on a bed with raised metal rails. She noted a darkened television screen bracketed to the opposite wall. A nightstand and recliner beside the bed.

I'm in a hospital.

She tried to sit up but couldn't. She was hooked up to machines. Lots of them. Fear pumped her heart into overdrive.

Why am I here?

Again she tried to move, but her body screamed in protest.

Burning pain. Throbbing pain.

Searing the skin on her back. Pulsing through her arm and gathering behind her eyes.

She tried to raise her left arm to touch her forehead but it felt heavy, weighted down, lost in its own gnawing sea of hurt. She glanced down and saw it bandaged and held against her chest by a blue cloth sling.

I've injured my arm. But how? Why can't I remember? And why do I feel so scared?

She took a deep breath.

Don't panic. Take your time. Think.

Once more she inhaled, held it for a second, and forced herself to ever so slowly release it. Repeating the process a couple more times helped her regain a sense of calm.

Okay. She could do this.

She opened her eyes and stared into the darkness.

"Sarah?"

Sarah? Is that my name?

Why can't I remember?

Her heart almost leaped from her chest when one of the shadows moved.

The man had been leaning against the wall. She hadn't seen him standing in the shadows until he stepped forward. He obviously wasn't a doctor. His garb seemed familiar yet somehow different. He wore black boots, brown pants held up with suspenders and a white shirt with the sleeves rolled to his elbows. He carried a straw hat.

"I thought I heard you stirring." He approached her bed and leaned on the side rail. She found the deep timbre of his voice soothing.

The faint glow from the overhead night-light illuminated his features. She stared at his clean-shaven face, the square jaw, the tanned skin, his intense brown eyes. She searched for some form of recognition but found none.

"I'm glad you're awake." He smiled down at her.

She tried to speak but could only make hoarse, croaking sounds.

"Here, let me get you something to drink." He pushed a button, which raised the head of her bed. He lifted a cup and held it to her lips. There was something intimate and kind in the gesture, and although she didn't recognize this man, she welcomed his presence.

Gratefully, she took a sip, enjoying the soothing coolness of the liquid as it slid over her parched lips and trickled down her throat. When he moved the cup away, she tried again.

"Who…who are you?"

His large hand gently cupped her fingers. She found the warmth of his touch comforting. His brown shaggy hair brushed the collar of his shirt. Tiny lines crinkled the skin at the sides of his eyes.

"My name is Samuel, and I'm here to help you."

Her throat felt like someone had shredded her vocal cords. Her mouth was so dry that even after the sip of water, she couldn't gather enough saliva for a good spit. When she did speak, her voice reflected the strain in a hoarse, barely audible whisper.

"Where… What…" She struggled to force the words out.

"You're in a hospital. You've been shot."

Shot!

No wonder she had felt so afraid when he'd moved out of the shadows. She might not remember the incident, but some inner instinct was still keeping her alert and wary of danger.

"Can you tell me what you remember?" There was kindness in his eyes and an intensity that she couldn't identify.

She shook her head.

"Do you remember being in the schoolhouse when the gunman entered? Did you get a good look at him?"

Schoolhouse? Gunman?

Her stomach lurched, and she thought she was going

to be sick. Slowly, she moved her head back and forth again.

"How about before the shooting? Your husband was inside the building constructing bookshelves. Do you remember bringing a basket of treats for the children?"

His words caused a riotous tumble of questions in her mind. She had a husband? Who was he? *Where* was he? She tried to focus her thoughts. This man just told her she'd been shot inside a school. Had anyone else been hurt? Hopefully, none of the children.

"Hus…husband?"

"Sarah. There's no easy way to tell you. Your husband was killed in the shooting."

The room started to spin. Sarah squeezed her eyes shut.

"I'm so sorry. I wish there had been an easier way to break the news." His deep, masculine voice bathed her senses with sympathy and helped her remain calm. "I hate to have to question you right now, but time is of the essence." The feel of his breath on her cheek told her he had stepped closer. "I need you to tell me what you remember—what you saw that day, before things other people tell you cloud your memories."

A lone tear escaped and coursed its way down her cheek at the irony of it all.

"Can you tell me anything about that day?" he prodded. "Sometimes the slightest detail that you might think is unimportant can turn into a lead. If you didn't see the shooter's face, can you remember his height? The color of his skin? What he wore? Anything he might have said?"

He paused, giving her time to collect her thoughts, but only moments later the questions came again.

"If you don't remember seeing anything, use your other senses. Did you hear anything? Smell anything?"

She opened her eyes and stared into his. "I told you." She choked back a sob. "I can't…can't remember. I can't remember anything at all."

His wrinkled brow and deep frown let her know this wasn't what he had expected.

"Maybe you should rest now. I'll be back, and we can talk more later."

Sarah watched him cross to the door. Once he was gone, she stared at her hand and wondered why the touch of a stranger had made her feel so safe.

Sam stood in the corridor and tried to collect his thoughts.

Sarah.

He hadn't expected to be so touched by her unfortunate circumstances. He had a policy to never let emotions play a part when he was undercover or protecting a witness. Sarah Lapp was a job, nothing more, and he had no business feeling anything for her one way or the other.

But he had to admit there was something about her. He'd been moved by the vulnerability he saw in her face, the fear he read in her eyes. She was terrified. Yet she had stayed calm, processing everything he had to tell her with quiet grace.

She'd been visibly upset when Sam had told her about the shooting. She'd seemed shocked when he informed her that her husband had been killed. But learning that she had had a husband at all seemed to affect her the most.

He hadn't had an opportunity yet to talk with Sarah's

doctors about the full extent of her injuries. Was she really suffering from memory loss, and if so, was it a temporary setback or a permanent situation?

Sam often relied heavily on his gut. His instincts this time were warning him that he had just stepped into a much more complicated situation than he had first thought.

He needed to talk with the doctor.

When he glanced down the hall, he saw Dr. Clark, as well as several members of the police force, including his superior, with three Amish men in tow. Dr. Clark ushered the entire group into a nearby conference room and gestured for Sam to join them.

Once inside, Sam crossed the room and leaned against the far wall. He saw the men shoot furtive glances his way and knew they were confused by his Amish clothing.

He didn't blame them. He was disconcerted by it, too. He hadn't donned this type of clothing for fifteen years. Yet his fingers never hesitated when he fastened the suspenders. The straw hat had rested upon his head like it was meant to be there.

Jacob Lapp, identifying himself as the bishop of their community and acting as spokesperson for their group, addressed Captain Rogers.

"We do not understand, sir. Why have you brought us here?"

"Please, gentlemen, have a seat." Captain Rogers gestured toward the chairs around the table. "Dr. Clark wants to update you on Sarah's condition."

They pulled out chairs and sat down.

Dr. Clark spoke from his position at the head of the table. "Sarah is in a very fragile state. She was shot twice in the back, once in the arm and once in the head. She has a long road to recovery, but I believe she *will* recover. To complicate matters, she is suffering from amnesia."

"Will her memory return?" Jacob asked.

"I'm afraid I honestly don't know. Only time will tell."

The man on Jacob's left spoke. "Excuse me, sir. My name is Benjamin Miller. I do not understand this thing you call amnesia. I had a neighbor who got kicked in the head by his mule. He forgot what happened with his mule, but he didn't forget everything else. He still remembered who he was, who his family was. Why can't Sarah?"

The doctor smiled. "It is common for a person not to remember a traumatic event but to remember everything else. What is less common, but still occurs, is a deeper memory loss. Some people forget everything—like Sarah."

"When she gets better, she will remember again, *ya?*" Jacob twirled his black felt hat in circles on the table.

"I hope that once she returns home, familiar surroundings will help, but I cannot promise anything," the doctor replied.

The men looked at each other and nodded.

"There is something else. Sarah is sixteen weeks pregnant."

Sam felt like someone had suddenly punched him in the gut. Wow, this woman couldn't catch a break. As if amnesia, gunshot wounds and widowhood wasn't enough for her to handle. He raised an eyebrow, but steeled himself to show no other reaction to the news.

The doctor waited for the men at the table to digest the information before he locked eyes with Jacob. "Mrs. Lapp has informed me that Sarah has had two prior miscarriages."

Jacob nodded but remained silent. The information regarding this pregnancy seemed to weigh heavily upon him.

"I'm sorry to inform you, Mr. Lapp, that even though she has made it into her second trimester, she still might lose the child. She has experienced severe trauma to her body, and currently she is under emotional stress as well."

"With my son gone, this will be our only grandchild." Jacob's eyes clouded over. "What can we do to help?"

"You can allow me to protect her." Sam pushed away from the wall and approached the table.

The bishop's expression revealed his confusion. "Protect Sarah? I don't understand, sir. The man who hurt Sarah is gone, *ya?* She is safe now." Jacob looked directly at Sam. "Excuse me, sir. We do not recognize you. What community do you call home?"

Captain Rogers nodded permission for Sam to answer the questions.

"My name is Detective Samuel King. Standing to my left is my partner, Detective Masterson. To his right is Special Agent Lopez from the FBI. We believe Sarah is in grave danger."

"From whom?" Benjamin spoke up, gesturing with his arm to the men sitting on either side of him. "Her family? Her friends?"

Sam addressed his words to Bishop Lapp. "Since I was raised Amish, Captain Rogers thought it might be easier for me to blend in with your community as Sarah's protective detail."

All three men gasped, then turned and whispered in their native Pennsylvania German dialect commonly known as Pennsylvania Dutch.

Sam understood not only the words, but also the emotions and objections the men were expressing. The Amish do not care for law enforcement and try to keep themselves separate from the *Englisch* way of life.

"With respect, sir," Jacob said, "although grateful, we do not feel we need your protection, and neither does Sarah."

Sam sighed heavily. "You are wrong." When he had their full attention, he said, "If you do not allow us to help, Sarah will be dead before this week is over, as well as her unborn child and many of the kids who were inside that schoolhouse when the shooting occurred."

Samuel noted the sudden pallor in Jacob's face. He recognized bewilderment in the other men's eyes and glimpsed hesitation in their body language, but they continued to listen.

Sam pulled out a chair and faced the men. He explained about the diamond heist and the murders of the other thieves, which led to the shoot-out in the school.

Matthew Kauffman, the third Amish man in the group, spoke up for the first time. "If you were once Amish, then you know that we cannot allow police to move into our homes. It is not our way."

"I understand your dilemma," Sam responded. "I assure you that although I left my Amish roots behind, I never abandoned my respect for the Amish ways."

"You do not speak like us," Benjamin insisted. "You sound like an *Englischer*."

Sam slipped easily into the lilt of the Pennsylvania Dutch dialect. "Many years of living with the *Englisch,* and you can start to sound like one, ain't so?"

"Why did you leave your home, sir?" Benjamin asked.

Sam took a moment to decide just how much he was willing to share with these men.

"In my youth, I witnessed too many things for a young boy to see. I witnessed theft of Amish goods that went unpunished. I witnessed bullying and cruelty against the Amish people, yet I could not raise my hand to retaliate."

The men nodded.

"I witnessed worse. I witnessed drunken teens race their car into my father's buggy just for the fun of it. My parents did not survive their prank."

Several heartbeats of silence filled the room as everyone present absorbed what he'd said.

"The Amish forgive." Sam shrugged. "I could not. So I left."

"It is difficult sometimes to forgive, to not seek vengeance and to move on with life." Jacob's quiet voice held empathy. His eyes seemed to understand that Sam's emotional wounds had not healed and still cut deep. "I understand how hard it can be. I just lost my only son. But…" He looked Sam straight in the eye. "It is not our place to judge." When he spoke, his voice was soft and sad. "Judgment belongs only to God, *ya?*"

"And vengeance belongs to the Lord, not us," Benjamin Miller added.

"I am not talking about vengeance," Sam said, defending himself. "I am talking about justice."

Jacob scrutinized Sam as if he were trying to determine his character from his words. "How do you know whether what you call justice, Detective King, is what God would call vengeance? Is it not best to leave these matters in God's hands?"

A sad ghost of a smile twisted Sam's lips. "I believe God intended for us to love one another, to help one another. I believe He expects us to protect those who cannot protect themselves. Children. Unborn babies. An innocent woman who doesn't even know the gravity of her loss yet. Isn't that God's will?"

Jacob remained silent and pensive.

Sam had to work hard to control his emotions. There was no place in police work, particularly undercover police work, to let emotions control your actions or thoughts. But he understood these people. He'd been one of them. He knew they were pacifists who refused to fight back. If a gunman walked up and shot them dead on the street, they'd believe it was God's will.

How was he going to make them understand the danger they were in? Or worse, defend against that danger? Jacob was their bishop. He was the one he had to win over. Sam knew the only hope he had of convincing Lapp to go along with the plan was to drive home the pain the man was still feeling from his loss. He challenged him with a hard stare.

"Are you willing to accept responsibility for the deaths of your loved ones, Bishop? Your neighbors' loved ones? To never see your grandchild? To attend the funerals of your neighbors' children? Because you will be killing them just as if you held the gun and shot them yourself."

Sam's voice had a hardened edge, but he made no apologies for his harshness. He had to make these men understand the seriousness of the situation if he stood any chance of saving their lives.

"Please, sir, listen to me," he continued. "A stranger entered your Amish schoolhouse on a beautiful, peaceful spring afternoon. He cared only about diamonds, not about God or the sanctity of life." Sam placed his forearms on the table and leaned closer. "This isn't his first crime. We suspect him of many other crimes, but have been unable to bring him to justice.

"No one who would be able to describe him has lived to talk about it—except Sarah. Don't be fooled. He will return. He will find a way to walk freely among you. He is not above using your children—perhaps killing your children—to accomplish his goals. You will never sense the danger until it is too late."

The three men shot concerned glances at one another.

"Please," Sam pleaded. "Even *with* your help, we cannot promise that he won't succeed. We are chasing a shadow."

Sam paused, letting the men absorb his words. He gestured toward the other law-enforcement officers in the room.

"We are not asking you to take up arms or fight back. But we cannot protect you from the outside alone. If we stand any chance of stopping this man, then we must be close. We must be on the inside. We are asking for your help."

Jacob's head bent, and his lips moved in silent prayer. After a few moments of silence, he wiped a tear from his cheek and turned to the other Amish men.

"How can we not help?" he asked. "This is our Sarah. Hasn't she been hurt enough? These are our children he speaks of. Is it not our duty as parents to protect them?

And what of the innocent child Sarah carries? Must we not protect that child, too?"

"Jacob, you know if this horrible thing he speaks of happens, then it is the will of God." Benjamin's voice was insistent. "We must accept the will of God."

Jacob nodded slowly. "*Ya,* Benjamin, you are right. We must accept the will of God." After a moment, he made eye contact with Benjamin. "Your Mary was in that classroom…and your Daniel and William." Jacob glanced from him to the other man. "Matthew, your children, Emma, Joseph, John, Amos…they were there that terrible day, too." His eyes implored both men. "Are we so eager to let the wolf snatch them away that we stand aside and open the door?"

Benjamin blanched as the realization of what was at stake finally hit him. Visibly shaken, he lowered his head, his voice almost a whisper. "But if it is God's will…"

"I agree. We must accept God's will." Jacob leaned forward and placed his hand on his friend's shoulder. "But I have to ask you, Benjamin, how many detectives do we know who used to be Amish? Maybe sending Samuel to us *is* the will of God."

The men exchanged looks, whispered together in hushed tones and then nodded their heads.

This time, Jacob looked directly at the police captain. "We will agree to this. But please, sir, find the man you seek quickly. We cannot endure this situation for long."

The captain stood and thanked the men for their co-operation. "We will be placing undercover officers in your town. They will deliver your mail, pick up your milk and serve in your local shops and restaurants.

But only one will actually enter your home—Detective Samuel King."

Sam hadn't been back on Amish soil for more than a decade. He'd have to keep his emotions in check, his mind clear and his thoughts logical. A woman's life, and that of her unborn child, were at stake. The gravity of the situation weighed heavily on his shoulders, and he prayed he'd be up to the challenge.

Chapter Two

Sarah stared out the window. It had been one week since the shootings, two days since she'd awakened in this hospital room and they still hadn't caught the shooter.

She watched the people below in the parking lot.

Was he out there? Waiting? Plotting? Biding his time like a poisonous snake in the grass, coiled and ready to strike?

Would he come back for her? And if he did, this time…

Sarah didn't have to remember the past to know that she had no desire to die in the present.

She studied the men passing beneath her window. Did any of them look up in her direction? Was the killer watching her even now?

Fear shuddered through her.

How could she protect herself when she didn't even know what the man who posed a threat looked like? How could she help the police catch him before he could hurt more people if her mind continued to be nothing more than a blank slate?

Her mother-in-law, Rebecca, and the doctor had filled her in on what they knew of the details of that day.

The story they had told her was tragic. But she had no emotional connection to that schoolroom, or to the children who had fled out the back door and summoned help, or, even worse, to the man who had once shared her life and was now dead and buried.

She knew people expected an emotional response from her—tears, at least—but she felt nothing.

Surprise? Yes.

Empathy? Of course.

Pain? Grief?

No. They were the emotions she saw every time she looked at the sadness etched in Rebecca's face. She had lost a son.

Sarah had lost a stranger.

Earlier Rebecca had told Sarah that she'd been raised *Englisch* until the age of eight. Try as she might, she couldn't find any memory of those childhood years.

Following her mother's death, she'd been adopted by her Amish grandmother, who had also passed on years ago. Then she'd come to live with Jacob and Rebecca, embraced the Amish faith and married their son. Sarah found it more difficult to come to terms with the person she was supposed to be than to try to summon grief she couldn't feel.

She was a pregnant Amish widow recovering from multiple gunshot wounds and suffering from amnesia. That was her reality. That was the only world to which she could relate.

She couldn't conjure up the slightest recollection of Peter Lapp. Had he been of average build? Or was he tall? Had he had blond hair like his mother? Or maybe brown?

Rebecca had told her they'd been married five years and were happy together.

Had they been happy together? Were they still as much in love on the day of his death as they'd been the day they married? She hoped so. But can true love be forgotten as easily as a breath of air on a spring day? If they'd been soul mates, shouldn't she feel *something?* Have some sense of loss deep in her being, even if she couldn't remember the features of his face or the color of his hair?

Rebecca had also told her that she'd had two prior miscarriages. Had Sarah told her husband about this pregnancy? Were they happy about this blessing or anxious and fearful that it, too, would fail?

A surge of emotion stole her breath away. It wasn't grief. It was anger.

She wanted to be able to grieve for her husband. She wanted to be able to miss him, to shed tears for *him.* Instead, all she felt was guilt for not remembering the man. Not the sound of his voice. Not the feel of his touch. Not even the memory of his face. What kind of wife was she that a man who had shared her life was nothing more to her now than a story on someone else's lips?

She was no longer a complete human being. She was nothing more than an empty void and had nothing within to draw upon. No feelings for her dead husband. No feelings for an unborn child she hadn't even known she carried. No memories of what kind of person she had been. She was broken, damaged goods and of no use to anyone.

Please, God, help me. Please let me climb out of this dark and frightening place.

In the stillness of her empty room, the tears finally came.

Sam stood up from the chair outside Sarah's door and stretched his legs. Hours had passed since Rebecca had left with Jacob. He hadn't heard a sound lately, and the silence made him uneasy. Quietly, he opened the door and peeked inside.

He was surprised to see Sarah out of bed and standing at the window. Her floor-length robe seemed to swallow up her petite, frail figure. The swish of the door opening drew her attention.

"Hi." Sam stepped into the room. "Are you supposed to be out of bed?"

Sarah offered a feeble smile. "The nurses had me up a few times today. I won't get stronger just lying in bed."

Sam could see she wasn't having an easy time of it. Dark circles colored the skin beneath her eyes in a deep purplish hue. The telltale puffiness told him that she'd been crying. Her sky-blue eyes were clouded over with pain and perhaps even a little fear.

"It is kind of you to show concern, Detective King." Her voice sounded fragile and tired.

"Please, call me Samuel."

He flinched at the sound of his true Amish name slipping from his lips. Donning Amish clothes had returned him to his roots. But the sound of his given name instead of Sam sealed the deal. He had stepped back in time—and it was the last place he wanted to be.

"Samuel." The sound of his name in her soft, feminine voice drew his attention back to her. She smiled again, but it was only a polite gesture. Happiness never lit her eyes. "What can I do for you?"

"I thought I'd poke my head in and make sure you're all right."

"Thank you, but you needn't bother. I'm fine." A shadow crossed her face.

Fine? He didn't think so. Lost in his thoughts, he hadn't noticed the puzzled expression on her face until she questioned him.

"Who are you, Samuel?"

She stood with her back to the window and studied him.

Who was he? He'd told her he was a detective. Was her loss of memory getting worse?

Sarah went right to the point. "You dress like an Amish man. Our men are not detectives." Her eyes squinted as she studied him.

She looked as if she might be holding her breath as she waited for his answer.

"I assure you, Sarah, I am a detective."

"And the Amish clothes? Is it a disguise?"

"Yes—and no. I was raised Amish. I left my home in Ohio and joined the police force about fifteen years ago."

"Ohio? You are very far from home, aren't you?" she asked.

Was that empathy he saw in her eyes? She was feeling sorry for *him*. Didn't that beat all?

"I wanted to get as far away as I could." Sam shrugged, and his mouth twisted into a lopsided grin. "Memories aren't always good."

She pondered his words before she spoke again. "Don't the Amish shun you if you leave?"

He found her words interesting. She could pull the

definition of shunning from her memory banks but talked about it as if it wasn't part of her own culture, as if the term was nothing more than something she had read in a dictionary.

"I have no family to shun me."

The gentlest of smiles teased the corner of her lips. "Everyone has a family at one time or another, Samuel."

Her words hit a tender spot. She was getting much too personal. He didn't want to open that door for her. He didn't want to share that pain. He was acting as her bodyguard, nothing more, and the less emotional connection between them the better.

Attempting to change the subject, he said, "I'm sure you've been up and about enough for one day. Why don't you let me help you get back into bed so you can get some rest."

She allowed him to hold her elbow and support her as she crossed the room. "It must have been difficult for you to leave your Amish religion behind."

Her soft blue eyes stared up at him.

Sam smiled. He was fast learning that she was a stubborn woman, not easily distracted when she wanted to know something, and right now it was obvious that she wanted to know about him.

"I left religion behind, not God," he replied. "I carry God with me every day—in here and in here." He pointed to his head and his heart. "Memories were the only thing I left behind, painful ones."

Since her left arm was useless because of the sling and the IV bag and pole still attached to her right hand, Sam put his hands on both sides of her waist to lift her up onto the bed. Although tiny and petite, he couldn't help but note the slightly thickening waist beneath his touch. The signs of her pregnancy were starting to show, and the protective emotions that surfaced surprised him.

Her saucerlike eyes shimmered with unshed tears, and he fought not to lose himself in their beauty.

"I wish I had some memories," she whispered.

The minty scent of her breath fanned his face, and the slightly parted pose of her lips tempted him to lower his head and steal a taste of their tantalizing softness.

Instead, he removed her slippers and, after she positioned herself back on the pillows, he covered her with a blanket.

"Memories aren't all they're cracked up to be, Sarah. I have memories, but no one to love me. You don't have memories, but you have people who love you very much."

She acknowledged his words with a nod and a pensive expression.

Her fragile beauty spoke to him, stirring emotions and feelings better left dormant. Stepping back, he subtly shook his head and reminded himself of his own rules.

Rule number one: never get emotionally involved with anyone in a case.

Rule number two: remember, at all times, that when working undercover none of it is real. You are living a lie.

"So, you didn't answer me. Why are you dressed like an Amish man, Detective King?"

He searched her face, looking for any signs of fear or weakness. He found instead only interest and curiosity.

"This shooter is highly intelligent. He managed to pull off a massive diamond heist without leaving a trace. No images on surveillance cameras. No witnesses. No mistakes. Until now." He took a deep breath before continuing. "This time he left behind a pouch full of diamonds. The doctors found the pouch pinned inside the waistband of your skirt when you were brought into the emergency room."

He heard her sharp intake of breath, but otherwise she remained still and waited for him to continue.

"This time he was sloppy. He left behind a witness. You." His eyes locked with hers. "He believes that you still have the diamonds in your possession. And he doesn't believe in leaving witnesses behind. There is no question. He will be back."

Fear crept into her eyes. "But you told me the doctors found the diamonds. I don't have them anymore, do I?"

"No. But he doesn't know that."

"Then I have to go away. I have to hide. I can't be around anyone who could be hurt because of me."

His admiration for her rose. She was worried about people she couldn't remember, and not about the imminent threat to herself.

"The safest thing for you and for everyone else is for you to return to your community. It will be harder for him to reach you and easier for everyone involved to recognize an outsider."

"Is he a threat to anyone besides me?"

"He is a really bad man, Sarah. He will stop at nothing to get what he wants. He could snatch a child. Harm one of your neighbors while looking for information. He is evil in human form." Gently, he tilted her chin up with his index finger and looked into her eyes. "But you and I will work together, and we will not let that happen. I promise."

Sam couldn't believe he had just said what he did.

Promise? The two of them working together? Was he crazy talking to her like this? Like they were a team fighting against evil?

Had he lost his mind?

"How can I help? I seem pretty useless to everyone these days." She smiled but seemed totally unaware of how the gesture lit up her face like a ray of sudden sunshine.

He liked making her smile. He liked easing her pain and stress. He tried to identify this tumble of feelings she stirred within him despite his attempt to stay neutral.

Pity? No. Sarah Lapp was too strong a woman to be pitied.

Admiration. Respect. Yes, that was it. He refused to consider there was anything more.

"I will be moving back to the farm with you," he said. "I'll be your bodyguard while the rest of the police force concentrates on finding this guy. With my Amish background, it makes me the perfect choice for the job. I can blend in better than any of the other officers. I can help maintain respect for the Amish way of life."

"Move in? With me?" Her eyes widened. Her mouth rounded in the shape of a perfect letter *O,* and a pink flush tinged her cheeks.

"We will both be staying with Rebecca and Jacob. We believe you will be the primary target because the shooter still believes you possess the diamonds. You also saw his face and lived. He can't afford to let you talk to the authorities. He will try to make sure that doesn't happen. If we can apprehend him when he makes his move, then everyone else will be safe as well."

"So I am going to be the bait to hook the fish?"

Now it was his turn for heat to rush into his face. He felt embarrassed and ashamed because she was right. He was using her as bait.

"It's all right, Samuel. I understand. I will do this

thing if it will help keep the others safe. When do we begin?"

"Soon." He gave her fingers a light squeeze. "You will be in the hospital a little while longer. You still need time to heal. But try not to worry. I will not let anything happen to you while you are in my care."

"I am not in your care, Samuel." Her smile widened. "I am in God's hands."

"Then that is a good thing, *ya?* With God on our side, we can't lose." Sam grinned, hoping his cavalier attitude would build her confidence and help her relax. "Concentrate on regaining your strength. Let me worry about all the bad guys out there."

The door pushed open behind them. Captain Rogers and Sam's partner, Joe Masterson, stood in the doorway. "Detective King, may I see you in the hall for a moment?"

Sam released her hand. "I'll be back. Remember, no worrying allowed. Everything is going to work for good, just the way the Lord intends."

Sarah tried to still the apprehension that skittered over her nerve endings when she found herself alone in the room. The police were going to use her as bait to catch a killer. Her breath caught in her throat, and she could feel the rapid beating of her heart beneath her hand on her chest. Was she strong enough, brave enough?

You can do this. You must do this. These people need you to help them.

These people? Where had that thought come from? These were her people, weren't they? Her family? She knew she felt a warm affection for both Rebecca and

Jacob. They had been wonderfully kind and attentive to her since she'd come out of her coma.

But as much as she hated to admit it, she couldn't feel a connection to them. At least not the kind of connection they seemed to expect. They were kind people. Loving people. But were they *her* people?

She tried again to conjure up a memory, even the slightest wisp of one, of Peter. Rebecca had told her that they'd grown up together and were the best of friends. They were happily married. They were expecting a child.

Sarah placed a hand on her stomach, feeling the slight swell beneath her touch. Their child. And she couldn't even remember Peter's face.

A stab of pain pierced her heart. She must be a shallow person to not remember someone she had obviously loved. Love goes soul deep, doesn't it? Love wouldn't be forgotten so quickly, would it?

Maybe it hadn't been love. Maybe it had been friendship or convenience or companionship. Maybe it was an emotion that hadn't claimed her heart at all. She would never know now.

Her eyes strayed to the hospital room door, and her thoughts turned to Samuel.

She was certain if a person were to fall in love with Samuel, it would be a deep, abiding love. It would be two souls uniting before God. It would last a lifetime and not be forgotten by injury or time.

Her heart fluttered in her chest at just the thought that she might be starting to have feelings for Samuel, before she angrily shooed them away.

Foolish notions. That was one thing she was quickly learning about herself. She was often a victim of foolish notions.

Chapter Three

"There's been another murder."

Apprehension straightened Sam's spine. "Another murder? Who? When?"

"Not here. Follow me." Captain Rogers, Joe and Sam strode briskly to the conference room and took their seats. The tension in the room was almost palpable.

Sam stole a moment to study his superior's face. The past seven days had made their mark. He noted his captain's furrowed brow, the lines of strain etched on each side of his mouth, but what caught his attention the most was the bone-weary fatigue he saw in his eyes. The political pressure to find a quick solution to a complicated, ever-worsening scenario was taking its toll.

The captain folded his hands on the table. "There's no sugarcoating this, so I'm just going to say it. Around 2:00 a.m. last night, Steven Miller was murdered."

"Steven Miller?" Sam leaned back in his chair. "Isn't that the name of the second diamond-heist robber?" He threw a hurried glance at both men. "Didn't we have him in custody?"

"Yep. Same guy." Joe's expression was grim. "We

had him under armed guard in a secluded room in a medical center in the Bronx."

"Special Agent Lopez called me first thing this morning." Captain Rogers wiped a hand over his face and leaned back in his chair. "The man was suffocated with one of his own pillows."

"How could something like this happen? He was under armed guard. Did they at least catch the guy?"

"No. He did it on the graveyard shift, when there would be fewer people roaming the halls or in attendance. Once Miller's heart stopped, the monitors went off at the nurse's station. By the time the nurse and crash cart personnel arrived at the room, he had disappeared."

"Any leads? Witnesses?" Sam tried to calm his racing thoughts. This shooter had walked into a hospital and murdered a man in police custody. The degree of difficulty to keep Sarah safe just rose several more notches.

"We believe it was the ring leader of the group," Rogers said. "The same guy we're expecting to show up here. We figure he left here right after the schoolhouse shootings and returned to New York. He spent the week tracking down the whereabouts of his partner in crime, did his surveillance of the medical center and set a plan in motion. He's never left anyone alive who could identify him. He wasn't about to leave one of his team in the hands of the enemy."

"I don't believe this guy." Sam ran his hand through his hair. He could feel his blood throb in a rapid beat on each side of his temple. "You're telling me that he just walked up to a guarded room, slipped inside, killed our witness and left? Why didn't our guards stop him? What did they have to say when they were questioned?"

"Nothing." Joe's expression grew grimmer. "The perp slit the guard's throat. Nobody knows whether it was coming or going, so we're not sure if that's how he gained access or how he covered his tracks when he left. But we think it was on the way out, because a nurse reported that she had stopped and asked the police officer if he'd like a cup of coffee only moments before. She'd just sat down at her desk when the monitor alarm went off."

"What about the surveillance cameras?" The throbbing in Sam's temples became a full-blown headache. He closed his eyes for a second or two and rubbed his fingers on the tender spots beside his eyes before locking his gaze on Rogers. "We're not chasing a shadow. He's a flesh-and-blood man just like the rest of us. Somebody had to see something."

Captain Rogers frowned. "Lopez identified someone he believes is the perp on the tapes. The suspect shows up in multiple camera shots and hides his face every time. Lopez sent the digital images to the FBI labs for further enhancement."

"How did he get into the room in the first place?" Sam shot a glance between his partner and Captain Rogers. "We discussed his security plan with Lopez before he left. It seemed solid."

"It was solid." Rogers sighed heavily. "There was a police presence visible at the elevator banks, both in the lobby and the floor in question. There was an officer at the door of the patient's room as well. Matter of fact, Lopez had created a dummy room with an armed guard, so it wouldn't be easy for someone off the street to easily identify the actual location of our prisoner."

"Yeah, I thought that part of the plan was brilliant

myself," Joe said. "I guess the dog we're chasing is smart, too."

"I don't get it." Sam was finding it difficult to process this new information. When he spoke again, he addressed his captain.

"Lopez told me he had a dual checkpoint in place. Every person entering that room would have had to be cleared—not just the doctors and nurses, but housekeeping and dietary would have had to follow the same protocol. They had to be wearing a photo identification badge, and as a fail-safe that photo ID had to match the image in the guard's laptop.

"Even if this guy did manage to create a fake badge, are you telling me that he was able to hack into the hospital personnel files and upload his picture so he'd pass the guard's scrutiny?"

A slow, steady burn formed in his gut and spread through his body. Sam leaned back and threw his arms in the air. "If the guy is that good, we need him running the FBI, not running from it."

"He found a loophole," Captain Rogers said.

Sam arched an eyebrow. "Ya think?"

Rogers ignored the sarcasm.

"Lopez set up a failsafe plan for hospital personnel. He even went one step further and insured that the same police personnel rotated shifts on the door so anyone would question a stranger in uniform, and the officers would recognize their replacements. The guard would also log the time in and out of the room for each visitor."

Sam leaned forward, waiting for more.

"What Lopez didn't consider was that the culprit would create a fake FBI identity. There wasn't anything on the laptop for FBI because Lopez intended to be the only one accessing the room. Unfortunately, he failed to make sure the guards knew it. That's how we figure he got past the guard. He pretended to be one of Lopez's own."

"I told you," Joe said. "The guy's smart."

Sam jumped to his feet. "Sarah…"

Captain Rogers waved Sam back down.

"Sit down, King. We're taking care of it."

"We need to move her to another floor ASAP," Sam urged.

"I already talked with her doctor," Joe said. "She's stable enough to be moved out of ICU, so they are making arrangements for a private room as we speak."

"Our men will be handling security on the door—not FBI, not hospital security guards—us." Rogers glared at both of them. "Nothing, absolutely nothing, is going to happen to that woman on our watch. Understood?"

Sam's heart started to beat a normal rhythm for the first time since he'd heard of Steven Miller's murder. He didn't know how this guy could keep slipping through traps, avoiding surveillance cameras and sidestepping witnesses, but it didn't matter. No matter what it took, Sam wasn't going to let the jerk anywhere near Sarah or any of the people who loved her.

With renewed determination, he shoved back from the table and stood. "Captain, with all due respect, don't you think we've talked enough? The ball is in our court now. We'd better get busy setting things in motion. The FBI botched this one, but we can't afford to. If he shows up here, I intend to make sure he's sorry he didn't stay in New York—deadly sorry."

"King." The censoring tone in his superior's voice cemented his feet to the floor. "Your Amish background gives you a leg up over my other officers. I picked you because I believe you can deal with the nuances of this case the best. But for that same reason, you need to be careful. You can't let your emotions color your judgment and jeopardize this case. Everything by the book. Got it?"

Sam nodded.

"Good. Now get back to Sarah. I'm going to finalize the room move with the hospital administrator while Joe coordinates the shift coverage outside her door."

Sam didn't need to be told twice. He was halfway down the hall with the door easing shut behind him before the captain had stopped speaking.

The man made a final adjustment to the fake beard that covered the lower part of his face, being sure to keep his upper lip clean, as was the Amish custom. He stared at the reflection in the full-length mirror on the back of the door and admired his handiwork.

The blond shaggy wig brushed the back of his neck. It made him twitch the way one might with an errant insect racing down your arm, and he shivered with disgust.

He was a man who took great pride in his appearance. His chestnut-brown hair was always faithfully groomed in a short, concise military cut. His fingernails were manicured at all times, his clothing choices impeccable. He'd be glad when this distasteful costume was no longer necessary.

He leaned in for a closer look at the blue contacts he'd worn to conceal his brown eyes. He finished off the look by donning a pair of plain, wire-rimmed glasses. The transformation was amazing.

He glanced down at his outfit. His clothes looked like they'd been woven a century ago. What kind of people willingly dressed like this?

He couldn't wait to get out of this outfit and back into one of his expensive Armani suits. He longed to sit in his butter-soft leather chair, sip the prime Scotch from his private collection and gaze out his plate-glass window overlooking the ocean.

He hooked his fingers behind his suspenders, turned sideways and grunted with satisfaction.

One obstacle still remained.

He glanced at his immaculate nails. He'd have to go outside and dig in a flower bed. The thought of dirt under his fingernails actually caused his stomach to roil. But these men worked on farms. He imagined they grew used to the feeling of soil and debris as their manicure of the day. The thought made his lips twist into a frown of disgust.

Well, it wouldn't be for long. Diamonds valued in the billions were definitely worth this ridiculous costume and a little dirt, weren't they?

He sighed heavily. He'd have a very limited opportunity to interrogate the woman. But he wasn't worried. If he couldn't get her to tell him where she'd hidden the diamonds before he eliminated her, then he'd find them another way.

He rolled his white sleeves up to his elbows and smiled with satisfaction. Even his own mother wouldn't recognize him. If she had still been alive, that is. He paused for a moment and allowed himself to remember the look of panic and fear he'd seen in her eyes moments before he squeezed the life out of her.

He'd learned many things in his lifetime. One of

the most important lessons was that when you needed to infiltrate enemy lines, it was best to blend in, give off an air of confidence, act like you belonged exactly where you were.

It had served him well over the years. His enemies had never sensed his presence—even though he was often right in their midst, hiding in plain sight, as the saying goes.

He stepped back, donned his straw hat and headed to the door.

Nighttime in hospitals always gave Sam the willies. Fewer staff. People speaking in whispers. Tonight his "willies alert" was operating on full throttle. Some cops called it gut instinct. Either way, Sam hated the tension that shot along his nerve endings, the fingers of unease that crept up his spine.

The only discernible sound as he moved through the empty corridors was the soft whirring of machines from open doorways, an occasional whimper of pain or a soft snore.

He was tired. Bone tired. He hadn't had more than two hours of uninterrupted sleep in the past thirty-six hours, and it was beginning to catch up with him. He wasn't a kid anymore—thirty-four on his next birthday, and he needed those eight hours of sleep. Or at least six. Who was he kidding? He'd settle for four if he could snatch them.

He glanced into the rooms as he passed by. They'd taken a risk when they'd moved Sarah to the pediatric floor. He didn't want to imagine the uproar the parents of these children would unleash if they had any idea that the bait to catch a killer had just been moved into their midst.

Captain Rogers had arranged the move. He firmly believed this would be the last floor in the hospital the perpetrator would expect to find Sarah. The captain didn't seem worried about the sensitive location. He was certain that even if the killer did locate Sarah, the children would be safe because they weren't his target. Sarah was.

Sam moved past the rooms filled with sleeping children. He offered a silent prayer that the captain hadn't made a horrendous mistake. As he drew near Sarah's room, he recognized the officer sitting in front of the door.

"Hey, Fitch, how's it going?"

The policeman folded his newspaper and grinned when he saw Sam approach. He gestured with his head toward the door.

"You'd think she was a Hollywood celebrity or something. Orders came down from the top that this is the last day allowed for visitation. It's been a steady stream of Amish folks in and out all afternoon saying their goodbyes. First thing tomorrow morning, the only Amish visitor allowed to visit is her former mother-in-law, Rebecca Lapp. No one else. Period."

Sam nodded. "Good. How did everyone else take the news?"

"Truthfully, I think they were a little relieved. They've been taking turns keeping vigil at the hospital all week. I'm sure they want to return to their homes and their farms."

Officer Brian Fitch stood and stretched his back. "I must admit I'm glad they've cut back on visiting. Less work for me. I hear the Amish go down when the sun does, so that's probably why it's been quiet the last few hours." Fitch shot a glance at Sam's Amish attire. "No offense intended or anything."

Sam grinned. "None taken. You're right. The Amish do go to bed early because they are up before dawn each day to begin their chores. Running a farm is not an easy task."

Sam leaned his hand flat against the door and then paused before he pushed it open. "You look beat. Why don't you go stretch your legs? Maybe grab a cup of coffee while you're at it? I'm here, and I'm not going anywhere."

"You sure?"

Sam opened his jacket and patted the gun in his shoulder holster. "I'm still a cop. Remember?"

Fitch grinned. "Yeah, well, you sure could fool me. You look like a natural fit with the rest of those folks. If I hadn't recognized you from our precinct, I'd be checking your ID and trying to talk you out of visiting altogether."

Sam grinned. "That coffee is calling your name, Fitch."

"You want me to bring you something back?"

"No, I'm good."

Taking advantage of Sam's offer to cover the room, the guard nodded and hurried to the elevator banks, not giving Sam a chance to change his mind.

The telltale *ding* of the arriving elevator filled the silence of the night, and Fitch waved. Sam gave him a nod and then entered Sarah's room.

Chapter Four

The night-light above the hospital bed cast the room in a soft, white haze. Sam looked down upon the sleeping woman, and his breath caught in his throat.

With stress and pain absent from her expression, she looked peaceful, young and surprisingly beautiful.

Long blond hair poked from beneath the bandages that swathed her head and flowed like golden silk over her shoulders. Her cheeks were flushed, giving her smooth complexion a rosy glow. Lost in sleep and probably dreaming, her lips formed a tiny pout. For the second time in as many days, he had to fight the temptation to taste the softness of those lips.

She was young and vulnerable and…

And she took his breath away.

Although he'd found her attractive when they'd first met, he'd been consumed with the business of ensuring her safety and nothing else.

But now…

In the quiet semidarkness of the evening, she reminded him of a sleeping princess and, for one insane moment, he felt an urge to awaken the princess with a kiss.

Shocked by that unexpected and traitorous thought, he stepped back from the bed as quickly as if he had touched an electrified fence, and then chuckled at his foolishness.

His eyes fell on a white *kapp* resting on the hospital tray table beside Sarah's bed. Rebecca must have placed it there. Sam wondered why. Rebecca had to know that Sarah's injuries would not allow her to wear the *kapp* for quite some time.

Then he glanced around the room and grinned. The middle-aged woman was sly like a fox. This room was a sterile slice of the *Englischer's* world. Monitors. Hospital bed. Even a television hanging on the far wall. This *kapp* resting in plain sight and at arm's length would be a constant reminder of the Amish world waiting for Sarah's return.

He glanced at Sarah's sleeping form one more time before he forced himself to turn away. Before exiting the room, he stepped inside the bathroom. He needed to throw some cold water on his face and try to wake up. His exhaustion was making him think crazy thoughts, have crazy feelings.

He used the facilities and washed his hands. He turned off the water and was drying his hands on a paper towel when a sound caught his attention. He paused and concentrated, listening to the silence.

There it was again. Just the whisper of sound, like the soft rustling of clothing against skin as a person moved about.

He crumpled the paper towel into a ball, tossed it into the trash can and pushed open the bathroom door.

It took his eyes a moment to adjust to the change from bright to dim light as he reentered Sarah's room. A tall man dressed in Amish clothing stood in the shadows on the far side of Sarah's bed.

A feeling of unease slithered up Sam's spine. Why would an Amish man be visiting at this time of night, and without a female companion in tow? Sam slid his jacket aside for easy access to his gun and stepped farther into the room.

"May I help you?" he asked in Pennsylvania Dutch dialect.

The visitor didn't reply. He removed his straw hat and nodded as a person who was apologizing for the late-night visit might. He sidestepped around the bed.

Sam stood too far from the light switch at the door to be able to fully illuminate the room. He had to rely on the soft glow from above Sarah's bed. Because the visitor held the hat higher than normal, Sam was unable to get a clear view of the man's face. His gut instincts slammed into gear. He drew his gun and aimed for the middle of the man's chest.

"Don't move." Sam made no attempt to hide the steel resolve beneath his words. Slowly, he stepped toward the main light switch. He shifted his glance just long enough to see how much farther he had to go.

The visitor immediately took advantage of this momentary distraction, dived sideways and simultaneously threw a pillow at Sam.

Instinctively, Sam raised an arm to protect his face. He pushed the pillow away, recovered quickly from the unexpected gesture and fired his weapon at the man's back as he sprinted out the door. The splintered wood of the door frame told him he'd missed his mark.

Sam sprang forward in pursuit. He'd almost reached the door when his right foot slid out from under him. He struggled to regain his balance and not fall. When he got his footing again, he glanced down and saw a syringe poking out from beneath his foot. He bent down and picked it up.

Suddenly, the monitor beside Sarah's bed erupted in a loud, continuous alarm. Sam's gaze flew to the screen and horror filled his soul. A flat, solid green line moved across the screen. Sarah's heart was no longer beating.

Before Sam could react, the door burst open. The room flooded with light. A nurse, quickly followed by another, burst into the room and rushed past him to Sarah's bed. While one nurse tended to the monitor and alarms, the other began CPR on Sarah. Seconds later, several other staff members hurried into the room with a crash cart pulled by the doctor close behind.

Sam knew he should be chasing the man who had done this, but his feet wouldn't budge. His eyes flew to Sarah's face. She lay so still, deathly still. He couldn't believe this was happening and, worse, that it had happened on his watch. Feelings of failure were quickly replaced first with fear that he'd lost her, and then by a deep, burning rage that he was helpless once again.

Sam had to leave—now. But he could barely find the inner strength to pull himself away from Sarah's side. This was his fault. But there was nothing he could do for her now. She was in better hands than his, and he refused to let the lowlife who did this escape. Not this time. Not ever again.

Sam pressed his hand on the shoulder of the nearest nurse. When she turned to look at him, he shoved the syringe in her hand. "I found this on the floor. I believe something was injected into her IV."

As soon as she took it from him, he raced for the hospital room door. Before he could pull it open, a woman's scream pierced the air, and the sounds of chaos filled the corridor. Something was terribly wrong. Had the mystery man grabbed a hostage or, worse, hurt one of the children?

Whispering a silent prayer for Sarah, Sam wrenched open the door and darted into the corridor.

A small gathering of people congregated at the end of the hall around the elevator banks. One woman had collapsed on the floor. Sam figured from the shocked expression on her face as he drew near, and from the sobs racking her body, that this was the woman who had screamed. An older gentleman hovered over her and tried to offer comfort.

A man dressed in green scrubs knelt half in and half out of an open elevator. Another man, also dressed in hospital garb, leaned close behind.

Sam pushed his way through the few gathering spectators and up front to survey the scene. For the second time that night, he felt like a mule had kicked him in the gut.

Officer Brian Fitch was sprawled on the elevator floor. One look at his open, sightless eyes and the trail of blood pooling beneath his body said it all. The officer hadn't made it downstairs for coffee.

Sam remembered the sound of the elevator arriving. Their surprise night visitor must have been on it. When the door opened, Fitch was busy nodding to him and must have been caught unaware. One quick, deadly slice across the officer's throat guaranteed that Fitch would never need coffee or exercise again.

Sam pulled out his badge and ordered everyone back, including the hospital staff. There was nothing any of them could do for Fitch now, and he had to protect whatever forensic evidence they'd be able to gather. Sam called hospital security on his cell phone, which he had put on speed dial for the duration of Sarah's hospital stay.

But somebody else had beaten him to it. The second elevator bank hummed to life. He held his hand on his gun and watched two startled guards emerge and stare at the carnage in front of them.

Sam identified himself as an undercover police officer, despite his Amish garb, and flashed his detective's shield and identification. He hoped he hadn't just blown his cover, but at the moment it couldn't be helped.

"Shut down every possible exit," he commanded. "Do it now."

Without hesitation, one of the guards barked orders into his radio while the other attended to crowd control. Sam offered a silent prayer of thanks that if this had to happen, it had happened late in the evening and gawkers were at a minimum.

He hit speed dial on his phone and barked orders the second his partner answered.

"Joe, we have a problem. Get over here, stat."

They'd been partners long enough that when Joe heard the tension in his voice, he was on full alert, and any drowsiness in his tone from interrupted sleep was gone.

"What happened?"

"Fitch is dead. Sarah might be, too. It's total chaos here."

Muttered expletives floated through the receiver. "On my way."

"Notify Rogers and call for backup."

"Okay. Where can I find you?"

"Making sure that every window, door and crack of this hospital is sealed shut so this piece of slime doesn't escape."

Sam ended the call and shoved the phone back in his pocket. He stole one more precious second to glance down the hall at Sarah's door. Every fiber of his being wanted to know what was going on in that room. Had they been able to save her? Or was she dead? The fact that no one had come out of the room yet must be a good sign, right? He had to fight the urge to run back and see what was happening. But no matter what was going on inside that room, he would not be able to help. This time logic won out.

He did what he was trained to do. He compartmentalized his emotions and focused on doing his job. He sprinted down the stairwell, his feet barely touching the stairs, and made it from the fourth floor to the lobby in record time. The sound of approaching sirens and the sight of flashing red-and-blue lights as vehicles slammed to a stop in front of the building told him that both Joe and hospital security had also gone straight to work.

Security guards were already at the entrance. They looked confused and highly nervous, but Sam had to admire how quickly and well they had sprung into action. No one was getting in or out of the building right now except cops.

Sam met with the head of security and asked to see the building's floor plans. Once they were in hand, he began to coordinate a thorough hospital search room by room, floor by floor, while making sure that all exits were covered. For the time being, no one would be allowed to exit, for any reason, from anywhere.

Twenty minutes after he'd called Joe, Sam saw his partner flash his badge and hurry through the front door. He breathed a sigh of relief and stepped forward to greet him.

Joe stopped short when he saw Sam approach. He shoved both hands into his coat pockets and scowled. "Want to tell me what happened?"

"The killer entered Sarah's room dressed in Amish garb." Before Joe could ask, Sam said, "He killed the police officer assigned to guard the door. It was Brian Fitch."

The detectives knew the officer well. A deep frown etched grooves on both sides of Joe's mouth.

"Has anybody notified his wife?"

"Not yet."

"And Sarah?"

"I think the guy injected something into Sarah's IV to stop her heart."

"Is she dead? Were they able to resuscitate her?"

"I don't know. I haven't had a chance to check. I've been organizing the search."

Joe's shocked expression echoed the one Sam was sure he wore as well. "How did this happen? Nobody can be this lucky. The guy's a ghost."

"The guy's no ghost. He's as much flesh and blood as you and me."

"I just don't understand. What happened?" Joe shot a bewildered look at Sam.

"I was there, Joe. Right there." The remorse in his voice was evident. "He got past me anyway and got to Sarah."

"Were you hurt? Did he hit you over the head or something?"

A red-hot flush of shame and embarrassment coated Sam's throat and face. "Sarah was sleeping. I'd stepped into her bathroom to throw some cold water on my face. I didn't hear him come in until it was too late. The room was dark. He threw something at me. It distracted me enough that he was able to get past me."

Joe nodded. "Don't beat yourself up over it. It could have happened to any of us."

"But it didn't. It happened on my watch. Mine, Joe."

Joe grimaced. They'd been partners long enough that Sam knew Joe understood this was about more than what was happening now. This shame and pain and anger stretched back to another time and another place, when Sam had been helpless to save loved ones or bring perps to justice.

Joe patted Sam's arm, empathy evident in his eyes, and then changed the subject. "Where do we stand with the search?"

"The best I've been able to do is get all the exits covered. We're dealing with graveyard shift. We don't have a lot of warm bodies in the security department right now."

"Where do you want me?"

"Downstairs." Sam walked with Joe to the elevator bank. "I don't believe the guy will try to walk out any of the obvious exits. He's got to know they're the first places we'd shut down. Check every single room in the basement. Housekeeping has storage rooms, supply rooms. I think there are even some employee lockers and break rooms down there. And, of course, the morgue and the autopsy rooms. I've sent security guards to the loading platform by the morgue, but I'll feel better if one of us is checking things out."

"You got it."

The elevator doors opened, and Joe stepped inside.

"Be careful. Fitch was found dead with his throat slashed."

"Great. Just what I want to hear." His mouth twisted in a wry grin just as the doors shut.

Within thirty minutes of the initial alert, the SWAT team, special weapons and tactics, arrived, quickly followed by Captain Rogers. Sam shared what he knew, and they took over command of the ongoing search.

They hadn't located the perpetrator yet. But the hospital looked like a military camp in Afghanistan for all the uniformed and armed personnel swarming the halls. They'd catch him.

Sam threw a glance at his captain and saw the man in a deep conversation with both the SWAT team leader and the head of hospital security. Everything that could be done was being done. Finally, he'd have a moment to find out what had happened to Sarah.

Adrenaline hammered through the intruder's blood stream, and the beat of his heart thundered in his chest. Who knew all those morning jogs along the beach outside his home would have prepared him for the race of his life? He'd made it down five flights of stairs into the basement without anyone seeing him and, he was certain, before anyone could even sound the alarm.

What a rush! He thought it had been too simple when he caught the cop sneaking away for a break. But that's why he loved operating during the graveyard shift. People often snuck away or fell asleep. Made his job so much easier.

But when he'd slipped inside the darkened hospital room, he'd never expected someone might be in the bathroom.

The man had been dressed like an Amish guy, but he wasn't any more Amish than he was. Not carrying that 9 mm Beretta he had fired at him. He was probably an undercover cop.

Undercover cop. Undercover villain. Both disguised in Amish garb. The whole situation was laughable—and dangerous.

He stood with his back against the wall of the storage closet, trying to quiet the sound of his heavy gasps.

He could hear the pounding of feet racing down the corridor and hear the anxious, high-pitched whispers the guards shot to each other as they did a quick search of every room.

The sounds grew louder as the men approached his hiding spot.

He pushed into the far back corner of the room and crouched behind a utility cart with a large white mop and aluminum bucket attached. His hand tightened around the pistol grip of his gun, and he waited.

The door to the closet swung open. One of the security guards scanned the room with a flashlight. Just as quickly, he was gone.

Idiots.

They hadn't even bothered to throw on the light switch or step into the room. No wonder hospital security guards had the reputation of being toy cops. How did they expect to find anyone with such a lazy, half-done search?

He grinned and relaxed his hand, lowering his weapon.

Lucky for them they were stupid, or they'd be dead security guards just about now.

He stepped out from behind the cart when a sudden flash of light made him squint and raise his hand to his eyes. Someone had thrown on the switch, illuminating the room, and it took his eyes a second to adjust.

"Don't move! Drop your weapon and slide it over to me. Do it now!"

This wasn't a security guard. He looked into eyes of cold, hard steel. This must be a detective. A smart one, too.

Slowly, he lowered his weapon to the floor and kicked it in the detective's direction.

The detective moved farther into the room, never lowering his gun. He stepped to the side and withdrew a pair of handcuffs with his free hand. "Nice and easy now. Put your hands out where I can see them, and slowly walk over here."

Again, he did as requested.

The detective clasped a cuff onto his right wrist.

With speed resulting from years of martial arts training, he spun, released the blade sheathed on the inside of his sleeve and slashed the detective's throat.

The killer grinned. He always loved the look of surprise and horror on his victims' faces, and this detective looked shocked, indeed.

He removed his Amish clothes and quickly donned the detective's cheap brown suit. His lips twisted in disgust. The pants were about two inches too short, the waist at least two sizes too big, and the sleeves of the suit jacket revealed too much forearm. He shoved some towels under his shirt and cinched his belt tight to hold them in and his pants up.

He glowered at the pant length. When a scenario like this played out in the movies, the exchanged clothes were always a perfect fit. Just his luck this wasn't a movie. But he'd have to make do.

He slipped the detective's badge onto his belt, retrieved both guns from the floor and took one last look around to make sure he left nothing of significance behind. His eyes paused on the dead body.

"Sorry, buddy. You were good. Much better than those security guard wannabes. But I'm better. You never stood a chance."

He used a towel to wipe away fingerprints on the light switch and doorknob. He shut off the light, glanced up and down the empty corridor, stepped into the hall and leisurely walked away.

Chapter Five

Sam couldn't breathe.

He tried. But only shallow wisps of breath escaped his lips.

As soon as he could move...or react...or feel anything but pain, he'd remind himself to inhale deeply.

Yep. He'd do that. Just as soon as the world stopped spinning.

"Do you recognize this man?" A male nurse kneeling beside the body on the floor glanced up at him. "Is he one of yours?"

Tears burned Sam's eyes. His throat clenched, making it impossible for him to speak. The nonchalance of the strangers doing their jobs roiled his stomach. To them, this was just another body. To him...

Sam glanced at the body of the man, dressed only in underwear, lying on the utility room floor. He hated what his eyes relayed to his brain, but he couldn't seem to turn away.

How did this happen? Dear God, why?

"Hey, are you all right, buddy? You look pretty gray in

the face. You're not getting sick on me, are you? You're a cop. You see dead bodies all the time, don't ya?"

"Bert, give him a minute." The female nurse gently touched Sam's forearm. "You know this man, don't you, detective? He's one of yours."

One of yours.

Sam nodded.

Yes, he was one of his. His partner. His best friend. His only family. And now he was dead.

"His name is Detective Joseph Masterson. He was my partner."

"I'm so sorry." Her eyes supported the truth of her words. "Is there anything we can do to help?"

Sam took a deep breath and steadied himself. Rational thought returned, and his inner cop took command.

"I need both of you to step away from the body and try not to touch anything else on the way out of the room. This is a crime scene now. Please wait in the hall for a few minutes until I can get your names and contact information." He ushered them out of the room and grabbed the closest officer in the hallway. "Who discovered the body?"

The cop pointed to two women waiting at the end of the corridor. "Guard this door," Sam said. "No one comes in—absolutely no one—until our forensic team arrives. Make sure to take contact information from these nurses while I speak to the women at the end of the hall."

The cop nodded and did as requested.

Sam approached the women and flashed his detective shield. "My name is Detective King. I'd like to ask you a few questions." He glanced at their name tags. The younger female was a nurse. The matronly woman's tag identified her as custodial staff. "Ms. Blake," he spoke to the nurse. "I'm told you're the one who called us."

"That's right." She seemed perplexed at his Amish garb, but accepted the badge at face value.

"Did you find the body?"

The body.

He couldn't believe he was able to treat this like any ordinary crime scene when, internally, he was reeling in pain.

Dear Lord, continue to give me the strength I need to do my job and get through this night. First Sarah. Now Joe. Help me. Please.

"She found the body." Ms. Blake nodded to an older woman sitting beside her. "This is Mrs. Henshaw. She went into the room to get supplies, and then I heard her scream…."

Sam arched a brow and studied the drawn features of the elderly woman. It was evident that the shock of her discovery had taken its toll, and he knew he needed to tread lightly. "Thank you for speaking with me, Mrs. Henshaw. I'm sure you want to get home. I'll try to keep my questions short and to the point."

The woman looked up at him, her eyes glazed and distant.

"How long ago did you discover the body?"

She glanced at her watch. "I'm not sure. Thirty minutes, maybe."

Mrs. Blake nodded. "At least. Maybe a bit longer. We checked the body for vitals before I made the call."

"Do you remember touching anything in the room?" Sam asked.

"No. When I saw his throat had been cut, I knew he was dead, but I checked his carotid for a pulse anyway. Then I pulled out my cell and called it in."

Sam took a deep breath and fought to keep the images she relayed out of his mind.

"Do either of you remember seeing anything or anyone suspicious? Anything out of the ordinary?"

Both women shook their heads.

"Do you remember passing anyone in the hall?"

"Policemen," Mrs. Henshaw said. "There were security guards and police officers running up and down the halls. I wasn't sure what was going on. I waited for the halls to clear before going to get my supplies." A moment passed, and her face crunched in concentration. "There was something…"

Tension tightened Sam's body as he waited for her to continue.

"I didn't think much about it at the time but…" The woman looked directly at him. "I did see a man. He came down the hall after everyone else had already gone."

Sam honed in on her words. "Did he do or say anything?"

"No."

"What caught your attention? Why do you remember this particular individual?"

"Well, he was walking kind of slow, like he was taking a leisurely stroll in the park, and I guess I noticed that because everyone else had raced past."

"Anything else, Mrs. Henshaw?"

She frowned. "Yes. His pants. They didn't fit. They were about two inches too short."

The shooter had changed into Joe's suit.

"Thank you both. If I have any more questions, how can I reach you?" He pulled a small pad out of the inside pocket of his jacket.

Both women gave him their contact information.

"King!"

Sam glanced over his shoulder, then thanked the women for their help and joined the captain. It took only a few minutes to bring his superior up to speed.

The captain wiped a hand over his face and sighed heavily. "I'm sorry, Sam. Losing a good man is never easy for any of us. Worse if it's your partner."

Sam nodded. "Any word, Captain? Has anyone caught him?"

"Not yet. Unfortunately, we suspect he has already slipped past us." The captain nodded toward the utility room. "Everyone's been looking for a man in Amish garb. I've got a BOLO out now on him using Joe's suit, badge and gun as a description."

"That sounds like a plan. Be on the lookout for a detective when every detective and cop on the force is part of the search. Don't want to bet on the success of that one." Sam couldn't hide the bitterness and sarcasm in this voice. "We've got to get this creep. If it's the last thing I ever do…"

The captain clamped a hand on his shoulder. "I've got this one covered. Go home, son. Get some rest."

"I need to call Cindy." The last thing he wanted to do was have to tell his partner's wife that her husband wasn't coming home. His distaste for the assignment must have been evident in his eyes, because the captain slapped his shoulder a second time.

"It's been handled. I sent a squad car and a couple of our most empathetic men over to her place. Didn't want to take a chance she'd hear it from another source. Now get some rest. Go see her after you've gotten some sleep."

"Thanks, Captain."

Sam pushed open the stairwell door and sprinted up the steps. No way was he going home. Not until he found out what had happened to Sarah.

When he entered the fourth floor, the first thing he noted was the absence of guards in front of Sarah's room. His mind raced with a variety of scenarios on why no one would be posted there, but the only one that made sense was the one thought he refused to believe. Sam's feet felt as if they were encased in cement, each step forward harder than the one before.

He paused outside the room, threw his shoulders back and then pushed the door open.

A black mattress, empty and stripped of its sheets, waited silently for its next occupant.

The air gushed out of Sam's lungs.

Where was Sarah? Was she...

His mind couldn't even complete the thought.

He blinked hard and continued to stare at the empty bed. She couldn't be dead. A sense of failure, mixed with a multitude of other emotions, washed over him.

Oh God, please...

Sam was glad God could read hearts, because at the moment he was totally incapable of completing the prayer.

"May I help you?"

Startled, he spun toward the voice. The nurse's expression registered suspicion, even a tinge of fear, as she stood in the doorway, poised to run if necessary.

"Can you tell me what happened to Sarah?"

The nurse eyed him skeptically. Of course she'd be wary. The entire hospital was in shutdown mode. They'd been told the killer had been dressed in Amish clothes—and here he stood in Amish clothes. The staff had also been told the killer had stolen a detective's badge and gun, so showing his identification probably wouldn't help this frightened nurse feel any better.

"Are you family?" she asked.

Not up to explanations, Sam simply nodded.

The nurse pushed the door wider, but made sure not to enter the room and kept in plain view of people in the hall. Smart lady.

"Sir, I'm sure Dr. Clark will be happy to speak with you. Take the elevator to the seventh floor and ask for him at the nurse's station."

"Can you at least tell me if Sarah is alive?" Sam heard the hopeful tone in his voice and realized this case was quickly becoming more personal than he had intended it to be.

"Please, sir. The doctor will answer your..."

Sam sidled past her and bounded toward the elevator before she had a chance to finish her statement. He tapped his foot impatiently and watched the numbers light from floor to floor. A sense of anticipation filled his senses as he got off the elevator and skidded to a stop at the nurse's desk.

"I'm looking for Sarah Lapp."

Don't say she's in the morgue. Please don't.

The nurse looked up from her paperwork. "I'm sorry, sir. Mrs. Lapp is not allowed visitors."

She's alive. Thank you, God.

A tsunami wave of relief washed over him. Now if he could just get this nurse to give him the information he needed. He pasted on his best smile and tried again. "You don't understand—"

"Sam."

He turned his head at the sound of his name. Dr.

Clark approached, stretched out his hand and grasped his in a firm handshake.

"Sarah made it? She's going to be okay?" Sam asked, not paying any attention to Dr. Clark's quizzical expression at the emotion evident in his voice.

Dr. Clark ushered Sam away from the nurse's desk and asked him to walk with him. As they moved down the corridor, Sam could see a uniformed guard sitting in front of one of the ICU rooms.

"Sarah's going to be fine. Thanks to you. The vial you gave the nurse held the remnants of potassium chloride. A large enough dose can stop a heart. We were able to act quickly and bring her back."

"Will she be all right?"

The doctor nodded. "She's going to be fine." He raised his eyes. "Someone up there must be looking out for her. I can't believe everything this woman has survived over the past two weeks. Unbelievable."

Sam frowned. He felt awkward asking, but he needed to know. "The baby?"

"As far as we can tell, the baby is as strong as the mother. All is well."

It felt like one of those old-fashioned leaded vests had just been lifted off his chest. His lips twisted into a smile for the first time that day.

"Thanks, Doc."

"You're welcome. Please tell me that you apprehended the man who committed these horrible crimes." Worry creased the doctor's forehead into two deep, parallel furrows.

"Not yet."

Dr. Clark's frown deepened. "The best thing we can do for all concerned is to make other arrangements for

Mrs. Lapp. Under the circumstances, the hospital cannot accept responsibility for her safety...or the safety of our other patients."

Sam nodded.

Dr. Clark continued, "I believe that with some medical precautions put in place, moving to a safe house or, perhaps, to a more familiar environment will help with her recovery. Her stress level here is off the charts. Understandably, of course."

They walked the last few feet to her door, but stood outside to finish their conversation. Sam recognized the officer on duty, acknowledged him and turned his attention back to the doctor. "How quickly can we move her?"

"I want to keep her under observation for another twenty-four hours. Barring any unforeseen complications, she will be released then."

"Does the captain know?"

"Not yet. I haven't seen him since the hospital shut down."

"I'll fill him in. We'll start making arrangements on our end. Is Sarah awake? I have a few questions."

"Yes, she's awake. Her mother-in-law is with her. But please keep your visit short and try not to upset her. She needs her rest."

Sam nodded, and the doctor walked away.

Sarah's alive. She's going to be okay and so is her child.

Despite the nightmare this evening had become, he couldn't help but smile as he pushed open the door and stepped into the room. He was going to see Sarah.

Chapter Six

Sarah caught movement in her peripheral vision, turned her head and smiled. "Detective King."

"Samuel." He gestured at his clothing. "It won't do me any good to dress like this if you announce me as an undercover cop every time I walk into a room."

A giggle escaped her lips, seeming to surprise them both. "You're right. Sorry, Samuel."

Sam respectfully inclined his head toward the older woman and acknowledged her presence.

"Do you have any information for us?" Rebecca's face wore lines of concern. "Have they found the man who did this terrible thing to our Sarah?"

"I'm sorry—not yet. But I'm sure we'll hear something soon. The hospital has been shut down. Every floor and room is being searched as we speak."

Rebecca seemed satisfied with Samuel's reply. "My husband went home at dinnertime. I was sleeping in one of those reclining chairs in the family waiting room when Dr. Clark sent a nurse to tell me what had happened." She squeezed Sarah's hand, and tears glistened in her eyes. "God is *gut,* Sarah. He has returned you to us twice, *ya?*"

Sam leaned a hand on the bed rail. "I hate to have to do this now, but I need to ask you a few questions."

"It is all right, Samuel. Do what you need to do." Sarah looked up at him and waited.

"Do you remember anything that happened this evening? You were asleep when I first entered the room. Did you wake up at any time?"

Sarah offered a weak smile. "Of this, I remember, Samuel." She locked her gaze with his. "I had been sleeping, but I started to wake up when you came into the room. I was—what's the word?—groggy? My eyes didn't want to open, but I knew you were there." Her smile widened. "When I did coax them open, I saw your back as you walked into the bathroom. I closed my eyes again. I think I started to drift back to sleep. I know this is not helping you."

"You're doing fine."

Her heart skipped a beat and fluttered like a symphony of dancing butterflies in her chest when he smiled at her. Before she could ponder the strange feelings she seemed to experience in this man's presence, he encouraged her to continue her story.

"The man must have entered the room as soon as I stepped out. Did you see him?"

"Yes."

Samuel's eyes widened, and she sensed his anticipation and tension.

"Can you describe him?"

She chewed on her bottom lip as she tried to bring the memory of the man's face into her mind. "I… I'm not sure. The light in the room was dim. I had been sleeping."

"Do your best, child." Rebecca patted her hand. "Anything you can tell Samuel will help him."

Sarah broke eye contact with both of them and stared at the ceiling as she tried to remember every detail she could. "He had blond hair and a yellow beard that reached the top of his chest. He was dressed in Amish clothes. He looked…ordinary."

"Did you recognize him, Sarah? Was he one of the men at the school?" Rebecca asked.

"I don't remember anything that happened at the school."

"Still nothing?" Rebecca asked. "No one?"

Sarah knew the woman kept hoping that she would someday remember her son, Peter. But today wasn't that day.

She couldn't bear to see the disappointment in Rebecca's eyes or the anticipation in Samuel's. She squeezed her eyes shut and tried as hard as she could to remember something, anything. When she opened them again, she looked from one to the other and knew she had nothing to offer. Sadness almost overwhelmed her.

"I'm so sorry. I can't help you."

"What happened when he approached your bed?" Sam tried to prod her memory. "Did he say anything to you? Think, Sarah. It might be important."

"Yes. I remember that he did speak to me. I knew from his words that this was the man who had killed my husband and who had shot me."

Rebecca gasped. Her hand flew to her chest, but she remained silent.

"Take your time, Sarah. No one can hurt you now.

Try to remember what he said." Sam's calm, warm voice encouraged her.

"He asked me what I did with the diamonds. He said he knew I had the pouch." An increasing anxiety caused her voice to tremble. "I told him I knew nothing about his diamonds." Fear slithered up her spine at the memory. "His eyes were so dark, so cold and…and evil."

Sam reached out and clasped her hand. "Go on. You're doing fine. What else did he say?"

Sarah found Sam's touch strangely comforting, and the way her body trembled with fear, she needed all the comfort she could find.

"He grinned at me," she said. "I remember thinking how perfect his teeth were. Really white and straight and clean. His breath… I remember a cloying, minty scent when he leaned close…almost too minty…my stomach turned. He leaned close to my ear and whispered, 'I will find where you hid those diamonds. I don't need you to do it.'"

Her heart galloped inside her chest, but this time it was fear that caused the pace. "That's when I saw him pull something out of his pocket. He held it against the tube attached to my arm. My chest became tight, like something very heavy was sitting on me. I couldn't draw a breath. That's all I remember." A tear slid down her cheek. "I woke up in this room with Rebecca by my side. She told me what had happened. That is all I know."

"She has answered your questions. You must leave her now," Rebecca insisted. "She needs to rest."

Sam nodded and released Sarah's hand. He stared into those mesmerizing blue eyes. "Thank you."

"I have been of no help."

"That is not true. You have helped quite a bit. Thanks to you, we know that he will stop at nothing to find the diamonds. He was bold enough to walk into enemy camp and risk being recognized as an intruder. In New York, he dressed as an FBI agent, and here, as an Amish man. So our belief that he would return has been proved correct."

Sam sighed heavily. "You have also proved our theory that he would not leave behind any survivors. He tried to kill you. He did kill the one member of his team we had in custody in New York. He also killed the guard who had been sitting outside your door." The darkened intensity in his eyes told her that he had more to say, and it was very difficult for him. "He also killed my partner." His voice broke as he tried to conceal his grief.

Rebecca gasped. "Detective Masterson has been killed?"

Sarah looked into Sam's eyes and thought her heart would break when she saw nothing but pain staring back at her.

"I am so sorry, Samuel."

He hung his head in silence.

"You said the man guarding my room was also killed?"

Sam nodded and didn't seem to be able to meet her eyes. When he did look at her, he reminded her of a little boy in pain who needed cuddling and comfort, but this brief glimpse of vulnerability didn't last more than an instant before the hard-edged detective reappeared.

"I apologize. I let my guard down. It almost cost you your life. It did cost the life of a good officer, as well as the life of my partner."

"This was not your doing, Samuel. You must not

blame yourself." Sarah knew from his reaction that her words held little comfort.

"I was standing in the room with you. Just feet away, and I let him slip by. I promise I will not let anything like that happen again."

"God willing."

Both of them glanced at Rebecca after she spoke.

"God is in control, Samuel, *ya?* He will decide what does or does not happen." Her steady, unflinching gaze caught his.

Sam straightened his shoulders. The tone of his voice was harsher than normal when he replied. "Sometimes God needs a little help to bring the bad guys to justice, Rebecca. That's my job, and that's what I intend to do."

"Justice, Samuel? Or vengeance?"

Sam bristled beneath the censure. "Call it what you want. If I hadn't been there this evening, if I hadn't stepped out of the bathroom when I did, Sarah wouldn't be with us right now."

Rebecca shot a loving glance Sarah's way. "It was God's will that Sarah remain with us. He may have used your presence, Samuel, and for that I am most grateful."

Ashamed of himself for lashing out at the woman, he lowered his head and apologized. "I'm sorry I spoke harshly. You're right. God uses many things to bring about His will in this world...and many people."

Rebecca smiled at him and nodded.

The door opened. Sarah thought Captain Rogers looked even more exhausted than Samuel, if that were possible.

"What are you doing here?" he growled in Sam's direction. "I thought I told you to go home and get some sleep."

"I will. I had a few loose ends that I needed to tie up first, sir."

The captain glowered, but refrained from any further admonishment.

"Have you found the man who did this terrible thing?" Rebecca asked.

The captain's face wore the strains of exhaustion. "No. I'm sorry. He got away."

"But how?" Sarah asked. "There were so many of you looking for him."

Captain Rogers sighed heavily. "He killed one of my detectives and switched clothing with him. When we initially started our search, my men were told to look for someone in Amish garb. They weren't looking for one of their own. By the time we got the word out about the wardrobe change, we believe he had already escaped."

"We are so sorry to hear about the death of your men, Captain." Rebecca folded her hands. "They lost their lives trying to protect us. We will remember them and pray for their families."

Sarah shot a glance at Sam and was again moved by the pain she saw in his eyes. The loss of his partner cut deeper than he was willing to admit.

"Thank you, ma'am," Captain Rogers replied.

"Do you think he is gone for good?" Sarah asked. "No man would be foolish enough to come back again when the whole police force is looking for him, would he?"

"That is exactly what he is going to do, Sarah." The captain's steely gaze and no-nonsense voice held her attention. "He plans on killing you, the teacher and the children who were in that classroom. We've suspected that from the beginning. His actions in the past two days have confirmed it."

Sarah's stomach twisted into a tight, painful knot. The anger and determination she saw in both men's eyes upset her. She didn't need past memory to recognize the tension and fear in the room now.

She was willing to accept God's will for her life, and she trusted Him to protect her. But her throat constricted when she thought about the children. She knew in her heart that God would protect them, too. But she had looked into the stranger's face. Pure evil had stared back.

A chill shivered down her spine when she thought of the stranger's threats.

She glanced at Samuel, and a sense of peace calmed her.

Maybe Samuel was right. Maybe God used people to help carry out His will, and He could be using Samuel. She certainly hoped so. She would pray about it.

"What happens now?" Rebecca asked, swinging her gaze around to everyone in the room.

"Dr. Clark will be releasing Sarah tomorrow," Sam said.

Captain Rogers looked surprised. "So soon?"

"Yes, he told me just a few moments ago. He feels Sarah will be safer somewhere else. And, of course, the administration is screaming about liability."

"I'll need time to get the wheels in motion." Rogers looked at Rebecca. "Can we count on your help, Mrs. Lapp? Will Sarah be going home with you? Are you still willing to let Detective King accompany you?"

"Of course we will be taking Sarah home." Rebecca moved closer to the bed and busied her hands, gently tucking the blanket around Sarah's body as a mother might when tucking in a child for the night. When she finished, she looked at the two men.

"As for Samuel, my husband has already given his permission, and Jacob is a man of his word. Nothing that has happened here tonight will change that." She sent a kind, warm glance Sam's way. "Besides, Samuel has had a great loss of his own. Losing a partner must be a difficult thing, *ya?* Like losing a member of your family? It will be good for Samuel to be in a quiet place where he can reflect and pray and feel the tender mercy of God's healing touch."

He cleared his throat. "Okay, then. Let's get this thing started. We have twenty-four hours to make it happen."

"No. We have sixteen hours," Captain Rogers corrected. "Both of us need sleep. I don't want to see your face for at least eight hours. That's an order."

Sam nodded. "Understood, Captain. I'll be here first thing in the morning to take Sarah home."

Home.

A place she couldn't remember, but just the word made her long to get there. She tried hard to conjure up a mental image. What did the house look like? Did they have a barn? Horses? Cattle? Were they farmers tending fields of grain, or did their fields contain rows of corn? With all that had happened, would the Amish community still gather for celebration and praise? Or would the death of the bishop's son change everything?

Once Sarah saw the house and the farm, would it help refresh her memory? She held current memories of many faces that had come to visit her during this ordeal. They had claimed to be her friends. Would she be able to rekindle those relationships once she returned home? She hoped so. Maybe she wouldn't feel so lost and alone anymore.

In twenty-four hours, she would know the answer to all the questions tumbling around in her head. Somehow the thought of returning to a place where she had once forged roots, a place where she had once belonged to a community and a family, was strangely comforting... and oh so terrifying.

Chapter Seven

Sarah glanced down at her clothing. Gone was the print hospital gown. She wore a black apron that covered a good portion of the light blue dress beneath it. The dress draped her body loosely, fell slightly below her knees and brushed against her black opaque stockings. She smoothed her hand across the material.

Because of the many visitors she had had over the past week, Sarah knew this was typical Amish garb. So why didn't it feel familiar? Why couldn't she picture in her mind another time and place where she might have been dressed this way?

"Is something wrong?" Rebecca's heavily lined face wore a quizzical expression. "Are you feeling ill? Is this task too difficult for you right now?" Before Sarah could reply, Rebecca hurried forward. "Here, let me help you with your shoes."

"Thank you, but I can put on my shoes." But when Sarah bent down for the shoes, her head spun, and pain seized the left side of her temple.

Rebecca leaned over and retrieved the shoes. "You are not yet fully recovered. You are going to need some help with things you used to do for yourself. Do not let pride make you stumble before the Lord."

Sarah accepted the chiding with a respectful nod. But was it pride? Or a fierce determination to get better as quickly as possible and regain her independence?

A knock on the door drew their attention.

Sarah's heartbeat skipped when Samuel poked his head inside. She hadn't seen him for more than a moment or two since yesterday. He'd been making arrangements for her safety after she left the hospital. She'd missed him—and that thought surprised and unsettled her.

Samuel nodded a polite greeting to Rebecca as he entered, and then froze. The intensity of his gaze as his eyes roamed over her Amish clothing made her self-conscious. She smoothed her apron and wondered if some piece of clothing looked silly or out of place.

Rebecca coughed, breaking Samuel out of his reverie.

"Forgive me," he said. "I apologize for staring." He smiled at Sarah. "It is a surprise to see you out of hospital gowns. You look—" he seemed to search for the proper word "—healthy." His smile widened. "You look like you're ready to get out of here and go home."

Sarah smiled in return. "That I am."

Dr. Clark had told her that familiar surroundings might help her regain some of her memory. Sarah was counting on it with an anticipation so intense she found it almost hard to breathe.

"Are you ladies ready?"

"Almost." Rebecca slipped the white *kapp* that had been lying on the nightstand on top of Sarah's bandages.

It was a tight squeeze, but she got it placed properly. She tilted Sarah's face up. "We are ready now, *ya?*"

Sarah squeezed Rebecca's hand. She had grown fond of the woman, grateful that she came every day regardless of how difficult it must be for her. It didn't take black clothes to show that Rebecca was grieving. All someone had to do was look at the pain and fatigue evident in her eyes, body language and facial expressions. Yet still she came, every day, and sat beside her and told her stories of the farm, and occasionally stories of the life she'd shared with Peter.

Sarah learned they had not only known each other since childhood but had been good friends, which was a bit unusual in the Amish community, since boys and girls often had separate activities and chores. But Sarah had been a bit of a tomboy as a child. She loved to climb trees and play baseball and fish. Rebecca's eyes would light up when she'd tell Sarah tales of her escapades— the catfish she'd caught that weighed more than any of the boys' and the tale of her broken arm when she'd been spying on the boys swimming and had fallen out of the large oak tree on the back of their property by the pond.

"You always pushed boundaries. I had to practically tie you down when it came time to teach you how to cook and sew." Rebecca actually smiled for the very first time since this nightmare began.

"Why didn't my mother teach me those things? Why did it fall on your shoulders?"

A dark cloud passed over Rebecca's expression, but she quickly recovered. "That is another conversation for another day, *ya?* Right now I think it is best to get home."

Sarah held her tongue, but she couldn't help wondering why Rebecca seemed reluctant to talk about her mother. Was there some dark secret no one had told her about? And if Rebecca was hiding behind secrets, how could she be sure that what she told her about Peter and their marriage was the truth?

Before Sarah could question the older woman more, a nurse entered the room pushing a wheelchair. "These are your discharge instructions. Your medications are listed. So are signs and symptoms that you should report immediately to Dr. Clark if they occur."

Sam took the papers from the nurse's hand. "Thank you. We will go over these with a fine-tooth comb once we get home." He folded them and tucked them inside his jacket. "Sarah won't be needing the wheelchair. You can take it out with you."

"It's hospital policy that every patient is wheeled safely to the curb," the nurse insisted.

"Her safety is exactly the reason we can't afford to have her leave in a wheelchair." Sam shifted his attention to Sarah. "I was afraid the news media would catch hold of this story. After the hospital lockdown and the two murders, they have. National news crews have been camped outside all night, hoping for a picture for the tabloids or a few quotes for their papers. They've been trying to locate your room and slip in to see you. You wouldn't believe how creative and sneaky some of them have been. Hospital security has had their hands full. If we push you outside in a wheelchair, they'll descend on us like vultures."

"So what must we do?" Rebecca twisted her hands together and looked at Sam with concern on her face. "Sarah is not strong enough for such attention."

Sam looked at Sarah with a steady gaze. "Are you strong enough to walk out of here if I help you?"

Her stomach flipped under his scrutiny. When he looked at her like that, she wanted to please him. She just wasn't sure she could. "I think so but..." She lowered her voice and her eyes. "I'm willing to try, but I'm not sure I can."

"That's my girl. I knew I could count on you to give it a try. Don't worry. I'll be with you every step of the way."

My girl? Had he just said that to her?

He turned to Rebecca. "Do you have any extra Amish clothes with you? Perhaps a *kapp,* and possibly a shawl?"

"Yes," Rebecca replied. "I have some extra clothes with me. I have been sleeping in one of those fancy chairs that tilt back. Jacob brought me a bag from home so I could change and freshen up in the public bathrooms."

"Good." Sam grinned at the nurse. "I think you will look lovely in a white *kapp,* don't you?"

The nurse stammered and sputtered a weak protest as she realized he intended to put *her* in the wheelchair. She glanced at the two Amish women. Their faces were pale with fright and concern. She looked back at Sam and smiled. "Why not? I love pranks. This should be fun. Maybe I'll even make it on national TV."

Sam gently cupped Sarah's elbow, and the heat of his touch sent waves of tingles through her body. When he spoke, his voice was warm and tender. "How do you feel? Are you able to do this?" His eyes locked with hers, and she thought she'd drown in their darkness. "Am I asking too much of you? If you can't do the

walking, we will use the wheelchair. We'll try to cam-
ouflage your exit."

Her pulse beat like war drums against the soft tis-
sue of her wrist. She wasn't sure if it was the result of
her anxiety about evading the press and going home,
or whether it was a reaction to the strong, masculine
presence of the man standing beside her. The man who
had been kind and supportive and…and almost irresist-
ibly attractive from the moment she'd opened her eyes.

"How far must we go?"

"Not far. We'll take the elevator to the basement and
slip out the morgue entrance. I will be with you every
step of the way."

Rebecca clasped Sarah's other arm. "So will I, child.
God will be with us too." Rebecca handed a *kapp* and
shawl to the nurse. "I hope these will help."

Sam asked an officer to push the disguised nurse in
the wheelchair through the front entrance while they
headed toward the elevators.

Just as the three of them were about to make their
exit, the door opened again.

"Jacob." Rebecca looked at her husband in surprise.
"What has happened? Why are you here?"

"You are my wife. Sarah is my daughter-in-law. You
need me. Where else would I be?"

Although there was no physical contact between
them, there was a sense of intimacy. They obviously
loved each other and it showed…in the kindness of
their words…in the gaze of their eyes…in the gentleness of their voices. Sarah couldn't help but wonder
if this was what her relationship with their son, Peter,
had been like.

A deep sadness flowed over her that she felt no feelings for Peter. Neither good nor bad. She couldn't even draw his image into her memory. The Amish did not approve of pictures, so Rebecca was unable to show her a wedding photo or any other.

Sarah glanced at Samuel. There was kindness and gentleness and something else with this man. She felt more fondness for this stranger than she did for the man who had been her husband. It wasn't the way it was supposed to be, not the way she wanted it to be. And it troubled her greatly.

Almost as if he could read her mind, Sam seemed to assess both the change in the atmosphere of the room and its possible reason. Instantly, he took charge.

"Come." He spoke with authority. "We have to slip out before the press realizes that isn't Sarah we sent out front."

Without a word, they hurried from the room. They rode the elevator in silence. Sam exited first, checked that the corridor was empty then summoned them to follow.

Sarah knew he shortened his steps to keep pace with hers. She moved as quickly as she could down the long, empty corridor, but her rubbery legs had no strength. She feared they would crumple beneath her at any moment. Her heart beat in her chest like a runaway horse, and for the first time in many days, fear threatened to claim her composure.

Sam had arranged for a driver to be waiting for them at the morgue loading dock. The four exited the building and crossed the dock with synchronized movements to the steps to the parking lot.

Beads of sweat broke out on Sarah's forehead. She felt as if the blood had drained from her face, leaving her light-headed and dizzy. Her chest hurt, and suddenly it became difficult to breathe.

"Wait! Please." She began dragging her feet. "I can't... I can't breathe." Her hand flew to her chest, and she gulped for air.

Jacob and Rebecca had reached the car, and they turned to see what delayed them. Sam gestured them on. "It's okay. Get in the car. We'll be there in a second."

Sam faced Sarah. He clasped both her forearms in his hands and locked his gaze with hers. "Sarah?"

"I don't know what's wrong. My chest...it hurts... and I... I can't breathe."

"Listen to me. You're having a panic attack. Dr. Clark warned me that you might, once you left the hospital and the stress hit you." He locked his gaze with hers, the intensity of his stare mesmerizing her. "I'm not going to let anything happen to you." He drew her closer, almost as if he could transfer his strength to her. "You can do this. But you have to trust me."

"There they are! On the loading dock!"

Sam and Sarah looked in the direction of the voices. Two women, each holding a microphone in hand, raced toward them. A couple of men carrying cameras sprinted behind the women.

"We have to get out of here," Sam said.

Sarah's legs trembled as if they were made of gelatin instead of flesh and bone. "I can't." Certain her legs would no longer support her weight, she leaned heavily against his chest. "I'm sorry, Samuel."

Without hesitation, he scooped her off her feet.

She could feel his muscled strength supporting her legs and back as he carried her to the car. She clenched his shirt, its softness rubbing against her cheek. The clean scent of fresh linen mingled with the appealing, warm scent of his skin as she clung to him, and for a crazy moment in time she had no desire to release her grasp.

By the time they'd reached the first step, her heartbeat had slowed and her breathing returned to normal. Raising her eyes to meet Samuel's, Sarah knew that everything would be okay. God would protect her... and He would use Samuel to do it. Peace and gratitude replaced the terror that had been flowing through her veins just moments before. She smiled up at the man who held her in his arms.

"Take me home, Samuel. Please, I just want to go home."

Chapter Eight

It was early evening when they arrived at the house. Looming in the shadows of twilight, the two-story white clapboard house looked much like many of the others they'd passed along the way. A large red barn loomed to the left. They passed a multitude of fenced areas. In the distance, two horses grazed in the meadow.

Once the driver stopped the car, Jacob got out and hurried ahead to ready the house. Sam came around and helped both Rebecca and Sarah out of the vehicle.

Sarah stood for a second and looked around the property. She breathed in the heavy smells of fertile earth, manure and animals common to a working farm. She climbed the steps to the front porch, all the while trying to retrieve memories of times past, but none came.

Jacob met them just inside the door. Several kerosene lamps bathed the home in a warm, soft glow. "It is *gut* to have you home, Sarah." He helped Rebecca take off her coat and then helped Sarah with hers.

"I will make us some hot tea." Rebecca crossed to the propane-powered stove and put the kettle on.

Sarah glanced around the living room. She noted a

sofa, several chairs and scattered tables, but the focal point of the room was an impressive stone fireplace.

"Please, sit. Rest." Jacob gestured toward the kitchen table. "I have to bring in my horses. I will be back shortly."

"Do you need help?" Sam offered.

"*Danki,* no. Sit. Rest. It was a long trip, and I believe you have gotten little sleep in the past weeks."

Rebecca placed hot tea and a plate of fresh, home-made cookies in the middle of the table.

The scent of chamomile and chocolate chips teased Sarah's nostrils and made her realize she had barely touched her dinner.

"There's nothing better to ward off a night's chill than a hot cup of tea and a sweet treat. Come, both of you. Sit. Eat," Rebecca said.

"*Danki,*" Sam answered in the Pennsylvania Dutch dialect, his tone light and friendly. He bit into a cookie. "*Gut.* Did you know the *Englisch* have a saying that the way to a man's heart is through his stomach? These cookies are probably what prompted the saying."

A smile teased the corner of Sarah's mouth when she saw the blush of pleasure stain Rebecca's cheeks. What do you know? She wasn't the only one to succumb to this man's charm.

Rebecca, mindful of Sarah's arm in a sling and her frail health, poured her a cup of tea and placed two cookies on a small plate in front of her.

The three of them sat in companionable silence, enjoying the quiet and the treat, comfortable enough with each other not to feel obligated to fill the silence with idle conversation.

Sarah felt at home amidst the simple, plain surroundings, even though she had no concrete memories of ever being here before. But it only took a glance outside, now that twilight had ebbed to darkness, to remind her that until this man was caught, she would have no safe haven.

The back door opened, and Rebecca waved her husband inside.

"Come, Jacob. Sit. The tea grows cold."

Jacob took a seat and grinned. "I'm coming, *lieb*. I already know the secret that I am sure Samuel has just discovered. A bite of your cookies on a person's lips is a moment of pure joy."

Rebecca's blush deepened, and she placed an extra cookie in front of her husband.

Sarah grinned. Cookies might bring joy to the men, but for her, it was witnessing the strong and loving bond between the two people who were turning out to be the only family she had.

Sam and Jacob kept the conversation at the table flowing. They discussed hopes for the fall's harvest, the farmer's market prices, the plans for next year's planting.

Sarah smothered a yawn with her hand, and immediately Rebecca rose from the table. "You must be exhausted after today's journey, child." She picked up one of the oil lamps. "Come, I will show you your room."

Sam stood, clasped Sarah's elbow and helped her to her feet. His touch sent a surge of energy through her body, leaving tingles and confusion in its wake.

"Rebecca is right." Sam gently trailed a finger down her cheek. "You need your rest."

His eyes darkened with an intensity Sarah didn't understand. As they gazed into each other's eyes, there was an intimate pull between them, almost as though they were the only two people in the world.

More confused and disconcerted about the feelings that were growing for this man, Sarah broke eye contact and took a step away.

They were right. She was more than tired. She was exhausted, weak and disheartened. She'd expected a flood of memories to burst forth once she'd seen the farm, and she could barely hide her bitter disappointment when it did not happen.

Sarah followed close behind Rebecca, her path illuminated by the oil lamp Rebecca had given her. Rebecca paused outside a door to the right of the stairs, opened it and stood aside, looking hopeful and expectant.

Sarah recognized Rebecca's expectation. She was hoping that once Sarah entered the bedroom, her memory would return. She couldn't fault the woman; she longed for the same thing and dreaded that it wouldn't happen.

She stepped inside. The oil lamp bathed the room in a soft glow. She noted the pretty patchwork quilt on the double bed, the plain curtains at the two windows, the rocking chair beside a sturdy table that held a Bible.

Sarah's eyes missed nothing, and her heart grew heavy. She released the breath she'd been holding. Nothing. No memories. No feelings. No past. She could barely turn to face Rebecca.

The older woman forced a smile to her face, hurried to the chest against the wall, pulled out a clean, fresh, cream-colored floor-length flannel gown and laid it out on the bed. "Will you need me to help you dress?" Rebecca glanced at Sarah's sling.

"No. I'll be fine."

Rebecca nodded. "This should keep you warm, but if you find the gown and quilt are not enough, please come and tell me. The nights this time of year can sometimes chill a person to their bones." She crossed to the door. "If you need anything, child, anything at all, our room is only three doors down on the right."

"Danki." Sarah answered in the Pennsylvania Dutch dialect, but she wasn't sure if it was something she was pulling from her memory or something she'd heard so many times over the past few weeks that it felt natural saying it.

After Rebecca left, she placed the oil lamp on the nightstand. It was a struggle to get out of her clothes and don the flannel gown, but she managed. Sitting on the edge of the bed, she glanced around the shadowed room. That's how her mind felt—a mixture of clear images, shadows and darkness. Would she ever remember her former life?

It was frustrating not to remember anything of her childhood, her teens, her adulthood. Questions swirled through her mind.

What kind of person was she? Was she kind and loving, or did she have a selfish streak? Was she hard-working or lazy? Had she laughed easily, loved deeply, or was she more withdrawn and quiet?

Everyone in this small community knew the answers to her questions. Why couldn't she find those answers within herself?

A tear slid down her cheek. She felt so afraid and alone.

But she wasn't alone, was she? The thought brought her comfort, and she began to pray.

* * *

In the bright light of morning, Sarah took the opportunity to study her surroundings. The room was clean, neat and simple. A plain wooden oak chest stood against a far wall. Small oval rag rugs rested on each side of the bed to warm one's feet against the chill of the wooden floor. Two hooks hung on the wall next to a small closet. Were they to hold the next day's clothing? Or perhaps a man's hat? Peter's?

The thought reminded Sarah that in the not too distant past, she'd shared this room with someone. Someone she'd been told she loved. She spread her hands over the slight swell of her belly. That love had created this new life.

Even if she had no mental images of Peter, she was certain she'd have a clearer picture of the man when this child was born. She would only have to look at the child's eyes, or the color of hair, or the tiny baby smile, and she would be able to "see" her husband. If nothing else, she was certain that at that moment she would feel love for the man who had given her such a precious gift. But would she ever remember Peter himself, and the life they'd shared?

Dr. Clark had warned her not to expect too much of herself, that memories would come gradually, if they came at all, and not to stress over it.

Easier said than done.

Sarah couldn't deny that she'd had huge expectations when she'd come home. As foolish as it might seem now, she'd believed that once she actually saw her home, her memory would return. Disappointment left a bitter taste in her mouth and her heart heavy. But she wouldn't let it color the day. She would be grateful that she was home and healing.

Sarah followed the rich, mouthwatering aroma of coffee and freshly baked bread downstairs to the kitchen. "Good morning, Rebecca."

The woman spun around from the sink. "*Guder mariye*. Did you sleep well?"

"Yes, *danki*. The trip home must have tired me more than I thought. I fell asleep as soon as my head hit the pillow."

"Did sleeping in your own bed help you remember anything?"

Rebecca's expression held such hope, and Sarah's inability to give the woman the answers she longed for filled her with guilt and sorrow.

"I didn't remember anything. I didn't even dream last night." When she saw the light in Rebecca's eyes dim, pain seized her heart. "I'm so sorry. I know you were hoping for more from me."

"The only thing I am expecting from you, child, is for you to do your best to regain your health. Nothing more. You will remember in God's time if He desires it." Her brow furrowed. "Should you be out of bed? I was fixing a tray to bring to your room."

"I was just about to ask that same question."

Sarah didn't have to turn around to know that Samuel stood behind her. He filled every room he entered with a strong, masculine presence. Besides, she would recognize the deep, warm tones of his voice anywhere.

The polite thing to do would be to acknowledge him and answer his question. She glanced over her shoulder to do just that, but the smile froze on her face and her breath caught in her throat. He stood closer than she'd expected. Close enough that she should have been able to feel his breath on the back of her neck.

Mere inches separated her from the rock-solid wall of his chest. She couldn't help but remember how warm and safe and protected it had felt to be held in those muscled arms, cradled against that chest.

She took a step back and stumbled awkwardly over her own feet. Sam's hand shot out to steady her. "See, it is too soon. You should be in bed." Concern shone from his eyes and etched lines in his face.

"I'm fine." She eased her arm out of his grasp. "I tripped over my own feet. I don't know if I was an awkward oaf in my old life, but it looks like I am now." She grinned. "And yes, I should be out of bed. I've been in bed for two weeks. I may not remember much about my old self, but this new self, this person I am now, can't stand being cooped up for one more minute."

Rebecca chuckled behind her. "That's not a new self, Sarah. That's who you've always been. A dervish of activity from sunup to sundown, even as a little one." Rebecca patted her hand on the table. "Come. Both of you. Sit down. Eat."

"I can't remember the last time I sat down to a meal that didn't come out of a hospital vending machine. I'm starving." Sam beat Sarah to the table and pulled out a chair for her before he sat down.

Rebecca laughed. "Good. I like to feed people with healthy appetites." She carried a heavy, cast-iron skillet to the table and filled his plate with potatoes and sausage. Scrambled eggs were already in a bowl on the table. She set out a second small plate filled with slices of warm bread and a Mason jar of homemade strawberry jam.

"Yum." Sam's stomach chose that moment to growl loudly, and both women laughed.

Sarah watched every movement he made while pretending not to notice anything at all. She noted how long and lean his fingers were when he lifted a slice of bread. She smiled to herself when she saw the tiniest bead of jam at the corner of his mouth.

A warm flush tinged her cheeks when she realized how happy she was when he was around, and then she grew confused and unhappy with herself for that same reason. Should she be allowing anything, even friendship, to develop with this man? He was an *Englischer*. She was Amish, or at least that's what everyone told her she was. She wished she felt Amish, or English, or anything from anywhere—if she could only own the memory.

One thing she did know for sure. She was an assignment to Samuel, and he would be leaving as soon as his assignment was over. Didn't she have enough chaos in her life without adding unreturned feelings to it?

She stole another glance at him. She couldn't help but admire his strong, chiseled features, the square chin, the pronounced cheekbones, the angular planes and the deep, dark, intense eyes that seemed to be able to look at a person and see into their soul.

Was she gravitating toward him because, besides Rebecca, he had been the only constant in her life for the past two weeks whom she could rely on in an otherwise frightening, blank world of strangers and fear?

Or was the reason simply a woman being drawn to an attractive, kind man?

Either way she had to learn to dismiss these new feelings in an effort to discover the old ones. She had to concentrate on remembering the past and forget the temptation of daring to think about a future. There was no future for Samuel and her. There never would be.

"Where is Jacob?" Sam smeared jam on a second slice of warm bread. "I'd like to ask him if there is anything close to the house that I might help him with today. Maybe muck the stalls in the barn?"

"Jacob is mending a fence in the back pasture," Rebecca replied. "He left at first light. I am expecting him back anytime now."

No sooner had the words had left her lips than the back door opened and Jacob strode into the room. He hung his coat and hat on the hooks by the door, slid out of his boots and padded in his socks to the table.

Rebecca slid a mug of hot coffee in front of his chair before he even sat down.

"*Guder mariye,* everyone. The skies are clear. The air is sweet. Looks like a good day for working in the fields." Jacob rubbed his hands together in anticipation and took a slice of bread from the basket.

"What can I do to help?" Sam asked. "I know work is never truly done on a farm, but I am limited in how far I can wander from the house. I was hoping you might have something for me in the barn. I can muck stalls, feed animals. I also saw carpentry equipment."

"*Ya,* that was Peter's work. He built cabinets and furniture. He was working on a new table and chairs to present to Josiah and Anna. They are to be married this month."

"Aren't weddings held in November, after the harvest?" Sam asked.

"*Ya,* but this is a special occasion. Josiah has a *gut* job opportunity with an Amish family in Ohio. Peter finished the chairs he was making for them, but not the table." Jacob's eyes dimmed. "I will have to find time in my schedule to finish it for him."

"Let me."

Jacob cocked an eyebrow. "You know woodworking?"

Sam shrugged. "I am better working in the fields, but my father taught me to sand and stain and varnish. I need to be close to the house to protect Sarah, but it doesn't mean I can't share in the work."

Jacob nodded, and a new respect crossed his expression. "That is *gut. Danki,* Samuel. I will accept your help with the table."

Sam glanced out the kitchen window. He tensed and rose to his feet. "A buggy passed by the window," he said in answer to the questioning looks on everyone's faces.

Pounding on the front door drew their attention.

Jacob rose to answer it, but before he could the door opened like a burst of wind had pushed it, and Benjamin Miller stormed into the house. He strode to the kitchen doorway, his demeanor angry.

"Forgive me, Jacob, for entering without your permission, but the matter is urgent."

Jacob's tone of voice was low and calm but stern as he faced his friend. "What could be so urgent, Benjamin, that you could not wait for me to open the door? You have frightened my wife and Sarah."

Sam remained standing. Sarah thought he looked like a panther poised to strike, his hand subtly hidden within the folds of his jacket. He must be wearing a gun. The thought made shivers of apprehension race up and down her arms. She did not like guns, and she did not want to be reminded that Sam was as comfortable wearing one as he was his pants or boots.

Benjamin removed his hat. "I apologize." He pointed an accusing finger at Sam. "But I told you that allowing this man into our homes would only bring trouble to us, and now it has."

"What are you talking about? What trouble?" Jacob asked.

"There is a man in town. He is going business to business asking where he can find Sarah—and the man protecting her."

Chapter Nine

"*Kumm,* sit." Jacob gestured to a vacant chair at the table. "Rebecca will pour you a cup of *kaffe,* and you can tell us what you know."

Benjamin glared at Sam as he stepped past him. After he took a sip of his coffee, he leaned in toward Jacob as if he was the only person in the room to hear.

"I was at the hardware store when Josiah came in and told me. The whole town is in a dither. No one knows what to do or say."

"What are folks saying?" Sam tried not to appear annoyed when Benjamin directed the answer to Jacob as if he was the one who had asked.

"We cannot lie. Everyone has simply said that we cannot help him."

"Did you see this man?" Jacob asked.

"*Ya,* he came into the hardware store just a few minutes after Josiah. He was of average height and dressed in an *Englisch* suit and tie. He had bushy, bright red hair and wore wire-framed glasses."

"Did you hear what he said to the store clerk?" Sam

asked. "Did he have an accent? Any distinguishable features like a scar or mole on his face?"

Still ignoring him, Benjamin finished his coffee and then spoke to Jacob. "He pulled out some kind of wallet and flashed the badge inside. He said he was a police detective."

"But that is a lie." Jacob glanced between Sam and Sarah, who had paled like the milk in the glass in front of her. "If he truly was a police detective, he would know where Sarah lives, and he would know Detective King."

"*Ya,* he is lying. Everyone knows it. He brings trouble to our town." For the first time since sitting at the table, Benjamin made eye contact with Sam. "He is following you. You should not have come here."

"Benjamin, please tell us what else the man said." Rebecca refilled his coffee cup.

"He told the store clerk that the woman he was searching for, Sarah Lapp, had been kidnapped from the hospital by the man who was claiming to protect her. He asked if anyone could tell him what farm or family she belongs to, or if they'd seen her in town."

Sam ignored the accusatory glare directed his way. "Could he have been a newspaper reporter? They have been known to use less than truthful tactics to get a story."

Benjamin shrugged. "The town is full of reporters. They travel in packs like wolves. They carry cameras and climb in and out of big motor vans. They wear their pictures on a badge on their clothes."

"So what do we do?" Rebecca held fingers to her chin, and concern filled her eyes. "We cannot let this man near our Sarah."

"I don't intend to let that happen, Rebecca. Don't worry," Sam assured her.

"Maybe I should leave this place." Sarah joined the conversation for the first time. Her eyes were earnest, her tone anxious. "If I go away and hide someplace else, maybe the man will follow me. Maybe it will keep the *kinner* safe."

"The children will not be safe, Sarah, no matter what you do. It is not beneath him to use them to flush you out, even if you did hide someplace else. It is better for you to stay here. It will be easier to protect you."

"Is there anything we can do to help?" Jacob asked.

"Yes. Talk to everyone you know. Ask them to keep their silence. Tell them it is not only Sarah's safety they will be protecting, but also the children's."

Sarah stood. Her legs wobbled beneath her, and she held on to the table edge for support. "I cannot let this man hurt the *kinner.*"

Sam hurried to her side and supported her right arm with his hand. "The only thing I want you to do right now, Sarah Lapp, is to rest. You must get stronger if you expect your memories of that day to return. If they return, that is when you will be the most help."

"Samuel is right, child." Rebecca took Sam's place at Sarah's side. "You've had enough excitement for now. Let me help you back to bed. You haven't been out of the hospital an entire day yet."

Sarah looked at each man at the table, and then fixed her gaze on Sam. "What happens now, Samuel?"

"We wait."

"That's it? Just sit and wait for a madman to come and hurt our *kinner,* or kill me, or both?"

Benjamin jumped to his feet and shouted. "You must

go! Maybe if you go, he will leave and we can all go back to our lives."

Benjamin flailed his arms in anger, but Samuel saw beneath it and recognized the fear. He kept his voice calm and his tone reassuring.

"Tell me, Benjamin. If a wolf stalks a man's sheep, will the wolf go away because the shepherd decides to leave the flock and go home?"

Sam paused while he waited for the other man to consider the wisdom of his words. When Sam spoke again, his voice, though calm, held a note of steel.

"This man will come for Sarah...and when he does, I will stop him."

Sarah thanked the good Lord that the day had ended much quieter than it had started. She gently rocked back and forth on the front porch and watched the sun set over the newly planted fields. Despite the disturbing news at breakfast, once the discussion had ended, the men had gone about their chores, and the day had passed peacefully.

Samuel had kept busy in the barn with the table he had promised Jacob he would finish. Although he rarely left the barn, Sarah could feel his eyes upon her whenever she stepped out of the house. At first it was unsettling and made her uncomfortable, but after she'd had some time to think and pray about it, she realized his intention was to keep her safe, and she was grateful.

Rebecca crossed the porch and sat down beside her. "Let me help with the string beans."

Sarah laughed. "Please, I may not be able to use my left shoulder, but my hand works. I can break string beans into smaller pieces for dinner."

Rebecca glanced into the bowl resting on Sarah's lap. "And it is a good job you do."

Once Rebecca had settled into a soft, rhythmic rocking beside her, Sarah dared to broach the subject that had been weighing heavily on her mind all day.

"Rebecca, tell me about my family. In the hospital you changed the conversation when I mentioned my mother. No one has claimed me as daughter or sister or aunt. Do I have a family? Beside you and Jacob… and Peter, of course."

A shadow crossed Rebecca's face, and her rocking quickened.

"I do not wish to cause you any grief," Sarah continued. "But of course, you must understand how difficult it has been for me not to know who I am, who I come from. I am afraid those memories may not return, and you…you could help me with some of the answers to this darkness inside."

Rebecca dropped her head and remained silent.

"Was I an evil person? Did I come from a bad family? Is that why talking about it is difficult for you?"

Rebecca's eyes widened, and her mouth opened in a perfect circle. "Lord, help us. Where would you get a notion such as that?"

"Because the question brings you pain. I assume it is bad memories I am asking you to recall."

"Nothing could be further from the truth, child. The pain I feel is that of loss and grief for all the wonderful people who were part of my life and are now home with the Lord."

Rebecca reached over and patted Sarah's knee. "Your grandmother and I grew up together. We were best friends. Her name was Anna. She married when she was still in her teens and had a daughter soon after, a beautiful girl named Elizabeth.

"Elizabeth was a dervish of energy, a tornado of sunshine and light…just like you were, child. Elizabeth met an *Englisch* boy and left our community to marry him and live in his world. It broke Anna's heart but…" Rebecca shrugged. "She understood this thing called love."

"When your father was killed in a factory accident, Elizabeth brought you home. You were about five at the time. Such joy! Such happiness you brought to Anna's eyes every time she looked at you." A cloud passed over Rebecca's expression. "And when your mother took ill and died, you were the only thing that kept Anna's heart from shattering into a million pieces."

Rebecca smiled at her. "Your grandmother died just before your tenth birthday. Jacob and I brought you into our home and raised you like one of our own. We were overcome with joy when you married Peter and became a true daughter, not just one of my heart."

Rebecca's eyes glistened with tears, pain, grief—and something else, something she found harder to identify. "You are all Jacob and I have left now. We have lost Anna and Elizabeth and…and Peter…" The catch in her words gave her pause.

"I'm so sorry. I didn't mean to cause you pain."

"Ack. Sometimes life is painful, child. That is what makes it life and not heaven." She smiled broadly. "But it is not all pain. We still have you, *lieb*. And the child you carry is God's blessing to all of us. He knows how painful it has been for me. Not to see my son's smiling face or hear his voice or watch him hammer away on the furniture he crafts in the barn. Part of my heart shattered that day in the school house. But not all of it…"

She cupped Sarah's chin in her hand. "God made sure He left me with enough of a heart so I could fill it with love for you and for my grandchild. He took Peter to be with Him. That was His will, and sometimes it is hard to understand His ways. But He left a little part of Peter with us. For that, I am so very grateful. God is *gut*."

Rebecca stood. "*Kumm*. It will be dark soon. The men will be tired and hungry. I am sure there is something I can find for you to help me with despite your sling. It will be like old times, fixing dinner together for our family."

The two women embraced and then walked together into the house.

Later that evening, Sam saw Sarah standing on the porch. She stared up at the night sky and seemed to be studying the stars.

"For a person who just got out of the hospital, I find you spend most of your time outside." Sam's boots scraped loudly against the wooden floor of the porch.

Sarah turned her head and tossed a smile his way. The light from the kerosene lamp danced softly across her features.

"I've been cooped up much too long. I like to feel fresh air on my skin." She turned her eyes back to the sky. "Have you ever really looked at the sky, Samuel? God is an artist, and He uses the sky as His palette. I watch in awe as the patterns and colors change from dawn to dusk to the inky blackness of night. Even then, He decorates the darkness with stars to light our way and to give us hope."

Sam stepped behind her and wrapped a quilt around

her shoulders. "If you insist on living on the porch, you must start wearing a jacket or sweater. The days are pleasant, but the temperatures still dip in the mornings and evenings. You're going to be a mother. You must keep yourself warm and healthy."

Almost on cue, a rush of cool air brushed past them and he could feel her quiver beneath his touch. She pulled the quilt tighter and burrowed into its warmth.

"You have looked at the sky for hours, Sarah. Even God has gone to bed," he teased her.

Sarah chuckled. "True, I suppose. I find it easier to think when I'm out here."

Sam gestured to a rocker. "I have been standing all day. I would like to sit now, and I can't if I am supposed to be protecting you. How about protecting me for a little while? Sit with me so I can give my legs a rest."

She did as requested. "I think it would be your eyes that need rest, Samuel. They bounced in my direction and then back to your chores so often, I'm surprised you can still see straight."

He laughed hard and deep, the booming sound breaking through the silence of the night. No words needed to be spoken as they rocked together in perfect unison.

"You are right, Sarah," Sam said. "You created quite a dilemma for me. A bodyguard cannot guard a body if he is not watching it, and a man cannot be a man if he stays in another man's home and does not attempt to pull his own weight. So my poor eyes got a work-out for sure." He rested his left ankle on his right knee.

"How is the table coming along? I saw how hard you worked. You went over every inch, your movements steady, your attention to detail evident."

"Tomorrow I will do the final touches and it will be

ready." He reached over and squeezed her hand. "Maybe you will take pity on my eyes and sit with me in the barn."

"Breathe in fresh air on the porch, or inhale the smell of hay, manure, animals and varnish in the barn? Sit in shadows when I can be outside and feel the warmth of the sun on my face. Hmm?" She held an index finger to her lips as if seriously considering the proposition. "Sorry, I think not, Samuel. You will just have to finish your chores faster and come sit in the sunshine with me."

"I do sit in the sunshine whenever I am with you."

The unexpected compliment seemed to surprise them both. A heavy silence fell over them. The only sound on the porch was the rhythmic swishing of the rockers. When Sam spoke again, his tone was thoughtful and serious.

"Talk to me, Sarah. What deep thoughts trouble you so much that you stare into the horizon for hours searching for answers? I know the past two weeks have been difficult. I understand. I am just wondering if there is something more…something deeper that troubles you."

A tear slid down her cheek, and she hurried to wipe it away.

"You can talk to me, you know. Listening is part of bodyguard duties and comes absolutely free of charge."

In the soft glow of the kerosene lamp, Sarah saw warmth and empathy in his eyes. She knew she could feel safe baring her soul to this man because he was a stranger. She didn't have to choose her words with care for fear of saying the wrong thing or having something she said cause pain, like it sometimes did when she talked with Rebecca or Jacob. She felt she could talk to him about anything—except the unsettling feelings and questions she had about him, of course.

He reached out and clasped her hand. "Talk to me. I can be a good listener."

She inhaled deeply. Maybe it would be helpful to talk with someone who might be able to understand the disappointment and fear gnawing inside. Grateful for an open ear, she kept her voice low so as not to disturb Rebecca or Jacob inside.

"I thought coming home would end all my troubles. I thought when I saw the house, when I returned to familiar surroundings and slipped back into a normal daily routine, that everything would be okay."

Silence hung in the darkness between them.

"I expected my memory to return. Expected answers to the thousands of questions I have inside."

"I take it you haven't had any flashes of memory?"

She shook her head, oblivious as to whether he could see the movement in the dim light.

"Dr. Clark warned you, Sarah. He said your memories would probably come back slowly, maybe in flashes, and you should be patient. He also told you that they may not come back at all."

"I know." Her voice was a mere whisper on the wind.

"Can you live with that? Can you cope with the fact that your memories may never return?"

The warmth of his voice flowed over her, filled with concern and offering her waves of comfort, but still she felt lost and defeated. "I'm not sure. I don't know how it will be if this is a permanent situation. The only thing holding me together right now is hope…hope that it will all come back, that I will remember again."

"And if you don't?"

The silence became heavy and oppressive, stealing her breath, causing her fingers to tremble and her toes to nervously tap against the wooden floor.

"Calm down, Sarah. You're starting to have another panic attack. Take a couple of deep breaths. It will be all right."

He stopped rocking, pulled his chair around to face her and moved in closer so she could see his face in the dim light.

"You're scared."

She nodded.

"What frightens you the most?"

She thought for a moment, and then locked her gaze with his. "I'm scared to death that I will never know who I am, who I was…" She nodded with her head toward the house. "Who they expect me to be." She lowered her eyes. "They are good people. They have been hurt enough. What if I can't be the person they want me to be?"

A burst of anger raged through her. "Why did this happen? What am I supposed to do with all this emptiness?" She jumped to her feet, held on to the porch rail and stared out into the night.

"Do you have any idea what it feels like to be me?" she asked. "I can't remember the people around me, the same people who shower me with love and gaze at me with such high hopes and expectations." She sighed deeply. "I can't even remember *me*.

"I am told I was an *Englisch* child who was raised by an Amish grandmother and then adopted by the Lapps after her death. But what does that make me? Am I *Englisch* because I was born in your world? Or am I Amish because I was raised as a child in this one? I can't remember anything about either world, so how can I answer that question?

"I am told I was a dervish of energy. Is that why I want to be busy all the time? Why I long to be outside and moving? Or is it fear and restlessness from thoughts I cannot bear that drive me?"

She paced, and Sam didn't speak or try to stop her.

"Do I like strawberry jam? Scrambled eggs? Sausage? Can I cook? Can I sew? Do I have friends? Do I care about anybody? Am I a person who should be cared about?"

Sarah's fears shone through her eyes.

"I was married to a man I can't remember. There isn't even a picture I can look at so I can try to remember his face. Married, Samuel. Partners in life, in love. I can't remember any of it. Does Peter deserve to be forgotten? What kind of person does that make me?"

Her voice rose. She could hear the frustration and anxiety in it, but she couldn't control it.

"I'm pregnant. I'm carrying a precious gift, a blessing. But what kind of mother will I be? How will I teach this child the ways of the world when I can't remember ever taking the path myself? How can this child grow to love me? How can *anyone* love me when I don't know me well enough to love myself?" Her voice rose an octave. "I have to remember. Everyone needs me to remember. I don't know what I will do if I can't."

Sarah had to physically fight the urge to dart away, to flee into the darkness and try to outrun the fear.

Sam stood and gathered her into his arms. She nestled firmly against the warmth of his chest. The sound of his voice rumbled against her ear. She could feel the gentle breeze of his breath through her hair with each word of comfort.

The words he spoke were not important. They were comfort words. It was the strength of his embrace, the solid wall of his presence that soothed her. He offered her a safe haven to air her fears without judgment. He offered her friendship and empathy. Sarah may not be able to prevent disappointing the people who knew her in the past, but Samuel wasn't a part of her past. He knew her only as she was now. She truly believed that God had sent him into her life to help her when she needed it most…and that thought brought her peace.

"I'm sorry." She eased out of his embrace.

She didn't have a chance to finish the sentence before he cupped her chin with his hand and forced her eyes to lock with his.

"You have nothing to apologize for, Sarah. You are as much a victim in all of this as anyone. Remember that."

He brushed his fingers lightly against the path of tears on her cheek. "You can sit and wallow and feel sorry for yourself. You have the right to do that." He smiled down at her. "Or you can look at this as God's gift…an opportunity to be anyone you want to be."

She arched an eyebrow.

"You tell me you don't know if you were a good person or bad, selfish or kind? Okay, so choose. It doesn't matter who or what you were. None of us can change one moment of the past, no matter how much we might want to. But God has given you the present and it is a gift, isn't it? Decide what kind of person you want to be. Will you be loving and kind to others? Will you be hardworking and helpful? Your choice, isn't it?"

He smiled down on her. "You will be a wonderful

mother because you care for your child so much, and he or she isn't even here yet. Think about it, Sarah. You can take the journey with your child. The two of you can learn to play in the sunshine. You can both decide together whether you like the taste of turnips or prefer the taste of corn. You can read books together each night before bed. You might find that you enjoy them just as much as the child because you will be reading them for the first time.

"Who cares if you can cook? If you can't, you can learn. Who cares if you can sew? Try it. If you can remember the stitches, *wunderbaar*. If not, it is only another lesson to learn. You can start your life over again, Sarah. Many people I know wish they could have that chance."

The truth of his words washed over her, and she felt a new resolve, maybe even a little happiness blossom within. She chewed on her bottom lip. "But what of Jacob and Rebecca? What if I can't be the person they remember?"

He slipped his arms around her waist and drew her close again.

"They loved the person you were. Now they will love the person you will grow to be."

She smiled and allowed herself to burrow against him one more time. She closed her eyes. He felt so warm and comforting and safe.

Suddenly his body tensed. She raised her head and searched his face.

"What?"

He didn't speak but stared hard into the darkness. The tension in his body made his formerly comforting hands tighten to steel. His grasp almost hurt as she eased out of his hold.

She turned her head and followed his gaze. A tiny ball of light shone in the distance. She squinted and tried to focus to get a better look. As she stared harder across the dark, empty fields, the light grew larger, brighter.

"Samuel, what is it?"

His features were stone-cold, his expression grim. "Fire."

Chapter Ten

"Fire? Are you sure?" Sarah grasped the porch post and stared hard at the horizon. What had begun as a tiny glimmer was now an ominous orange light that grew in height and width even as they watched.

The sharp clanging of a bell broke the silence of the spring night. Seconds later Sam's cell phone rang, the musical notes clashing with the continued clang of the farm triangle. He mumbled a few words in reply to whatever he was hearing, shoved the phone back in his coat pocket and raced for the barn.

"Samuel?"

"Stay there. Don't move!" he yelled over his shoulder as he ran.

Sarah watched in alarm as the light became a looming two-story-high monster of flame on the horizon.

Jacob and Rebecca raced onto the porch.

"What's happening?" Jacob stumbled toward Sarah in a half hop as he bent down to pull one of his boots on. Rebecca, tying the sash of her robe over her long flannel nightgown, was close on his heels.

Before Sarah could respond, Jacob yelled, "That's

Benjamin's place! There's a fire!" He turned and clasped his wife's forearms. "I must go. I'll be back as soon as I can." He kissed her on the forehead.

Rebecca nodded. "God speed and keep you safe."

Just as Jacob moved to the steps, Sam ran out of the barn, pulling one of the horses behind him. He brought it to a stop at the base of the stairs. "I thought it would be faster to saddle the horse than hitch the buggy."

"Danki," Jacob replied, throwing his foot in a stirrup and mounting up. The horse, sensing the tension and probably smelling the smoke, pawed the ground and tried to rear, but Jacob took control of the reins and had the steed settled and listening to commands in no time. "Take care of the women."

Sam nodded and watched Jacob gallop away. He climbed the steps and joined the women. They watched in silence as what had been a glimmer of brightness now filled an uncomfortable stretch on the horizon, with ominous fingers of light that seemed to touch the sky.

"Let us say a prayer." Rebecca clasped their hands. They bowed their heads and prayed for safety of all who faced the flames, for strength to deal with whatever lay in wait, for hope that no life would be lost. They knew that material things could be replaced.

"What do you think happened?" Sarah asked. She removed the quilt from her shoulders and tucked it around Rebecca, then sat down beside her.

"I don't know." Rebecca sounded as surprised and confused as the rest of them. "It is late. I'm sure the propane stove was turned off. No engines would be running in the barn at this time of night. Perhaps a kerosene lamp was knocked over. But…" Her words trailed off, and worry lines etched her face.

"But what?" Sarah asked.

"A kerosene lamp should not be sufficient to cause that size flame," Sam said. His hardened features looked like they were carved in granite. He didn't seem able to pull his eyes away from the horizon. "Even if a lamp had been knocked over onto something flammable, the lamp would not have been unattended, and the resulting fire should have been easily contained."

Sarah gasped. "Are you saying this fire was deliberately set? Who would do such a thing?"

Sam stared hard at her. His silence and the truth she saw in his eyes chilled her to the bone, more than his words ever could.

"*Nee,* Samuel. I refuse to believe anyone set the fire." Rebecca rubbed her hands together against the chill that raced through her body. "In your world, you are accustomed to meeting evil every day. I understand your mind jumping to that thought. But in our community, accidents are usually just that—accidents."

Rebecca patted Sarah on the shoulder. "*Kumm* inside, child. You are still recovering and must not stress yourself. You, too, Samuel. There is nothing you can do out here to help. I will make some hot chocolate." She stood and folded the quilt over her arm. "I would appreciate it, Samuel, if you would bring in some extra wood for the fireplace. It is going to be a long night for all of us."

Rebecca stepped toward the door, but spun back around when she heard Sarah gasp.

"Look! Over there!" Sarah pointed her index finger to a spot a considerable distance west of the fire. "Do you see it? Tell me I'm not seeing what I think I see."

Sam and Rebecca huddled beside her. The three of them stared at the small flicker of light in the distance.

Terrifying moments passed as they watched the light intensify and grow.

"It can't be. That's not another fire, is it?" Sarah held her breath. She hoped it was a reflection of something, or that her overactive imagination was spooked and creating worst-case scenarios.

A second bell began clanging furiously, the frantic sound wafting across the night air.

"That's the Yoder farm." Rebecca's voice was little more than an awestruck whisper. "The Yoders have a fire."

The three of them stood in silence and watched the light quickly become an orange wall against the night.

Over the horizon and harder to see, another light appeared. Another clanging bell joined the unwanted symphony of the night.

"Oh God, please Lord, help them." Rebecca's eyes widened, and shock was evident on her face. "It is too far to be certain, but I think that is coming from Nathan and Esther's place. They just had a baby last week. Please God, let them be safe."

"Why is this happening? I don't understand." Sarah tried to keep the panic out of her voice as she counted at least three yellow-orange walls of flame shooting high in the night sky.

Sam wiped a hand over his face and then threw his arms over the shoulders of the two women huddled together in front of him.

"Evil is no longer out in the *Englisch* world, Rebecca. Evil is here."

The sunshine streaming through her bedroom window brought Sarah fully awake. She arched her back like a sleepy cat upon awakening, stretched her right arm over her head, and then used it to push up into a sitting position. She adjusted the sling on her left arm and winced at the pain still throbbing in her left shoulder whenever she jarred it.

Her thoughts wandered to the night before. Had it all been a horrible nightmare? It took her a moment to orient herself. No, it had been only too real.

She'd sat with Rebecca for hours in front of the fireplace, sipping hot chocolate, reading the Bible together and waiting. Sam had paced like a caged animal. He slipped outside every thirty minutes or so to check the Lapp barn and the perimeter of the house before hurrying back inside. He was a man whose emotions were torn. Sarah knew he'd wanted to go with Jacob and help the men, but she also knew he would never shirk his duty of protecting Rebecca and herself.

She dressed hurriedly, pulled the *kapp* over her bandaged head and walked to the bedroom door. It had been almost dawn when Jacob had come home. His body had screamed of fatigue. The haunted look in his eyes told them it had been as bad as they had suspected.

She wondered if anyone else was up yet. She eased the door open and heard the sound of men's voices below.

Padding softly down the stairs, she saw Jacob surrounded by men. She recognized Benjamin, Nathan, Thomas and several others she'd met but still couldn't place names to faces. The deep rumble of conversation wafted up the steps and then ceased when they sensed her approach.

"*Guder mariye,* gentlemen. Please don't let me interrupt." Sarah smiled and nodded as the men returned her greeting. She passed them and headed into the kitchen, stopping abruptly when she saw at least a half-dozen Amish women gathered around the table.

"*Kumm,* Sarah, join us." Rebecca waved her to the table, lifted the pot and poured her a hot cup of *kaffe.* "We are discussing the troubles of last night and dividing up the workload."

"*Ya.*" Elizabeth Miller passed Sarah apple butter and fresh bread. "Our barn was first, but there were four more barns burned to the ground last night."

"Five barns?" Sarah couldn't keep the surprise from her voice. She'd seen three fires. There'd been two more.

"*Ya,* five barns. There was no way the fire department could reach even one of the barns in time, let alone five. There was nothing we could do but keep the fires from spreading," Elizabeth said.

"That's how Esther got hurt," Rebecca said. "She ran out to help Nathan. Part of the barn collapsed on her. She got a pretty nasty burn on her back."

Sarah gasped. "Isn't she the woman who just had a baby last week?"

"*Ya,*" Rebecca replied. "We are just discussing a schedule on how we can help with chores and dinner. She will have her hands full taking care of her *boppli.* We will help with everything else until she is recovered."

"What can I do?"

"Sarah, dear, you must work on getting better yourself." Elizabeth patted her hand. "You have only been out of the hospital two days, *ya?*"

"Maybe so, but I'm not helpless. There must be something I can do, especially since…"

"What?" Elizabeth asked.

Sarah felt even worse when she saw the kindness in

Elizabeth's eyes. She lowered her gaze. "Since every-one here knows it is my fault the barns were burned."

"Nonsense," Elizabeth said, and the other women at the table murmured their agreement. "You did not burn our barns. You did not hold our children hostage in their school. You did not kill one of our own and severely injure another of our loved ones." Elizabeth's eyes welled with tears. "This bad thing has happened to all of us, Sarah, and I'm thinking you have suffered most of all."

The other women at the table nodded.

"We will put this in God's hands," Rebecca said. "It is not our way to seek vengeance or punishment. It is our way to help. So let's divide the work, for there is much to do."

"Sarah and I will prepare three *yummasette* casseroles and three pies. We will deliver them to the Yoders, the Burkholders and the Zooks."

"*Gut.* Hannah and I will cook for Elizabeth and Benjamin."

Elizabeth started to protest, but Hannah waved her silent. "*Nee,* Elizabeth, you are not going to work all day, helping with Esther's house and *boppli,* and think you are coming home to your own chores, too. We will have a hot meal for you and Benjamin by the end of this day."

Elizabeth nodded. *"Danki."*

"We will all be working to help each other," Rebecca said. "Now let's finish our *kaffe.* There is much to do."

The men decided as a group to rebuild one barn at a time rather than scatter their labor force. Once that decision was made, Jacob pulled out Peter's wagon and went to town for lumber while the other men left for

Benjamin's. The women scattered to their own homes to prepare the meals they'd promised.

When Rebecca returned to the kitchen, she had a surprised look on her face.

Sarah looked up from her preparations. "What? Is something missing?" She glanced down at the bread, soup, ground beef, onion, peas and noodles she had collected on the table.

Rebecca smiled. "*Nee,* everything is there. I am just happy to see you remember."

Sarah froze and then smiled. "I guess I do remember." She glanced at the ingredients in front of her and then at Rebecca. "I don't have a definite memory of making this particular casserole, but when you mentioned it I knew right away what ingredients to gather. Did I make this often?"

"One of your many talents was your cooking. After you married Peter, you took over preparing the main meal for all of us each evening. Rarely would you even let me step inside the kitchen." Rebecca smiled at her. "I suppose that is why I started making huge breakfasts for everyone."

Rebecca clasped her hand. "This is a *gut* thing, Sarah. Soon now, God willing, you will remember even more."

Sarah smiled at the older woman, but it was only a smile for show—it didn't touch her heart. Yes, she knew the ingredients for *yummasette* casserole. Just like she knew how to brush her teeth or wash her face. It came naturally to her, ingrained deep inside like breathing. But she still had no flashes of memory where she could see herself preparing the dish. She didn't want to dash Rebecca's hopes, but she was beginning to fear she would never remember the past again.

Not wanting to give Rebecca any more grief—five neighbors' barns burning through the night had caused enough of that—she squeezed the woman's hand, and the two of them began the day's cooking.

Samuel kept himself scarce for most of the day and allowed the women to work in peace. He was always on the periphery, doing what chores he could while still keeping himself within shouting distance of the kitchen. Every now and then he'd step inside under the guise of getting a glass of water. He'd snitch a piece of sliced apple or a piece of cheese, and Rebecca would puff up like a mad hen and smack at his fingers and scoot him away, but he never strayed far.

Many times through the course of the morning, Sarah could feel his eyes on her. She'd look up to see him gazing in through the kitchen window or pausing in the doorway. It should have annoyed her, but instead it made her feel cared for and protected.

Sarah sensed his discontent. She'd see him gaze in the distance toward the neighboring farms. She knew he was itching to pick up a hammer and help the men. But the moment would pass, and he'd seem to settle into his routine of barn chores and watching the women.

Samuel seemed relieved, even happy, when Rebecca asked him to hitch up the buggy so they could deliver the food.

Rebecca offered to drive the buggy herself and urged Sarah to stay behind and rest, but Sarah would have none of it. She was tired, sure. She was pretty certain they were all exhausted by now after having such little sleep. But her pain level was tolerable, and no matter what the women told her this morning, she did feel responsible for their troubles. No one would stop her from delivering this food. It was the least she could do.

Samuel sensed this. When she glanced his way, he was already standing beside the buggy and extending his hand to help her inside. They'd known each other for little more than a few weeks, and yet he seemed to know her so well—guessing correctly what she would do or how she would feel before she even knew those things herself. How could this stranger become a friend so quickly? How could they be so attuned to each other's thoughts and feelings? And what kind of pain was she going to feel when he left?

When those thoughts entered her head, she shooed them away. Samuel had become a good friend and confidant. He'd sit and talk with her for hours. Although, if she was honest, she did most of the talking.

Samuel was a great listener. He didn't judge. He didn't offer unsolicited advice. He didn't seem to expect her to be anything other than who she was. She could relax with him. She didn't have to be constantly striving to recall the past or deal with others' disappointments when she couldn't.

"Well, are you coming or do I have to carry you to the buggy?" Sam grinned and shook his waiting hand, as though she may have missed seeing it held out for the past few minutes.

"I'm coming. Hold your horses."

Sam jiggled the reins in his other hand. "That's exactly what I'm doing."

Sarah laughed and allowed him to help her into the buggy. She adjusted the basket she carried on her lap and anchored it between the sling on her left arm and her body to keep it from falling.

Sam helped Rebecca into the seat beside her, handed

up the basket she carried and raced around to climb in the left side of the front seat.

"Okay, ladies. This is your last chance. Do a quick mental checklist. Do you have everything? This horse doesn't know how to turn around. It only goes forward."

Both women chuckled and assured him it was safe to leave, and he clicked his tongue and jiggled the reins.

The buggy ride was more painful than Sarah had expected. Each bounce and jolt sent shooting pains into her left shoulder and down the side of her back, but she didn't complain. She kept a smile pasted on her face and offered a silent prayer that the ride would soon be over. Gratitude washed over her when a little while later they pulled up in front of the Miller home. Benjamin's three children hooped and hollered as they raced each other to the buggy.

Rebecca nodded toward the approaching children. "You may not have your memory back yet, Sarah, but the *kinner* remember that you always bring cookies with you when you come to visit."

Samuel helped Rebecca out of the buggy. She took her basket up to the house just as William, Benjamin's oldest boy, squeezed past her into the seat she'd vacated.

"Hi, Sarah. Did you bring any chocolate chip cookies with you?"

"*Mamm* will be mad at you for asking for cookies." The little girl, who was standing on a wheel hub and leaning into the buggy, was adorable. About five or six years old with golden blond hair and brilliant blue eyes, she looked like a living, breathing doll. "But if you did bring cookies, I want one too, please."

Sarah laughed. "Well, lucky for both of you I just happen to have a fresh batch of cookies in my basket."

The children squirmed and bounced in anticipation while Sarah slipped her hand inside and pulled out one cookie for each of them. "Don't you have another brother?" She handed them their treats. "I think someone told me there are three of you."

The girl giggled, and the high-pitched melody sounded like wind chimes on a breezy day. "You're silly, Sarah. You know there are three of us—William, Daniel and me." She hung by one arm off the buggy and swung back and forth.

"You're right. How silly of me to forget." The child was so adorable. Sarah couldn't help but wonder whether her child would be a girl or a boy, and if that child would be as cute and impish as these two.

"I'll take his cookie and give it to him," William volunteered.

Sarah chuckled. Somehow she didn't think it would reach his brother without at least a little nibble out of it, if she gave the cookie to the boy.

"Where is Daniel?" she asked.

William pointed his finger. "Over there, standing by Daed and the other men in the field."

For the first time, Sarah turned her attention their way. Samuel had already joined them. She shielded her eyes from the glare of the setting sun and squinted for a better look. She noted it wasn't just Amish men standing in the field. There were two police cars parked where the rebuilding of the barn had begun, and some uniformed officers stood talking with the men. A large area of field was roped off with yellow tape.

"I wonder what's going on over there," Sarah said aloud.

"The policemen want to look at the words somebody wrote on the ground," William mumbled through a mouthful of crushed cookie.

"I don't like going over there. It's scary," the little girl said.

"It isn't scary," William corrected. "I told you, Mary, it's just spilled paint."

"Messy red paint. I don't like it. It looks like blood."

"Well, it isn't blood. It's paint. It's messy 'cause Daed said the man did it in a hurry after he set the fire in the barn."

"It's still scary. I'm gonna stay here with Sarah… and the cookies."

Her smile warmed Sarah's heart, and she had to fight the urge to pull the child close and squeeze her tight.

"Daed told us not to go over there, anyhow. He said it was adult business and we should stay away. So I'll keep Sarah company, too…and the cookies."

Sarah reached inside the basket. "Okay. You win. I can't resist your beautiful smiles. You can have another cookie."

After handing them another cookie each, she glanced over again at the men. "William, do you know what words the man wrote in red paint?"

"*Ya,* but they didn't make any sense." He bit his cookie.

"Why don't you tell me? Maybe they'll make sense to me."

"It was only four words. I don't know why everyone is so upset about them."

"What did the words say?"

He swallowed his last bite of cookie and then said, "'Give her to me.'"

Chapter Eleven

Sarah gasped and then, not wanting to upset the children, she pretended to cough. "Well, *danki*. Go play now. Shoo. I have to get these goodies in the house while I still have some left."

She slid across the seat, but before she could attempt to climb out of the buggy, Sam had returned and was standing below her. He took the basket out of her hand and placed it on the ground. Instead of offering his hand, he clasped her waist and lifted her high, as if she were as light as a flower in the breeze. Heat seared her cheeks as the firm touch of his hands on her waist sent her pulse flying. The heat deepened when she stared into his eyes and saw he knew the effect he was having on her.

"Danki," she said when he placed her on the ground. Trying to hide her reaction to his nearness, she glanced over at the men still gathered by the field. "William told me about the words written in the field."

Sam picked up her basket, clasped her right arm with his hand and guided her toward the house. "This is why I became a police officer in the first place. The

Amish people are not accustomed to the evil that exists in the world."

"And you are?"

He stopped midstride and shot a look her way. "Yes, Sarah. I have met evil face-to-face many times. The Amish are my people. I chose to devote my life to protecting them because they are peaceful people who will not protect themselves."

"They depend on God for protection, Samuel. Certainly you do not think you are God?"

The words sounded harsh even to her own ears, and instantly she wished she could recall them. She hadn't meant to be unkind. She was just trying to understand what drove a man who loved God, his family and his people to leave them behind.

Sam's hand tightened on her arm, and his body bristled. The red flush on his throat was the only physical sign that she had hit a nerve, and it had angered him. "No, Sarah, I know I am not God." He gestured toward the field. "But He seems to be a little busy someplace else right now, so I thought I'd give Him a hand."

She knew she couldn't take back what she had said or soften its blow, so she continued walking beside him in silence.

"There they are." Rebecca's voice carried on the air. "See, I told you they were right behind me." Rebecca and Elizabeth peered from the doorway and beckoned them inside.

Sam handed the basket to Elizabeth and spoke to Rebecca. "I'll leave Sarah in your safe hands."

Even though his words were light, Sarah knew Samuel well enough by now to feel the anger emanating from him. He didn't even glance in her direction as he marched off to rejoin the men.

Sarah gazed at his back as he moved farther away, and wished she could rewind the past few minutes and eat her words. Since she couldn't, she followed the other two women into the house and vowed to apologize to him later when they could find a moment or two alone.

But the time never presented itself.

The afternoon slipped into evening in a flurry of activity. Jacob and Rebecca drove the buggy home with Sarah in the second seat while Sam brought up the rear with the lumber wagon.

The next few days fell into a similar pattern. The women cooked all morning, delivered the food to various farms in the afternoons, helped with cleanup and returned early evening just in time to finish their own chores, say their prayers, get some sleep and do it all over again.

Their visit to the Yoder farm had the most impact on Sarah. With her left arm still in a sling, she wasn't able to cradle and rock the Yoders' new infant as the other women did. But she had managed to steal a private moment with the newborn.

Sarah couldn't resist tracing her finger across the silken softness of the baby's cheek, and a smile tugged at the corner of her mouth at the strength of the fisted hold the child had on her finger. She counted the ten perfect little fingers and ten perfect little toes. She watched the tiny lips pucker in a sucking motion as the baby slept. She breathed in the clean, fresh baby-powder scent and, for the first time, longed for the day when she would be hovering over the cradle of her own child.

Almost as if the child she carried could read her

mind, Sarah felt a slight stirring, like butterfly wings fluttering in her stomach, and she knew this was her baby moving about, letting her know it wasn't a story a doctor had made up, but that this child was very real and would soon be in her arms.

The thought comforted her—and frightened her, as well. She didn't know the first thing about giving birth or raising a child. And she would have to do it alone, without a husband to help and guide her.

Raising a child would be the most important job she would ever have. She offered a silent prayer that God would be with her each step of the way so she could raise the child in the ways of the Lord—with love and patience, without fear or self-doubt.

"Sarah?"

She spun around at the sound of Sam's voice.

"I'm sorry. I didn't mean to startle you." He stood a few feet from her and held his hat in his hand. He glanced at the baby in the cradle and then looked back at her. It was as if he could look into her mind, into her very soul, and he smiled. "Soon you will have a *boppli* of your own. That is exciting, *ya?*"

His features scrunched up as he studied her, but after a moment, a slight smile teased his lips. "I know life has been hard for you lately, but we will find this man. This will be over soon, and you will be happy again. I promise."

"Only God can promise such things, Samuel." Before he could respond, she raised a hand to stop him. "I apologize for the harshness of my words a few days ago. I did not mean to insult you by implying you thought yourself like God. I do not think such a sinful thing, or think you are prideful."

She softened her voice. "I was just trying to understand why you made the choices you did. And if you ever regretted those choices." She lowered her eyes.

Sam tilted her chin and looked into her face. "I had my reasons for leaving, Sarah. Good reasons. And no... I do not regret the choice I made. I am no longer Amish, and I will never return to this way of life. My time here will end when my job is over."

Sarah's heart clenched. She didn't want to be reminded that he was only here for a short time. She didn't want to imagine how empty her days would be without seeing him at work in the barn or sitting across from her at the dinner table. She didn't want to think what it would be like not to sit beside him in the evenings and count the stars. Not to have him near so they could talk.

So she wouldn't think about it. For now she would pretend that he would always be here—and she'd deal with the pain later, when he left.

"What is so important, Samuel, that you sneak up behind me and startle me to death?"

He grinned. "Rebecca asked me to fetch you. She went to join Jacob in the buggy. They are ready to go home."

"Well, why didn't you say so?" She brushed past him in a huff, unable to hide her annoyance. It wasn't his delay in telling her that Rebecca was waiting for her that bothered her. It was the fact that no matter how much she wanted to or how hard she tried, she couldn't forget that soon Samuel would leave.

Sarah gazed out the window. The skies were gray, and the smell of rain was in the air.

The sun did its best to break through the clouds but

was losing the battle. It would be dusk soon, and the men would be coming home, looking for a hot dinner and a good night's rest.

She pressed her face against the windowpane. She should be able to see Samuel from here. He'd told her he wouldn't go far. He needed to help Jacob mend some downed fencing before the worst of the impending storm hit, but the barn obstructed her view.

Samuel had not said anything else about leaving since their discussion a couple of days ago. But the subject hung in the air between them. She knew he saw the sadness in her eyes when she looked at him, but she couldn't help it. He had become a dear and close friend. Why would she be happy about his going?

Sarah was pretty certain that Samuel wasn't happy about going, either. She had seen a deep, pensive expression on his face more than once when he thought she wasn't looking. She knew she wasn't imagining it. Samuel liked her, too. They had become friends.

And friends harbored a fondness for each other.

Friends would miss friends if they parted.

And sometimes…friendships deepened. Feelings grew. If Samuel started having deeper feelings, it might be hard for him to say goodbye. Right? She could only hope…and wait…and pray.

She rubbed her hand against the glass, trying to erase the moisture her warm breath had caused on the cold pane. Still no sight of him. She had to stop acting like a mooning teenager and get downstairs and help Rebecca with dinner.

She noticed that she had more fluid movements these days. She wasn't due to see the doctor again for a couple of days, but she was optimistic about the visit. She knew her body was healing. She didn't tire as easily. Her pain had lessened, and she was looking forward to getting the sling off her left arm and the bandages off her head. All she wanted to do was soak in a hot bath and shampoo her hair. Who would have thought that the idea of such a small thing promised so much pleasure?

"I was just going to call you." Rebecca, her face flushed from standing over the hot stove, waved her over. "I need to go out to the barn. I forgot to bring in the pickled beets and corn. The bread is rising nicely but needs to be watched. The stew needs to be stirred. Will you please watch the meal? I will be right in."

Sarah gestured for her to stay where she was and grabbed her sweater hanging on the hook by the front door. "You're the cook. Who better to tend the food? I'll fetch what you need."

"Are you sure? It's going to start pouring any minute."

"Yes, I'm sure. I've been looking forward to catching raindrops on my tongue."

Rebecca laughed. "I must be getting old. That thought never entered my mind."

Sarah smiled back. "Do you need anything else while I'm out there?"

"Will you be able to carry more than two Mason jars with just the use of one arm?"

"Of course."

"*Gut,* then please bring me a jar of sliced apples, too."

Sarah nodded and hurried out the door before Rebecca could change her mind. She stopped midway between the house and barn and lifted her face to the sky. Thick, dark clouds were rolling in rapidly. A breeze caught the leaves of the trees and teased the dust of the ground into swirls around her feet.

Maybe spring was one of her favorite seasons. She didn't have any specific memories to draw from so it was only a guess, but she was pretty sure she was right. She loved the smell of freshly cut grass, the flowering buds that poked their heads through the last of the winter's snows, the warmth of the day followed by the chill of evening where she would sit in front of a roaring fire and sip a cup of hot chocolate.

Samuel was right. If she still couldn't recover memories of the past, she could decide what pleased her now and form new memories for the future. Today she decided that spring was definitely her favorite season.

She unlatched the barn door. Before she opened it, a sound caught her attention and made her pause. She looked over her shoulder. Had Jacob and Samuel returned?

She couldn't see anyone, but an inner awareness told her that she wasn't alone.

"Hello. Is anybody there?"

Her words were swallowed up in the impending storm. She squinted her eyes and tried to focus as she let her gaze wander around the yard. Darkness was descending on the farmyard and the first, fat drops of rain began plopping on the ground. She knew she needed to hurry with her task, find the items and get back to the house before Rebecca started to worry. But still she hesitated. Her senses told her she was being watched, even if her eyes didn't see anyone.

"Samuel? Jacob?" she called out as loudly as she could. Nothing but silence.

Apprehension crept up her spine.

Hurriedly, she let herself into the barn. The wind had picked up, and she had to exert all her energy to pull the door shut behind her. She briskly walked to the pantry in the far corner of the barn, opened the doors and started to search the shelves for the items. So much food. Rebecca must have cooked and canned all last summer. She had enough stored in here to feed an army.

But of course, being the bishop, Jacob often had people to the house for a variety of reasons. He likely presided over weddings, counseled those in need, met with the elders of the church and occasionally took his turn conducting church services. Plus, Rebecca had told her that she often delivered food to the sick and shut-ins throughout the year.

Sarah found the beets and corn quickly. It took a few minutes more to find the apples since Rebecca had jars of pears, peaches and a variety of berries, as well. She slipped two of the jars inside her sling and grinned at how she was finding many other uses for this sling besides just holding a useless arm. With the third jar clasped in her right hand, she shoved the pantry door shut with her forearm.

She had turned to go back to the house when the sound of metal upon metal froze her in place. Someone tinkered with the handle of the barn door.

"Hello? Jacob? Samuel?"

Someone was out there. It was probably one of them, but why hadn't they answered when she called?

The barn door swung open, and a man stepped inside. She knew with just one glance that this wasn't anyone who should be here this late in the day. This man's dress was *Englisch*.

A shiver of anxiety shook her from head to toe. Why

was a complete stranger standing in their barn in the middle of an impending thunderstorm? Panic made her want to run. Logic and common sense kept her calm and standing in place. There had to be a simple explanation.

The storm! That must be it. Perhaps he was afraid he couldn't outrun the storm, and he wanted someplace safe to wait for it to pass. Or maybe he had lost his way and just wanted directions to town. No reason to panic.

"Can I help you?"

The man didn't reply but, instead, took several strides in her direction. Just as quickly, Sarah stepped back. Something was wrong. This man didn't belong here, and he wasn't answering any of her questions.

Her heart thundered in her chest.

Please God, help me. Is this the man who burned the barns? Who killed Peter and shot me? Has he come to kill me?

"Who are you?" She tried not to reveal her terror, but her voice betrayed her.

The man sprinted forward.

Startled by his actions, Sarah dropped the jar from her hand and cried out. She turned and ran toward the back door of the barn. She had almost reached it when she lost her footing and tumbled onto the barn floor. The impact of her body on the barn floor broke the jars hidden in her sling. Glass sliced her skin. The force of the fall shot fresh pain radiating through her arm and shooting into her shoulder.

Dear Lord, protect my child. Please don't let this man kill me.

Stifling a groan, she rolled onto her back to face her assailant. She wouldn't go easily. She intended to fight for her life—for her child's life.

But it was too late. The stranger loomed over her, and she was unable to get to her feet or run. Something was in his hand, but he moved it too quickly for her to identify it.

Please Lord, don't let it be a gun.

The man raised his hand high and pointed the object at her.

She flung her arm up to protect her face, squeezed her eyes closed and screamed.

Chapter Twelve

Sarah tried to prepare herself for the sound of gunfire and the slamming pain she expected at any moment from bullets entering her body. Still, she refused to give up. She crab walked on her back as quickly as she could in a last-ditch attempt to scurry away from the stranger.

Instead of gunfire, she heard a muffled *oomph*.

Sarah opened her eyes and couldn't believe what she saw. As if caught in a tornado, the stranger was lifted straight up into the air. His body flew several feet to her right and slammed hard into one of the barn's support beams. She leaned up on her elbows for a closer look, but before she could react she felt hands pulling on the back of her arms.

"*Kumm,* Sarah, let me help you." Jacob helped her to her feet. "Are you all right? Did he hurt you?"

Sarah brushed at her clothing. "I'm fine, Jacob. Just scared."

The sound of a strangled scream caught their attention, and both of them hurried toward the stranger.

"*Nee,* Samuel, don't." Jacob tried to pull Sam's hands off the man. Samuel had a fisted hold on some kind of binding around the man's neck and was holding the stranger several inches off the ground by it. The man looked terrified, his face red, eyes bulging, breath coming in gasps.

"Stop, Samuel. Let him go." Jacob tried to insert his body between them. "This is not our way."

With a ferocity that Sarah had never witnessed before, Sam pushed Jacob away and refused to release his hold on the stranger. "I am not one of you. Remember? This is my way, so step back."

Sarah rushed forward and gently placed her hand on Sam's shoulder. "But is it God's way, Samuel?"

Sarah wasn't sure whether it was the truth of her words, the sound of her voice or her touch, but Sam froze. He seemed to struggle for a few minutes with his anger, but gradually gained control. He released the hold on the binding around the man's neck and let him fall to his feet. The stranger doubled at the waist and coughed and gasped for breath.

"Who are you?" Sam loomed over the man. His tone of voice threatened more violence if he didn't receive the answers he wanted.

"Roger… Roger Mathers." The stranger started to reach inside his pocket.

Sam drew his weapon with lightning speed and had it aimed at point-blank range at the man's chest before the gasp left Sarah's lips.

"Don't move," he ordered.

The stranger did as he was told. "I was just going to show you my credentials." His voice trembled.

"Do it slow and easy." Sam's tone of voice and stern expression brooked no hesitation.

Roger pulled out a plastic card with his photograph

and name printed on it. His fingers trembled as he offered it to Sam, who snatched it from his grasp and
read it.

"A reporter? I don't believe it." He threw the identification back at the man. It bounced off his chest and
landed on the dirt floor. "You're working for a sleaze-
bag tabloid?" Sam muttered something unintelligible
under his breath. "What are you doing sneaking around
out here?"

"I'm sorry. I didn't mean any harm. Do you know
how much money I could get for an exclusive picture?
Everyone knows the Amish don't like their pictures
taken. But a picture like this one…" He hung his head.
"My wife's sick. I need the money."

For the first time, Sarah took a good look at the
man. She saw the camera hanging from a thick cord at
his neck. That's what he'd pointed at her—a camera,
not a gun. A wave of relief flowed over her. She noted
the bright red marks on the man's neck from the camera strap and felt sorry for him. "What is wrong with
your wife?"

"She needs an operation." He looked hopeful. "Just
one picture would guarantee that for me."

Sam grabbed the man and slammed him back against
the wood. "Knock it off, Mathers. Stop trying to play
on her sympathies, you creep. You don't have a sick
wife. Tell them the truth." He knocked him back again.
"Tell them."

"Okay!" He raised his hands. "So I don't have a wife.
So what? Get your hands off me before I press charges."

"Call the sheriff. Go for it. I'd love to see what happens when a trespasser calls in to report his own crime."

Mathers's face contorted into an angry grimace, and he swatted Sam's hands away.

Sarah's mouth fell open. No wife? No operation? How could a person lie so convincingly? Worse, how much evil had Samuel witnessed that he would recognize it so quickly and easily?

Jacob had remained silent through it all, but now Sarah heard low murmured prayers behind her. Apparently, Jacob was uncomfortable in the presence of evil, too.

"How did you find her?" Sam folded his arms over his chest and returned the glare.

"Easy." He moved his hand toward his inside coat pocket, waited for Sam to nod permission and pulled out a folded paper. "The dry-goods store sells these church directories."

Sam took the paper from his hand and looked it over, then he glanced at Jacob. "Why didn't you tell me about this? This paper not only has all the names and addresses of everyone in the community, but it also has a map to each farm."

Jacob blinked and looked confused. "Of course. Many Amish communities publish this information. We do not want anyone who wishes to attend a church service to get lost or to forget who is having the service that particular week." Jacob looked puzzled. "Have you been gone so long, Samuel, that you forgot something as common and simple as this?"

A flush of red crept up Sam's neck. Instead of responding to Jacob, he grabbed Mathers by his coat collar and shoved him toward the door. "Get out of here. Don't set foot on this property again, or you'll get more than my hands on you. I guarantee I'll be the one calling the sheriff. You'll have a one-way handcuffed trip to jail for trespassing on private property."

Without a backward glance, Mathers ran out of the barn.

Sam watched Mathers's back. Not because he wanted to make sure the man was gone. Like the cockroach he was, he knew the man would scurry into the night. No, he needed the few precious moments to gain control of his emotions before he could turn and face Sarah.

The sound of her screams still echoed in his head. His heart hammered in his chest. Adrenaline raced through his blood.

"What's going on? Who was that man?" Rebecca, her coat flapping open and her *kapp* askew, rushed into the barn. "Is everything all right? I came out to check when Sarah hadn't returned."

Jacob slid his arm over Rebecca's shoulders and pulled her close. "*Ya,* everything is as it should be. We are all fine and hungry. Ain't so, Samuel?"

Sam didn't respond. Instead, he turned toward Sarah. He knew he shouldn't, but he couldn't stop himself. As if in a slow-motion movie, he reached out and drew her to him. His arms encircled her waist. He felt her cheek press against his chest. With his left hand, he cradled the top of her head against him.

"Sarah…" It was all he could say—and it said everything. The anguish, the fear, the concern. His emotions coated his words, and there was no hiding the feelings behind them.

Rebecca gasped at the sight of the sudden intimacy.

"Samuel." Jacob's voice was firm and censuring.

Sam couldn't process Jacob's words or his tone. All

he could think about was how close he'd come to losing her—again.

"When I saw that man standing over you, it was like a switch went off inside of me, and all I felt was rage." Samuel loosened his hold enough to let her move a step back. "Not just for the threat he presented. But mostly at myself, I think, because I let you down again."

"Shh." Sarah placed her fingertips on his lips and looked into his eyes. "You did not let me down, Samuel. You saved me."

The shimmering in her brilliant blue eyes and the smile on her perfectly shaped lips clenched his heart as tightly as if it were squeezed in an iron fist. He was developing feelings for this woman. He couldn't deny it anymore to anyone, not even himself.

But he couldn't let it continue.

He was her bodyguard. Her protector. He had to keep his emotions in check, his mind sharp so he'd be able to do the job. There was a definite, though invisible, line drawn between every bodyguard and victim, a line he couldn't cross. Not now. Not ever.

And in Sarah's case, it was more than a line. It was a canyon-size gorge, impossible to bridge. She was a pregnant, vulnerable *Amish* widow. He was an *Englischer* who would return to a world that held no place for the sweetness or softness of Sarah. Whether he harbored feelings for her was no longer the question. He did. But if he didn't want to hurt her, he had to bury those feelings. Permanently. Right now.

"Samuel!" This time Jacob's voice demanded attention. When Sam looked at him, he said, "Rebecca can tend to Sarah. We should go into the house and clean up for dinner."

Their eyes met. Jacob's gaze was stern, clearly showing displeasure in the inappropriate affection Sam had just shown Sarah. Sam's eyes held both shame for dishonoring these kind people, as well as challenge that he wasn't able to express his heart.

It was Rebecca's gaze that made him feel guilt and hang his head. She looked shocked and disappointed and wary...as if a trust had been broken. And it had.

"Kumm." Rebecca rushed past him to Sarah's side. "I don't know what happened, but you can tell me all about it while we get dinner on the table."

Sarah glanced down at her soiled sling and dress. "I'm so sorry, Rebecca. I broke the Mason jars when I fell."

"Were you hurt?"

"I banged my shoulder pretty hard." She grinned humorously. "Just when the pain went away, now it is back again."

"Let's go inside. We'll get you in dry clothes and make sure you didn't do more damage to yourself. It is a good thing you are scheduled to see Dr. Clark in the morning. He will fix you up good as new."

"But the vegetables..."

"It doesn't matter. We have more. Jacob, please bring in some corn and beets." Wrapping her arm around Sarah's shoulders, she ushered her toward the house, but not before shooting a warning glance at Sam that said it all.

Stand back. Keep away. She belongs to us, not you.

And she was right.

Jacob didn't say anything. He didn't have to. He handed Sam a Mason jar, clapped his hand a couple of times on his back as though consoling him, and then the two men walked in silence to the house.

* * *

The following morning Sam offered his hand to Rebecca and helped her out of the back of the car. He wished he'd been able to be the driver that morning when he'd accompanied the women to see Dr. Clark. It would have made the trip go faster and less stressful.

He was sure his cover had been blown, anyway. News travels quickly in an Amish community, and he could tell from the nods and glances sent his way that everyone knew by now who and what he was. It also stood to reason that the stranger in town who'd been seeking Sarah and the "man protecting her" had a pretty good idea that he was a cop and not an Amish farmer.

But undercover meant *undercover.* Until they were certain his cover was no longer in place, he had to act as if it were.

So he had climbed into the backseat and let one of the other police officers act as driver today. He'd been smart and had made sure to sit between the door and Rebecca, setting himself an acceptable distance from Sarah. He had no desire to endure another day of sharp, disapproving glances from Rebecca as he had through dinner last night. It seemed to work. The less attention he gave Sarah, the more Rebecca relaxed.

Once Rebecca exited, he turned to offer a hand to Sarah. He kept his face an unreadable mask. He was certain no one could see in his expression just how lovely he thought Sarah's blond hair looked now that the bandages had been removed from her head. Even tucked beneath her white *kapp,* enough errant strands escaped to glisten like gold and make his fingers itch to see if it felt as silky as it looked.

He didn't allow a smile to cross his lips when, free

of the sling she no longer had to wear, she stretched her left arm across the back of the seat.

And he was particularly careful to keep any tenderness out of his eyes when he noted how her dress stretched across the growing swell of her body as she scooted across the seat.

"*Danki,* Samuel." She smiled that beautiful, sweet smile of hers and he thought he'd melt at her feet. Before he made a fool of himself, she turned away.

Jacob met them in the yard with a horse already hitched to a wagon and waiting.

"Are we going to Nathan Yoder's house now?" Sarah asked when she saw him. "It's our day to help with the *boppli* and the housework, isn't it?"

"*Nee,* it is my day to help," Rebecca replied. "You had a long trip back and forth to the city today. You heard what the doctor said. You are healing nicely and getting stronger, but you need more rest. He does not want you to overdo it."

"But…"

"You can be helpful without coming with me."

Sarah gave her a questioning look.

"It would be *wunderbaar* to come home to a hot meal. I have a pot of stew that needs tending."

"That is not much of a chore, Rebecca, to stir a pot of stew every now and then."

"Your job today is to rest. You can work your fingers to the bone tomorrow."

Jacob finished loading the back of the wagon with supplies. "*Ya,* Sarah. I would appreciate a hot bowl of stew when I finish the repairs on Nathan's barn. I understand that, to you, it does not seem like much of a chore.

To us, it is a task we hope you will do well because we will be looking forward to the rewards all day."

The small group laughed. Sarah nodded and threw up her hands in surrender. "Okay, Jacob. I will stir the stew."

"Danki." Jacob helped Rebecca into the wagon.

Sarah watched them pull away. "Be sure to kiss the *boppli* for me," she yelled as the wagon moved down the lane. Her words were answered with a wave from both of them.

"Should we go into the house?" Sam stood near the porch steps and waited.

"Nee, Samuel. I need you to prepare the buggy for me. I'm going into town."

Sam frowned at her but refrained from offering what he knew would be a useless argument. When Sarah set her mind on something, she was not easily swayed from doing it.

"Where are we going?" he asked.

Sarah opened her mouth to speak and then shut it. "I don't suppose I could convince you to stay behind?"

Sam scowled.

"I didn't think so. We're going into town. A hot, steamy stew should be accompanied by a hot, sweet dessert. I found a wonderful recipe in a cookbook I was looking at the other day. I want to try it, but Rebecca does not have all the necessary ingredients."

"Dessert. Ah, you found my soft spot. I'll have the horse hitched up in no time."

"Good. But we must hurry. I need to get back in plenty of time to tend the stew and make the dessert."

They rode in companionable silence for a good part of the journey. The brisk morning air kissed her cheeks, but she enjoyed the feel of the fresh breeze against her skin. The billowing, uncut grass in the meadows and the bare tree branches rapidly being clothed with green leaves made her smile. She thanked God for such a beautiful day.

"Are you going to give me a hint about what kind of dessert you'll be making?" Sam grinned at her.

"Nee."

"No? You'd really torture me like that? I'm sitting here thinking up one thing after another, each one better than before, and my stomach is growling. Can't you hear it?"

"I won't tell you, but you can try to guess."

He laughed, and the deep rumble in his throat made Sarah's smile widen.

"A homemade cherry pie," he guessed.

"Nee."

"No? Then pumpkin. Or sweet potato, maybe."

"Not even close."

"Apples. You're making crisp apple strudel or baked apples and cream."

Sarah shook her head.

"Give me a hint."

"We are not shopping for fruit, Samuel. Rebecca has more than enough. I need chocolate and heavy cream and marshmallows and—"

Before she could finish, Sam grabbed at his chest as if he was having a heart attack. "Oh, you're killing me. I love chocolate. I am a chocolate fool. It's my deep, dark secret that I can be easily manipulated with just the promise of chocolate."

Sarah giggled at the silliness of their game. But then Samuel always brought a smile to her face, made her feel happy and content, sometimes by doing nothing more than walking through a door.

Suddenly, their horse flung her head in the air and moved slightly right and then left.

Sam stopped the teasing banter and turned his attention to the horse. He tightened his grip on the reins and spoke to the mare. "Easy, girl. Take it easy."

The horse tossed its head again and whinnied.

"Something is spooking her." Sarah checked both the road ahead and the landscape. "I don't see anything that should be frightening her."

Sam pulled back on the reins and continued speaking in a calm, soothing voice. "Whoa, girl. Quiet down. You're okay." He slowed the mare from a brisk trot to a steady walk.

Within seconds, the roar of a car engine sounded behind them.

"What the…" Sam threw a glance over his shoulder and then turned back to soothe the horse, who grew more agitated as the car approached.

"That car is going awfully fast." Sarah clasped the frame of the window and leaned her head out for a closer look. "But Molly shouldn't be scared. She's used to cars on the road."

The driver of the car revved the engine and sped even faster toward them.

"This one isn't operating like the normal drivers Molly is used to," Sam said. "No wonder she's spooked. The fool shouldn't be speeding on a country road like this. It's dangerous." Samuel edged the mare to the side of the road, being sure to leave plenty of space for the car to pass, and then brought the buggy to a stop. "Let's wait and let him go by."

Within seconds the car flew past. His tires spewed an arc of gravel and dust. Samuel ducked as he was pummeled with the spray. Although Sarah couldn't hear the words he muttered under his breath, she was certain he wasn't happy.

Once the car passed, Sam made a clicking sound with his mouth, bounced the reins and eased Molly and the buggy back onto the lane. They'd gone only a few dozen yards when Molly stopped dead in her tracks and whinnied loudly.

One look told Sarah all she needed to know. "Samuel." Her blood froze in her veins. She tried to keep the anxiety out of her voice when she spoke. "He's coming back. Why would he be coming back?"

Sam didn't answer. By now he had done all he could do to control the frightened horse. Again he moved them to the shoulder of the road, and again the car rushed past at a dangerous, accelerated speed, veering toward them like a bull charging a matador.

"Did you see the driver?" Sam asked. The set of his square jaw and a grim frown on his face revealed his own tension regarding this strange and unforeseen situation. "Could it be teenagers playing a dangerous prank?"

"I don't think so, Samuel." Sarah strained her neck to see behind them. "I'm certain I only saw one man in the car."

Within seconds the car came back—faster, closer, more threatening. This time the side of the car actually scraped against the buggy. Molly whinnied, pawed the earth and tried to run to the right. Samuel struggled to keep control of the terrified animal. While he fought with the reins, he yelled, "Get my cell phone out of my pocket. Hurry!"

Sarah didn't hesitate. She scooted over as close as she could get, allowed her hand to slide across the warmth of his chest until she located the small cell phone tucked in the pocket of his shirt. She withdrew it immediately and held it in an outstretched palm.

Once Molly had calmed, Sam chanced loosening his grip on the reins and grabbed the phone out of her hand. Within seconds he had called his sergeant, given their location and asked for immediate backup.

But the call was too late.

Sarah watched in horror, unable to believe her eyes. The car crested the rise and increased its speed until it seemed to be flying. Sarah clutched his sleeve and pointed. "Samuel, look. He's driving right at us!"

Already pulled as far off the road as possible, Samuel had nowhere else to go. The car was to their left and closing the distance between them. The horse, against the fence to their right, whinnied in fear. She reared to her hind legs in panic.

"Get out!" Samuel yelled and pushed hard. She fell between the buggy and the fence.

The horse reared to her hind legs. Seconds later the car smashed into the buggy. Sam flew through the air and landed with such force, he momentarily blacked out.

When he opened his eyes, he pulled himself to a sitting position. He grabbed his head in an attempt to stop the waves of pain and dizziness trying to claim him. Taking a deep breath, he dared to look at the carnage. His brain didn't seem to want to register what he saw. Pieces of buggy were strewn all over the road and well into the fields on both sides of the lane. The car, although it must have sustained considerable damage, had managed to drive off and was out of sight.

Sam scrambled to his feet, stumbling and half running toward the fence. He stopped abruptly when he was only a few steps away, an expression of relief on his face which was immediately replaced by one of anxiety.

Tears streamed down Sarah's face.

"Sarah? Are you all right?" He stepped closer but didn't touch her.

Sarah laughed uncontrollably and she could see by Sam's expression that he didn't know what to make of it but she couldn't stop. Her anxiety level was high and the laughter seemed to be her body's way of coping.

"Look!" Sarah pointed toward Molly, and a fresh wave of giggles erupted from her. "Molly is ready to take us home."

Sam looked in the direction she pointed. The horse stood docilely by, still in harness. The remnants of what was left of the front seat of the buggy were wrapped in the reins. To a passerby, it would look like the horse forgot the buggy altogether and waited for her master to take their seats so she could pull them home.

Sarah took a second glance at him and came to his side instantly. "You're hurt."

"It's just a scratch."

She probed his wound. The soft, feathery touch of her fingers against the heat of his skin was almost his undoing. He clasped her wrist and stilled her hand.

Their eyes locked. Sam thought he would never be able to pull his gaze away from the glistening blue pools staring back at him. Her lips were slightly parted and only a breath out of reach—and he wanted to reach, to taste, to lose himself in a stolen, forbidden kiss.

"Samuel?" The whisper of his name on her lips brought him back to sanity. He was her bodyguard, her protector, and he couldn't let himself pretend or even hope for one moment that he could be anything else.

"It's just a bump." The huskiness in his voice made a lie of his sudden aloofness. But still, he had to try. "How about you? Are you okay? Are you hurt?"

Sarah stared hard at him, searching his face for something, an answer to an unasked question that hung in the air between them. Slowly she smiled—a sad smile, an understanding smile—and she withdrew her wrist from his grasp.

"I'm fine," she whispered.

He knew she didn't understand his emotional withdrawal, and a deep, clenching pain seized his heart with the knowledge that he was causing her pain. But he had a job to do—and a different world to go home to.

Turning away, Sarah crossed the few feet to her horse and lovingly stroked the mare's neck. "Good girl, Molly." She ran her hand along the animal's back and crouched down to run her fingers over all four legs. When she seemed satisfied that Molly was uninjured, she looked over her shoulder at him.

"Why, Samuel?" Her face still wet with tears, her laughter faded to hiccuping breaths. "Poor Molly could have been hurt or worse. We could have been killed. Why would anyone do such a careless thing?"

"It was not careless, Sarah. It was deliberate and premeditated. Just like the shooting in the schoolhouse. Just like the fires on the farms."

He withdrew his gun from his shoulder holster.

"What are you doing?" Sarah looked at the weapon in his hand as if he held a poisonous snake.

"I won't be caught unprepared again. I never should have agreed to Jacob's terms. I will no longer carry an empty gun for fear of offending Amish sensibilities."

"No, Samuel, please. There must be another way." She choked and had difficulty forcing out her words.

The pain on her face seized his heart and made it difficult for him to draw a breath. Right now he hated himself for what he knew she must be thinking of him. She was seeing a side of him she'd heard about, knew existed, but until now hadn't seen.

She straightened and stared hard at him.

"Violence is never the Amish way, Samuel."

He broke his gaze away from her pleading eyes and slammed the clip into the base of the weapon.

"I've told you before, Sarah. I am not Amish. Not anymore. Not ever again."

Chapter Thirteen

Captain Rogers offered Sam a cup of hot coffee. Sam was pretty sure it had been the captain's coffee, but he accepted it gratefully.

"That's a pretty good knot on your forehead. Maybe you should get it checked out. I can put someone else on Sarah's protection detail until you get back."

Sam glanced across the dozen yards that separated him from Sarah. Past the local police and state trooper cars. Past the flashing strobe lights. Finally resting on the ambulance that had pulled up a short time ago.

He could see Sarah sitting in the back as the paramedics checked her out. He'd done a cursory check of her before they'd arrived, and other than suffering a few bumps and bruises from being thrown out of the buggy, she appeared physically fine.

Emotionally, however? She hadn't spoken a word to him since he'd loaded his weapon, and he couldn't help but wonder if she ever would again.

He couldn't erase the memory of the look on Sarah's face. For the first time since they'd met, the reality of what he did for a living had seemed to come crashing down on her. She'd seen him in cop mode, gun in hand, ready to kill—and her look of horror pierced his soul.

"Sam? Did you hear me? Are you okay?"

"Yes, Captain. I heard you and I'm fine. No need to replace me. Thanks."

"Did you see who did it?"

"No. It happened too fast, and I needed to focus my attention on controlling the horse. I couldn't get a license plate number. It was a dark blue sedan. Didn't look like a foreign model, and probably wasn't more than a year or two old. What I am sure about is that the perp held pedal to the metal. This was deliberate." He dumped out what was left in his cup. "Sarah confirmed that it was a sole driver."

Captain Rogers nodded. "Luckily I'd driven up from the city this morning to take a look at the situation for myself. I was with the sheriff when the call came in. We set up roadblocks the second you called it in. He put out a BOLO for any car in the area with body damage, but so far it hasn't turned up anything."

"We both know it was our guy."

Rogers planted his hands on his hips. The scowl on his face as he stared out over the accident scene said it all.

"He's leaving bodies in his wake, and we can't touch him." His superior scratched his head. "He burned down five local barns in one night. He attacked the two of you on the road. And he's still a ghost. No name. No picture. No leads." He rubbed a hand across his face. "He's a cocky character. Always one step ahead of us. No question he knows we've got state troopers, local police and undercover officers in place. Nothing deters him. He's fearless."

"We'll see how fearless he is once I get my hands on him."

"Is that your brain talking, King, or your emotions?" Captain Rodgers clapped a hand on Sam's shoulder. "You've got to keep your wits about you if you're going to catch this guy. He's smart, Sam…and deadly."

"You think?" Sam laughed mirthlessly. "He administered an almost lethal dose of potassium to Sarah right under my nose. He killed the relief cop guarding her door. He killed my partner. You think I don't know the evil I'm dealing with?"

Captain Rogers returned a hard, steady gaze. "Evil, huh? You know, I've never discussed your religious beliefs with you before, Sam. But this time you might be right. If we are dealing with evil personified, it wouldn't hurt if you took a moment and had a conversation with the man upstairs. We sure could use some help on this one."

Rogers walked back to join the sheriff just as Jacob and Rebecca's buggy pulled up.

The two of them spoke briefly to one of the officers, and then Rebecca raced to the back of the ambulance. After another short conversation with the paramedics, Rebecca wrapped her arm around Sarah and ushered her to their buggy. Before she climbed on board, Sarah threw a glance over her shoulder and her gaze locked with his. Without a word, she climbed into the buggy.

Jacob followed her gaze, spotted Sam and walked over to where he stood.

"You've been hurt."

"It's nothing."

The man studied his face, looked as if he was going

to argue that statement and then decided to keep his counsel.

"Please, can you take Sarah home? She's been through a lot and must be exhausted." When Jacob turned to go, Sam clasped his arm. "Make sure you ask the sheriff to send one of his men with you until I finish up here and can get back. And Jacob, keep Sarah inside the house. Period."

Jacob nodded and walked briskly back to the buggy. A police cruiser, lights flashing, pulled out and slowly followed the buggy as it turned and headed back the way it had come.

Sam stood at the side of the lane and watched until they disappeared over the rise. He couldn't erase the memory of what he'd seen in Sarah's eyes when she looked across the distance between them. He saw confusion and shock. He saw vulnerability and fear and sadness. And he saw something else he couldn't quite identify.

Please, Lord, don't let it be disgust.

Sam hung his head. For the first time in over a decade, he wished he wasn't a cop.

Captain Rogers arranged for additional men on the property. Jacob and Rebecca bristled beneath the added police presence. Jacob felt their agreement had been breached. Sam was the only officer who was supposed to be on his property, and Jacob didn't like the betrayal. But at least they were trying to make the best of the situation. Rebecca invited the officers to join them for dinner. Jacob treated his guests with the hospitality of the Amish. The officers sensed the polite but distant ambience of their hosts, and nobody at the table was happy right now.

Rebecca offered a platter of fried chicken to one of the men. "Would you like some more, Officer Jenkins?"

The man smiled and raised a hand in a halting motion. "No, ma'am. I couldn't eat one more bite. Everything was delicious. Thank you for the invitation."

"A man needs to eat." Jacob glanced at his guest. "I wouldn't want you to go away hungry."

The officer hid his chuckle in a napkin. Jacob did little to hide how much he hoped the officers would be getting ready to leave.

Both men stood up. "Thank you again for your hospitality. We'll be sitting outside in our squad cars if you need us. Just call."

The other man, Officer Muldoon, gave a curt nod in agreement with that statement and reached out to grab a chicken leg off the platter. "I'm gonna save this piece for later, if you don't mind." He raised it in the air as he backed toward the door. "I can't remember ever eating chicken so good."

"Will you be staying all night?" Jacob scowled at the men.

"Yes, sir. Our replacements will be here first thing in the morning."

"You can't sit in the car all night." Jacob's gruff tone caught everyone's attention. He placed his napkin on the table and rose. "*Kumm,* I will make a place for you in the barn. I have an oil burner. It will be warm."

"Thank you, sir. That would be much appreciated." They stood and followed Jacob out to the barn.

When the men left, the silence around the kitchen table became stifling. Sam glanced back and forth between Rebecca and Sarah. When neither woman spoke, he turned his attention to his meal. Although the aroma of fried chicken mingled in the air with the scent of cinnamon atop baked apples, Sam found no enjoyment in the dinner. It was simply fuel that his body needed. When he was finished, he thanked them and walked out of the room.

He grabbed a hurricane lamp and stepped out on the porch. Placing the lamp on the table, he sat down in one of the rockers and stared into the darkness.

Waves of pain washed over him as memories of days past entwined with the emotions of today's events. Pieces of buggy scattered and strewn in multiple directions. The sound of screams in the stillness of the night. A frightened whinny of a horse. A racing, reckless driver making stupid, irresponsible, dangerous choices. The sight of blood and lifeless bodies crumpled beneath wreckage as he scrambled through the carnage, begging and praying for survivors, only to find none.

His breath came in short, shallow gasps. Faces, sounds and sights raced through his mind.

He hadn't allowed himself to go to this deep, dark place for more than a decade. But here it was again. As though it had just happened, the pain fresh and intense.

He couldn't take it anymore. He bowed his head, cupped his face in his hands and sobbed.

Sarah helped Rebecca clear the table. She washed the dishes while Rebecca dried and put them away. Rebecca tried to maintain idle chatter, and when she realized Sarah was in no mood to talk—not about what to make for dinner tomorrow or even about how well Nathan's wife was recovering from her injury, and definitely not about the horrible events of the day—she finished her chores in silence.

Sarah couldn't think of anything but the day's events and the haunted look she saw in Samuel's eyes every time he looked at her. What had she done wrong? She knew she shouldn't have tried to stop him from loading his gun. He was a police officer, and that was a huge component of his job. But had that been enough to cause the anger and pain she saw in his eyes?

Still, she couldn't shake the way he had looked at her. Something was terribly wrong.

Once the chores were complete, Rebecca shooed Sarah into the living room. She told her to go sit in front of the fire. She'd make them a kettle of tea as soon as she was finished washing the floor.

Sarah left the kitchen but she didn't sit by the fire. Instead, she donned her sweater and slipped outside to find Samuel. She didn't have to go far. As soon as she stepped outside, she saw him sitting on the far end of the porch. He was hunched over, his face covered with his hands. She couldn't be sure, but from the muffled sounds she heard and the shaking of his shoulders, she thought he might be crying.

"Samuel?" She hurried to his side and placed a comforting hand on his back.

Sam startled at her touch. He jumped up from the rocker, dragged his forearm over his face and turned away.

"What are you doing out here? You should be resting."

She heard the catch in his voice, witnessed the effort it took him to regain control. She waited for a moment before speaking. "Can I help?"

He drew in a deep breath. Slowly, he turned to face her. "I'm sorry. I lost control for a moment, but I'm okay now. Truly, Sarah, go inside and go to bed. You need to rest, if not for yourself, then at least for your *boppli*."

He stayed in the shadows, and she couldn't see his face.

"Are you upset with me? I'm sorry I tried to stop you…"

"This has nothing to do with you, Sarah. Now please, go inside."

She stepped closer. So close they were both swallowed in the shadows cast by the hurricane lamp. She touched his arm. "Talk to me, Samuel. Tell me what torments you so."

For a moment, she didn't think he was going to answer her. When he did, his voice was gruff and harsh.

"It happened a long time ago. More than ten years now. Today stirred up those memories." He made a gruff sound. "Like I told you before, Sarah, memories are not always good things to have."

"Talk to me." She ran her hand down his arm and clutched his hand. "You have been such a good friend to me. Let me be a friend to you." She moved closer still, watching the kerosene light play across his features. "Tell me of this thing that troubles your soul."

He stepped into the light, and she was taken aback by the terrible pain she saw in his eyes. His expression reflected his indecision about whether he was going to talk to her about it. When he finally spoke, his words tumbled out with the force of a breaking dam.

Sarah never removed her hand from his. She smiled gently, encouragingly, and listened—until she thought her heart would break under the weight of his words.

"I was seventeen when I experienced the worst day of my life. Thanks to *rumspringe,* most of the restrictions my *daed* had enforced in my life were lifted. He turned a blind eye to the radio I'd sneak into the buggy when I'd take it to town. He'd pretend he didn't hear when I'd play music in my room and sing at the top of my lungs. When I'd had a few sips of beer that one of my *Englisch* friends had given me, I knew he smelled the alcohol on my breath. He scowled, his expression telling me he didn't approve, but he kept silent."

Sam turned his face away and stared into the darkness, but not before Sarah saw a tear trace its way down his cheek.

"But the one thing he wouldn't budge on was my curfew."

Sarah remained still, afraid to move, even breathe. She felt as if she was standing on the edge of a deep, dark crevice, and knew that whatever Sam was about to tell her had been buried for a very long time and had cut deep.

"I disobeyed the curfew. I didn't want to lose face with my friends. I was afraid they might taunt me for running home to Daed." He looked at her, and the pain she saw in his eyes seared her soul. "Friends? I can't even tell you the name of one of those boys today. Yet on that night they were more important to me than my father...or his rules."

Her eyes filled with tears. She wasn't even sure why. She just knew Sam was suffering, and there was nothing she could do to help him—except stay strong and silent and listen as he spoke about this thing, maybe for the very first time.

Sam's voice seemed wooden, his tone flat, empty. He

stared off into the darkness. He might be standing here on the porch in front of her, but his spirit was gone—to another place, another time.

"It was dusk. Dark enough to trigger the streetlamps along the main street in town, but still light enough to recognize my father's buggy. I can still remember seeing him snap the reins when he saw me standing outside the local general store with my friends. Our horse fell into a trot, and the buggy headed in my direction.

"Some of my friends recognized my father's buggy, too. A few of the *Englisch* teens we were with had been drinking. They thought it was funny that my *daed* was out looking for me. They teased me, taunted me. When I didn't respond, they decided it might be more fun to taunt my father. They jumped in their car, revved their engines and drove down the street toward him."

Sarah's heart seized. She relived today's sound of an engine revving and the fear of watching a car swoop past their buggy. Her pulse pounded in her ears with fear as she remembered how hard Sam had fought to control the panicked horse. Suddenly present and past converged, and Sarah understood Sam's pain.

Today's incident had opened a portal into Sam's past, and everything he'd experienced came flooding back. She wanted to silence him. She wanted to pull him away from what she knew would be ugly, hurtful memories. But it was too late. Sam was already standing in front of that general store, watching a car full of drunken teens descend upon his father.

"I didn't even know those boys. They were friends of a friend. Mere acquaintances. Older than me and the boys I was with." Sam rubbed his hand over his face. "They'd been drinking, and it affected their driving.

They didn't mean to hit him. They thought it would be fun to scare him a little. But they were driving too fast and they lost control...."

Sam's words faded away, but it didn't matter. Sarah was with him now, standing beside the teenage Sam as he apprehensively watched his father approach, feeling the panic when he saw the car driving too fast and too close to the buggy. She held her breath and tightened her hold on his hand. She needed him to tell her the rest— and simultaneously wished he wouldn't.

"My father wasn't the only passenger in the buggy that night. My *maam* was with him. I didn't know it at first. I didn't know until after the buggy shattered into a million pieces, and I found their bodies in the rubble."

Sam looked at her. Flickers of lamplight danced across his face, but not even the shadows of the night could hide his tortured expression. "My mother was dead when I reached her. God was merciful. She died upon impact and didn't linger or suffer. My *daed*... his back was broken, his legs twisted at an odd angle beneath him, his breathing shallow and difficult. I remember he stayed awake and alert for a long time. Long enough for the police to arrive. Long enough for the paramedics to confirm my mother was dead.

"He held tight to my hand, and he kept saying the same words over and over again. I heard the words but they didn't really register...not then...not for years to come."

Sam drew his hand out of her grasp and ran his index finger softly down her cheek. His voice fell into a whisper. "My *daed* kept saying, 'I love you, son. Do not blame yourself. It was an accident.'" Sam's eyes glistened with fresh tears. "Isn't that the Amish way? To forgive the person who sinned against you?"

Sam stared off into space for several minutes before he spoke again, but when he did his words carried the pain and guilt of a young, frightened teenage boy who'd been unable to face his past.

"How could he do that, Sarah? Forgive? I killed my own family. Even God will never be able to forgive me."

Chapter Fourteen

"Hush, Samuel, don't say such a thing." Sarah wrapped her arms around him and pulled him close. "God knows our hearts. He can forgive us anything if we ask." She released her hold and cupped his face with her hands. "It is a terrible thing that happened that night. Terrible. But I agree with your father. It wasn't your fault."

"I broke curfew."

"*Ya,* just like hundreds of other teenagers trying to find their own way in this world. That's all you did."

"If I hadn't broken curfew, my parents would not have been in that buggy looking for me."

Sarah smiled tenderly at him. "Ah, Samuel, that is the hurt child inside of you speaking now. The man who stands in front of me knows that we do not have control over other people. Everyone made their own choices that evening. Your *dat* to search for you. Your *maam* to go with him. Those boys to drink and then drive recklessly."

She let her fingers trace a path down his cheek. "It would be prideful and foolish to think that we have power over other people, over life. Only God can claim that right, *ya?*"

"God?" Samuel scoffed. "Where was God that night? He allowed it. How could He permit such a terrible thing?"

"It is not our place to question God's plan. We do not know why He allows these things or how they affect His plan for our lives." The gentleness in Sarah's voice soothed him. "God never promised us that bad things wouldn't happen, Samuel. Just the opposite. The Bible tells us we will suffer many trials in this life. We only know He promises to be at our side to help us through when bad things do happen, and that somehow, in time, He makes all things work out for good."

"How is watching the murder of my parents a good thing? What good came of their deaths?"

Sarah folded her hands in front of her and smiled softly into his face. "I don't know. No more than I understand why Peter was killed or why my memory was erased. I don't understand why my neighbors are being punished because I am still alive. And, *ya,* I know how guilt can creep up on you and make you think that everything is your fault. But aren't you the one who told me everything that is happening now is not my fault? Did I shoot my husband? Terrorize the children in the school? Burn down my neighbors' barns?"

"No, of course not."

Sarah's smiled widened. "You're right. I am not responsible." She waited a heartbeat to allow her logic to penetrate his pain. "And you are not responsible for the tragedy that befell your family."

"You make it sound so easy."

"Easy? *Nee.* Suffering through trials is never easy.

Simple? *Ya.* Put your faith in God, Samuel. Trust Him to run the world. He's been doing it for a very long time."

"How did you ever get to be so smart?"

"I don't know. I can't remember."

Sam laughed at her attempt at a joke, and Sarah joined in. When the moment passed, he drew her close. "Thank you." He wrapped one of the ties of her *kapp* around his finger. "I haven't spoken to anyone about that night. I thought I had dealt with it and buried it long ago. But today... I found myself reliving everything."

Sarah smiled up at him. "I'm glad I could be here for you."

His expression sobered. "I've never had anyone be there for me." He drew her close. His lips hovered inches above hers.

Sarah's pulse raced like birds taking flight, and a delightful shiver danced along her spine. She held her breath in anticipation. She didn't need to wait long.

When Sam lowered his head toward hers, he ignited feelings inside that she could no longer deny. She loved the feel of his breath as it whispered across her skin. She loved the softness and taste of his mouth as he claimed hers in a tender kiss. She loved the warmth and strength of his arms wrapped around her, holding her close, close enough that when she slid her hand along his shirt, she could feel the beating of his heart against her palm. She loved—

A bright light shone in their faces. Instinctively, they broke apart. Sarah raised a hand to shield her eyes.

"Um, sorry. I saw Mrs. Lapp come out onto the porch." The officer lowered his flashlight. "I didn't see you, Detective King. I thought she was alone, and when she disappeared into the shadows… Well, um, I thought I should check and make sure she was okay."

Even in the dim light from the kerosene lamp, Sarah could see a deep red flush on Sam's neck.

"You did the right thing, Officer." Sam stepped forward. "But, as you can see, Mrs. Lapp is unharmed."

The officer glanced back and forth between them. "Well, okay then." He gestured with his flashlight over his shoulder. "I'll just head back to the barn." He took a few more steps away. "And please thank Jacob for us again, Mrs. Lapp. The spring nights are still pretty cool, and that heater made it real comfortable in there."

Sarah watched him walk back to the barn. When he disappeared, she chanced a demure glance toward Sam. Suddenly, she felt awkward and unsure of herself—of them. What had really happened between them tonight? Had it been a simple kiss? An expression of gratitude when his emotions were running high? Or could it be something more? Could he be drawn to her as powerfully as she was to him? Could their friendship be turning into something deeper, something lasting, something that gave her hope for their future?

But she didn't find the answers she sought. His expression was inscrutable. There was no lingering sign of the tears he'd shed for his family. No warmth or tenderness directed to her after their kiss.

"You should go back inside, Sarah. It's not safe for you to be out here at night." His dismissive tone pierced her heart. It was like he could reach inside his mind and flip a switch from being a warm, tender, attentive man—*flip*—to a hard, cold, professional cop. A slow, seething anger surfaced inside.

"Not safe? From whom, Samuel? The man trying to kill me?" She stared hard at him. "Or you?"

She walked away and thought her heart might break because he didn't ask her to stay.

The wedding ceremony of Josiah and Anna had been simple but beautiful. Each time the bride smiled demurely at her groom, or the groom beamed his smile over the congregation, everyone could see how much in love the two of these young people were. At the conclusion of the ceremony, the women gathered to set up the food for the reception. The men moved the benches apart and squeezed as many tables as possible into the small space.

While setting plates and utensils on the tables, Sarah noticed Sam walk across the yard toward the barn. She smiled and greeted people as they inquired of her health and took their seats at the tables. She helped Rebecca carry out the hot casseroles and fresh bread. But her mind was elsewhere. She wondered why Sam had left the reception and what he was doing in the barn.

Sarah could barely squeeze through the cramped spaces between tables. Normally, Jacob would have erected a tent for the reception outside, but the heavy rainstorm from the other night had left puddles of mud and downed tree branches in its wake and changed those plans. Instead, the living room furniture had been pushed to the walls, and smaller chairs stored in bedrooms and outdoor tables and benches were overflowing through the great room, into the kitchen. One even rested at the entrance to a hall.

You'd think the cramped space would have put a damper on the wedding plans and upset the bride and groom, but it seemed to have a totally opposite effect. Everyone laughed and talked and rubbed elbows and laughed some more like one big happy family gathered for a holiday meal.

Then Sarah realized that that was exactly what this small community was—one large happy family. She smiled at the thought, and then gave a wistful sigh. She wondered if she would ever get her memory back. Even though everyone had been kind and helpful, she had no memory of them, no relationships with them, and she couldn't help but continue to feel like an outsider, always watching and never truly belonging.

She was making her third trip from the kitchen into the great room when she glanced out the window and saw Sam. Now she understood why he'd left the group and gone to the barn. A smile tugged at her lips.

Sam waited while the groom pulled his wagon up to the barn entrance, and then jumped out and circled around the back to help. He removed the protective sheet he'd put on top of the table.

Josiah moved a hand lightly over the waxed-to-perfection table. "*Danki,* Samuel. You honored Peter's memory with this fine work."

Sam, embarrassed by the rare compliment, acknowledged it with a curt nod. "I hope Anna is pleased."

"Ah, how could she not be?" He stepped back, hands on hips, and studied the table. "It is a fine piece of furniture, is it not? Simple and plain, but sturdy and attractive too, *ya?*" He helped Sam cover the table, and then the two men lifted it into the back of the wagon. "This table will serve us well, Samuel. As our family grows,

God willing, it will be the focal point of our home for prayers, meals, conversations. *Ya,* this is a good table."

They shook hands, and then both men headed back to the reception in the house.

Sam couldn't stop thinking about the table and the words Henry had spoken. It was true. The table was sturdy, well built and would service the family for years to come.

Peter had been the carpenter. He'd carved the wood lovingly with his own hands, building a piece of furniture that would withstand a baby banging a cup against it, support children doing their homework, bring a family together with hands joined and heads bent for prayer.

Sam wondered if Peter had thought about his own family when making the table. Jacob had told him that Peter was planning to start building his own house on the property in the spring—a place he was certain God would bless with the laughter and love of many children. Sarah and Peter had endured the emotional pain of two miscarriages. Sadness tugged at Sam's heart because Peter hadn't seen that prayer answered.

Sam was glad he could finish the gift that Peter had made for his newlywed friends. But now there was one more thing he could do in honor of the man's memory. He could find the man who had taken his life and threatened to end the life of his wife and unborn child. This is why he'd left his Amish ties so many years ago. To protect those unable to protect themselves. And with God's help, he would.

"Hurry, *kumm,* you are letting all the cold air into the house." Sarah laughed, braced the door open with her hands and ushered Sam into the house. "Josiah moved as quickly as a jackrabbit to get inside. You have been poking along like a turtle, and all the while I'm holding this door open for you."

Sam hung his hat on a peg by the door. "Do you know the rest of that story, Sarah? I believe it was the turtle who won the race."

Sarah's eyes widened with bewilderment. "What nonsense are you saying? When did you ever see a jackrabbit and a turtle race each other?"

Sam threw his head back and laughed. "Never mind. Go stand by the fire and warm yourself."

Sarah's smile was all he needed to feel warm. He watched her weave in and out between the tables, stopping for a quick word and always sharing a smile with many of the folks who spoke to her on her way. When she reached the fire, she shot him a quick look and then rubbed her hands together near the open flame.

"She looks happy today, *ya?*"

Sam had been so absorbed in watching Sarah that he hadn't heard Rebecca approach, and the sound of her voice startled him.

"Hello, Rebecca. Yes, she looks very happy today. It must be Josiah and Anna's wedding. The festivities seem to have lifted everyone's spirits."

"Not everyone's spirits were lifted today. Some of our hearts are still heavily burdened with loss." Her eyes glistened. "Let me ask you, Samuel. This man—the one who kills our loved ones, who burns our neighbors' barns…" Rebecca's voice choked as tears threatened to fall, but she took a deep breath and held them at bay. "How much longer do you think it will be before you find this man?"

"Soon, Rebecca." He hurried to reassure her and ease her pain. "He is getting careless and sloppy. He is out of his element now, in the country, not his familiar city setting, having to work quickly without help and not having the luxury of time to plot and double-check and plan. He is getting careless and frustrated and desperate. I believe it will be very soon when he will make a mistake that he will not be able to fix. Then we'll get him."

Rebecca considered his words and nodded. "*Gut.* Sarah needs this to be over. We all do."

Sam glanced in Sarah's direction and smiled. "Meanwhile, she is getting stronger and healthier each day."

Rebecca nodded. "*Ya,* that is true. Because she is home now, where she belongs—with her family and her community surrounding her, loving her, supporting her."

Sam straightened and tried not to bristle at the poorly veiled meaning behind her words.

Rebecca folded her hands in front of her and spoke just loud enough for him to hear. "I see the way you look at her, Samuel. More importantly, I see the way she looks at you."

He opened his mouth to protest, but Rebecca raised a hand in a silencing motion. "It is natural for her to have feelings for you. You are a *gut* man, strong, kind, protective. She feels vulnerable and afraid, and she has no memories of the man she loved...of the man whose child she carries...so she turns to you. I understand."

Sam didn't want to have this conversation, didn't want to hear what he knew Rebecca was about to say, but he remained silent and showed her respect by listening.

"You must be the strong one, Samuel. You must be the man whom all of us have come to know and respect. You must find this man—and I believe with God's help, you will—and then you must leave. Quickly. To ease her pain at seeing you go. We will take care of her when you are gone. After all, we are her family."

Rebecca locked her gaze with his. Sam almost had to look away from the pleading look in her eyes. "I have loved her as my own daughter since she was a small child on a neighboring farm. Often, she would come to our farm to play. I watched her grow into a beautiful young woman. I was so happy when Peter fell in love with her and asked her to be his wife."

She paused and stared off into space, reliving those distant memories. When she turned her attention back to him, she wore her pain like a heavy shawl.

"She carries my grandchild, the only part of Peter that I have left. Sarah's world is with us, and your world—" She shrugged her shoulders. "You made your choice many years ago, *ya?*"

Pain ripped through his heart as physically as if she had struck him with a dagger. But she was right. He had no intention of returning to the Amish community—and they would shun Sarah if he tried to take her with him.

"Be a *gut* man, Samuel. Be strong. Protect her from the evil of your world."

Anger bubbled beneath the surface and raced through his body. "Do you want what is best for Sarah, or what is best for you? Have you discussed this with her? Would she leave with me if I asked her to go?"

Rebecca sighed deeply. "No, Samuel. We did not speak of such things." Her gaze wandered to the other side of the room. Both of them watched Sarah as she teased and played with some children at a nearby table. Her laughter floated through the air like the tinkling of wind chimes and hovered over the rumble of conversations at the tables.

Rebecca turned her attention back to him. "I am not too old to remember what it feels like to give my heart to a man. When Sarah looks at you, I see it in her eyes. I think she has already given her heart. I think maybe she would go with you if you asked."

Rebecca stepped closer. "But just because someone *can* do something, Samuel, does not mean they *should* do it. Sometimes the wrong decision brings only heartache and pain. Be a *gut* man. Help Sarah make the right decision. You may not like my words, but you know my words are true. Sarah belongs here with her people, not in your world of evil and killing and pain."

She patted his hand like a mother who had just scolded her child, but wanted to assure the boy that he was not bad, just his actions.

He hadn't felt that motherly admonition for many years, and it was just that action that made him face the truth. She was right. He had to leave—soon—and if he loved Sarah, then he would be leaving alone.

Overcome with emotion, he grabbed his hat, donned his coat and stepped outside. He checked in with the other two officers watching the house, told them he would be out of contact for a bit and to keep a sharp eye on Sarah.

With bent head and heavy heart, he walked away.

The man's teeth chattered, and he salted the air with a string of curses. He should be home. He envisioned himself standing before a roaring fire with a snifter of brandy in his hand as he looked through the wall of glass to the ocean below. That's where he belonged.

Not here, perched in a tree, hidden by leaves and clinging to branches so he wouldn't fall to his death.

He cursed John Zook. Why had he ever allowed the man to join his team? What a colossal mistake that had been, and he wasn't a man who made many mistakes.

Who would have ever believed that stupid Amish lout would find the backbone to steal his diamonds? Steal! From him!

He should have cut his losses and called an end to this long ago. After all, he certainly didn't need the money. His expertise at ridding the rich of their wealth had served him well over the years. A smile bowed his lips when he pictured some of the art and fine gems in his collection.

No, it was not the loss of the diamonds. Money could always be replaced. And what did it matter, since none of it had been his in the first place?

It was the betrayal he couldn't forgive.

No one betrayed him and lived.

So he'd followed Zook and punished him appropriately. He hadn't anticipated the resulting mess. The Amish husband rushing to his wife's defense. The woman surviving—twice—but unable to remember. Yet.

He definitely had a mess on his hands, and he didn't like messes.

But it would soon be over.

If he killed the woman, then none of the others would dare come forward. He'd read that the Amish were big on forgiveness. They often didn't prosecute offenders and rarely testified in courts. Yep, kill the woman and the others would be so afraid for their children—and themselves—that he would feel safe to return home, where he belonged. He couldn't bear being away for even one more night.

Today it would end.

He glanced at the sky. The sun would be setting shortly. The party at the Lapp residence would soon be over. He'd have to act fast. He'd thought it over and decided it would be easier to strike when hundreds of people milled about the place rather than try to isolate her when she was on her own.

He wasn't worried about the cops. Oh, they kept watch over her, sure. But they could be easily distracted. They weren't as invested in her well-being as that one who'd followed her here from the hospital. There was probably something going on between the two of them. But he didn't care. He hoped the guy got what he wanted from his lady friend because their little romance was coming to an end real quick.

He lifted binoculars to his eyes for another surveillance of the party and couldn't believe his good fortune. That cop—the undercover one who thought he could fool him by dressing Amish—was leaving.

He adjusted the lens and took a second look. He watched him consult with the other two cops and then walk off. He watched his hurried gait, his bent head, his stooped shoulders.

Uh-oh. Something had happened. A love spat, maybe? This guy didn't look happy, and he definitely didn't look like he was coming back.

It was time. He smiled in anticipation. Soon this would be over. He would be home and safe. He could almost taste the brandy on his lips.

With agile movements, he lowered himself to the ground. He had to move fast—and it had to be now.

Chapter Fifteen

"William, you forgot your sweater." Sarah stood in the doorway, waving them in front of her. The boy rushed back, took the sweater from her with a hurried *"Danki,"* and ran off to join the mass of children playing in the yard.

Benjamin came up beside her in the doorway. *"Danki,* Sarah. I worry about that boy. His head is always in the clouds."

"He is young still, Benjamin. He will settle down soon enough."

Benjamin frowned. "Sometimes he seems so distracted, I worry he can't walk a straight line across the yard." Benjamin shook his head. "Always getting into trouble, that one. Not bad behavior. Just foolish behavior from not thinking things through."

"How old is he now? Seven? Eight?"

"Seven. Old enough to stop all that daydreaming."

"Who knows? Maybe William will use his creativity to be a great writer or painter."

Benjamin frowned. "Sarah, you should know by now

that the Amish do not take great stock in those foolish things. I will be happy if he is a great farmer."

Sarah chuckled. "Ah, but Benjamin, think about it. The good Lord created all of us. Each one of us is the same, yet different. It is those differences, those individual talents, that make us unique and special, *ya?*"

Before he could reply, both Benjamin and Sarah ducked as a baseball flew past their heads and crashed through the front window.

"Sorry, Daed. I was trying to throw the ball to you." William, wearing a worried expression, stood at the bottom of the steps looking up at them.

Benjamin frowned. "Throw it to me? Did you call my name? Did you let me know the ball was coming my way? Look what you've done to Bishop Lapp's window. Think what you could have done if you had hit me in the head!"

William hung his head. "I'm sorry, Daed. I will do chores for the bishop to help pay for the broken glass."

"That you will!" Benjamin looked at Sarah. "See what I mean? Now I must speak to Jacob about this." Sighing heavily, he reached down to retrieve his hat, which had fallen to the ground, plopped it on his head and went back inside.

"I didn't mean to hit the window," William said, his gaze trailing after his father.

"I know you didn't." Sarah lowered her voice to a whisper. "But next time you aim for your father, William, make sure he knows it is coming. Now go back and play." She shooed him away.

Sarah stepped back inside the house. Most of the adults were preparing for their trip home. The women finished washing dishes and wrapping up leftover food.

The men carried the benches out to the wagon used to transport them from farm to farm for services, and then they collapsed and stored the long plastic picnic tables for future use.

"Anything I can do to help, Mrs. Lapp?"

Sarah glanced at Officer Muldoon. He looked too young to be a cop. She bet his *maam* found it difficult to watch him don the uniform and walk out the door with a gun strapped to his side each day. Sarah placed a hand on her swelling belly and thanked God she would never have to carry that worry in her heart for her child. The worst that could happen to him or her was to be kicked by a horse or hurt by some farm equipment.

She'd found it difficult to see Samuel carry a gun. He hadn't liked it, but had complied with her wishes when she asked that the gun be put away for this occasion. There were so many women and children attending today's wedding. This was not a time or place for guns.

Sarah glanced around and then looked back at the officer. "Have you seen Detective King anywhere?"

"He left about an hour ago. He asked us to keep an eye on things."

"Left?" A frown twisted her lips. "Where did he go?"

"Don't know. Didn't ask. But you're in good hands, don't worry."

"I'm not worried, Officer Muldoon. I am sure you will do a good job."

Sarah smiled and then walked away.

How strange. Even in the hospital, Samuel had barely left her out of his sight. Since they came home from the hospital, he'd never been farther than the sound of her voice. So why would he suddenly leave without a word of his whereabouts to anyone? It seemed so unlike him.

Seeing the bride and groom preparing to leave, she hurried over to offer her congratulations and best wishes for their future together. En route, she said her goodbyes to several other families that were heading out. When she'd accomplished her task, she sat down in front of the fireplace to rest—and think.

She still couldn't understand Samuel's sudden disappearance. She knew he didn't owe her any explanation—but still. She thought back to the last time she'd seen him, and then remembered him standing by the front door speaking with Rebecca. Maybe he'd said something to her.

Sarah found Rebecca in the kitchen putting away the dishes. "Do you need any help?"

"*Danki,* child, but no. This is the last of it. Many hands made the work disappear fast." Rebecca sent a puzzled look her way. "Is everything all right? You look troubled."

"Everything's fine. I was just wondering if Samuel might have said something to you before he left. I saw him talking with you earlier, and I haven't seen him since."

Rebecca's cheeks flushed a bright red, and she averted her eyes. If Sarah didn't know better, she would have thought the woman felt guilty about something. But that certainly couldn't be the reason for the flush, could it?

"Rebecca?"

The older woman tucked pots into lower drawers on the stove, and then pretended to wash an already clean countertop.

"Do you know why Samuel left? Or where he went?" Sarah asked.

Rebecca turned and planted her hands on her hips. "I think you pay that young man much too much attention. We both know that his job brought him here, and when the job is done he will leave. It is best you remember that and go about your business."

Stunned by her harsh tone, Sarah simply nodded and stepped away. She'd never heard Rebecca utter a stern word before, and it shocked her. Of course, she couldn't remember if there had been any harsh words spoken between them in the past. She could only base her opinion on her experience with the woman now.

Maybe the stress of the past month, along with everything that happened since Sarah had come home, was catching up with Rebecca. Yes, that must be it. The woman was tired and still grieving. A bit out of sorts. Anyone would be. She'd have to be a little kinder, a little quicker to offer help.

But still…

Something didn't feel right. Sarah thought Rebecca knew much more than she was saying.

Wrapping a shawl around her shoulders, Sarah stepped onto the front porch. Maybe a little walk would do her good, make her feel less restless. She told herself that she was just getting some exercise. She would not allow herself to believe she was looking for Samuel.

"Going somewhere, Mrs. Lapp?"

"Officer Muldoon, please call me Sarah. I have trouble remembering to answer to Mrs. Lapp."

"Yes, ma'am."

Sarah smiled. "And please don't call me ma'am. In our language, that means mother." She squelched a giggle at the bashful and embarrassed look he sent her way.

"Yes, ma'am…uh, Sarah." He looked around and

then asked, "Are you walking alone? Would you like me to accompany you?"

"No, that won't be necessary. I'm not venturing far. I just feel the need to stretch my legs."

As they spoke, Officer Jenkins appeared. "Everything okay here?"

Sarah laughed. "How could it not be with so many attentive gentlemen watching over me?" She folded her hands in front of her. "I just wanted to stretch my legs. You can both sit on the porch. I promise I won't leave your sight. I just want some time alone with my thoughts."

"Seems to be a lot of that going around lately."

Sarah raised an eyebrow in question.

"Detective King told me the same thing not so long ago." Jenkins nodded toward the porch. "We'll wait over there. But please don't leave the yard."

Sarah acknowledged his words with a nod and continued her walk.

Samuel needed time alone with his thoughts?

Once again the niggling feeling that Rebecca knew more than she was saying returned. She'd only strolled a few yards when the ground shook beneath Sarah's feet, and the sound of an explosion deafened her.

Children who had still been playing in the yard raced for the safety of their parents' arms. Screams rent the air. Men's voices of alarm and concern added to the cacophony. The police officers scrambled off the porch. Jenkins ran to their vehicle. Muldoon hurried to her side.

Jenkins shouted to Muldoon. "Get her back in the house, and don't let her come out until we know what's going on!" His voice brooked no argument. Muldoon nodded.

Sarah watched the patrol car, lights flashing, speed down the lane.

"C'mon, Mrs. … Sarah, let's get you inside."

They were hurrying toward the house when Jacob rushed past. Sarah reached out to stop him. "What's happened?"

"I don't know." Jacob pointed in the distance to a large plume of black smoke. "There's been some kind of explosion in the west end of my cornfield. But nothing is there to cause such a thing. Stay calm. It will be all right. We will follow the police officers and find out what is happening. Stay inside with the rest of the women." Before Sarah could respond, he hurried to a buggy hitched at the rail, climbed aboard and snapped the reins, leading the horse in the direction of the smoke.

When they reached the bottom step of the porch, Officer Muldoon released her arm. "Go inside, Sarah. I'm going to make a fast check of the perimeter of the house and the barn, and then I'll be right in."

Before she could reply, he disappeared around the corner of the house.

Sam leaned against a bale of hay and glanced toward the house. The loft of a barn had been his favorite spot as a child to find a quiet, private place to be with his thoughts, and he found it worked for him as an adult, too. The slow, steaming anger he had felt toward Rebecca at her blatant request for him to leave slowly dissipated.

She was right. How could he be angry with someone who spoke the truth? So he cooled down and gave her words some more thought. It didn't take long for him to realize that he'd never really been angry with Rebecca. He was angry with himself.

What had he been thinking? He knew better than to mix his professional life with his personal life. That was rule number two in undercover work. Rule number one was to stay alive at all costs. He should never have allowed himself to get too close to Sarah, to care about her. He shouldn't have—but he did.

He rubbed a hand over his face. He couldn't deny it anymore. It had begun as sympathy for a wounded widow, then admiration for her spirit and determination. It had progressed to appreciation of her gentle nature and enjoyment of her sense of humor until, without knowing exactly where or when, he'd fallen in love with her. When he looked into her eyes, he could see that she had fallen in love with him, too. That was the worst part.

The fact that he had never intended to hurt her didn't mean much when he knew that he would. There was no future for them. He couldn't return to the Amish way of life. He'd left it more than a decade before, and although he still retained a love for the Amish people, it was no longer his world.

And Sarah…

Even though she had no memory of this life, she still had strong, loving ties. What was he supposed to do? Take her away from the people who loved her? Ask her to sit in his small apartment all alone because he was off for days, weeks, sometimes even months on undercover jobs? What kind of life would that be for her? For her child?

No. Rebecca was right. If he loved her—and he did—then he needed to leave as quickly as possible, just as soon as this was over. One broken heart was enough. Best it be his.

Satisfied that he was making the right decision, he began to crawl out from behind the bale of hay. He intended to climb down the ladder, relieve the other two officers and have a heart-to-heart talk with Sarah.

The sound of an explosion froze him in place.

He scrambled toward the ladder, but stopped when he saw a stranger enter the barn. It was the stealth of the man's movements, the way he kept looking over his shoulder, that made Sam pause.

Mary and William Miller were playing on the barn floor below.

Sam couldn't believe what he was seeing, and he had to force himself not to move when the man grabbed Mary roughly by the arm and dragged her toward the far end of the barn. The intruder stood just below him, which made it difficult for Sam to get a clear view of what he was doing without exposing his presence and putting Mary at greater risk.

Sam's brain raced a million miles an hour. Who was this man dressed in Amish clothing? He'd seen him before. It definitely wasn't Benjamin. As strict as Benjamin was, he loved his children and would never treat them in such a rough, unkind way. Sam was just about to speak up and reveal his presence when recognition slammed into him with the force of a semi truck.

This was the man he'd fought in Sarah's hospital room. Even though it had been dark and he'd only seen him for a moment, he was sure it was the same man.

This was their killer.

As he watched in horror, trying to formulate a plan, William ran to Mary's defense. Like a charging bull, he pushed against the man, then yelped like an injured puppy and pulled his hand back. The man had sliced the palm of William's hand with a knife.

Fury seethed within him. It took every ounce of strength he had to stay where he was. But he'd seen the silver glint of a blade pressed firmly against Mary's throat. Sam knew this man wouldn't hesitate to use the weapon if he were startled or if he discovered his presence.

Sam dared to lean forward. He took another glance at the situation. His heart melted when he saw tears streaming down Mary's cheeks. He hoped she'd do what she was told and remain still. This particular intruder had no conscience. He wouldn't care in the least that the life he ended would be that of an innocent child.

As quietly as possible, Sam crept back into the shadows. He needed to signal for help. He moved to the loft door to see if he could spot the other officers. He didn't catch sight of either one of them. But what he did see turned his blood to ice.

Sarah had reached the top porch step when she thought she heard someone calling her name and turned around. William stood at the base of the steps, looking up at her.

"William?" Sarah's heart clenched. The boy's face was as white as the sheets on the line, and his entire body trembled. She hurried down the steps, crouched in front of him and placed a comforting hand on his shoulder. "What's wrong?"

The little boy's lips trembled. He spoke in a whisper, and she had to lean closer to hear. "He...he told me to get you. He told me to bring you to the barn."

Sarah glanced toward the barn and then back to the boy, who was literally shaking in his boots. "Who told you, William? What man?"

"A bad man, Sarah. A very bad man." William's eyes were wider than she thought his little face could hold.

"Okay, honey. Let me get Officer Muldoon, and we'll come into the barn."

As Sarah started to rise, the boy grabbed her arm with both his hands. "No! The man said nobody could come but you." Then the boy collapsed into her arms and began to cry.

"Shh, William, everything will be okay." She held the child against her, rubbing his back in comfort while searching the yard for help. Seconds ago there had been people everywhere. Since the explosion, there wasn't a person in sight. Sarah continued to pat William's shoulder. "Your parents are inside. Let's go talk with them."

"No!" William looked terrified. "We can't tell my parents. We can't tell anyone or he'll kill her. He told me so."

Sarah felt the blood in her body drain away. "Kill who? William, tell me everything, please, right now." She tried to remain calm and keep her voice controlled so the boy wouldn't panic. The strength seemed to drain out of her legs, and she didn't know how much longer she trusted them to hold her up.

"We were playing in the barn when a man ran in, grabbed Mary and pulled her into one of the horse stalls. He held her real tight so she couldn't run away. He told me to come and get you. He told me to make sure we didn't bring anyone else."

"We don't listen to bad men, William. Of course we are going to bring people with us to help Mary." Sarah placed one foot on the lower step, but William threw himself at her, almost as if he were trying to tackle her.

"Please, no." His eyes pleaded with her. "If you tell anyone, then he said he will cut her worse than he cut me." He held out his left hand.

Sarah took hold of his tiny hand. Her eyes could barely pull away from the sight of the thin red line slashed across the boy's palm.

"Dear Lord, help us. Why didn't you tell me that he'd hurt you?" For the first time, she noticed the stark droplets of red on the ground at the boy's feet. She quickly untied her apron and used it to tend to the boy's wound. She applied a steady pressure against his palm.

After a moment, she lifted the material and breathed a sigh of relief. The cut had been superficial and not deep. The bleeding stopped immediately. No permanent damage had been done. He wouldn't need stitches or even have a scar.

"Danki, Lord."

William couldn't hold back tears anymore, even though they both knew his father would find it a sign of weakness for a boy to cry. His breathing came in hiccups. "He…he is holding a knife against Mary's throat. She can't even try to run away, or he will cut her. Please. You have to help Mary."

Sarah hugged him close. When she released him, she held his forearms and stared hard into his eyes. "I am going to go into the barn and try to help Mary, but you must help me. Do you understand?"

The boy nodded.

"Good. You stay here. You count to ten very slowly. Then you run inside and tell your father everything. Counting to ten will give me time to get into the barn.

After the bad man sees that I am alone, he won't be expecting anyone else. It will be safe for you to tell your father and let him bring people to help me." She gave William's shoulders a gentle shake. "This is important, William. Do you understand? Count to ten slowly, and then go inside and get help."

Although the boy nodded, she didn't like the dazed expression on his face. This was not a time for William to get distracted or daydream as he frequently did, but she didn't have a choice except to trust him. If this man had used a knife on William, she had no doubt that he'd use one on Mary, and she couldn't let that happen. She offered up a silent prayer that the boy would do as she'd requested, and she hurried to the barn.

Stopping right outside the entrance, she took a deep breath to steady the trembling that seized her body. She glanced over her shoulder. William stood right where she'd left him, his eyes riveted on her. She did her best to smile reassuringly. She nodded in his direction and then, slowly pushing the door open, stepped inside. Her breath caught in her throat the moment she spotted the stranger. He stood at the far end of the barn in the entrance to one of the stalls. The knife he held pressed against the little girl's throat was clearly visible.

"Don't cry, Mary. Everything is going to be all right. Try not to move, honey." Although the beat of her heart galloped like a wild stallion on stampede, Sarah kept her voice steady and her outward composure calm.

Please, God, be with this child. Please keep her as still as possible until William can bring help.

"Come in, Sarah. Shut the door behind you." The tenor of the intruder's voice rose and fell in a singsong rhythm. "I've been waiting for you."

Chapter Sixteen

Fear danced up and down Sarah's spine. "Please. Let her go." She took several steps toward the man. "She is just a child. She has nothing to do with any of this."

The man stepped out of the stall, dragging the girl with him. He sneered, and for a moment Sarah couldn't believe she was even looking at a human being. He seemed to have no heart, no compassion. She found herself looking into the eyes of pure evil.

"Where are my diamonds?" he demanded.

Sarah had to take several breaths before she was able to calmly answer. "I have never seen your diamonds. The police told me they found them on my body when they took me to the hospital. They must still have them."

"Police, huh. Figures." He yanked the child closer, and she whimpered with fear. "So what are you going to do to make it up to me, Sarah? What can you offer me in exchange for my diamonds…and for the life of this girl?"

Sarah's legs shook so badly that she felt they would dump her on the dirt floor at any moment. Her mind raced, but she couldn't come up with any plan of action that would ensure the girl's safety, and she knew there was little hope for her own. She prayed that William had done what she requested and that help would be racing through the open barn door at any moment. She moved closer so she could throw herself against the man and try to save Mary as soon as she heard help coming.

"Stop right there!"

The command in his voice froze her in place.

"Do you think I'm stupid? I can see exactly what you have in mind. It's written all over your face. You think you can wrestle this knife from me and save the child. I may even let you do it." He let out a maniacal laugh. "I'll even do one better. I'll give you a choice. I can slit this child's throat right now…or you can step forward so I can claim the life of the child you carry."

In horror, Sarah's hands flew to her belly, and for a moment she couldn't move, couldn't think.

"That's what I thought. So it will be the girl." Before he could move his hand across her throat, a small voice echoed in the barn.

"No! Let my sister go!" William had crept into the barn behind Sarah and now stepped out into the open, drew something from his pocket and, before anyone could blink, launched an object into the air.

It took only seconds for Sarah to realize that William had a slingshot in his hand, and his stone had hit its mark.

The stranger groaned and automatically lifted his right hand to his forehead, freeing the knife from Mary's neck. The girl dropped to the barn floor and scrambled away on all fours. Sarah and William raced forward to help her. At the same time, a large, dark object fell out of the loft and landed on top of the stranger.

"Help! Somebody help us. Help!" Sarah screamed

at the top of her lungs as she pulled William and Mary toward the open barn door. It wasn't until they'd cleared the barn and were standing safely in the yard that Sarah sent the children racing to the house for help and dared to turn and look behind her to see what had fallen on the intruder.

Her eyes widened in horror. It wasn't a thing. It was Samuel. Both men were in the fight for their lives as they wrestled on the dirt floor of the barn.

Glancing over her shoulder, she saw the children burst into the house.

Sarah ran back into the barn, grabbed a pitchfork and hurried toward the men. She never had to wonder whether or not she'd be capable of piercing the man with it. She couldn't get a clear poke at him. His back would be toward her for a split second, then just as quickly it would be Sam's.

Sarah danced around the two men looking for an opportunity to help, but she needn't have worried. After a few well-aimed punches, Sam had the situation under control. He straddled the man, holding the stranger's hands behind his back.

"Sarah, place that pitchfork on the back of this man's neck."

Nausea rose in Sarah's throat.

"Do it. Now," Sam commanded.

It took a moment of supreme trust in Samuel, but Sarah did as he asked.

Sam grabbed the weapon from Sarah's hands. "I'm holding this pitchfork now, and I will not hesitate to use it on the likes of you. Understand?" He exerted a little more pressure, and the man stayed absolutely still. "Smart decision," Sam said. Then he glanced up at Sarah. "Find Officer Muldoon and get him out here. Then go and get my gun."

Sarah ran from the barn just as a half-dozen Amish men rushed past her into the barn. When she returned, the gun held at arm's length in front of her and hanging gingerly from her fingers, Sam looked like he was trying not to laugh at her. The Amish men, armed with sticks, baseball bats and a second pitchfork, had formed a circle around him and the intruder. They seemed to be doing their best to look threatening, but Sam knew that not one of them would connect a blow, and the entire scene was staged for support, not protection.

Sarah hurried forward, and he took the gun from her fingers. He loosed his hold on the pitchfork, ordered the other Amish men to step away and hauled the intruder to his feet.

Officer Muldoon stumbled into the barn. The back of his head and the shoulder of his jacket were coated with blood. Despite his injury, he moved forward, drew his weapon and stood next to Sam.

"I'm sorry, Detective King. I was checking the perimeter of the house when someone got me from behind."

"Meet the somebody who clocked you. You okay?"

"I will be."

"Good. Cuff him and get him out of here."

Sam supervised the cuffing and had started to walk with Muldoon to the car when Jenkins raced into the barn, assessing the situation in an instant. He stepped forward, replaced Sam's hold on the perp's arm and helped escort him to his patrol car.

Sam thanked the Amish men for their support and

watched as they filed out behind the police officers. Sam smiled again.

Finally, he had a chance to focus his attention on Sarah. He clasped her forearms and felt the trembling beneath his fingers cease. Her eyes, filled with concern and caring, caught his gaze and melted him to the spot. His heart thundered in his chest. His pulse raced.

Before he could give it a moment's thought, he pulled her into his arms and kissed her. This kiss wasn't tender or tentative. All of the emotions he had tried to hide surfaced in an embrace of passion and fire and need.

And she kissed him back.

She fit in his arms as naturally as if she'd always belonged there. She threaded her fingers in his hair and wrapped her other arm tightly around his waist. She tasted of strawberries and coffee and tears.

It was a delicious, intoxicating kiss—and he wanted more. When he lifted his mouth, the flush of her skin and the brightness in her eyes made him smile.

"Are you all right?" he asked. "Did that man hurt you?"

"*Nee,* I am fine." She smiled so widely it barely fit her face. "Samuel, you saved us."

"I wish I could have done something sooner, but he had too tight a hold on Mary for me to take the chance. If it wasn't for William's bravery..." He directed the words to Benjamin who had just reentered the barn, closely followed by Jacob and the others. "That is a brave, fine boy you have."

Benjamin's voice croaked. "*Danki,* Samuel. William was very brave today, it's true."

Although the Amish try not to show favor, pride shone from Benjamin's eyes, and Sarah believed God would forgive this moment of transgression.

"Who was that man, Samuel?" Aaron Miller asked from the middle of the crowd.

"That is the man who shot Sarah and killed Peter. He is a career criminal who has made a lifetime of stealing art and fine gems to support his expensive lifestyle. He made fatal mistakes when he entered a world he was not familiar with. No one will have to worry about him again."

"What happens now, Samuel?" Jacob stepped forward. "What will they do with that man?"

"He will go on trial. Based on the evidence we have against him, he will spend the rest of his miserable life in a cell. He will never be a threat to you or your family again."

Jacob nodded. "*Danki,* Samuel."

"Don't thank me. Everyone worked together. The children, Sarah, yourselves. You graciously allowed the intrusion into your home and into your lives. But it's over now."

"Yes, it's over." Rebecca stepped out of the shadows and stood beside her husband.

Sam took one look at the expression on her face, and he knew that she had witnessed the kiss.

"We must say a prayer of thanksgiving to the Lord," Rebecca said. Her gaze locked with his. "God is good. Sarah is safe. The man has been captured. He will be punished in an *Englisch* court under *Englisch* law. And our lives can return to what they should be." Rebecca stared hard at him. "Isn't that so, Samuel?"

Sam's stomach clenched. His arms still ached with the feel of Sarah within them. His lips still tasted her lips. He knew what the woman expected of him. Now he had to ask himself if he was man enough to do it.

* * *

Sarah watched the exchange between Samuel and Rebecca. She heard the words. Nothing out of the ordinary had been said, but something unspoken hung in the air.

Seconds of silence stretched between them, and then Samuel nodded. "Yes, Rebecca. Now is the time for your lives to return to normal."

"Gut." She stepped forward and hugged Sam. "You are a *gut* man, Samuel. God bless you."

Sarah wasn't sure what she had just witnessed, but a sense of dread overcame her.

Rebecca ushered the others out of the barn to regroup, check on the children and have a cup of coffee before their departure. Sarah had started to go with them when Sam's hand shot out and stopped her.

"Sarah…"

She stared into his eyes and almost had to look away from the pain she saw looking back at her.

Gently, he cradled her face with his hands.

"Sweet, sweet Sarah."

His eyes glistened, and for a brief moment she thought he might cry.

When the others were out of sight, he pulled her to him. He kissed her again—a passionate kiss, a desperate kiss—and suddenly Sarah knew. It was a goodbye kiss.

She lifted her eyes and searched his face, hoping she was wrong, but the shuttered look in his eyes told her she wasn't. Still, she tried to deny the inevitable. She offered him a tentative smile. "When you are finished with whatever you have to do for your job, you are welcome to join us for dinner. Rebecca is making a pot roast, and I still have some of your favorite apple pie left."

"Sarah…"

"If you can't make it back this evening, that's okay. We understand you have many things to do. You are welcome to join us tomorrow night."

He placed his hands on her waist and held her in place.

"It's over. My job here is done. It is time for me to go home."

Her breath seized in her throat, and her heart refused to beat. She had known this moment would come, but she'd hoped…she'd prayed…

"Your home could be here, Samuel. You are Amish. You could return to your roots, study, get baptized. Our community would welcome you."

"I am not Amish. I haven't been for more than a decade." He trailed a finger down her cheek. "You are a very special woman. A loving woman. Smart. Kind. Brave." Boldly but gently, Sam placed his hand on her stomach. "God knew what He was doing when he chose you to be the mother of this child."

She placed her hand on top of his and clasped his fingers. "Samuel…please, don't…"

"I will always cherish the moments you allowed me to share with you." He removed his hand. "We both knew this time would come, and now that time is here. I must return to my world—and you must stay in yours."

"But is this my world?" Sarah's eyes filled with tears. "I have no memories of this life. I have no memories of *any* life. As you told me yourself, I can be whoever I want to be. The future has not yet been written."

He smiled sadly. "You will have a wonderful future here with your family—raising your child and surrounded by the people who love you."

"What about who *I* love?" She challenged him with her eyes. "Don't my feelings matter?" She hesitated and then took the chance and spoke. "I... I don't remember Peter. You are the only man I know. You are the only man I... I..."

He placed a finger against her lips before she could finish.

"Shh. Think, Sarah. You love Rebecca. You love Jacob. And they and all the people in this community love you in return. They are your family. You belong here." He drew her into his arms and hugged her tightly. His breath was like a gentle breeze through her hair. "Go with God, Sarah. Be happy. It is best you do not dwell on everything that happened in this past month. Try to put it all behind you and move on."

"Is that what you truly want, Samuel? For me to forget you, too, as I have forgotten everything else?" She stared defiantly into his eyes, daring him to look away.

He released her. He tilted her chin up and kissed her on the forehead. His tenderness ripped at her heart. "In those quiet moments of the evening, when you sit on the porch and stare at the sky, I want you to know that the feelings we had for each other were real. The respect. The friendship. The warmth."

"The love?" Sarah could barely whisper the question.

He dropped his gaze from hers. "Our time together was special. Something to be cherished. A memory, Sarah. A memory that no one will ever be able to take away."

He placed a gentle kiss on her lips, and Sarah could have sworn she tasted the salt of his tears. When she opened her eyes, she stared at his back as he walked out of her life as suddenly as he had swooped in.

Chapter Seventeen

"I wish you had stayed home," Rebecca scolded as she stepped down from the buggy and turned to help Sarah down as well. "Soon you will be delivering that wee one. These bumpy carriage rides cannot be helping."

Sarah grasped Rebecca's hand and used it to steady herself as she moved her cumbersome girth and stepped down. Her foot twisted, and she started to fall.

Rebecca gasped and reached out to try to grab her, but her hold was too weak to help.

Before Sarah hit the ground, two strong hands grabbed her from behind and righted her. When she regained her footing, she turned with a smile to thank the person who had helped her, but the words locked in her throat.

Tears welled in her eyes. She had truly believed she would never see him again. But here he was. Not an apparition or a dream, but a flesh-and-blood man standing mere inches away from her.

"Samuel?"

He shuffled his feet and stared at the ground. It was

obvious he was as uncomfortable with their encounter as she was.

"What are you doing here?" She held her breath and waited for his answer.

"I quit my job in Philadelphia. I got a job here with the Lancaster Sheriff's Department." He dared a quick glance her way and shrugged. "I kept telling everyone I became a cop to protect the Amish community. Figured if I planned to really do that, then I belonged here with the Amish."

His sheepish grin tugged at her heart.

He was back. For good.

What did that mean? Did she dare hope?

"Are you telling me that you live here now...in Lancaster, I mean?"

"Yes." He tucked his thumbs into the utility belt on the waist of his police uniform.

Sarah's eyes couldn't get enough of him. He looked tall and dangerous and absolutely delightful. And he was back.

"I bought a place not far from town," he said. "The older couple who had owned it couldn't keep up with the repairs. I'm fixing it up little by little on weekends and any hours I have away from work."

"Are you talking about the Townsend farm?" Rebecca asked. She hid her shock at seeing him as well, but the tremor in her voice gave her away. "I'd heard they'd sold their property to a young investor and moved away."

Sam laughed. "I don't consider myself an investor. Don't know if I'd qualify as young these days, either. But yes, I bought the Townsend place."

The sound of his deep chuckle sent a wave of warmth through Sarah's veins.

He's back. Sam came back.

"The Townsend place…isn't that the farm down the hill from ours?" Sarah asked.

Sam locked his gaze with hers. "Yes."

Had he come back for her? And if he had…

Sarah glanced at Rebecca and saw the question and fear residing in the older woman's eyes.

Myriad emotions raced through her. Could she leave the Amish community knowing they would shun her? She'd never be able to continue her relationship with Rebecca and Jacob. Could she bear that? Would she be any happier in the *Englisch* world than she had been in the Amish one? Since her memory had never returned, how would she be able to answer the questions tumbling through her mind?

And then she knew.

It wasn't her mind that would answer those questions. It was her heart…and her heart belonged to Samuel.

She stared at him, waiting for him to say the words she longed to hear. She tried to understand his silence, searched for a hidden message in his eyes, an invitation, but she didn't see one. Her exhilaration and hope quickly faded.

"It was good seeing the two of you again. I expect we'll bump into one another now and again. Give Jacob my best."

He was getting ready to walk away…again.

Please, God, not again. Please.

"Well, you ladies have a nice afternoon."

Sarah couldn't believe it. He hadn't returned for her. He wasn't here to ask her to be his bride. She stared at his back in silence and wondered just how many times her heart could break before there wouldn't be any pieces left.

Walking away from Sarah for the second time was one of the hardest things he had ever had to do. He loved the woman. He'd always love the woman. And that's how he found the strength to leave.

She belonged with Rebecca and Jacob. She was close to term with her pregnancy, and the birth of this baby would seal her role within their family.

He knew he should have stayed in Philadelphia. What had he been thinking?

Sam hadn't been thinking. He'd been feeling. He knew he couldn't have a life with Sarah, but he couldn't live a life without her, either. So he satisfied himself with the occasional glimpse, the few idle words spoken on the street. And he prayed, something that hadn't come easily to him but was now part of his daily life. He prayed that somehow God would perform a miracle and find a way for them to be together, and that He'd give him the strength to continue to do what was right if that miracle didn't come.

And Sarah...

Her weekly jaunts into town became almost daily buggy trips. She seemed to have the same need he did to see each other on the streets, to nod at each other in passing, to steal a few spoken moments and words.

Sam leaned against his car door in the parking lot of one of the local restaurants and watched the buggy approach. When it came to a stop beside him, he approached the driver.

"Are you sure about this?"

Benjamin shrugged. "We have to try. Get in."

Sam walked around the horse, and he climbed into the buggy. The irony of the situation did not escape him. He settled onto the seat beside the man who had once been against his presence in this community, and now not only welcomed him but wanted to help.

Benjamin snapped the reins and turned the buggy onto the open road.

"How is Sarah?" Sam could barely wait for Benjamin's reply. He had been on pins and needles since he'd received word that she'd gone into labor.

"The midwife is with her, as well as Rebecca. I am sure all will be well."

Sam's stomach clenched. He wished he could be as confident.

Benjamin laughed. "You would think, the way you pace and worry, that you are the papa. Relax. The women know what they are doing."

Sam tapped his fingers against his knee and looked out over the fields they passed. The harvest complete, the fields stood empty and waiting for the first taste of winter's snow.

It was time for rest, renewal and hope.

Sam's stomach twisted into knots when they turned into the lane leading to the Lapps' farm. As they approached the white clapboard house, his pulse raced and his knees literally knocked together. He hadn't felt so unsettled and unsure of himself since he was a teen.

Benjamin pulled the buggy in front of the barn. Sam hopped out, circled around and met Benjamin as he climbed down.

"I don't know if this is a good idea. Maybe I shouldn't be here, especially today."

Benjamin tilted his head and studied Samuel's face. "Where else should you be on the day Sarah delivers her *boppli?*"

Sam began to pace. "What if this idea of yours doesn't work?"

Benjamin laughed, and the sound startled Sam. He didn't think he'd ever heard the man laugh at anything.

"Where is the brave man we all came to know?" Benjamin asked. "You can capture killers, *ya?* But you cower at the thought of seeing the woman we both know you love?"

"I shouldn't have come. The situation is impossible."

"Nothing is impossible with God." Benjamin put down the reins and gestured with his hand. "I have been praying. I believe God has given me an answer to those prayers."

"What if it doesn't work?"

"Have faith, Samuel. It is in God's hands. Whatever He wants will be. Now let's go inside."

The men had turned toward the house when Benjamin reached out and grabbed his arm. "Wait…"

Sam faced him.

"I think I hear Jacob's voice coming from the barn. It would be best if we spoke to him privately before approaching Rebecca or Sarah."

Sam agreed, and the two men quietly entered the barn.

Jacob's voice drifted from inside one of the far stalls. "I can't believe you are coming to me with this request. Do you know what you are saying? Do you know what it would cost us?"

"Of course I do." Rebecca's voice, timid and filled with tears, reached their ears. "It is all I have thought about…all I have prayed about for weeks. Ever since Samuel came back to town."

Sam knew he should make his presence known and not eavesdrop, but something about the serious tone of the conversation stopped him. Apparently, Benjamin felt the same way. The men glanced at each other and remained still, continuing to listen.

"When Samuel left, everything changed. You know that. Sarah did her best. She is a good and obedient child. She tried to adjust to his absence and commit herself to the Amish life. She did chores, attended services but…"

Rebecca placed her hand on Jacob's arm.

"She can't hide the longing in her eyes from us, Jacob, or her pain. She is still a stranger to herself. She is a stranger even to us. This is *not* our daughter-in-law, Jacob. Not the Sarah we knew."

"What nonsense do you speak? Of course it is."

"No." Rebecca shook her head. "I love her just the same, but she is different. You know what I say is true. Sarah stayed for us so we could see our grandchild. But her heart…it left with Samuel."

Sam's heart constricted when he heard Rebecca's words.

"That will change with time."

"Will it, Jacob? It has been months, and I have seen no signs of this change. It is even worse now that Samuel has returned."

"Ah, but now she has a daughter. Peter's daughter. Our grandchild. Now she will be happy again."

Sam grinned widely and gave a friendly slap to Benjamin's arm. Sarah had given birth to a baby girl. He wondered if the child had hair the texture of golden silk like her mother. It was all he could do not to run into the house and see for himself.

"Sarah stayed for us, Jacob. She didn't want to hurt us, and with time I believe she has even grown to love us. But asking her to continue to stay for us would be wrong."

Sam's breath caught in his throat. Sarah had missed him. Sarah had had as much trouble letting go of him as he had of her. Maybe there was hope.

"What are you asking of me, Rebecca?" The pain in Jacob's voice was evident in the harshness of his tone.

"I'm asking you to love her, Jacob…as much as she has come to love us. I am asking you to love her enough to let her go…to let her find her heart again…to let her be happy. Hasn't she been through enough? Isn't it selfish to keep her here when we know her heart is elsewhere?"

"But the *boppli*…"

"I know, Jacob. I know." Rebecca's voice choked on sobs. "But she is not happy, and without Samuel I don't believe she ever will be."

As Benjamin and Sam slowly moved forward, they saw Jacob throw his shovel to the ground.

"What you are asking of me is too much. If she leaves, we must shun her. We could not speak to her again. We would have to turn away if we passed her on the street. We would lose Sarah forever, just as we lost Peter, and we would lose our only grandchild. I cannot, Rebecca. I cannot do this."

Rebecca stepped into his arms and held him tightly. "But you will, Jacob. You will let her go because you love her. You will let her go because it is what is best for Sarah."

Sam's throat constricted, and his admiration and affection for this couple grew. He saw the tears and pain etched deeply in Jacob's expression, and it tore at his heart.

"Perhaps there is another way."

Jacob and Rebecca startled at the sound of Benjamin's voice and stepped apart.

Benjamin entered the stall with Sam close behind. "Excuse us for this surprise visit, Bishop, but I believe what I have to say might help."

Jacob blinked in surprise. "Benjamin, what is this about?"

He glanced between the two men. "What are the two of you doing here?"

"Forgive me for the intrusion in what is obviously a private conversation, but I think it is time to speak the truth," Benjamin said.

"What truth?" Rebecca asked.

"The truth that we all lost Sarah the day we lost Peter."

Rebecca gasped, and her hand flew to cover her mouth.

"It's true." Benjamin hurried to finish what he wanted to say. "Do not misunderstand me. We love this Sarah. She is kind and sweet and loving. But she is not the same woman who stepped into the school-room that day. She has no memories of that Sarah. She has no memories of us or our way of life. All of us have watched and waited for many months for that woman to return, and she hasn't."

Benjamin stepped forward and placed a comforting hand on Jacob's shoulder. "You know I speak the truth. This is a new woman—in Sarah's body, *ya*—but it is not the Sarah we knew. It is not the woman who was married to Peter. It is not an *Amish* woman."

Jacob opened his mouth to protest, but Benjamin raised his hand to stop him.

"Listen to me, Jacob. She speaks *Englisch* and can only remember some words of our language. She attends our services but can't participate because she does not understand the words of the songs or service. She is not Amish, Jacob. She is *Englisch*. She was born and raised *Englisch*. And after the shooting…" Benjamin looked steadily into Jacob's eyes. "It is the *Englisch* woman who came back to us."

"What are you saying?" Jacob shook his head and stepped away from the three of them, his expression showing how hard he was trying to deny what he knew he had to do. "You are telling me that I should let her go? That I should shun her?"

Benjamin smiled widely. "We do not shun the *Englisch*, Jacob. We befriend them. We welcome them into our homes for visits. We welcome them to join us in our services and gatherings, *ya?*"

A smile creased Rebecca's face as understanding dawned on her. "And this would be acceptable to the community, Benjamin?"

"Forgive me, but I have already taken the liberty to speak to the elders. They agree that the woman residing in Sarah's body is more *Englisch* than Amish. They love her but…" Benjamin shrugged his shoulders. "If God has wiped away her memory, if God has erased the Amish part of her and replaced it with her *Englisch* roots, then it must be God's will, *ya?* And who are we to question God's will?"

All four adults stood in silence as each processed the conversation.

Sam's heart pounded so hard in his chest, he thought it might burst. This was it. The moment of truth. If the bishop and the elders decreed that Sarah was not Amish but *Englisch,* then they would not have to shun her. She could remain an active part of their lives.

Hope filled every pore of his body. Sam bowed his head and prayed. He prayed harder than he had ever prayed before. And he waited.

When an eternity seemed to pass, Rebecca clasped her husband's hand. "Jacob?" Her eyes never left his face as she waited for his answer.

Jacob brushed the tears from his face. "It is true that Sarah was born and raised an *Englisch* child." He turned to face them. "It is also true that since that horrible day in the school, she has no memory of the Amish ways. She does speak the *Englisch* language well, and she struggles to learn ours. It is true that she loves God, but she does not know or understand our *Ordnung,* our Amish rules and laws."

Jacob smiled widely. "What happened to Sarah was God's will, and I will never go against God's will. Sarah is *Englisch.*"

Rebecca flung herself into Jacob's arms, and even though public displays of affection were frowned on in Amish life, this was an exception that all four adults could live with.

Jacob slid his arm around his wife's waist and faced Sam. "Sarah is inside. I am sure she would like you to meet her daughter."

Chapter Eighteen

Sarah couldn't tear her eyes away from her daughter. She traced her finger across the baby's soft skin. When she saw the child's lips pucker and suck in sleep, she smiled with joy. She examined the exquisite, perfectly formed little fingers. She grinned at the way her tiny golden tufts of hair stood up at attention, and she wondered if it would remain that way as she grew.

For the hundredth time today, she offered a prayer of thanksgiving to God for blessing her with this tiny miracle.

A light rap sounded on the door. She made sure she was properly covered with the blanket and then called, "Come in."

The door opened.

"Samuel."

The word escaped her lips as a gasp of surprise. Her mouth fell open. Her pulse raced. She must be dreaming. This couldn't be real. Her eyes took in every inch of the apparition standing in front of her. The dark brown hair that still wanted to fall forward across his forehead. The rasp of a day's growth of beard. The dark, compelling eyes that stared back at her with such longing, she didn't think she could draw another breath.

"Can I come in?"

Unable to speak, Sarah simply smiled and nodded.

Sam fell to his knees beside the bed and gazed at the tiny infant held in her mother's arms. The touch of his index finger to the child's fist caused the baby's fingers to startle open, and then they fisted tightly around his finger.

"She's so beautiful, just like her mother."

A warm, tingling sensation flowed through her body when his eyes caught hers.

Thank you, God.

Samuel had come. He was here with her on one of the most important days of her life and was meeting her daughter. Her eyes welled with tears.

"Samuel, what are you doing here?"

"Where else would you have me be?" The baby still clutched his finger, and Samuel seemed hard-pressed to claim it back. He glanced up at her, and the look of awe and joy in his eyes stole her breath away.

Sarah glanced at the open doorway and then back at Samuel. "Do Jacob and Rebecca know you are here?"

"Yes, of course. They are in the barn with Benjamin. They gave me their blessing and sent me in to see you."

Sarah's mouth fell open, and for a moment she didn't have any words. When she finally found her voice, she could no longer hide the tears that flowed down her face.

"I don't understand. Gave you their blessing? What does that mean?"

Sam grinned and placed the index finger that wasn't being held in the baby's fisted grip against her lips. "It means God has answered our prayers, *lieb*. He in His infinite wisdom devised a way for us to be together, and I will fall on my knees in thanksgiving every day for the rest of my life."

He replaced his finger with his lips in a kiss so sweet, so tender, that she thought she'd never forget this moment of absolute joy.

This wasn't an apparition. This was real. The feel of his touch on her skin. The taste of his kiss on her mouth. Samuel was here, with her, on one of the most important days of her life. He was crooning over her baby. He was smiling down into her eyes and stroking her cheek. She didn't understand it all, but at that moment it didn't matter.

"We have much to talk about, Samuel."

"We do, *lieb*. But we also have time…lots and lots of time."

Why had Samuel suddenly appeared at her door? How could he possibly have Jacob and Rebecca's blessing? But Sam had proved himself to be a man of his word. For now, just seeing him was enough.

Overwhelming waves of emotion gripped her. Tears tracked down her cheeks like streams escaping a dam. But they were good tears, happy tears. For what could make this day more perfect than to be sharing it with her newborn daughter and gazing at the man she loved with all her heart?

She swiped the back of her hand against her face. *Must be hormones setting off these endless tears.*

Sarah quietly watched Samuel interact with her daughter.

"Hello, little one," he whispered in the deep, caring voice she had come to love. His tender expression as he gazed down at the baby touched Sarah's heart. When he glanced up, his eyes glistened. Hmm. *Was he having a surge of hormones, too?*

They spent the next few hours sitting, the three of them—talking, laughing, enjoying their first day together.

Rebecca had come into the room twice. Once just to see if anyone needed anything, and then hours later with a tray laden with sandwiches, fruit and tea.

Samuel took the time to repeat the conversation that had occurred in the barn. He told her that Benjamin had approached the elders, and after several hours of deliberation, they came up with the solution that everyone believed was the right one, one all could happily live with.

Once again Samuel fell to his knee beside Sarah's bed. This time he wasn't focused on the sleeping child in her arms. This time he clasped her hand and looked deeply into her eyes.

"I love you, Sarah. I think I have been in love with you from the very first moment you opened your eyes in that hospital room. You were so vulnerable and lost and frightened." He grinned widely. "But you were also strong, resilient and determined." He drew her hand to his lips and kissed her palm. "From the moment I looked into those beautiful blue eyes of yours, I knew my life was about to change."

Samuel reached into his pocket, extended his hand and opened it.

Nestled softly on his palm was a simple silver band with a small diamond stone. "I know the Amish do not exchange wedding rings. But neither of us are Amish,

Sarah. We are *Englisch,* and I would be honored if you would accept this ring and agree to be my wife."

Sarah stared at the ring.

Was this really happening? Had God truly answered her prayers?

She smiled such a wide grin that her face hurt. "Yes, Samuel. I will wear your ring. I will be your wife."

He slipped the band on her finger and clasped her hand in his.

"The repairs on my house are almost finished. I think you will like the house, Sarah. It has a large kitchen and lots of windows for light. There is a stone fireplace in the living room, and there are four bedrooms upstairs."

"Four? Are you planning for us to have several children, Samuel?"

Sarah almost laughed out loud at the embarrassed flush that colored his neck.

"Would that be acceptable to you?" He looked at her earnestly.

"More than acceptable, my love. I want to fill our lives and our home with many, many children."

"I do have one thing I must talk to you about."

She was surprised by the seriousness of his tone, and she waited for him to continue.

"I am a cop, Sarah. I've been a cop my entire adult life. I don't know any other way of life." He gazed deeply in her eyes. "But I'm willing to try to be something else. A farmer, maybe. Or perhaps I can learn woodworking. I did a decent job on that table I finished."

Sarah cupped his face in her hand. "I do not know Samuel the farmer. Nor have I met Samuel the woodworker. I only know the man I met and the man I love with all my heart…and that man is a cop. A very good cop, I might add. And I wouldn't want him to try to be anything that he is not."

"Are you absolutely certain? I want you to be happy, Sarah. I do not want you to have any regrets."

"No regrets. But one ironclad rule."

He arched an eyebrow in question.

"There are never to be guns in reach or sight of the children. Not ever."

"I promise." Samuel leaned forward and sealed the promise with a kiss.

"Speaking of children," Sam said, turning his attention to the sleeping infant in her mother's arms. "What have you decided to name this precious one?" Sam gently stroked the wisps of golden locks that continued to stand straight up in the air.

"I don't know yet," Sarah replied. "I've been holding her for the last few hours and trying to decide what name best suits her."

"I know what we should call her."

We? Did he say "we"?

Sarah's heart felt like a bird thrashing in her chest. The three of them were going to be a family. She didn't believe it was possible for a person to be so happy.

"Faith." Sam's eyes locked with hers. "Let's name her Faith."

When Sam's lips touched hers in a passionate kiss full of promises for the future, Sarah knew he was right. Faith was the perfect name. Sarah had complete faith that they had a long and happy future stretching out in front of them. Their future was in God's hands—and God was good.

Epilogue

Jacob snapped the reins, and the horse and buggy cleared the curve and approached the white house on the hill.

"What time will Samuel be joining us?" He glanced over at his passenger and smiled. "Rebecca has baked a fresh apple pie, and she will not allow anyone near it until Samuel arrives."

Sarah grinned. "He won't be long. He got called over to the Millers' farm. Someone tampered with his fencing, and his cows are scattered up and down the road."

Jacob chuckled. "That must be a sight. Cars and cows on the same roads. Perhaps the cows will win, and the *Englisch* drivers will go away—permanently."

Sarah laughed. "You know you don't mean a word of that, Jacob. The tourists provide an excellent market for your produce and Rebecca's pies."

Jacob pulled up to the hitching post.

"I know. I know." He waved his hand dismissively. "But I cannot help but wish I could steer my buggy into town without horns blasting and my horse being skittish each time the cars rev their engines or rush past."

Jacob jumped out of the buggy and tied the reins to the post.

"*Kumm, kumm,* everyone has been waiting." Rebecca beckoned to Sarah and stretched out her arms. "Let me have the *boppli.*"

Sarah smiled as she handed her sleeping daughter down into her grandmother's waiting arms. Jacob came around and offered her a hand getting out of the buggy.

Sarah followed the two of them to the grove, where picnic tables covered by white tablecloths dotted the horizon. Even from this distance, Sarah could recognize most of her neighbors already socializing.

"Sarah, Sarah!" William and Mary raced across the lawn in her direction. "Did you bring any cookies with you?"

Sarah laughed. "Get the basket off the floor of the backseat of the buggy. Carry it over to the table, and I will let each of you sample one cookie apiece."

The children dashed off.

Benjamin followed them with his gaze. "They should not be asking you for cookies, Sarah. I will speak with them."

"Nonsense, Benjamin. They are children. Let them be."

"Only if I am also allowed to sample the wares."

Sarah's eyes widened with surprise, and she laughed. "Well, Benjamin, if I didn't know any better, I would swear you are just a big kid yourself."

The sound of her daughter's voice caught and held Sarah's attention.

"Looks like someone just woke up from her nap."

Faith squirmed in her grandmother's arms and tried to get down.

"No, precious. If I put you on the ground, you will get dirt all over your hands. Let's sit down at the table, and Grandmom will fix you something to eat."

A car approached, kicking up dirt and dust as it sped closer.

Jacob shook his head from side to side. "There's something about cars and speed that appeals to Samuel, but I am afraid I will never understand."

"I understand it, Jacob. Samuel doesn't want to miss Faith's first birthday party. Why don't you and Benjamin join the others? I will wait here for Samuel, and we'll be over in just a moment."

The warmth of the sun beat on Sarah's face, and the light breeze ruffled the wisps of hair framing her cheeks. Sounds of laughter and conversations wafted on the air. The party was in full swing, and from her vantage point she could see her daughter basking in the love and attention.

Sam kissed her on the back of the neck, and Sarah startled and squealed.

"You saw me coming, *lieb*. How could I startle you?"

She wrapped her arm around his waist, and he encircled hers. "I was so lost in the beauty of the day, I didn't hear you approach."

As they walked toward the others, Samuel asked, "Have I missed anything? They haven't sung or cut the cake yet, have they?"

Sarah grinned. "You haven't missed a thing. We just got here."

Samuel nodded, happy that he'd made it in time.

"I can't believe it's Faith's first birthday. It seems like only yesterday we were sitting together in this very house and trying to decide on a name for our daughter."

Our daughter.

A flash of warmth and love flooded her being. Samuel had always treated Faith as his daughter from that very first day, and the child adored him.

"Have you told them?" Samuel asked.

"Without you? How could you think such a thing?"

Samuel's smile widened. "Let's tell them now." He steered her toward the gathering of friends and family.

After pleasantries were exchanged, Samuel clasped Sarah's hand and pulled her toward him.

"This is a very special day," Samuel said. "Faith is one year old today."

Everyone cheered and fussed over the child.

"It has been a good year, *ya?*" Benjamin asked. "Good weather. Good harvest. Good friends. And now time to eat good food!"

Everyone laughed as he reached for a chicken leg and Rebecca shooed his hand away.

Rebecca tilted her head and stared hard at Sarah and Samuel. Then a grin broke out on her face, and she clapped her hands together. "You have news, *ya?*"

Her words silenced the group, and all eyes turned toward them.

Sarah smiled up into her husband's face. It was a good face. Strong features. Strong jaw. Eyes that shone with intelligence—and love.

Her heart overflowed with emotion. God had brought such blessings into her life. Her smile widened so much, she thought it would no longer fit her face.

"You tell them," she whispered.

"Tell us what?" Jacob asked.

"They don't have to say a word. It's written all over their faces, Jacob. Can't you see?" Rebecca rushed forward, Faith wrapped in her arms and clinging to her neck. "Faith is going to have a little brother or sister, *ya?*"

Sarah smiled and nodded. The crowd cheered and congratulated them.

"That is great news," Benjamin said. "Now let's celebrate by eating."

Laughter filled the air as friends and neighbors resumed talking while filling their plates.

Sarah's gaze drifted to the horizon. From this distance, Peter's headstone was a mere shadow on the rise. A twinge of sadness touched her heart that no memories of the man had returned. But the sadness was immediately replaced with happy thoughts. She had a pretty good guess now what he must have looked like. She saw glimpses of him every time she looked into her daughter's face, and felt nothing but fondness and gratitude toward the man.

Sarah could feel the warmth of Samuel's breath on the back of her neck.

"Penny for your thoughts."

"I was thinking what a perfect day today is."

He spun her around and smiled down at her. His lips brushed hers softly and tenderly. She could smell the fresh, clean scent of mint and could taste a trace of coffee on his lips.

"Now it is a perfect day," he whispered.

Sarah reached up and cupped his face with her hand. She smiled into his eyes. Without a word, she stood on tiptoe and kissed him back, long and passionately, expressing all the love and joy her heart could hold. "Now, my love, it is a perfect day."

Samuel's eyes glistened. "How did I ever find someone as wonderful as you?"

"I was gift wrapped in bandages and express-delivered to your care by God," Sarah replied.

Samuel laughed. "That you were. And I will be forever grateful to the good Lord for such a wonderful gift." He clasped her hand and tugged her toward the picnic tables. "Speaking of gifts, Faith is waiting for us to open hers. Let's go and help our daughter eat her cake."

Sarah offered a silent prayer of thanksgiving as she crossed the lawn to join her family and friends. God makes all things good…and Sarah's life was good, indeed.

* * * * *

HER FORGOTTEN
AMISH PAST

Debby Giusti

In memory of

Betty Ramsdell
August 23, 1919–April 1, 2019

A faithful Christian, devoted army wife
and dear friend.

Thank you, Betty, for your love and support.

Hear me when I call, O God of my righteousness:
thou hast enlarged me when I was in distress;
have mercy upon me, and hear my prayer.
—*Psalm* 4:1

Chapter One

"Hello?"

Becky Taylor tapped on the door of the trailer, then glanced at the Montcliff Studio van parked nearby and raised her voice to be heard over the cold wind that whistled through the tall pines.

"Is anyone there?"

Disheartened to have her knock go unanswered, she pulled her black cape tight around her shoulders and adjusted the starched white *kapp* that covered her knot of unruly hair.

An Amish woman should be able to twist her mane into a smooth and compliant bun, her grandmother's voice from the past challenged. Instead, Becky battled the wayward wisps that danced in the swirling wind. Raking the chestnut strands away from her face, she glanced up at the dark clouds crowding the sky and the descending twilight that brought with it the smell of November rain and musky, red Georgia clay.

Concerned about the encroaching storm, she knocked again, then shrugged and dropped her hand to the knob that turned too easily. Needing to escape the fat drops of rain that, at that moment, started to fall, she stepped into the small entry space, fully intending to make her presence known. The sound of raised voices from a back room made her swallow down the greeting that had almost escaped her lips. Realizing she had over-stepped her bounds by entering uninvited, she reached for the door again.

Footsteps sounded behind her. She started to turn, but just that fast, something cold and hard slammed against the side of her head. A scream lodged in her throat.

Pain, like white lightning, exploded across her fore-head and ricocheted down her spine. She gasped for air and crumpled to the floor in a swirl of confusion.

A roar filled her ears as she floated in and out of consciousness. The sounds of a struggle followed by a woman's scream. Had she screamed? Someone lifted her hand, wrapped her fingers around a hard object and lowered her arm to the floor again. All the while, she remained dazed by pain and unable to move.

She drifted into a numbing darkness, then jerked awake at the sound of running water as if a person was washing in a sink. She blinked to get her bearings. Her head pounded, and a cloying smell filled her nostrils and made her stomach roll.

Air. She needed fresh air.

Rising to her knees, she reached for the door and hoisted herself upright. An object dropped onto the rug. She glanced down, seeing the knife someone had placed in her hand. Her heart stopped as she stared for a long moment at the trellis-print carpet and the blood.

The room shifted. Fearing she would be sick, she opened the door and stumbled down the steps, needing to get away, away from the blood and the knife and whatever had happened that she couldn't remember.

The rain had stopped, but the ground was wet and her feet slipped on the soggy grass. She staggered toward the dense stand of tall pine trees and hardwoods that edged the property. Her breath clouded the frosty air, and a pounding in her temple kept time with the rapid beating of her heart.

She glanced back and gasped. A man stood backlit in the doorway. Without seeing his face, she felt his gaze and knew instinctively when he spotted her in the descending nightfall. He shouted something, then leaped forward, like a wild animal lunging for its prey.

Run!

She pushed through the underbrush. Tripping on a gnarly root, she caught herself, then lumbered on. Fear compressed her chest, and her lungs burned like fire, but she had to keep moving.

From somewhere behind her, she heard a voice, calling for her to stop. She ignored the warning and pushed on. Bramble and briars tugged at the hem of her dress, catching the fabric and scratching her legs.

Her *kapp* nearly slipped from her head. She grabbed for the ties, hanging unknotted at her neck and glanced back. The sound of him thrashing through the underbrush made her heart pound all the faster.

She could hear his raspy intake of breath. He called out again, but the roar in her ears prevented her from understanding what he said. All she knew was that he was close behind her. Too close.

If she could hear him, he could hear her.

She turned off the path and pushed deeper into the brush. Her foot snagged on a root. She tumbled to the ground, landed on her hands and quickly climbed to her feet. She had to keep moving.

Branches scraped her arms and caught at her cape. She raised her hands to protect her face as she continued on, afraid to stop, fearing what he would do if he found her.

The terrain angled downward. She heard the surge of water and narrowed her gaze in hopes of seeing what lay at the bottom of the steep ravine. As if on cue, the dark clouds parted ever so slightly and a thread of moonlight shone over a rushing waterfall, swollen from the recent rain. Its beauty lost on her, she saw only the steep incline that needed to be navigated if she wished to escape. Far below, the falling water rushed into a cascading river that surged down the mountain.

Glancing over her shoulder again, she searched for her assailant, then turned back too quickly. Her feet slipped out from under her on the rain-slick slope. She screamed as the mountain gave way, sending her tumbling, head over heels down the incline. Rocks scraped and cut her flesh as she somersaulted, over and over again until she came to a stop on a small outlay of soggy soil.

Her shoulder hit the ground and her head crashed against a jagged boulder. Pain seared through her body. She couldn't see or feel or think of anything that had happened. All she knew was that the darkness surrounded her like the dead of night.

Movement on the roadway ahead caught Ezekiel Hochstetler's attention. He pulled back on the reins of his buggy and leaned forward, squinting into the darkness. His mare, Sophie, slowed to a walk and snorted, as if she too wondered what was undulating across the pavement. Surely not a bear. The creature was too slender.

Whatever it was stumbled and swayed as if drunk with muscadine wine or sick with fever.

The buggy drew closer and the moon broke through the clouds covering the night sky. Ezekiel's heart lurched as he spied the calf-length dress and flowing hair.

An Amish woman with her back to him. Was she sick?

Whether sick, or confused and disoriented, one thing was certain, she needed help.

Pulling the buggy to a stop, he hopped to the pavement and slowly approached her. "Ma'am?"

She glanced over her shoulder as if unaware of his approach. Fear flashed from her eyes.

"No," she cried, her voice little more than a whisper.

Turning as if to flee, her feet tangled, one upon the other. She gasped, splayed her arms and started to fall.

He caught her, pulled her close and held her tight as she whimpered and fought to free herself from his grasp.

"I will not harm you," he said, hoping to ease her concern. "You are safe with me."

She struggled, but her feeble attempts were little match for his firm, but gentle hold.

Staring down at her, his gut tightened, seeing the scrapes and cuts on her arms and cheeks. Brambles nested in her hair. Her *kapp* hung to one side of her head, held in place by a crisscross of hairpins. Streaks of blood stood out against the starched white fabric.

What had happened to this woman?

With a last surge of determination, she tried to pull free, and then her knees buckled and her eyes fluttered closed. She collapsed limp against his chest.

He lifted her into his arms and continued to hold her as he climbed into his buggy and flicked the reins. He could not leave her on the road, not in this condition. He would take her to Hattie's farm. His aunt would provide comfort for the woman and provide for her immediate needs. Water and nourishment, along with salve and bandages to cover her wounds.

Holding her close, Ezekiel was reassured by her breath that played across his neck. Although grateful she was alive, he shook his head in bewilderment. Why would a woman stagger along this desolate stretch of mountain road, far from town or any of the Amish farms that dotted the valley?

Another thought came to mind, but he shoved it aside. He could not dwell on the past. He had moved beyond the pain of Irene's death. At least, he thought he had. Yet something about this woman and the fear he had seen in her eyes brought back all that had happened.

Irene had left him shortly before their wedding, saying she needed time to experience life before she joined the Amish faith and married him. A few weeks later, he had followed after her, hoping to convince her to come back to Amish Mountain. He never suspected Irene had gotten involved with a drug dealer who cooked up methamphetamines in his cabin. Or that she had started using crystal meth.

He shuddered at the memories that welled up unbidden and glanced again at the battered woman in his arms. He needed to focus on her problems and not his own.

Hattie's farm was not far, and the mare covered the

distance at a sprightly trot. Zeke barely touched the reins before Sophie turned into the entrance drive, eager for the oats and hay that awaited her.

Zeke pulled the mare to a stop at the back porch of his aunt's home. Carefully, he climbed down, still holding the bedraggled woman close.

The kitchen door opened, and his aunt stepped onto the porch, her gaze drawn with worry.

"You are late in coming from town, Ezekiel."

As he approached the door, her eyes widened. "What have you brought?"

"A woman, Hattie. I found her wandering on the road."

"She has fainted, *yah*?"

"I fear her condition is far more serious."

Hattie held the door open. "Hurry her into the house and upstairs to the guest room."

Grabbing an oil lamp, his aunt followed him to the second floor and into the bedroom. She pulled back the quilt that covered the bed and stepped aside as he placed the injured woman on the fresh sheet that had dried in the sun and smelled of the outdoors.

Hattie removed the woman's *kapp* and pointed to the streaks of blood, then glanced up at Ezekiel who shared her concern.

"Someone has hurt her," he whispered.

His aunt nodded.

She slipped the black cape from the woman's shoulders and gasped. Zeke's gut twisted, seeing the blood that stained the front of her dress. More blood than would have come from her head wound alone.

"*Gott* help you, Zeke," his aunt said with a shake of her head. "Trouble has found you again."

Thoughts of the explosion and subsequent fire flooded over him again. He had carried Irene from the drug dealer's cabin and had tried to resuscitate her. The memory of her limp body brought the pain back anew.

Giving his heart to an *Englisch* woman over two years ago had been his first mistake. He had made so many, but he was wiser now and would not be swayed by a new pretty face, even if she was Amish.

For the last twenty-four months, he had found solace helping his aunt with the upkeep of her farm. Here in this idyllic mountain setting, he had holed up away from the world. He would not let anyone, even a woman in distress, disrupt his status quo and the tranquil existence he had created for himself.

He sighed at his own foolishness, letting out a lungful of air. The stranger had already thrown his peaceful life into confusion.

Chapter Two

The man was behind her. She heard his footfalls and his grunts and groans as he moved through the underbrush. Her heart pounded nearly out of her chest. She needed to run, but her legs were weighted down and wouldn't move.

She thrashed, trying to escape whatever held her back.

A scream tore through the night.

Hands grabbed her. She fought to free herself.

"No!" she cried.

"Wake up, dear. You are all right. No one will hurt you."

A woman's voice. Not the man who ran after her. She thrashed again.

A soft hand touched her cheek. "You need water. Sit up, dear, and drink."

Water?

She blinked her eyes open to see an older woman with a warm gaze and raised brow.

An oil lamp sat on a side table, casting the small room in shadow.

"My name is Hattie. My nephew brought you here earlier this evening."

"Nephew?" Had he been the man chasing her?

"Ezekiel found you wandering on one of the back roads. You collapsed. He was worried about your health and brought you home."

"I'm… I'm grateful."

"You must tell me your name so we can notify your family tomorrow. I am sure they are worried."

"My name?"

The older woman nodded. "Yes, dear."

"Ah…" Her mind was blank. She rubbed her hand over her forehead. "I'm not sure."

The Amish woman stared down at her for a long moment, then offered a weak smile. "We will not worry about your name now. You can let me know when you do remember."

She reached for a glass of water on the side table. "Sit up, dear, and take a drink. You are thirsty, *yah*?"

Her mouth was parched, like the desert sand. She raised on one elbow and sipped from the offered glass. The cool water soothed her throat.

"Not too much too fast," Hattie cautioned.

A noise sounded in the hall. The two women turned and looked at the open doorway where a man stood, holding a lamp.

He was tall, muscular and clean-shaven with a tangled mass of black hair that fell to his neck.

"Do you need help, Hattie?"

His voice was deep and caused her heart to pound all the more quickly.

"My nephew Ezekiel who brought you here," Hattie explained as an introduction.

She peered around the older woman, trying to see him more clearly. "Thank—thank you, Zeke."

"If you are hungry, I could get something from the kitchen."

"Maybe later."

Hattie patted her hand. "Dawn will come soon enough. Rest now, child. I will wake you for breakfast."

She nodded and glanced again at the doorway, disappointed to find Ezekiel gone. Had she imagined him? Her mind was playing tricks on her so that she struggled to know what was real and what was not.

Blood. She kept seeing blood.

She took another sip from the offered glass and then reached for the older woman's hand and held it tight.

"Hattie, may I ask you a question?"

"Certainly, dear."

She hesitated, unsure of what to ask when her mind was in such turmoil. Would Hattie think her foolish or, even worse, insane?

The older woman leaned closer. "You have been through so much. Perhaps the question can wait until morning."

She shook her head, knowing she needed answers now, at this moment, so she could end the confusion that played through her mind.

Hot tears burned her eyes, but she blinked them back and steeled her resolve. No matter what Hattie thought, she had to ask.

"Who...who am I and why can't I remember my name?"

Zeke had not been able to sleep, not when a strange woman was in the house, a woman who Hattie said did not know her own name. He paced back and forth across the kitchen and then accepted the cup of coffee his aunt offered once the pot had finished brewing.

"Instead of drinking coffee, Ezekiel, you should return to bed. Dawn will not find us for another few hours and there is nothing either of us can do until then."

He glanced down at the sweet woman who had provided not only a home but also acceptance when he needed it most. "I do not see you following your own advice, Hattie."

She chuckled. "Which means both of us are either *dummkopfs* or concerned about our guest."

"You are not a stupid person, although some have called me worse names. For this reason, we cannot get involved."

Hattie frowned. "What do you suggest we do? Throw the woman out with the dishwater?"

He leaned against the counter. "I should not have brought her here."

"As if you would abandon a woman on the side of the road in the middle of the night. Do I know more about you, Ezekiel, than you know about yourself?"

"I know that neither you nor I want our lives disturbed."

"Helping a person in need is more important than our peace and quiet."

He nodded. "You are right. Still, I worry."

"You worry because of what happened, but we learn from our mistakes. Some days I fear you learned too well."

"Meaning what?"

"Meaning you hole up on this farm and venture into town late in the evening and take the long way home as if you are afraid to see anyone. You do not go with me to Sunday church or on visits to friends. You have not spoken to your father for over two years."

He glanced through the kitchen window at the darkness outside. "My father is busy being the bishop."

Hattie tugged at his arm. "*Yah*, he is a busy man, but he is still your father."

Zeke met her gaze. "A father who is disappointed with his son."

She tilted her head and leaned closer. "Then perhaps you must earn his respect again. His love is ever present."

"You accepted me, Hattie."

"I am your mother's sister without children of my own. You have always been the son I never had."

"For which I am grateful."

"Your mother's life ended too quickly for both of us. Your father said it was *Gott*'s will, yet I do not believe *Gott* wills us pain."

"Do not let my father hear you say such things. He will have you shunned for going against the *Ordnung*."

"He did not shun you, Ezekiel."

"Only because I was not baptized."

She raised a brow. "Which you could change."

"Then I would be forced to attend services and listen to my father preach. We would both be uncomfortable."

Hattie tsked. "You are headstrong, like your father."

"I am determined, not headstrong."

"Then why are you running from life instead of facing it?"

He stared at her for a long moment, surprised by the truth in her statement. Hattie was right. She did know him better than he knew himself. He finished the coffee and placed the cup in the sink just as footsteps sounded on the stairs.

They both turned to find the woman staring at them. She was dressed in one of Hattie's nightgowns with a robe wrapped around her slender frame. A bruise darkened her cheek and her left eye was swollen almost shut. Bandages covered cuts on her forehead and lower arms where Hattie had tended her wounds.

"I heard voices," she said, her good eye wide with expectation.

Hattie stepped closer. "Dear, I am sorry we woke you."

"You didn't. I tried to sleep, but…" She glanced at the aluminum coffeepot on the back of the stove. "Do I smell coffee?"

"Forgive me." Hattie pulled a cup from the cabinet and filled it with the hot brew, then handed it to the woman without a name.

She took a sip and glanced at Ezekiel. His stomach churned, not from hunger, but from the way her gaze bore into him as if she could see into the deepest recesses of his heart.

"Thank you again, Ezekiel. A man chased me through the woods. I remember falling, then wandering in the dark, afraid and confused. After that, I awoke in your house."

"My aunt's house," he corrected. "Do you remember anything about the man?"

She shook her head. "I heard him call to me, but I never saw his face."

Turning to Hattie, she asked, "You bandaged my cuts in the night?"

"While you were sleeping. Your soiled dress is soaking. I will find clean clothes for you to wear after breakfast."

"Thank you, Hattie. You are both generous and hospitable."

"We are pleased you could join us. Sit, dear, at the table. It is early, but since we are all up, I will prepare breakfast. You are hungry?"

"I don't want to put you out."

"Ezekiel will slice the bread and fetch the butter from outside. The jelly is on the counter. At least, you will have something to eat while I fry ham and eggs."

"The bread will be enough."

"Perhaps for you, dear, but my nephew will need his breakfast, as well."

Never before at a loss for words, Zeke suddenly felt like the odd man at a sewing bee. Quickly, he sliced the bread and then hurried outside to get the jar of butter cooling in the pail of water by the pump. He dried the jar and returned to the kitchen.

Ham sizzled in the frying pan. The pungent aroma filled the kitchen and made his mouth water. He glanced at the woman who watched him wipe his feet on the braided rug by the door. The latest copy of the *Budget* newspaper lay open on the table.

"Your aunt thought reading the paper might trigger my memory," she volunteered. "I seem to have forgotten everything about my past."

"A blow to the head can cause temporary amnesia," he offered.

She gently touched the bandage that wrapped around her head. "Tell me it won't last long."

"I am certain your memory will soon return," he said with assurance.

"And if it doesn't?"

"My mother always said to take each day as it comes."

Her face lit up and she offered a weak smile. "Good advice."

"Have you read anything in the paper that seems familiar?" he asked.

"A few of the more common surnames. Yoder and Zook. Luke Miller caught my eye as well, yet so many Amish have similar names."

"And your own, dear?" Hattie turned from the stove to ask. "Have you remembered your own name?"

The light in the woman's gaze faded. She bit her lip and glanced down at the newsprint as if searching for a clue to her past. Ezekiel sensed her eagerness to uncover something—anything—that would reveal who she was. Surely, she was confused and frustrated and feeling locked in a world where she did not belong.

He had felt the same way when he had been in jail, awaiting his hearing on wrongful death charges and intent to manufacture a controlled substance, not knowing what the future would hold. At least his memory had not failed him, even if it took a good bit of time before his innocence had been believed.

The woman glanced up. "I think it's coming back to me."

"Have you remembered something?" Hattie asked.

"As I think of names. Becca swirls through my mind and won't let go of me."

"Your first name is Becca?" Zeke asked.

"I believe it could be, along with Troyer as a surname."

"Becca Troyer," he repeated.

She looked at Zeke and tried to smile. He thought again of the woman covered with blood wandering aimlessly alone in the night. Did amnesia provide the excuse she needed to keep her past hidden?

As much as he wanted to believe her, Becca could be a fraud.

He turned and started for the door.

"Where are you going?" Hattie called.

"To feed the livestock."

"Breakfast is almost ready."

"Later." He grabbed his hat off the wall peg, opened the door and stepped into the cold morning air.

We cannot get involved, he had told Hattie earlier.

Whether he wanted to admit it or not, he was already drawn to Becca Troyer.

Chapter Three

After breakfast, Becca helped with the cleanup and then studied the *Budget* over the next few hours, trying to find something that would trigger her memory. Finally, frustrated, she rubbed her forehead and moaned.

Hattie came closer to the table. "What is wrong, dear? You sound frustrated."

"I have a name, but I want to remember my past, yet nothing comes. What is wrong with me?"

"You have been injured. You have taken a bump to your head, and it has caused you to lose your memory. Give it time, dear. Relax and try not to fret."

Hattie went to the window and peered outside. "Ezekiel must be in the far pasture on the other side of the road. I need to sauté onions and peppers and brown some beef for the midday meal before I search for him."

The older woman's brow furrowed as she turned back to the counter.

Becca left the table. "You are busy, Hattie. I can get Ezekiel, if it would help you. The fresh air would be good for me, but I will need something to wear other than this nightgown and robe."

"I have Amish dresses that might be your size, but they are in the bottom of a trunk that will take time to unpack." Hattie's eyes widened. "But I bought *Englisch* clothing at the thrift shop in town last week."

"Why *Englisch* clothing?"

"For quilt fabric, dear. The colors were subdued and the fabric perfect for a quilt I plan to make. The clothing is folded on a chair in my bedroom. I washed everything. Go to my room and see if you can find something to wear."

Becca smiled. "Is it allowed for an Amish woman to dress in fancy clothing?"

Hattie smiled. "The dresses are plain. You should find something to wear. By the time you are back from the pasture I will have at least one of the Amish dresses hanging in your room. You can change as soon as you return to the house."

Grateful for the help Hattie had provided, Becca hurried upstairs and found the pile of clothing. Sorting through the dresses, she selected a simple tan dress that looked like it would fit. Although it was a bit shorter than what the Amish usually wore, she was thankful to have clothing and found a lightweight cotton jacket that would provide warmth when she ventured outside.

Hattie smiled her approval as Becca entered the kitchen wearing the secondhand clothing. "Take the water jug on the counter. The paper bag contains two rolls with butter and jelly. Tell Zeke to eat the morning snack now and to come home in a couple hours or so for our midday meal. He is a hard worker and sometimes forgets to eat."

"When did he start working on your farm, Hattie?"

"Two years ago. He had gone through a hard time

and needed a place to live away from townspeople who sometimes seem more interested in other people's business rather than their own."

"Zeke helps you," Becca said, "while you help him."

"We are good for each other, *yah*?"

Becca nodded. *"Yah."*

Grabbing the jug and paper bag, she stepped outside and breathed in the fresh mountain air. The day was cold but the sun was bright, which filled her with optimism. As Hattie had mentioned, her memory would return.

Hattie had pointed her in the right direction, and Becca walked along the road and hurried toward the pasture, all the while enjoying the beauty of the crisp fall morning.

In the distance, she saw Ezekiel sinking fence posts. Even from this far away, she could tell his strength by the ease with which he lifted the heavy posts and sunk them into the newly dug holes. For a moment, she almost forgot her own plight.

But that moment passed with the sound of a car engine.

Looking over her shoulder, she saw a black automobile heading down the mountain. Something about the vehicle made her pulse pick up a notch, or maybe it was being alone on the deserted mountain road that caused her to be anxious. She crossed the road, glanced at the pasture, and then studied the forest that surrounded it, hoping the trees and underbrush would provide enough cover if she needed to hide.

Her pulse accelerated as the car increased its speed.

The pasture where Ezekiel worked sat far from the road. He had his back to her and was probably unable to hear the vehicle. No doubt, he was focused on his work and oblivious to what she was beginning to believe was an encroaching risk.

Reacting to her gut instinct, she made her way into the wooded area and stepped behind a large boulder. Crouching down, she watched the car draw closer. She was probably overreacting, but after last night it would behoove her to be careful.

Relieved when the vehicle passed by, she started back toward the road but, once again, heard the sound of a car's engine. Glancing in the direction the black car had gone, she realized it had turned around and was coming back.

She returned to the boulder and hunkered down once again. This time her heart pounded even more rapidly.

The car pulled to the side of the road and a man exited from the driver's side. Early thirties with brown hair pulled into a man bun and a full beard. He had broad shoulders, stood well over six feet tall, and was wearing jeans and a pullover fleece.

He stepped away from the car and peered into the woods, his gaze homing in on the boulder where she hid. Her chest tightened and everything within her cried danger.

Not that she needed a warning. The man's scowl was enough to cause a wad of fear to jam her throat.

He took a few steps forward and stopped again to study the area. Her heart pounded so hard, she was sure he could hear its erratic cadence.

Glancing over her shoulder, she spied a cluster of large rocks farther from the roadway. Slowly and carefully, she scurried toward the hiding spot and stopped on the far side to catch her breath. She placed the water jug and rolls on the ground and peered around the boulder, relieved to find him still staring into the distance.

Leaving the bag and water behind, she again retreated, going farther into the woods.

A twig snapped. She glanced back, fearful.

He stared in her direction, then started running.

She raced deeper into the woods, leaping over downed trees and skirting low patches of underbrush. The branches and brambles tugged at her dress and scraped her already raw hands and legs. Her side ached and her head pounded.

She glanced back, hearing him trample through the underbrush and hoping he couldn't hear her footfalls over the noise he was making.

Ezekiel continued to focus on the fence. She yearned for him to glance up and notice the man who had picked up his pace and seemed to be running directly toward her.

She caught her next breath, then ran to the pasture. She could see Zeke at the far end of the cleared area, still intent on his work. She waved her hand, hoping he would see her.

The gate to the pasture lay ahead. She heard the man behind her. Trembling with fear, she struggled with the latch, pushed open the gate and sprinted forward.

A snort sounded to her left. She glanced in that direction and came to an abrupt halt. A huge bull stood staring at her.

From some place deep inside her, a warning bubbled up. She did an about-face and rapidly retraced her steps. Without taking time to shut the gate, she turned right and ran toward another cluster of boulders. Collapsing against the rocks, she drew in a breath and watched the man race through the open gate, into the pasture, oblivious to the danger.

The bull charged.

The man turned around, rapidly retraced his steps and slammed the gate closed barely in time to stop the angry bull. Heaving for air, her pursuer glanced around, no doubt searching for her, then staggered back to his car.

Becca rested her head against the boulder. Tears of relief stung her eyes. She wiped them away, needing to be strong, and turned her attention back to the pasture.

Ezekiel must have seen what had happened because he was running along the outside of the pasture. The bull charged the fence. Big as he was, Becca wasn't sure the wood barrier would hold.

She hurried forward, slipped out of her jacket and waved it in the air. Her distraction worked. The massive animal eyed Becca, then made his way back to the center of the pasture.

Zeke rounded the fence and ran to where she stood. He grabbed her hand, and both of them raced behind the boulder and hid.

A motor sounded. Through the trees, they saw the black sedan drive away.

"Was that the man who chased you last night?" Zeke asked.

"I never saw the man's face last night so I'm not sure."

Becca's head pounded. If he wasn't the guy from last night, then two men had chased after her in less than twenty-four hours.

As they watched, the man pulled into Hattie's drive as if to turn around. He climbed from his car, hurried to the porch and pounded on the door.

"Oh, Zeke." Becca grabbed his hand. "That man is crazy."

Zeke pointed to the henhouse where his aunt peered from a window. "Hattie is gathering eggs. Hopefully, she stays put and doesn't try to engage the man."

He pounded on the door again, then turned to stare at the farm. Evidently he thought no one was home because he returned to the car and headed down the mountain toward town.

Both Zeke and Becca let out huge breaths of relief once he had driven away. "Let's hurry back to the house. I want to warn Hattie to get inside in case that guy returns."

"I'm so sorry, Zeke."

"You did not cause the man to chase after you."

"But I've caused so many problems."

He smiled, seeing her worry. "You are not the problem, Becca. The man is."

After retrieving the water jug and bag Becca had discarded, they crossed the road and hurried to the house. Hattie met them on the porch and filled them in on the unexpected visitor. Becca and Zeke shared their own plight and their concern for Hattie's safety.

Once inside, Becca went upstairs to change into the Amish dress Hattie had hung in the guest room.

"This man worries me." His aunt gave Zeke a troubling glance as she washed her hands and dried them on a towel. "The man sees Becca walking along the road dressed like the *Englisch* and starts running after her. I may be getting old, but my mind is still sharp, yet I do not understand what this means."

"It means Becca needs to be careful and so do you. Do not open the door if the man returns."

Her eyes widened. "You think we will see him again?"

"I do not know, but we will take precautions, *yah*?"

"I am grateful you are with me here on the mountain, Ezekiel. My worry would be even greater if I were living alone."

"Soon Becca's memory will return. Then we will know her story and who was running after her."

Zeke left the house and headed to the barn. The mountain had been peaceful before Becca had appeared in the middle of the night. As he had told her, she was not to blame for upsetting their peaceful existence, yet she had to be involved in something outside the norm since a man was so desperate to find her. Or had two different men chased after her?

He glanced up at the guest room window, thinking of her pretty eyes and smooth skin. Zeke wanted to know the truth about the stranger who was staying with them.

A question kept troubling him. Who had chased after her and why?

Chapter Four

The sun was high in the sky by the time Ezekiel finished the chores. He wiped his brow, thankful for the cool mountain breeze and glanced at the blue sky, wishing life could be as clear.

Yesterday morn he had worried about the price of corn and soybeans. Today was filled with thoughts of the woman he had found last night.

Since then, he had been in an emotional tug-of-war. His intellect cautioned him to be careful, whereas his heart wanted to trust the woman without a past.

Amnesia or prevarication?

Irene had lied to him all the while she had worked her way into his heart until he was unable to think clearly. *Besotted*, his father had called him. The fact that Irene's father and her brother, Caleb, had left the Amish faith only added to his own *datt*'s irritation about Zeke's choice of women.

Amish men only marry Amish women, his father had told him on more than one occasion, yet his father did not know Irene or what she had shared with Ezekiel.

I want to return to the Amish way with you, Zeke, Irene had assured him, *after I see the world.*

The world she explored had been the small town of Petersville, known for illegal activity and a police department that turned a blind eye to crime.

The kitchen door opened, and Becca stepped onto the porch. Ezekiel's throat tightened, recognizing the pale blue dress she wore. A wedding dress Hattie had made for Irene, the woman Zeke had planned to marry.

"Hattie said lunch is almost ready. You didn't eat breakfast so you must be hungry."

He had been hungry, but after seeing Irene's dress, his appetite left him. "I will join you soon."

Becca hugged her arms as if chilled by the mountain air. "Your aunt found this dress for me to wear until mine is washed and dried."

Once again he was at a loss for words. The woman needed clothing, other than the *Englisch* clothing from the thrift shop, and Hattie had solved that need. Why had her generosity unsettled him?

"Is something wrong?" Becca asked.

"No, of course not." But something was wrong. His quiet life had been turned upside down.

She stared at him for a long moment as if wanting to say something more, then with a nod, she turned and entered the house.

He let out an exasperated sigh. How could life become so convoluted overnight? He rolled up his sleeves and washed his hands at the pump and dried them on the towel. In the distance, higher up the mountain, three buzzards circled in the morning sky. He paused to watch their flight, then turned at the sound of a car coming down the mountain, a flashy sports car, traveling too fast over the narrow road.

He recognized the man at the wheel and waited until Caleb Gingerich, Irene's brother, braked to a stop. Tall, gangly and midtwenties, Caleb climbed from the cherry red convertible and extended his hand. "Good to see you, Zeke."

Hattie left the kitchen and stepped onto the porch.

"What brings you to this side of the mountain?" Zeke asked, irritation evident in his voice.

Caleb chuckled. "A piece of Hattie's pie."

Zeke glanced at his aunt. "She has not baked today."

On any other day, Hattie would insist on setting another plate at the table for anyone passing by, but this was not any other day, not with their mysterious newcomer inside.

No doubt hearing the frustration in Zeke's voice, the younger man's smile vanished. "After my sister's death, didn't we talk about moving beyond that which divides our families?"

"As I recall, you did the talking, Caleb. Besides, your father will never change."

"He grieves for Irene, but I thought we could move beyond the past. I forgave you."

Zeke's gut tightened. "There was nothing to forgive, no matter what your father says."

Seemingly exasperated by Zeke's response, the younger man turned toward the porch. "Expect someone from the movie studio to stop by, Ms. Hattie."

"A bearded guy?" Zeke asked, thinking of the man from this morning.

"A tall guy, clean-shaven," Caleb said. "The studio

needs an Amish farm on which to film a trailer for their next movie, and I mentioned your land. They pay well."

"Is that how you bought your new sports car?" Zeke asked, his tone sharp.

"Credit, Zeke. Something you Amish don't understand."

"It was not that long ago when you and your family were Amish."

"Things change."

Ezekiel knew that all too well.

Hattie hurried down the steps and walked to where the two men stood. "I still do not understand why a movie studio comes to Amish Mountain."

"For the idyllic setting." Caleb spread his hands and peered at the surrounding area. "Plus Georgia is considered the Hollywood of the South."

She shook her head with frustration. "Hollywood needs to stay in California."

Glancing at the convertible, she added, "You must be careful, Caleb. Driving so fast on the winding roads is dangerous."

He laughed. "Tell that to Zeke. There are more buggy accidents than automobile crashes on Amish Mountain. I bought the car because I'm working at the studio now."

Hattie raised her brow. "You are a movie star?"

"Maybe someday. Right now, I'm working in the commissary. You should stop by sometime. I could show you around."

"Commissary?" she asked.

"The dining hall where the crew eats," Caleb explained.

"They are filming there now?"

"For the next few days, they're shooting some extra

scenes in town. The leading lady is being a little can-tankerous. You know how temperamental movie stars can be."

Something Ezekiel did not know. He doubted his aunt knew anything about Hollywood types either.

"Seems she left the lot," Caleb continued, "and won't answer her cell phone. The director is putting up a good front, but from what I've heard, he's worried."

"Worried she will not return to complete the film?" Hattie asked.

"That's what I understand, although rumor has it she's been difficult since filming began. Some folks thought the director was ready to fire her, but the pro-ducer stepped in and insisted the movie wouldn't get the backing it needs without her."

"An actress leaves before the filming ends?" Hattie shook her head. "I do not understand how that could be."

"The ways of the world, Hattie, are not as the Amish live."

"*Ach*, it is so."

"I told Zeke that I stopped by for a slice of pie, but I really wanted to talk about buying some of your eggs. The studio cook who fixes meals for the cast and crew has been going to town for his supplies. I told him you might be able to provide fresh eggs from your chick-ens. I also mentioned your pies and cakes. He's inter-ested in purchasing your homemade desserts, if you have time for extra baking. You would be paid well for your efforts."

Hattie thought for a moment and then nodded. "*Yah*, this is something I can do."

Zeke touched her arm. "Are you sure you want to get involved with the studio?"

"What could be the harm?" She patted his hand as if to dismiss his concern and then turned to Caleb. "Yesterday, I baked cookies. You will take a dozen to the cook. He can decide if he is interested in buying my baked goods."

Hattie hurried inside and returned with a filled cookie tin that she handed to Caleb. "You will let me know?"

"I'm sure he'll agree to buy anything you can provide." Caleb placed the tin on the passenger seat and rounded the car to the driver's side.

Ezekiel glanced up and spied Becca at the kitchen window. Her expression made his breath catch.

"You mentioned the missing movie star," he said before Caleb climbed behind the wheel. "What does she look like?"

"I've got a picture of her on my phone. She's a nice lady, but evidently a little hard to handle. I downloaded her headshot." He tapped his phone and held it out for Ezekiel to see. "There she is. Vanessa Harrington. You wouldn't forget her if you saw her."

Ezekiel took the phone. Hattie stepped closer and both of them stared at the woman filling the screen. She was attractive with long black hair, big brown eyes, high cheekbones and a mouth that puckered into a half pout, half smile.

Relaxing ever so slightly, Zeke handed the phone back to Caleb. "She looks to be in her thirties," he said, hoping Hattie did not hear the relief in his voice.

"More like midforties, but makeup does wonders." Caleb swiped his finger over his phone and held up a second photo. "Here she is with the producer, Nick Walker, and Kevin Adams, her leading man. The producer's the big guy in the suit. The actor's the body-builder with a beard."

Zeke glanced momentarily at the second photo, noticing the younger man's arm around the actress's shoulders. The producer stood behind them, wearing a scowl on his square face.

"The producer does not look happy," Zeke stated the obvious.

Caleb chuckled. "Mr. Walker is not known for his good humor. He and Vanessa spent a lot of time together from what I've heard. Evidently their so-called friendship has cooled somewhat."

"And the younger man has moved in?"

Caleb shrugged. "Who knows? Although gossip at the studio is as plentiful as acorns on an oak tree."

"Has anyone else gone missing from the studio?" Zeke asked.

"Not that I know of." Caleb shoved his phone into his pocket. "Why do you ask?"

"Just wondering. I presume the behind-the-scenes folks in the movie industry change jobs frequently. It is probably hard to get good workers."

"I'm just glad they hired me." Caleb opened the car door and slid behind the wheel. "I'll stop by once I hear from the cook."

As he pulled out of the drive, the kitchen door opened. Becca appeared anxious as she stepped onto the porch. "Did you tell him about me?"

Hattie hurried up the stairs and rubbed her hand over the younger woman's shoulder. "You need not worry, dear. Caleb works at the movie studio nearby. The cook at the studio wants to buy some of my baked goods and eggs. We did not mention you."

Hattie glanced back. "Come inside, Zeke. You need to eat."

His aunt was right. He was hungry.

Climbing the porch steps, Zeke smiled at the newcomer, hoping to ease the tension that lined her pretty face. Her brow was tight with concern as she narrowed her gaze and stepped closer.

"Could there have been an accident on the mountain?" she asked, rubbing her arms as if she was cold.

Which he had not considered. An overturned buggy could be the reason for the blood on the woman's dress and the lump on her head, yet Becca had mentioned being chased through the woods. Could she have been involved in a buggy accident, as well?

Zeke looked again at where the buzzards had flown earlier. Now they were gone. Had they found a carcass and were picking it clean? A horse perhaps?

His gut tightened.

Or something else?

Becca hurried inside and then turned toward the door as Ezekiel followed her into the kitchen. His smile had vanished, and the frown he had worn earlier this morning had returned to darken his gaze.

Hattie stepped to the stove and stirred the hamburger mixed with a sloppy Joe tomato sauce. The scent of the simmering meat filled the kitchen with mouthwatering goodness. She said something to Zeke in a dialect that made no sense.

Just as before, Becca nodded as if she understood and hoped her response was appropriate. She didn't want Hattie or Ezekiel to know she had forgotten how to converse in the language common to the Amish.

Every thought that rumbled through her mind was in English, not German and not Pennsylvania Dutch.

Yet she *was* Amish. Wasn't she?

Evidently, not a very good Amish woman. The plain people were nonviolent, which meant she shouldn't have been running away from someone all the while wearing a dress stained with blood.

Something had happened in the woods. If only she could remember what.

Reaching around Hattie, she grabbed the coffeepot and poured a cup of the hot brew, then offered it to Zeke.

"Danki." He raised the cup to his lips, his eyes never leaving her face. Her cheeks grew warm and a tingle curved around her neck.

Abruptly, he lowered the cup and headed to the table, for which she was grateful. His nearness had unsettled her all the more. She returned the coffeepot to the stove and glanced at the stairway, longing to retreat to the guest bedroom so she wouldn't have to face her handsome rescuer whose mood swings confused her almost as much as her own lack of memory.

"Sit, dear." Hattie motioned her toward the table. "The sloppy Joes are almost ready to serve. You can help me then."

"Has anything new come to you?" Ezekiel asked as she slipped into the chair across from him.

"I have thought of nothing except what I cannot remember," she admitted. "And still I remember nothing."

Glancing down, she added, "I keep thinking of the Troyer family to which I must belong since the name seems so familiar."

She dipped her head. "While you were outside, Hattie placed a wet tea bag on my eye to draw the swelling. As you can see, thanks to her home remedy, it is better."

"Do not thank me, dear. It was the tannin in the tea."

"All the while the tea was working, I thought of the Troyers and what they must be like. Hattie mentioned a Troyer family living in the valley."

"The wife's name is Ida, dear. She and her husband have five boys." Hattie reached for a plate and heaped the meat mixture onto a bun, then held it out for Becca who hurried to the stove to help. "Serve Ezekiel first."

Zeke nodded his appreciation when Becca placed the plate in front of him.

Hattie handed a second plate to Becca. "It looks *gut, yah*?"

"And smells delicious." Becca stared at the fresh bun overflowing with the juicy mixture. Just as at breakfast, the portions were generous. "You've given me far more than I can eat, Hattie. This should be your plate."

"You ate little this morning, dear. I do not want you going hungry."

"Hattie, no one could go hungry in your house." Zeke chuckled from the table. "You are a bountiful cook."

His aunt seemed to appreciate the remark and said something in reply that Becca could not understand. A look of concern passed over the sweet woman's face before she repeated the statement in English.

"Surely you know the Amish saying, dear. When the man grows the food and the woman cooks the food, both eat to their fill."

Without commenting further on Becca's inability to comprehend the Pennsylvania Dutch dialect, Hattie pointed to the chair across from Ezekiel. "Sit, dear, before the food grows cold."

Taking her place at the table, Becca kept her hands on her lap, unsure of the midday meal routine. This morning she had started to eat and then noticed Hattie bowing her head to give thanks. She didn't want to make the same mistake twice.

Once Hattie was seated, Zeke lowered his gaze. Hattie did the same and Becca followed suit. From the recesses of her limited memory a prayer surfaced.

Thank you for this food and bless all of us today, especially those who cannot be here. Bring peace to our hearts, lighten our steps and help us to do all things according to Your Holy Will. Amen.

She should have been relieved to remember something, anything, but recalling the short prayer only made her want to remember more.

Was it an Amish prayer that she had said with her parents as a child? Or a prayer she said with her own children? How could a mother forget her little ones, those she should love most?

Ezekiel said something.

She glanced up to find him offering an open jar of pickles. She jabbed one with a fork and placed the pickle on her plate. *"Danki."*

Hattie patted her hand. "Is everything all right, dear? You look troubled."

"I'm concerned about upsetting you both by being here."

"Do not think such thoughts. We are happy to have you as our guest."

Becca glanced at Zeke. His eyes were on his plate. He didn't seem as enthusiastic as his aunt about having a stranger in the house, yet he had been the one to bring her here.

She shuddered thinking of what could have happened if he hadn't found her.

"Is that not right, Ezekiel?"

He glanced at his aunt, his brow raised.

"I said that we are both glad to have Becca with us, *yah*?" Hattie prompted.

He turned his dark eyes on her again, making Becca's breath catch as she lost herself for a moment in his gaze. If only she could read his mind.

She reached for her fork. "I am thankful you found me, Ezekiel. If you had not—"

She couldn't go on. Her mind failed to remember the past, yet it could bring forward terrible thoughts of what could have happened last night.

"All things work together for good," Hattie intoned with a definitive nod of her head.

Becca wasn't as sure. She took a bite of the meat mixture, but the food stuck in her throat. More than anything, she wanted to push back from the table and run upstairs to hide from Zeke's dark eyes and all the questions she saw in his troubled gaze.

She didn't want to bother this man and his aunt any longer, but before leaving, she needed to find out who she was, no matter how difficult the truth might be to accept.

"Did I hear you mention a nearby town?" she asked, needing something on which to focus other than the man sitting across the table from her.

"*Yah*, Willkommen," Hattie answered. "It is some miles away. Does the name sound familiar, dear?"

"Regrettably, nothing sounds familiar."

Zeke reached for his coffee cup. "You wish to go there?"

"It might help me remember if something triggers my memory."

"Willkommen has a sheriff," Hattie mused. "He might know of anyone who is missing."

"You mean he might have information regarding who I am and where I live?"

Hattie leaned closer. "*Yah*, but I must warn you, dear. If you go to town and ask questions, you could find more than you want to know."

"I don't understand."

She rubbed Becca's hand. "Think, dear. You were running from someone last night. If you notify the sheriff, he could tell the person who was chasing after you."

Hattie shrugged before adding, "A mean husband is someone to fear."

Becca glanced at Ezekiel, then turned back to Hattie. "I don't feel like I have a husband."

"And how would that feel, dear?"

"I... I'm not sure, but wouldn't I remember the man I loved?"

Hattie leaned even closer. "Perhaps you have a husband you do *not* love."

"Yet if I am married, there could be children."

Ezekiel's gaze darkened all the more. The direction of the conversation seemed to be unsettling to both of them. "I will go to town and see for myself without involving the sheriff," Becca said. "Perhaps then I will remember."

"Ezekiel will take you in the buggy," Hattie volunteered. "But you must dress so no one will recognize you."

"What are you suggesting?"

"You should wear men's clothing, dear. You are slim

and not so tall. People would think you a young Amish lad."

Hattie sat back and smiled with satisfaction. "Dressing as a man would be a perfect cover. Ezekiel's clothing is too big for you, but I kept a few of my husband's things. I will find something you can wear."

Ezekiel stared at Becca, as if she had been the one to suggest the idea of dressing as a man. Hattie was right. The costume would keep Becca from being recognized, especially from anyone who might do her harm, yet the idea of needing to hide her identity from others when she didn't even know who she was or where she lived weighed heavy on her shoulders.

The sound of a vehicle turning into the drive made Becca's heart stop. Zeke glanced at her as if he too was concerned.

"Stay here," he cautioned as he rose from the table and walked to the door, grabbing his hat before he stepped outside.

"Ach." Hattie patted her chest as if patting down a swell of apprehension, which was exactly what Becca had bubbling up in her own throat. "I do not know who would be coming to see us."

Hattie's gaze narrowed, and she pursed her lips. Then, with a shrug of her shoulders, she added, "We go for days without visitors and now they come one after the other."

Some friendly and some not, Becca thought, her stomach a jumble of nerves. Didn't Hattie realize they were coming because she was here?

Hattie pushed back from the table, hurried to the sink and then peered from the kitchen window. "It is a tall man who steps from a van. The Montcliff Studio logo is on the passenger door."

She glanced back at Becca. "I will go outside to learn the purpose of his visit. Perhaps it is the man Caleb mentioned."

"Please, Hattie, don't invite him in."

The older woman nodded, then reached for the doorknob and stepped onto the porch, leaving the door ajar.

In spite of the cool air coming through the open doorway, Becca moved closer, hoping to overhear what was being said. Her pulse raced when she peered outside. A tall, muscular man stood by the van.

The footfalls of the man who had chased after her last night played through her memory. From the sound of him stomping through the underbrush, he had to have been a big man, tall in stature and with a bulky build.

Her gaze homed in on the Montcliff Studio logo on the side of the van. Apprehension zigzagged along her spine as she stared at the black-and-white graphic, longing to remember why it drew her attention.

The man walked to the front of the van, closer to where Zeke stood.

A lump jammed Becca's throat as she saw the movie man's long legs and thick build. Hands on his hips, he stared at the barn and then the outbuildings as if searching for something.

Was he searching for her?

Tears burned Becca's eyes, but she forced them back. Why would an *Englisch* man from a movie studio be looking for her?

He extended his hand to Zeke. "The name's Larry Landers. I'm the location manager at Montcliff."

Zeke accepted his handshake without comment.

"The movie studio," Larry added as if for clarification. "As you probably know, we've been here for the last six months."

"I know about the studio, Mr. Landers," Zeke said. "It is located higher up the mountain on Levi Gingerich's land."

"That's right. We're almost finished with the production of our first film and hope to begin work on our next project in a few weeks. I'm looking for farmland on which to shoot a trailer and a few preliminary scenes, maybe as early as the end of the week."

"An Amish farm?" Zeke seemed perplexed by the statement.

Landers chuckled, although the gruff sound was anything but humorous. "I mentioned shooting, but not with a weapon, if that's what you're thinking."

Raising his hand, palm out, Landers quickly added, "I know you folks are pacifists."

Becca heard disdain in the man's voice.

"What I meant," Landers continued, "was shooting the film. And yes, we're scheduled to shoot an Amish story and are looking for an Amish farm, otherwise we might have to use someplace in town."

He pulled a folder from the van and handed the packet to Zeke. "The studio will pay to use your property for a week or two, depending on the weather. We'll need your authorization. Our landscape crew will arrive as soon as the contract is signed. Their job will be to enhance the property."

"The land is as *Gott* provided, Mr. Landers. It does not need to be enhanced."

"You're right, of course. Be assured you'll be compensated for your time and trouble."

Zeke glanced at the contract, then closed the folder and handed it back. "The farm belongs to my aunt. She is not interested in your contract."

"You didn't read the offer." Landers gazed at the barn and the pasture where the horses grazed. "You folks look like you could use some financial help. I can increase the payment by half to sweeten the deal."

"Sweet or sour, there is no deal, Mr. Landers."

"Look, I apologize if I've upset you. Perhaps if I talked to your aunt."

Noticing Hattie on the porch, he took a step forward. "Ma'am, if I could have a moment of your time."

"You would not hear anything different from her." Zeke's tone was firm.

"What about some of your neighbors?" Landers asked.

"You will find more farms in the valley. Some are owned and operated by *Englisch* farmers. Perhaps they would be willing to rent their land."

The guy shook his head with frustration. "You're missing an excellent opportunity."

Again, he played his gaze over the barn, then turned and stared at the kitchen door for a long moment.

Becca drew back, fearing he could see her. If so, would he recognize her?

He hesitated for a long moment and then added, "Have you folks seen anyone from the movie studio wandering around in the area?"

"Why do you pose such a question?" Zeke asked.

Larry offered a half-hearted smile. "The relationship between the Amish and our studio is not the best. I want to ensure we don't disrupt your way of life more than we already have."

"No one unknown has come through my aunt's property, if that is your question."

The guy glanced once more at the house. Becca's heart stopped. She held her breath, fearing he had seen her.

Abruptly, Landers turned and scanned the rest of the farm.

"Let me know if you change your mind about the land." He shook Zeke's hand, then threw the folder onto the passenger seat and climbed behind the wheel. Without further comment, he backed the van onto the road.

"Levi Gingerich never should have rented his property to those movie people," Hattie groused as she pushed on the kitchen door and wiped her feet on the entry rug. Zeke followed her inside.

"Levi may have needed money," she continued. "But we do not need a movie studio on the mountain. I have seen some of those people in town. They do not understand the Amish way. Plus, from what I have heard, they are a wild bunch who do not conform to Christian values."

"You are lumping them all together into one pot," Zeke cautioned. "I am sure the majority of the actors and actresses are *gut* people."

Hattie harrumphed as she walked past Becca and headed to the stove. Zeke returned to the table without comment.

Becca's heart beat erratically. The tall, muscular man had been looking for someone. Did Zeke and Hattie not realize he could have been looking for her?

She glanced first at Hattie and then back at Zeke. Grateful though she was for their hospitality, she was a stranger in their midst. A stranger with a made-up name and no knowledge of the life she had lived or even her age. A man had chased her last night, and she had been chased again this morning. Now another man with a haughty manner had stopped at the farm.

Tears stung her eyes, but they were a sign of weakness, at least that's what a little voice whispered in her head. A voice from the past perhaps? How could she know what was memory and what was her own mind playing tricks on her?

"Becca, are you all right?" Hattie asked.

"If you don't mind, I need to go to my room." She left the kitchen and climbed the stairs, stepping into the bedroom just as the tears started to fall.

She closed the door behind her and moved to the window, wanting to ensure the studio van was out of sight. Her heart lurched when she saw the vehicle stopped on the side of the mountain road. Larry Landers stood in front of the Montcliff Studio logo on the side of his van. He held binoculars to his eyes and was staring back at Hattie's house.

Becca jerked away from the window. Fear gripped her anew. Her pulse raced. Who was the man from the movie studio and why was he spying on her?

Pulling in a deep breath, she moved closer and peered again from the window. A black car like the one she had seen this morning had pulled behind the studio van and a bearded man with his hair pulled into a bun was talking to Landers.

Was he asking about an *Englisch* woman he had seen walking along the roadway? As she watched, the bearded man turned and stared at Hattie's house, seemingly zeroing in on the guest room window. Again, Becca stepped back, her heart in her throat.

She dropped her head into her hands. The worry and anxiety that had circled through her mind collided in a wave of emotion, like a giant tsunami washing over her. Hot tears ran down her cheeks and dampened her dress, but she couldn't stop their onslaught.

Struggling to remember anything, she thought back to the woods where the branches had caught at her dress. Was Larry Landers the person who had chased after her last night? Or could it have been the bearded man with the bun? If only she could have seen the man's face, but all she could remember was the blood on the carpet. So much blood.

She thought of something else that made her pulse race even more.

The knife.

Her heart stopped.

The knife that had dropped from her hand was covered with blood.

Chapter Five

"Tuck your hair into this hat," Hattie instructed the next afternoon as she handed a wide-brim black hat to Becca. "My husband's clothing fits you well, *yah?* The hat will sit low on your head and cover your hair. It will also cover the swelling on your head and the bruise on your cheek."

"And what happens if I go inside and need to remove my hat?" Becca asked.

"You will leave it on. A young boy will not be noticed but stay in the buggy if you are concerned. You will see with your eyes as Ezekiel drives through town. Something might bring back your memory. A store, a street, a person. You must be watchful."

Hattie adjusted the hat on Becca's head. "And you must be careful lest you see the man who chased after you through the woods."

As well as the man who had pursued her into the pasture and the tall man who had stopped by the farm yesterday. Becca's sleep had been fitful, interspersed with dreams of running from two men holding binoculars. She wouldn't worry Hattie, but the sweet Amish woman was right. Becca needed to be watchful not only in town but also here on Hattie's farm.

"I'll be careful, Hattie. You can be assured of that. Zeke is good to take me to town. I appreciate everything both of you have done."

"Soon your memory will return and you can decide whether to go back to the life you knew or to move on and make a new life for yourself. *Gott* will let you know the direction you must take."

"God might answer your prayers, Hattie, but He ignores mine."

The older woman tsked. "Hard though it might be to feel His love during difficult times, we must believe what Scripture tells us."

Becca tugged on the hat. "I'm not sure if Scripture was ever part of my life."

"You are Amish, dear. The Bible is important in your life. You can be sure of this."

Becca couldn't be sure of anything, not when she had no memory. She hesitated for a moment, searching for a Bible verse. None came.

Her stomach growled.

"You are hungry," Hattie stated as if any troublesome situation could be resolved with food.

Becca shook her head. "That's not the problem, Hattie."

The older woman nodded knowingly. "Then it is your concern for what you will learn today. You are anxious. Warm milk will soothe your stomach."

Becca wanted to laugh. Or cry. She wasn't sure which.

"You're making me feel like a young child. Warm

milk will not ease my concern, but I appreciate the offer."

She rubbed her hand over her stomach. "Once I am in town, everything will be better. Fear grows when we anticipate that which is never as bad as we imagine."

"You remember that from your past?"

Becca sighed. "I'm not sure."

Hattie smiled. "No matter who you are, Becca Troyer. You are a smart woman, *yah*?"

She nodded. "I hope I am smart enough to find out who I am."

"And who you were running from, *yah*?" Hattie added.

"Yah." Becca opened the bedroom door and stepped into the hallway. "I will come home from town with information about my past."

At least, that was Becca's hope. Who was she and who had been chasing after her? She needed answers to both questions and she needed those answers now.

Zeke harnessed Sophie to the buggy and led her to the back porch. The kitchen door opened, and an Amish lad stepped outside. Mentally Zeke knew who was wearing the black trousers held up with suspenders, white shirt and overcoat, but even then, he stared for a long moment as if confused by what he saw.

Becca widened her eyes. "The clothing does not work. I can see it in your gaze." She turned to flee back inside.

"Wait." Zeke reached to grab her arm, but she slipped past him.

"Becca," he called again.

She stopped and glanced over her shoulder at him.

"My expression," he quickly continued, "has nothing to do with your clothing, but with my own inability to put what I see together with who I know you to be."

He dropped his hand and paused again before adding, "Hattie was right. You will not be recognized."

Becca smiled weakly. "This is good, *yah*?"

He nodded. *"Yah."*

Not being recognized would be safer for Becca, but seeing her dressed in men's clothing confused Zeke even more. What was wrong with him? Ever since he had spotted her staggering in the middle of the road, his normally calm demeanor had been in turmoil. Was it because she was a woman or was it because she was this particular woman, with green eyes and a hint of coral in her cheeks, who caused him so much unease?

She drew closer and looked up as if somewhat perplexed. "How am I to climb into the buggy?"

Zeke wanted to laugh at her question and the cute way she pouted her mouth as she pondered her problem. Knowing better than to embarrass her, he kept his thoughts to himself and said instead, "You must learn now. When we are in town, I will not be able to help you lest someone wonder why an Amish boy cannot heft himself into the front seat of a buggy."

He pointed to the metal step. "Place one foot here and then swing up onto the seat."

She grabbed the front of the buggy for support, placed her foot where he had indicated and gracefully raised herself onto the seat.

"Gut," he said with a nod once she was settled.

"You will sit next to me?" she asked.

"Yah, but you must remember you are a boy, especially if buggies pass us on the road. Glance down or

to the side and keep your hat lowered. Amish children do not speak unless spoken to, which might be difficult for you."

She wrinkled her brow and turned her mouth into a coy grin. "Are you saying I talk a lot?"

"Not at all, but most women enjoy making conversation. A boy would not be as gregarious."

"A boy would be inquisitive and ask questions that would be posed one after the other."

Zeke's lips twitched. "You are forcing me to recall my youth. *Yah*, I had a million questions. It is how a boy learns."

"And I'm sure your father answered each question with patience and understanding."

"My mother answered my questions." He climbed into the buggy and sat next to her.

"And your father?" Becca pressed.

"My *datt* believed children should speak only when called upon to do so, which is something you, as an Amish lad, should remember." Zeke grabbed the reins and encouraged Sophie forward.

"Your dad sounds like a hard taskmaster," Becca said once they were on the main road.

"No more so than other fathers. As you know, the man is the head of the Amish family."

"True, but it sounds as if your *datt* took that role to heart." She hesitated before asking, "Is that why you're living here on the mountain with your aunt?"

"Hattie needs help with her farm," he offered as explanation, in hopes of satisfying her curiosity without having to delve into his own past.

"She could hire help," Becca mused.

"*Yah*, but a family takes care of their own."

"What about your parents, Zeke? Who helps them?"

How could he explain his estrangement with his father without mentioning Irene?

"My *mamm* died a few years ago," he replied, hoping it would suffice.

"And your father?"

"He works his own farm."

Zeke glanced at Becca, wondering how many more questions she would pose. She was as inquisitive as a dozen young lads, only there was nothing boyish about the arch of her brow or the wistful longing he read in her gaze.

She glanced at the passing countryside. "I wish I could remember my parents."

He hated hearing the pain in her voice.

Zeke flicked the reins, needing to think of something other than the woman sitting next to him.

What would Becca think of him if he revealed his own past? Some things were better left unsaid.

Except his memory would not let him forget how he had followed Irene to Petersville only to find her living with a man twice her age, a man who had a meth lab in his cabin and a wad of money in his wallet. A man who had stolen her heart and her common sense just as she had done to Zeke.

He had tried to save her from the burning cabin and had almost gotten killed in his attempt. The explosion played over in his mind, making him shudder.

He turned away from Becca and glanced over his shoulder, hoping she did not see the regret that colored his life. Had he really loved Irene or was he like all young men, running after a pretty girl who made him think not with his head but with his heart?

"Are you all right?" Becca touched his arm, the gesture warm with concern.

He shrugged out of her hold and turned his gaze back to the road. "It is nothing."

She folded her hands on her lap. "You're sure?"

He clenched his jaw and flicked the reins again, speeding the mare along the paved roadway. "I am sure."

The roar of a vehicle sounded behind them. Zeke tightened his hold on the reins just as a van raced around the buggy, going much too fast on the mountain road.

Becca gasped and reached for Zeke's arm as if fearing the passing vehicle's momentum would throw her from the buggy.

The logo on the side of the van read Montcliff Studio. The vehicle accelerated and continued on the road.

The mare balked.

"Easy there, girl. Easy."

Sophie shook her mane and swished her tail, letting Zeke know her upset.

"Was that the man who stopped by the farm yesterday?" Becca asked.

He rubbed her hand, hoping to calm her unease. "I did not see the driver's face. The man in the van who stopped by the farm yesterday is named Larry Landers. He works for the movie studio and wanted to shoot some scenes on Hattie's property."

"I overheard from the kitchen."

"Then you heard him claim the money would be good. He did not understand that some things cannot be bought."

Not love, not happiness, not a father's respect.

He thought of the man who was chasing Becca. What if he was her husband?

Zeke flicked the reins and wondered how things had gotten so convoluted. His status quo, as the *Englisch* would say, was in upheaval. Zeke could feel it in the core of his being. Nothing was in the right order. Not his life. Not his common sense. And not his heart. In fact, his heart more than anything was sending signals he did not understand.

He would not make a mistake about a woman again. Even a pretty woman whose need tugged at his heart.

Chapter Six

Rounding a bend in the road, Zeke's heart pounded a warning. He tugged on the reins, pulling Sophie to a stop.

"Get in the rear of the buggy, Becca."

She glanced at the cars and vans forming a roadblock. A number of men, all wearing jackets bearing the Montcliff Studio logo, had stopped a car heading to town.

"Should we turn around?" she asked.

"Perhaps." But just as Zeke was ready to nudge Sophie into the oncoming lane so they could head back to Hattie's house, a man at the roadblock motioned them forward.

"Pretend you are that young Amish boy."

Zeke knew from Becca's expression that she was worried. So was he.

As soon as she crawled into the rear, he flicked the reins ever so slightly.

"I do not see the man who chased me yesterday morning," Becca said, her voice little more than a whisper.

"That is *gut*. We will trust this is just a minor annoyance and not a problem."

"I hope you're right."

"*Yah*, I hope that, as well."

He pulled in a deep breath to calm himself. Zeke did not want to appear nervous, not when Becca's safety could be in jeopardy.

The car ahead of them had been waved through the roadblock. The vehicle accelerated and headed toward town. If only Zeke's buggy could also be waved through.

A burly man motioned him to a line in the road and then held up his hand, signaling he should halt.

Zeke tugged on the reins. Sophie stopped and shook her head. Perhaps the mare sensed his tension.

The road guard stepped closer. "Where you headed?"

"Is something wrong?" Zeke asked.

The man narrowed his gaze. "Just checking a few cars."

"And the reason for the check?"

The guy shook his head, visibly annoyed. "You Amish struggle with authority."

"I did not know Montcliff Studios controlled the public roadway."

"We've got a multimillion-dollar facility. We want to protect access to our property."

"Something has been stolen?"

The guy peered into the back of the buggy, stared for a long moment at Becca and then nodded to Zeke.

"Have a good day."

Returning the nod, Zeke encouraged the mare forward. Once the buggy had passed through the maze of cars, he encouraged Sophie to pick up the pace.

Becca climbed back into the front seat. "Why did you give him a hard time?"

"I did no such thing."

"You questioned what was going on. I thought he was going to search the buggy."

"And what would he have found?" Zeke asked.

"He would have found me." Her eyes widened as she jammed her thumb against her chest.

"Had I not questioned his right to be stopping vehicles and buggies, he might have been more aggressive."

"I think you're wrong."

"But we got through the roadblock, Becca. Everything went well."

She shifted away from him as if exasperated, or perhaps she was still frightened by the unexpected roadblock. Truth be known, Zeke had been nervous, as well.

Why were the people from the movie studio stopping those who traveled along the roadway? Was it because the movie star had gone missing? Or had someone else disappeared?

He glanced at Becca. Finding a woman in the middle of the road not far from where a missing movie star had worked and then to have people searching the area seemed more than a coincidence. Add the fact that one, if not two, men were running after Becca and the situation became even more convoluted.

Was Becca an Amish woman who had left her family or was she somehow involved with Montcliff Studio? If so, did she know anything about the movie star who had disappeared?

Becca remained silent as Ezekiel encouraged Sophie along the mountain road. She couldn't stop thinking about the roadblock and the two times she had been chased through the woods.

The cool afternoon air tugged at the felt hat she wore. Shivering, she yanked it down on her head, then wrapped the coat across her chest and held it tight at her neck.

Zeke glanced her way. "You are cold?"

"The breeze feels good and the air is fresh and clear."

"No one recognized you, Becca."

She breathed deeply, grateful for Zeke's support.

"Do you have any memory of the movie studio?" he asked.

She shook her head. "What would an Amish woman do there?"

"Perhaps you worked in the kitchen."

"Maybe. I could wash dishes and peel potatoes."

He smiled. "You do not give yourself enough credit. You could run the kitchen."

"I'm glad you have faith in me." She thought for a moment and then added, "Or maybe I live on an Amish farm in the area and have nothing to do with the studio."

"A movie star went missing, Becca, which is probably the reason for the roadblock."

She nodded, mulling over what he had said. Surely she had nothing to do with Montcliff Studio, yet something about the studio logo tugged at her memory.

"How did the studio end up here on Amish Mountain?" she asked.

He shrugged his broad shoulders. "Probably someone vacationed in the area. The *Englisch* rent rooms in town. The Amish community is starting to become a tourist attraction."

"But a movie studio in Georgia seems strange."

"The state gave the motion picture industry a cut on

their taxes. Anything to bring in jobs and grow business."

"Which is not what the Amish want."

"*Yah*, the Amish want their own land and to live without the interference of government. Some people find that difficult to accept."

He turned to face her. "Does this sound strange to you?"

"Why would it? It is the Amish way."

He smiled. Becca could not remember where she came from, but she thought like the Amish. If only she would learn more about her past.

"People gawk as they drive by the farm," Zeke continued to explain. "Perhaps they have never seen the Amish. I heard the studio needed mountainous terrain for a film. They shot a short documentary here first and then entered into a contract to rent the land."

"No doubt, from an *Englischer*," Becca added.

"An *Englischer* who had been Amish. Levi Gingerich left the Amish way and took his children with him, as well. He owns a sizable portion of land on the mountain, just as my father does."

"Yet your father doesn't live here."

"He lives closer to town and is now the bishop of the local district. He owns Hattie's farm and more acreage that is currently unsettled."

"Will your father pass the land on to you someday?"

Zeke shrugged. "I have a brother who would be his first choice."

"Older or younger?"

"Older, but he and his wife moved away from the area."

"Does the youngest son usually take care of the parents?" she asked.

"That sometimes happens, but my father does not want my help."

Something Becca doubted, but she remained silent and turned to study the scenery.

Dense forests of thick pine trees covered the land on each side of the road interspersed with barren hardwoods that had lost their leaves. Some still lay scattered on the ground, holding a portion of their fall colors.

The memory of running through the woods returned with a jolt. She wrapped her arms across her chest, recalling the footfalls of not only the man chasing her in the night but also the man who had come after her the next morning.

"Your memory will return," Zeke stated, as if he understood her struggle.

A farmhouse appeared in the distance. "This is the Troyer land, Becca. We will stop here before going to Willkommen."

She swallowed down the concern that filled her. "What if they recognize me?"

"They will see an Amish youth. Not an Amish woman. I will ask if they know of anyone missing in their family while you remain in the buggy."

Becca straightened her shoulders and peered into the distance.

"Slouch down," Zeke said.

"What?"

"Put your elbows on your knees and lean forward as a boy would do."

She followed his prompting, but kept her eyes focused on the farmhouse. Three young boys stood on the porch. Two older boys stepped from the barn as the buggy came to a stop.

Zeke hopped to the ground and turned as a man called to him from the nearby paddock.

"Is it Ezekiel Hochstetler?" the man asked jovially in greeting. *"Wie gehtes?"*

"Gut, Willie," Zeke responded. "And how is the family?"

"The children grow like weeds. Ida has coffee if you care for a cup."

"Not today but thank you."

"What brings you down the mountain?"

"I am going to town for supplies. We heard talk that a woman named Troyer had gone missing. Hattie wanted me to check to see if she could be your kin?"

Willie Troyer was medium height and stocky in build. He wiped a thick hand over his square jaw and peered into the distance for a long moment as if thinking if anyone had gone missing. "This I have not heard. Surely, we would know of anyone in the family. Was the woman in need?"

Zeke shrugged. "I know nothing more. News travels. Sometimes it changes as it goes."

"Like the game the children play," Willie said with a nod. "They whisper a statement from child to child that ends up different at the end. It is the same as we grow older. Only what starts as news, ends as gossip."

"I will tell Hattie that your family is well."

"Have you seen your father, Zeke?"

"He is busy."

"The years pass. Do not let them slip away before it is too late."

"He knows where to find me, Willie, yet I appreciate your concern."

Zeke turned back to the buggy.

"Who's the boy?" the farmer asked.

Becca's heart lurched. She glanced at the children as if she had not heard the question.

"A boy from the mountain. He helps Hattie at times."

"Did a man from the studio talk to you about renting land on which to film?"

"Larry Landers stopped by yesterday. Hattie rejected his offer."

Willie nodded. "Hattie made a wise decision. I told him my farm was not to be used for *Englischer* movies. He did not like my answer."

"He does not understand the Amish way."

"That is for certain. The bishop should talk to the studio manager so they understand us better."

"You tell the bishop what he needs to do, Willie. He will listen to you."

"He will listen to his son if you speak to him, Zeke."

Shaking his head, Zeke moved closer to the buggy. "Good to see you, Willie."

"Good to have you back on Amish Mountain, Ezekiel. A man is not held responsible for what he does in his youth before baptism, *yah*?"

"Perhaps you think that way. Some do not. Leaving the community was a grievous wrong as far as my *datt* was concerned."

"Time has passed. Things change."

"The seasons change, but my father's heart remains the same."

"Take care of yourself, Zeke."

"You, as well."

He climbed into the buggy and turned the mare back to the road. Becca remained silent as if she were truly that Amish boy, who lived on the mountain.

From what Ezekiel had said, the disagreement with his father was more than a family squabble. At least Zeke knew who he was and what had happened in his past.

Was Becca caught in the middle of a family squabble? She didn't belong to the Troyers who lived at the foot of Amish Mountain. Was there another family to whom she was related? Had someone from that Troyer family chased after her? Could that be the same man who had come after her today or were they two different people? She cringed thinking of terrible scenarios that could be part of her forgotten life.

After leaving the Troyer farm, Zeke guided the mare onto the main road, heading to Willkommen. The town would be bustling today and hopefully something or someone would trigger Becca's memory. He needed to be careful. Keeping Becca safe was his top priority.

"Evidently Troyer is not my last name," she said with a sigh.

"Troyer is a common Amish name. You are not part of that Troyer family, but there are others. The sheriff may know of a missing person report."

"I... I do not want to involve the authorities."

He glanced at her, seeing the concern that troubled her gaze. Was she wary of law enforcement because of her past? Or was she just being cautious?

"It is an option, Becca, and perhaps the fastest way to get information. I will be discreet."

"But you will not tell a lie."

"You know this about me?" he asked, surprised that she would make such a statement.

"You are a *gut* man, Ezekiel. I have seen how attentive you are to Hattie. I do not wish you to do anything against your will because of me."

"I would never lie, but all details do not need to be revealed, *yah*?"

She smiled and nodded. "You're right."

"You do not need to worry, Becca."

"I'm not worried."

"Ah, but now *you* stretch the truth. I see it in your eyes. You fear what you might learn today."

"Suppose I am married to a hateful man? Suppose he tried to hurt me? Suppose…suppose I have children."

"Would you leave children behind to save yourself?"

"Never."

"See, you have answered the question for yourself. You were running away from something, and yes, it could be from a husband. But you did not leave children behind. I am certain of this."

Becca's faint sigh of relief warmed his heart and made him see the folly of his own thoughts that she could be involved in something suspect. She was not the woman from his past. Irene had never been content on the mountain or with her own life. She always wanted more and was fascinated with the allure of the world. He had been young and fickle back then, not realizing the qualities he desired in a woman.

And Becca? his inner voice questioned.

Was she a desirable woman?

He flicked the reins, not yet ready to answer such a query. Not until he knew more about the real Becca Troyer.

Chapter Seven

Becca's heart pounded with apprehension as they drove into town. Shops lined the streets and people milled about on the sidewalks. Buggies were everywhere, along with Amish women in long dresses and white bonnets, ushering their children across the pedestrian walkways at various intersections. Bearded men wearing wide-brimmed hats guided their horses along the busy thoroughfares and turned into vacant lots at the rear of the businesses where the horses would be tethered while the families shopped.

"So many people are in town today," Becca said breathlessly, trying to take in all the activity around her.

"There is a cattle auction. Many of the farmers come to town and bring their families. They shop and then bid on cattle so the trip serves more than one purpose."

"The children are not in school?"

"Today there is no school because of the auction."

She glanced right and then left, all the while studying faces, the young, the old, men, women, Amish, *Englisch*.

"Drive more slowly, Zeke. I want to see everything."

There were so many people, and she feared missing the one person who would open up the past to her.

Zeke tugged back ever so lightly on the reins. The mare responded. "The cattle auction is on one of the side streets. We will drive there first." Zeke guided Sophie onto a more narrow road and then into the expansive complex that included an open-air pavilion and a large building with a sign over the door that read Cattle Auction.

Horses were tethered to hitching posts in front and rows of buggies lined the grassy knoll to the rear of the complex. A horse barn sat nearby.

Men chatted amicably in the central asphalt area. Young boys stood near their fathers and matched their own stances to the older men's. Women grouped together with the young children, and girls chatted nearby.

"Is there a flea market today?" Becca asked, reading the sign on the pavilion that mentioned the market.

"It is held once a month on the first Wednesday. We can come back then. I thought today might provide an opportunity to search for your family."

If only the search would be productive.

"See anything that looks familiar?" he asked.

She shook her head and tried to shrug off the discouragement that weighed her down as if a hundred-pound sack of potatoes rested on her shoulders.

"There is more to explore," Zeke assured her as he guided the mare toward the auction exit that returned them to the street.

Drivers in passing buggies waved, and Zeke nodded in response. Becca was careful to lower her eyes whenever anyone stared at her too intently. Thankfully most of the people were not interested in a young boy.

"The sheriff's office is on the next block," Zeke said.

"I do not want to stop there."

"We will pass by."

Her stomach churned. In the distance, she saw the sign for the sheriff's department. A number of men stood on the sidewalk, all with broad shoulders and thick necks. Could one of them have been the man chasing her? Was he there now, telling the sheriff about his missing wife or daughter or sister?

Glancing down a side road, Becca's chest tightened. She tapped Ezekiel's hand. "Look to your right. Is that the same van that passed us on the road earlier?"

Zeke peered at the vehicle. "Perhaps. Although the studio seems to have a number of vans. No telling who drove that particular vehicle to town."

Returning her gaze to the sheriff's office, she spied the tall, muscular man from yesterday, wearing a jacket that bore the Montcliff Studio logo.

She nudged Zeke.

"Yah," he said. "That is Larry Landers, who stopped by Hattie's farm."

"And the Troyer place."

Zeke nodded. "I do not think he will find any Amish farmers agreeing to give him access to their land."

Landers stared at Zeke and then flicked his gaze to Becca as the buggy passed the sheriff's office. Her mouth went dry, and a roar filled her ears. Something about his expression unsettled her.

She glanced away, trying to mimic a disinterested youth. Heat burned her cheeks, and she hoped her flushed face would not bring more scrutiny either to herself or to Ezekiel.

Grateful when Zeke turned at the next intersection, she glanced back. The man was still staring at the buggy.

Was there a connection between her and Larry Landers? Troubled as she was, Becca refused to share her concern with Zeke. If she did not understand her own feelings, he would not, as well.

Besides, she was probably overreacting. The man had startled her as he drove down the mountain, going much too fast. Surely that was the reason for her unrest. That and nothing else.

Then she thought of him watching Hattie's house with binoculars. The sweet Amish woman had told Becca to be careful, which meant she needed to keep her eyes on Landers. She didn't want to be taken by surprise and forced to flee for her life again.

Zeke guided the buggy through a number of side streets, hoping to trigger Becca's memory. "Do you see anything that brings back memories?"

She shook her head and sighed. "Nothing that I can recognize. What if this trip to town provides no clues to my past and turns out to be a waste of time?"

"Do not get discouraged, Becca. There is more to see. Besides, one clue could open up your past. We will not give up this soon."

At the next intersection, Zeke spied Larry Landers climbing from a studio van now parked farther down the street. He hurried into an office building. "Mr. Landers must have business in town."

"He seems to be everywhere, which worries me, Zeke."

"Do not let him concern you, Becca. He is probably still looking for that perfect location for the filming."

"We spoke of it earlier, but it does seem strange to have a movie studio in an Amish community," Becca said.

"What was once unheard of becomes the norm. It is the way of the *Englisch* world. We Amish keep our lives the same and trace our traditions back hundreds of years. There is something good about that consistency."

"It sounds as if you do not welcome change."

He thought of the new woman who had stumbled into his life.

Before he had a chance to answer, Becca added, "Sometimes things change without us wanting them to do so."

He understood her upset. "Your memory will return, Becca."

He leaned closer. "Glance down the street. Do you see anything familiar? Or do you recognize anyone?"

Slowly she studied the shops and the people who walked along the street and then turned back to Zeke. "I recognize no one except you."

She glanced again at the studio van parked by the curb. "But something about the logo on the van tugs at my memory."

"You saw Landers at Hattie's house. He is a man one does not forget, especially as he asserts what he thinks is his authority."

Zeke encouraged Sophie through an intersection. "Remember too that Landers has been stopping at farms in the area. Perhaps he stopped at the farm where you lived. You could have seen him there."

"If that is true, it means my home is not far from here." She scrunched down lower in the seat. "If so, someone might recognize me."

Seeing the concern on her face, he dropped his voice, hoping to reassure her once again. "You are dressed in men's clothing. No one will make the connection."

She nodded and started to say something, then stopped as they passed two men on the sidewalk. They both wore the Montcliff Studio logo on their jackets.

"Caleb mentioned the studio was filming in town," Zeke said. "Perhaps that is the reason so many movie people are here today."

Becca glanced at the men. "I don't recognize either of them."

"Does the logo on their jackets bring back memories?"

"Not like the van parked on the street. Perhaps it is the van and not the logo."

"Perhaps."

"Could we drive around the countryside before returning to Hattie's farm?" she asked. "If Larry Landers did stop at my home, then I must live close to Amish Mountain."

"This we can do after we have seen everything in town."

He turned onto another street and pulled up on the reins, bringing Sophie to a stop. The entire block was cordoned off by a wooden fence, more than fifteen feet tall, that prevented anyone from seeing into the enclosed area.

Signs tacked to the fencing read Montcliff Studio. Filming in Progress. A number of men dressed in navy blue uniforms patrolled the outside of the giant barricade. Montcliff Security was stamped on their jackets.

"Montcliff Studio likes privacy," Becca said. "They

put up fencing so no one can see what's going on at the filming."

Zeke nodded. "This is a first for Willkommen."

He spied one of the deputies that worked for the sheriff's department standing farther down the street. Zeke had known Mike Frazier in his youth.

"There is a hitching post behind the leather goods store," Zeke told Becca. "I will leave you there with the buggy while I talk to Deputy Frazier. He has only recently started working for the sheriff's department."

Becca grabbed his hand. "I told you I do not want to involve law enforcement."

"I will not reveal anything about you, Becca, but I need to let someone at the sheriff's office know about the roadblock. This is not something we want to face again. I also will ask about any missing person reports."

"And what if the deputy suspects I'm the person who's missing?"

"Trust me, Becca. Mike Frazier is a *gut* man."

The expression on her face told him she had a hard time trusting anyone. Truth be told, he could understand her concern about involving law enforcement. With no memory about her past and knowing she had been running away, Becca had to be careful.

Zeke guided the mare to the rear of the building where a number of other rigs were parked. He climbed down from the buggy and tied the reins to the post. "Stay here, Becca. I will be back shortly."

He hurried to the main street and waved a greeting. "*Gut* to see you, Mike. I heard you were working for the sheriff." Zeke smiled as he approached his friend.

"News travels even to Amish Mountain. What brings you to town, Zeke?"

"My aunt had some need of provisions, and I wanted to check out the cattle auction later today."

"I hear Hattie's farm is making a turnaround with your management."

Zeke shrugged off the compliment. "A woman of years living alone cannot do the work of a younger man. I am happy to help, and she provides a room and food that will make me fat if I do not curb my appetite."

Mike chuckled. "My father always said Hattie was the best cook in the area."

"How is your father?"

"Getting more and more infirmed. He's living at the assisted living center in town. With me working various shifts, there was no one at home to take care of him. His balance is not good and his mind is starting to wander. I worried about his safety in the hours that I was away from the house."

"It is hard to know what to do, *yah*?"

"I saw your dad last week when I took my father to the doctor."

Zeke's heart hitched. "My *datt* needed medical care?"

"Even the Amish get sick, Zeke."

"Yet my father has not been one to visit *Englisch* doctors."

"One gets older and wiser with years. He said it was a routine visit."

Even the mention of a routine visit did not ease Zeke's concern about his father's well-being. They had been estranged for two years, but the father-son bond would remain forever, even if his father was not interested in having a relationship with his wayward son.

"Montcliff Studio is a big attraction today," Zeke said, pointing to the giant fences.

"They're filming in town all this week, which means more traffic. Everyone wants to see a movie star. Thankfully, they've got their own security folks, but the sheriff's department is working overtime to make sure everything runs smoothly."

"Any problems?"

Mike shook his head. "Everything has been peaceful and that makes me happy."

Zeke thought of the woman who had disrupted his own peace. He had to be careful about what he said to the deputy. Zeke needed information, but he did not want to cause Becca harm.

"I stopped at Troyer's farm on my way to town today," Zeke said. "Hattie heard one of Willie's relatives was missing, but Willie Troyer said it was no one he knew. You have perhaps learned something about a missing person?"

Mike rubbed his chin. "No word on any Troyers. A man from Montcliff Studio stopped in and mentioned the star of the film they're working on left the area for a bit. He seemed concerned but didn't want to file a missing person report."

Zeke stepped closer. "Why would he tell you this?"

The deputy shrugged. "He acted as if he wanted information."

Which was what Zeke wanted, as well. "Did he tell you the name of the missing movie star?"

"Vanessa Harrington. He showed me her picture. She's a looker. Evidently married, but she's been separated from her husband for the last few months. The studio thinks she returned home, yet she's not answering her cell phone. The studio producer flew to California in hopes of bringing her back here to complete the film."

"Sounds like she thinks only of herself and not the other people working on the film. Has anyone else gone missing?"

The deputy looked quizzically at Zeke. "One missing movie star is enough."

Zeke smiled as if making light of his comment. "I wondered because of the roadblock the studio people put up on Amish Mountain."

"What are you talking about?"

"Men wearing Montcliff Studio jackets blocked the road with their vehicles. They stopped my buggy and glanced inside."

"Did they tell you why?"

"I thought it was because of that missing movie star."

The deputy let out a deep breath. "I'll pass the information on to the sheriff. Someone needs to inform the studio that the road is maintained by the county and patrolled by the sheriff's office. They have no right to set up any type of roadblock."

The deputy shook his head. "Thanks for letting me know, Zeke. By the way, Caleb Gingerich got a job at the studio."

"Have you seen him recently?" Zeke asked.

Mike smiled. "He showed me his new convertible. That guy lives above his paycheck, just like his dad. His sister had problems too, wanting what she didn't have and couldn't afford."

Zeke gut tightened.

Mike's eyes widened. "Look, I'm sorry, Zeke. I wasn't thinking. You and Irene were an item, as I recall. Didn't you follow her to Petersville? Terrible about the explosion and fire. Meth's a killer in more ways than one."

Zeke knew that all too well.

"If my memory serves me right, you had a run-in with the law," the deputy continued. "Didn't they suspect you were responsible for her death?"

"I was found innocent and released, Mike. That was a long time ago."

"A couple years, right?" He slapped Zeke's shoulder. "I'm really sorry I brought it up."

Zeke was sorry too, sorry he had talked to Mike and mentioned a missing woman. Becca had cautioned him not to get involved with law enforcement. He should have heeded her warning.

Chapter Eight

Becca had scooted to the front of the buggy where she watched Zeke as he talked to the deputy sheriff. No matter what he said about not revealing her identity to law enforcement, she was concerned that he might say something inadvertently.

Feeling somewhat conspicuous staring at them from the front seat, she had crawled down on the far side of the buggy and stood next to Sophie. Rubbing the mare's mane, she peered at the two men, feeling much less obvious.

She noticed the studio van parked farther down the street. Her stomach tightened as Larry Landers stepped out of one of the buildings. He hurried toward his van, then glanced at where she stood.

More than anything, she wanted to crawl into the back of the buggy and hide, but before she could do so, he started walking along the sidewalk, heading in her direction.

She looked over her shoulder and spied a narrow alleyway with a Dempsey dumpster that would provide the perfect cover if he drew near and passed by on the sidewalk.

When he stopped at the intersection, waiting for the light to change, Becca scurried into the alley and hunkered down behind the dumpster. From that hiding spot, she lost sight of Zeke. She didn't want him to return to the buggy and then wonder where she had gone. She especially didn't want Zeke to act upset about not finding her when Larry Landers was nearby.

Hearing the footfalls of an approaching pedestrian, she peered over the top of the dumpster, then ducked as Landers came into view. He stopped for a long moment before stepping into the alley.

Becca trembled, expecting to be found out.

A car horn sounded. Landers hurried back to the corner as if to see what had happened.

Wanting to evade discovery, Becca ran along the alleyway and turned onto the next street. She stepped toward a nearby store and stopped to catch her breath. Although worried Zeke would return to the buggy and discover she wasn't there, she was even more worried about Landers.

She watched the street for a few minutes. A studio van turned at a distant intersection, heading in the opposite direction from where she was standing. Evidently Landers had left the area. Relieved, she retraced her steps, needing to return to the buggy.

As she hurried around the corner, she stopped short and almost collided with the tall man from the movie studio.

"Why are you running away from me?" Landers lunged for her.

She ran back to the main street, past the store where

she had caught her breath and turned onto another side street.

Glancing over her shoulder, she saw him racing after her. Her head felt like it would explode, and her mouth went dry as his footsteps grew louder.

She slowed at an intersection snarled with traffic.

He caught up to her and grabbed her arm. She gasped, jerked free and ran into the street, directly in front of an oncoming vehicle. The driver braked to a stop, then laid on the horn and raised his fist.

Ignoring his show of anger, she dashed around the car and raced to the opposite curb.

A gust of wind tugged at her hat, lifting it from her head. She caught it in time, but not before her long hair spilled around her shoulders.

She looked back.

Surprise washed over Landers's angular face.

"Stop!" he called from the far corner, still stalled by the traffic.

The light changed, and he crossed the street. "Wait up!"

She turned down another alleyway. The path forked left. She took it, her feet pounding the pavement.

Her chest burned, and she gasped for air, but she pushed forward, needing to distance herself from the *Englischer.* If he caught her, he might haul her off to the very place from which she had tried to escape.

She pulled in another deep breath and counted the cadence of her feet slapping the pavement to keep her mind off the danger following much too closely.

The main road through town appeared in the distance. She glanced right, then left. Where could she hide?

Her hair hung free. She shoved it into her hat and yanked the wide brim down on her forehead.

A farm truck turned left at the corner, hauling a steer in a wire pen.

The auction. She raced around the corner, relieved to see the outdoor pavilion and a crowd of people who would provide the cover she needed.

After leaving the deputy, Zeke returned to where he had parked the buggy, expecting to find Becca hiding in the rear. When he peered inside, his gut tightened. The buggy was empty and Becca was gone.

His stomach tightened, and a warning rang in his ears.

Zeke clutched his fists, anger and fear bubbling up within him, anger at himself for not keeping better watch over Becca and fear for her safety.

He hurried to the corner and glanced in both directions, searching for some sign of an Amish lad. A number of women chatted amicably in the distance. Two young girls in black bonnets and long dresses stood near their mothers. He was looking for a slender Amish boy with expressive eyes and a fearful gaze.

Where was she? Why had Becca gone missing again?

Becca slipped through the throng of people milling around outside the cattle auction, hoping to elude Larry Landers. A number of Amish families stood together near the Flea Market Pavilion. The children, a mix of boys and girls, chatted nearby.

Sidling closer to the group, she stopped long enough to glance back. Landers stood at the entrance to the parking area, hands on his hips, and studied the crowd.

Not wanting to draw his attention, she stepped even closer to the Amish youth and hoped no one would ask who she was and why she was standing so near to them.

All the while, she kept her gaze on Landers. Tall as he was, the location manager was easy to spot. He walked around the periphery of the market and kept staring into the fray. Thankfully, he didn't pick her out of the crowd. After what seemed like an eternity, he shrugged and walked out of the market area. Becca watched as he headed back to the street and turned north, retracing his steps.

Relieved he was gone, she moved away from the other youths and breathed out a lungful of pent-up air. Although grateful for the Amish gathering, she needed to find Ezekiel. After all this time, he had probably finished his conversation with the deputy and had realized she was missing. As generous as he and Hattie had been, she didn't want to cause him more concern.

Needing to return to where he had parked the buggy, she started toward the exit and passed through a thick crowd of Amish folks heading toward the auction house. A few of the people offered a greeting, which warmed her heart. Instead of being recognized, the Amish community was embracing her. Becca smiled at the thought and let down her guard.

Someone grabbed her arm. "What are you doing here?"

Her heart stopped as she looked into the Amish man's eyes. He was tall and muscular, with a full beard and a clean-shaven upper lip. His shoulder-length hair was topped with a black felt hat. As authentically Amish as he appeared, something about his expression seemed artificial.

Peering more closely, she realized his face was covered with a heavy layer of pancake makeup. Dark pencil colored his brows and lined his eyes. The man wasn't Amish, he was acting the part.

"You're coming with me," he snarled.

She shoved him with her free hand. "Get away from me."

He tightened his grip on her arm.

A group of real Amish men stood nearby. "Help me," she called, trying to jerk free of his hold. "He's hurting me."

Oblivious to her plight, the men smiled and nodded among themselves.

Raising her foot, she kicked the guy's shin.

His eyes widened.

She kicked him again and again. "Help!"

He groaned. His grip eased ever so slightly.

She jerked free of his hold and ran into the crowd.

The actor followed after her, favoring his good leg.

She dashed toward the stable, hearing the man's footfalls behind her. The cloying scent of straw and horse surrounded her as she ducked into the dark interior. An Amish boy, probably thirteen or fourteen years old, was mucking one of the stalls.

He stopped and leaned on his rake. "Is something wrong?"

"A man's following me. I need to get away from him."

Glancing through the open doorway, she saw the actor drawing closer to the stable.

"How can I get to the main road?"

The kid pointed to an exit in the rear. "Turn right at the dirt road. It will take you there."

"Danki." She raced out of the stable.

Looking back, she saw the man trip and fall. The kid apologized for his rake getting in the way.

"An accident," the stable boy insisted, all the while the actor raised his voice and shook his fist at the boy.

His raucousness attracted a number of other Amish men who streamed into the stable, no doubt, to determine what was amiss. Becca would have chuckled if she hadn't been so unnerved by what had happened.

Everyone seemed to be after her. A man in a black car with a man bun, Larry Landers and now an actor dressed like an Amish man. Her heart sank as she followed the dirt path that headed toward the main road. If only she could jar her memory. What had she done to cause so many people to chase after her?

Chapter Nine

Ezekiel searched on foot throughout the downtown area, but he found no trace of Becca. His heart ached, fearing something terrible had happened.

Two years ago, he had lost Irene.

Now he had lost Becca.

Overcome with worry, he returned to his buggy and climbed into the seat he had shared with her earlier. He grabbed the reins and encouraged Sophie forward. As the mare trotted along the main road, Zeke studied the various businesses and shops and then peered down each of the side streets, hoping he could find her.

He started to turn the mare around so they could head back to where the studio was filming and search again.

Movement in an alleyway caught his eye. He eased back on the reins and stared at the spot, unable to determine what he had seen.

A swatch of chestnut hair? Or was it only his imagination?

He tethered Sophie to a hitching post and ran along the sidewalk.

Approaching the alley, he saw nothing and derided himself for his foolishness. Discouraged, he turned back to the buggy.

"Zeke?"

Glancing over his shoulder, he saw Becca peering at him from behind a doorway. Eyes wide, face drawn, she looked scared and frail and confused.

He ran to her and took her into his arms.

"Oh, Becca, I feared losing you." The words tumbled out, one after the other. "I searched but could not find you. Are you all right?"

"Larry Landers followed me to the cattle auction." She clutched his arms and stared into his eyes. "I disappeared into the crowd, and he finally gave up looking for me. I—I planned to find you when an actor dressed like an Amish man grabbed my arm. He wanted me to go with him."

"Did he hurt you?"

"No, because I ran away, just as I did before, but he was a hateful man who raised his voice and shouted at a young stable hand who helped me escape."

"Mike Frazier needs to know."

"The sheriff's deputy?" She shook her head. "Suppose I did something wrong, Zeke. Law enforcement might be looking for me, as well."

Zeke wanted to reassure Becca, but he knew her fears could be real. Much as he did not want to believe anything bad about her, people were searching for Becca. If only he knew why.

Becca shivered in Zeke's arms and wanted to stay wrapped in the warmth of his embrace. Instead he pointed her toward the buggy.

"We must hurry. It is not safe for you to be in town."

He was right, of course.

Stepping out of his arms, she sighed at the sudden letdown she felt.

"I… I'm so glad you found me, Zeke. I thought the main road led to the mountain, but I wasn't sure if you had already passed by here."

He put his hand on the small of her back and guided her forward. All the while, he glanced around them, no doubt to ensure they were not being followed.

Upon reaching the buggy, he helped her into the seat and climbed in next to her. With the flick of the reins, the mare started to trot, the buggy swaying in a steady side-to-side rhythm. Becca slid closer once they left town.

The air was cold, and he wrapped his arm around her as if realizing she needed his warmth and comfort after all that had happened.

Grateful that Zeke had rescued her once again, she eagerly shared how the man had chased after her.

"You are sure he was not the man who came after you in the woods?" Zeke asked.

She shrugged. "I am not sure. The man that night was shouting, and I couldn't make out what he said. Plus, I never saw his face."

Zeke turned to gaze into her eyes.

The concern she saw touched her to the core.

"The memory of running through the woods haunts me, Ezekiel, and comes in my dreams to wake me in the night."

"Yet the actor today knows you."

"Unless he mistook me for someone else. We need to

find out if the studio employs any Amish," she stated. "Maybe I did have a job there."

"Caleb Gingerich works in the studio's dining facility."

"The commissary?" she asked.

Zeke raised his brow.

"It's what the dining area is called," she explained.

"You know this how?"

She shook her head. "Perhaps because I did work there."

"The Gingerich house is on the way to Hattie's farm. We will stop there. Caleb may be at home."

"Can we trust him?"

Zeke thought for a moment and then smiled. "Caleb is more interested in his shiny new car than he is in anything else. Plus, I do not think he knows much about the movie business. He will not be a problem."

The word *problem* kept running through Becca's mind as they rode in silence up the mountain. She was a problem. A problem to Hattie and to Zeke, a problem without a past and no hope for the future until she knew more about who she was and what she had been running from two nights ago.

She glanced at Zeke, seeing the determination on his face. As much as she appreciated his help, she also worried about how he would feel once he learned the truth about her past. Suppose she was married or committed to marry someone else? Someone she did not know well enough or did not truly love.

Zeke was a good man. He had helped her so much. Could she be drawn to one man, all the while forgetting about another man from her past?

She tried to shake off the fear of the unknown that

was like a ball of fire in her stomach. Shrugging out of Zeke's hold, she scooted to the side of the buggy.

"Are you all right?" he asked.

"A bit woozy."

"You are sick?"

How could she tell him the sickness she was feeling was a sickness of heart, thinking of all that might eventually be revealed?

Tears burned her eyes. She didn't want to know the truth. She wanted to return to Hattie's farm and be surrounded by the older woman's warmth as she and Zeke got to know each other better. The future could be filled with wonderful expectation, if it weren't for the fact that she knew nothing about her former life.

She touched the knot on her head, wishing she would remember more about that night.

"You feel sick because of the bump on your head, Becca. It has not been that long. Rest on my shoulder."

But she didn't want to move closer to Zeke. She was already too close and too drawn to him.

She couldn't allow her heart free rein, like he was giving to the mare, when she had a whole history she needed to uncover.

She closed her eyes and rubbed her hand over her stomach, hoping to ease the unrest she felt.

Zeke was right in taking her to his friend's house. She couldn't live in this twilight world not knowing who she was and what had happened to her. She needed information, and the only way to learn about her past was to confront it head-on, no matter what she uncovered, and no matter who she had been or what had happened to her.

Chapter Ten

Zeke was growing more confused by the hour. Having Becca in his arms earlier had sent his emotions into a wild spiral so that he felt out of control and unsure of who he was or what was right about his life. Becca's expression proved she was equally confused.

Larry Landers and an actor had chased after her today. Two men running after Becca only doubled the problem. Add the man at Hattie's house and man who had chased her the first night and the number rose to four.

After Irene's death, he had promised himself to live a quiet life, working hard on Hattie's farm and staying away from anything that might pull him astray.

Yet here he was again, drawn to another woman, a woman who made his heart race and his chest constrict whenever she drew close. Like now.

Becca had snuggled next to him when they had first climbed into the buggy. Her nearness had made his heart warm. Then something had happened—was it something he had said?—and she had slipped away from him.

His father had warned him of fickle women who would steal his heart and leave him in the lurch, so tied up in knots that he would do anything to be with them. Case in point, Irene. He had been smitten by her charms, but he was young then and unknowing in the ways of love and the world.

He focused on the road ahead, needing to calm his upset and focus on finding information about Becca. He had to be firm and not let himself be drawn into another woman's drama, especially a woman who was clueless about her past. Or was Becca pretending to know nothing about the men who had chased after her?

He wanted to believe her, but he had been burned before. He would not play with fire again.

Going to the Gingerich farm was probably another mistake. He had made too many. Irene's father had accused him of causing his daughter's death. Losing a child was the greatest tragedy a person would ever have to endure, and if Levi Gingerich wanted to believe Zeke had caused Irene's death, he would allow the older man to wallow in the untruth. What good would it do to reveal that his daughter had died in a meth lab explosion, and that Zeke had carried her from the cabin and tried to save her life?

Zeke would not repeat the memory that was so painful and so tragic. Nor would her father accept what Zeke said. He was intent on blaming Zeke for his daughter's mistakes.

Levi Gingerich did not need to know the truth. And Zeke did not need to cause anyone more pain. Not Irene's father, not Caleb or his own father...and certainly not Becca.

When all this was over, Zeke would leave the area and find a new Amish community. Surely, someone would need an extra farmhand to help with the livestock and crops. He could trade his work for room and board. *Gott* would provide. At least, he hoped He would.

Zeke guided the mare onto a narrow dirt path that led from the main paved roadway.

"Hold on," he cautioned as they jostled back and forth.

Becca grabbed the side of the seat and then scooted away from the edge, as if fearing she would fall from the buggy.

"Levi needs to fill in the ruts," he told her. "The farm might be in as much disrepair as the access road."

Zeke's hunch was right. Rounding the next bend, he spied the Gingerich farm in the distant twilight. The house, a two-story, white sideboard with a front and back porch, listed as if pulled by the wind and gave evidence of needing refurbishment and repair. The fence posts had rotted and some appeared ready to topple over so that Zeke wondered how the livestock were contained, although when he searched the hillside, he saw only a few head of cattle. The fields looked barren and not because of a fall harvest. They appeared to have lain fallow for more than one planting season.

Uneasy about what he saw, Zeke turned the mare onto the path leading to the house and pulled to a stop near the back porch.

"Stay in the buggy," he told Becca under his breath.

Her eyes were wide as she took in the run-down farmhouse.

A few chickens pecked at the ground, searching for some morsel to eat, a bug or worm or piece of grain. Glancing at the barn, he spied the chicken coop with torn wire that would allow a hungry fox or coyote to take the chickens and their eggs.

Zeke had not seen Mr. Gingerich since the day he had returned to Amish Mountain. He had come here that afternoon to offer his condolences to Irene's grieving father. Only, he had been run off with a shotgun and Levi Gingerich's anger and the warning that he would shoot Zeke the next time he stepped foot on his land.

Hopefully, the old man had mellowed with time.

As Zeke hopped down from the buggy, the door of the house opened and the barrel of a rifle poked through the opening.

Mr. Gingerich stood in the threshold of the door. His eyes narrowed, and a sneer tugged at his thin lips.

"Get outta here, you varmint. Did you forget what I told you the last time I saw you?"

Zeke took a step forward. "No, sir. I remember, but I need to talk to your son."

"You killed my daughter. Now you plan to harm Caleb? Stay away from him so he doesn't wind up dead like Irene."

"Mr. Gingerich, I need to talk to Caleb about the movie studio where he works."

"You Amish don't want me to rent my land. You're trying to undermine my business agreement with the studio, just like your bishop dad."

Zeke's gut tightened. "You talked to my *datt*?"

The older man nodded. "He does not want the movie people in the area. None of the Amish are happy about the venture. They usually keep to themselves, but this time, the Amish are taking a stand."

He stepped onto the porch, the rifle still raised and aimed at Zeke. "Tell your father that I will not change the contract. The studio will stay whether he and his church district like it or not."

Zeke held up a hand. "That's not the reason I'm here."

The old man's eyes widened. "Then state your business before I decide to fill you with lead."

"It has to do with whether Montcliff Studio hires the Amish. Did Caleb mention seeing Amish employees at the studio?"

"Why would the Amish have anything to do with the movie industry?"

"That is what I am trying to determine, Mr. Gingerich."

"He's working tonight, but I doubt he'll talk to you. He knows the way I feel."

"Some things are not as they seem," Zeke insisted.

The man shook his head. "You're responsible for my daughter's death. I will never forgive you."

He glanced at the buggy and spied Becca, still dressed like an Amish lad. "Children are not safe in your presence. I thought I spread the word through the community that you are not to be trusted." He headed for the buggy.

"Come here, lad. You should not be with this man." Gingerich's beady eyes narrowed even more. "He might hurt you."

"Ezekiel Hochstetler is a *gut* man," Becca said from the buggy. "I am sorry about your daughter, but do not blame Zeke for something that was not his doing."

Levi narrowed his gaze. "Why would a young boy speak this way to an old man?"

"I mean you no disrespect, sir."

"We did not mean to upset you, Mr. Gingerich." Zeke climbed onto the buggy, grabbed the reins and encouraged Sophie forward. The old man was becoming deranged and even more militant, but he was right. Zeke should not have come to his farm, and he never should have brought Becca.

She gazed straight ahead, eyes wide, lips drawn. What was she thinking?

Probably that Zeke was as confused and misguided as Levi Gingerich.

Becca remained silent all the while Zeke encouraged Sophie along the bumpy access path and then onto the main roadway.

"Mr. Gingerich doesn't seem to like you," Becca finally said.

"An understatement for sure. He believes I was involved in his daughter's death."

"Why didn't you tell him the truth?"

"What would be the benefit? He does not want to hear anything bad about Irene, so I will not be the one to tell him."

"I'm a good listener if you feel like sharing?"

She waited, sensing his unease. When he failed to respond, she touched the sleeve of his jacket. "This woman was special to you, *yah*?"

He nodded. "I loved her." He hesitated a moment before adding, "At least, I thought I did."

The reins twined through his finger. "Have you ever been in love?"

Becca thought for a long moment, wishing she could answer Zeke's question. Had she loved someone once upon a time? Did she love someone now?

She shook her head and sighed. "I wish I knew."

He took her hand in his, causing her heart to lurch. She turned and looked into his eyes, seeing empathy and concern. Perhaps she had not answered Zeke's question correctly the way her neck tingled. Could the strange sensations have something to do with love?

"Forgive me?" he said.

She raised her brow. "Forgive you for what?"

"For asking a question about your past when you have no memory. I should have realized my query would cause you more upset."

"I wish I could tell you about my past, but it is a total blank, like a clean whiteboard that has no markings. I try to see beyond the present and I get only a void. Still—" She squeezed his hand. "Tell me about Irene and your relationship with her."

He turned his gaze back to the road.

"Irene was pretty," he started to explain. "She knew I was interested in being with her and smitten enough to agree to anything she suggested."

"She suggested leaving the mountain and moving to town?" Becca asked.

He nodded. "Irene wanted to experience life. At least, that is what she told me. I asked her to be my wife. Hattie made a wedding dress for her."

"The pretty blue dress Hattie gave me to wear. It was meant to be a bridal dress." Becca's heart sank, realizing the upset she must have caused Zeke when she wore the dress planned for his bride.

"That was long ago, Becca. The dress should be worn instead of hidden away in a blanket chest."

"Seeing me in the dress must have upset you."

He shook his head. "Irene is gone. There is no going back."

"Still—"

"Still, you are not listening. Irene found an *Englisch*

man who spent money on her. Drug money earned from the sale of the methamphetamine he cooked up."

"Oh, Zeke."

"The chemicals he used were highly flammable. There was an explosion and a fire. Irene was in the cabin at the time."

"I'm sorry." Becca's heart ached for the pain Zeke had to have experienced.

Mr. Gingerich's words came again to mind. *You're a murderer*, he had yelled.

She turned to look at Zeke. Hard as the question was to ask, she needed to know the truth. "If that's what happened, why did Mr. Gingerich say you murdered his daughter?"

"I had been with Irene minutes earlier. She was angry, and I could not reason with her so I left and had not gone far when the cabin exploded. I ran to save her. I…"

His voice was thick with emotion.

"I tried to resuscitate her. She started breathing but died in the ambulance as she was being rushed to the hospital."

"Yet her father claims you killed her?"

"The sheriff told him what happened, but he does not have ears to hear."

Becca wrapped her arms around her waist and leaned back, her gaze on the passing darkness.

Was Mr. Gingerich a cranky old man who failed to accept the truth or did he know something about his daughter's relationship with Zeke that was better left unsaid?

Becca hadn't told Zeke about the knife she saw in her dreams. Was he holding back something about Irene's death, as well?

Chapter Eleven

Zeke was heavyhearted as he encouraged Sophie up
the mountain to where Montcliff Studio was located.
Becca had been quiet and lost in her own world since
their brief discussion about Irene. Knowing she needed
time to sort through the information he had shared,
Zeke had remained silent, as well.

In the distance, he spied the two large soundstages
that rose like giants against the star-studded sky. Flood-
lights illuminated the area and brightened the various
buildings set in stark contrast to the dark night.

Becca sighed and finally spoke. "I don't have a good
feeling about this place."

"I understand your concern, but Levi Gingerich said
Caleb was working tonight. I want to talk to him."

"I told you the van with the Montcliff Studio logo
must mean something to me, Zeke. Suppose I worked
here as we talked about? If so, you're bringing me to
the very place where I might be recognized."

"The sun has set, Becca. The filming is taking place
in town. I doubt we will see anyone roaming about to-

night, but to ensure you are not recognized, hide in the rear of the buggy."

"What if someone grabs me, Zeke? Larry Landers chased after me today. Other men have, as well. You must realize my concern."

"Yet you need to find out why those men were chasing you, Becca. That is what we are trying to do. As I said before, everyone is in town. You will not be discovered. Trust me."

Her frustrated sigh as she climbed into the rear told him that was the issue. She did not trust him, although he could not blame her. She knew nothing about her past and knew little about him, so she was smart to be wary. Zeke needed to earn her trust. Hopefully with time, she would realize he wanted what was best for her.

"We will not stay long," he assured her.

"Long enough to be found out," she muttered under her breath.

A man stood at the entry gate and stepped into the road as Zeke guided the mare forward.

The guard held up his left hand. "This area is off-limits."

"I am here to talk to Caleb Gingerich. He works in food service."

"Come back tomorrow."

Zeke nodded. "This is something I might do depending on what he tells me this evening. Caleb Gingerich asked me to deliver fresh pastries and breads to the dining area. I need to know when the order is to arrive."

Zeke hesitated a moment and then raised a brow. "Unless you want to cancel the order of mouthwatering pies and cakes."

"Look, I'm just doing my job." The guard shrugged

and checked a clipboard he held in his right hand. "No one said anything about a delivery tonight."

"Not a delivery, but confirmation of an order." Zeke peered into the enclave, seeing a number of trailers and other temporary buildings. "Where can I find the dining hall?"

The guard pointed to the fork in the road. "Stay on this path. You'll pass the dorms that house the employees. Keep going straight until you come to a circle. The executive trailers and the office will be on the left. The commissary is directly to the right. The kitchen is on the far side in the rear of the building. You should find Gingerich there. If not, you'll have to come back tomorrow."

Zeke nodded his thanks and flicked the reins. Sophie's hooves clip-clopped on the pavement.

"He did not see you," Zeke whispered over his shoulder once the buggy turned at the fork.

Becca failed to respond, and he knew she was still worried about what might happen. "As I told you before, Becca. You will not be recognized."

"I don't share your optimism."

He glanced into the back of the buggy, seeing the faint outline of her oval face and the whites of her eyes opened wide with expectation.

"The studio looks abandoned. I do not see anyone wandering around the area. You can relax."

"I'll relax once we return to Hattie's house."

A circle of trailers appeared on the left. A sign in front of the building on the right read: Montcliff Studio Commissary. The front of the structure was dark. Rounding the corner, Zeke saw the well-lit kitchen. Caleb's red convertible was parked in a nearby lot.

Zeke pulled Sophie to a stop in a shadowed clearing

behind a hedge of bushes. "Stay in the buggy, Becca. I will not be long."

After hitching the mare to a nearby tree, he hurried forward and tried the door. Finding it locked, he knocked and peered through the window, then smiled with relief as he saw Caleb heading toward him, carrying a mop in hand.

Caleb unlatched the lock and opened the door, surprise written on his face. "What brings you here tonight?"

Zeke glanced at the bucket of sudsy water in the middle of the room.

"The floor needed to be cleaned," Caleb said without apology. "Come in. How about a cup of coffee?"

Zeke shook his head. "I wanted to check on the cook's order. Is he still interested in what Hattie can offer?"

"Definitely. He'll cut a check for her once he receives the baked goods. Tell Hattie to work quickly. He's eager to receive her items as soon as possible, otherwise, I fear he might hire someone else."

"My aunt cannot be hurried," Zeke said with a smile. "But I will encourage her."

"Knowing the hungry people are anticipating her homemade baked goods might spur her on," Caleb added with a chuckle. "Filming will be in town this week. They're working round the clock for the next couple days to get done early. I'll head there in the morning. Why don't I stop by Hattie's house on my way? If she has anything ready, I can take it with me."

"That sounds *gut*."

Zeke started for the door and then hesitated. "Do many Amish people work at the studio?"

"A few men have jobs in the carpentry department. They're the only Amish I've seen. Are you looking for employment?"

Zeke smiled and shook his head. "I just wondered, especially if Hattie delivers her baked goods here. Will she be the only Amish person at the studio?"

"No one will give her trouble, if that's what you're worried about."

"With the movie star gone missing—"

"I told you, Zeke, Vanessa Harrington is known to be temperamental. Although the sheriff is asking questions. Evidently someone notified them, expressing concern."

"Has anyone else gone missing?"

"Not that I know of, but then no one is as big of a star as Vanessa or as big of a problem. The leading man is well-known, but he's not a prima donna, if you know what I mean."

"Did anyone contact Vanessa's husband?"

"They talked to him, but he was clueless about her whereabouts. Law enforcement is waiting to hear from Mr. Walker, the producer, in case he had contact with her."

"And if not?" Zeke asked.

"Then the sheriff will open an investigation. They're calling this a missing person case, although from what I've heard, they're looking for evidence that might indicate foul play."

Zeke's chest tightened. "And if they find anything?"

"Some of the folks here think the missing person case could turn into a homicide."

"They think Vanessa Harrington was murdered?"

Gingerich shrugged. "People gossip about all sorts of things."

Just as Will Troyer had mentioned earlier today. Concern wrapped around Zeke's heart. He remembered Becca's bloody dress the night he had found her. He and Hattie had wanted to believe the blood was from the gash on Becca's head. Now he realized the blood could have been from another source.

Was Vanessa Harrington dead, and if so, could Becca be involved?

Becca huddled in the back of the buggy and stared into the night, aware of the sounds around her. From somewhere music played. A door opened and then slammed shut, and a man walked along the road, heading to one of the temporary buildings near the sound studios.

She climbed to the front of the buggy and peered out, hoping to get a better look at the man. He wore a baseball cap and had the collar of his jacket turned up, so she couldn't see his features.

Surely, he wasn't someone from her past.

After climbing down from the buggy, she sidled close to Sophie and patted the mare's mane. "Everything's okay, girl. Be quiet so no one sees us."

Becca peered around the corner of the commissary and stared at the row of trailers that sat in a circle around a central common area. One of the studio vans was parked in a distant lot. Again, she wondered about the logo. Did it hold a clue to her missing memory?

Turning her focus back to the commissary, she glanced through a large window into the kitchen, seeing Caleb and Zeke inside. As she watched, the two men shook hands, and Zeke opened the door to leave.

Grateful that she would not be alone much longer, Becca turned her focus back to the trailers, feeling a bit of déjà vu flood over her.

Even from this distance she could see a sign on one of the doors that read Vanessa Harrington. The missing movie star. A small light glowed from within the trailer as if someone had inadvertently left on a lamp.

Footsteps caused her to turn as Zeke rounded the corner and hurried to where she stood.

"A few Amish men work in the carpentry department," Zeke quickly explained as he reached for the reins. "Caleb has not noticed any other Amish employees."

Becca grabbed his arm. "See the trailer with the movie star's name on the door?"

Zeke stared in the direction she had indicated. "Vanessa Harrington?"

Becca nodded. "Caleb said she's not here now, so no one would be inside."

Zeke shot her a questioning glance. "I have a feeling you want me to be a Peeping Tom."

She shook her head. "Peeping Toms look at people. I want you to peer through the window and tell me what you see."

"I will see furniture, maybe a rug, table and chairs."

"The rug, Zeke. Tell me what the rug looks like."

He stared at her for a long moment. "Is there something you have remembered that you have not shared with me?"

She sighed. "I'm not sure if it has anything to do with

the movie star, but I've dreamed of a carpet with a geometric design. Do you know what a trellis pattern is?"

He pursed his lips. "Squares running on a diagonal?"

"I never thought of it that way, but yes. That's one way to describe it."

"So you want me to see if there is a trellis pattern on the rug? And you want to know this because you have dreamed about the pattern?"

"Twice."

"Why not go together?" He glanced around the central clearing. "Everything is quiet. Caleb said once again that the studio people are in town filming." He pointed to the wooded area adjacent to the star's trailer. "We can approach the trailer on the far side. The woods will provide cover."

"What about the buggy?"

"The hedge of bushes keeps it hidden from the main area. We will hurry."

He took her hand and they worked their way through the woods and approached the trailer located closest to the commissary. Zeke stepped toward the window and then motioned her forward.

Her neck tingled with apprehension when she glanced through the window and saw the area rug in the entrance foyer. Lime green trellis on a beige background. The pattern was identical to the rug in her dreams.

Except the rug in her dream was stained with blood.

A door opened on the far side of the clearing.

Her heart lurched when Larry Landers stepped outside.

Zeke grabbed her hand and they hurried back to the forested area.

"Hey!" Landers yelled. "What're you doing?"

Landers had chased her today. Becca couldn't let him find her tonight. She and Zeke ran deeper into the woods, needing to disappear. Just as before, branches grabbed at Becca's clothing and scratched her hands. Her foot snagged on a root. She tripped. Zeke caught her, and they stumbled on.

Her side ached. The last thing she needed was a cramp. She jammed her right hand under her ribs and pushed up, hoping to relieve the pain.

Zeke must have been aware of her struggle. He squeezed her left hand and guided her behind a large boulder. Collapsing against the rock, she struggled to catch her breath.

Holding his finger to his lips, Zeke motioned for her to be still.

She listened for Larry's footsteps, but heard nothing except her own ragged inhale and exhale of breath.

Had he given up the chase? Or had he stopped as well to study the terrain, searching for movement?

She envisioned him, ear cocked, listening for them to make a sound that would alert him to their whereabouts.

As the silence continued, she peered around Zeke and studied their surroundings. Through the trees, she could see lights from the studio enclave.

Zeke motioned that they needed to go deeper into the woods. Ever so slowly, they stepped away from the boulder and picked their way through the dense underbrush, stopping repeatedly to listen for the man's approach. At last satisfied that he was no longer behind them, they circled around the periphery of the studio and headed closer to the commissary.

Glancing through the heavy brush, they saw Landers standing in the clearing, hands on his hips, staring into the thicket where they hid.

The kitchen door opened and Caleb stepped outside. He called out to Landers, "Is something wrong?"

"Did anyone run past the commissary?"

Caleb shook his head. "I didn't see anyone. Why?"

"Someone took off running when I came outside. We've had a few things go missing recently. Probably a kid from town. This one wore a wide-brim hat like the Amish."

The door of a second trailer opened. Becca's heart stopped as another tall, muscular man stepped onto the stoop.

"What's going on?" he asked.

"Someone was snooping around." Once again, Landers stared at where Becca and Zeke hid.

She shivered. What if he saw them in the underbrush? She never should have come to Montcliff Studio. Something was happening here, and Becca was beginning to think she was involved.

Chapter Twelve

Zeke's mouth was dry and his palms wet. He kept his eyes focused on the two men talking among themselves. The sooner he and Becca left the area, the better, but the men kept pointing to the woods.

He had not prayed, really prayed, since he had pulled Irene from the fire. That night, he had called out to the Lord to save her. *Gott* had ignored his request.

Tonight was different. He feared for Becca's safety. Gazing up into the night sky, he removed his hat.

Protect her, Gott. Protect Becca or whatever her name might be.

His father would not approve of his silent prayer, but then, his *datt* did not condone any of Zeke's actions.

Although Hattie did not understand Zeke's reason for not attending Sunday services, she never condemned him, for which he was grateful.

His aunt was a *gut* woman, and she had provided refuge for Zeke when he had needed some place to hole up and heal his heart. Just as Becca had needed refuge the night he found her wandering along the mountain road.

Zeke feared the men would remain outside all night. At long last, they nodded their farewells and went inside.

Still concerned they might be seen, Zeke and Becca remained in place for another twenty minutes until the lights in the trailers went out and the men appeared to have settled in for the night. Zeke hurried to the buggy while Becca remained in their hiding spot.

Not wanting the clip-clop of Sophie's hooves to disrupt any of the studio people, he grabbed the reins and turned the mare toward a dirt path he hoped would weave through the forested area and eventually end up on the main road.

Sophie responded to Zeke's whispered commands and the tug on the reins. Staying off the pavement masked the sound of her hooves. The only noise was the occasional squeak of the buggy. Slowly, he guided the mare toward the dirt path. He glanced over his shoulder, searching the studio grounds, to make certain no one had seen him.

He stopped, stood still for a long moment and studied the entire area, his gaze moving from the dormer buildings to the tall sound studios, standing back-dropped against the night sky, to the Montcliff Studio van and the trailers sitting dark in the night. Light spilled from the commissary windows and allowed Ezekiel to find a narrow path into the underbrush.

His shoulders drooped as much as his heart as he urged Sophie forward. He was responsible for Becca's safety and his carelessness had placed her in danger. The pain that swelled within him made him want to scream in anger, which was not the Amish way. What would his *datt* say? No doubt, he would admonish Zeke for not being able to control his emotions. Perhaps his father had forgotten about love.

Zeke shook his head, unable to see his prim and proper father, pining for his mother—or any woman, for that matter.

Was Zeke pining now—pining and worried sick about whether he could get Becca out of danger?

As much as he did not want to admit his feelings, he was drawn to her.

"Zeke?" The brush parted, and Becca stepped onto the path.

Relieved to be reunited again, he opened his arms and pulled her into his embrace. She was warm and soft and fully alive. Everything that mattered most was with him at that moment and he never wanted to let her go.

Becca nestled into Zeke's arms feeling overcome with relief that the men from the studio had gone inside.

He glanced over his shoulder, all the while urging her forward.

"We must hurry," he told her. "Come, we will walk Sophie farther along the path, then we will climb into the buggy and head back to Hattie's house."

The trail wound through the woods, and Becca wondered if she had run along that same path two nights earlier.

The moon broke through the clouds, which helped them make their way. She studied the path as they walked, looking for any clues or signs that she had traveled this identical route.

Something caught her eye. She leaned down and pulled a swatch of fabric from one of the low-lying branches and held it up to the moonlight.

Zeke stepped closer. "What did you find?"

"A piece of material. I'm not sure in this light, but it looks blue."

"Your dress was torn," he whispered.

She nodded. "If this swatch of fabric matches my dress, then I ran along this path."

Glancing back toward the studio, her stomach roiled. "What happened on that studio lot that made me run for my life and made a man chase after me?"

Tears welled in her eyes. "Oh, Zeke, what if I've done something wrong. You saw the trellis-patterned carpet tonight. The rug I remember was covered with blood. What did I do? Did I cause someone harm?"

"Do not think such thoughts."

"Look." She pointed to where broken twigs and trampled underbrush curved left. "This is where I left the path. We need to follow that trail."

Zeke took her hand. "Not tonight. It is late. Hattie will be worried. She thought we were just going to town, but we have been gone so long. We can come back tomorrow."

"You wouldn't mind returning? If we follow the trail, we might find something that would provide a clue as to what happened."

She shivered.

"You are cold. Let me help you into the buggy. Wrap yourself in the blanket. The road is not far."

Becca appreciated his help as he guided her into the buggy. She slipped to the back seat and unfolded the blanket, a crocheted lap throw, and wrapped it around her shoulders. As much as she would have enjoyed the warmth of Zeke's arms, she needed to keep out of sight in case someone else was on the path tonight.

As Zeke urged the mare forward, Becca glanced back to the fork in the trail. She would come back tomorrow. She had to know more about where she had been that first night. The torn fabric from her dress confirmed her presence.

What else would she find on the trail?

A section of bloodstained carpet? A knife?

She shivered again.

Or a dead body?

Chapter Thirteen

⟿

Becca and Zeke were both relieved when they arrived back at Hattie's farm. Just as Zeke had suspected, his aunt had been worried about their safety.

"I knew you would be concerned," Zeke told her, "but one thing led to the next."

Zeke explained about stopping to see Mr. Gingerich and his less-than-hospitable welcome. "He still holds me responsible for Irene's death."

"His heart has hardened," Hattie said with a disapproving shake of her head. "He was never an overly friendly man, but he was not one to jump to the wrong conclusions. The pain of losing a child has made him bitter. I understand his grief, yet I cannot condone his accusations."

"He told us Caleb was working at the studio tonight," Zeke explained. "We were close and decided to stop by."

"How is the movie star?"

Zeke chuckled. "He was mopping the floor in the kitchen."

"Hard work is good for a man, *yah*? His father spoiled him along with his sister."

Zeke's face darkened. Becca glanced away, realizing he still had feelings for Irene. Why would he not? They had planned to marry.

She thought of the warmth of Zeke's arms around her on the path and in the buggy as they rode toward Levi Gingerich's house. Some thoughts needed to be buried. She could not think of Zeke as anything but a friend who provided her safe haven and support.

Then she looked at his expressive eyes and the curve of his lips. Some memories lasted forever.

"You look upset, Zeke, that I would say this," Hattie continued, unaware of the turmoil Becca was feeling. "Yet, you know yourself Irene was self-centered. She got what she wanted when she wanted it."

"Irene might have been self-absorbed, but she had a good heart."

The older woman tsked. "A good heart if everything was going her way. She was not to be trusted, as your father told you."

"My father told me a lot of things I did not accept."

"The young have a mind of their own, it is true. Now, come, we have talked too much about the past. You are hungry, *yah*?"

Becca smiled. "I know I'm hungry."

"Wash your hands. The stew is ready. Pour coffee, Becca, while I pull bowls from the cupboard. There's fresh baked bread, as well."

Becca did as Hattie asked and after washing her hands, she filled three cups with coffee and set them on the table. Hurrying to the pantry, she smiled, seeing the loaves of bread along with the freshly baked cakes and pies.

"You've been busy, Hattie."

"Busy hands keep the mind from too much worry. At least this is what I told myself. I wanted to get some baked items ready for the studio."

"Caleb said he will pick up anything you have ready in the morning." Zeke reached for a cup of coffee.

Becca glanced down at the trousers and shirt she wore. "Tomorrow I'll dress as a woman."

"I have a pale green dress that needs only to be hemmed," Hattie said. "You can wear that tomorrow. A different-colored dress might be enough of a change in case you see anyone throughout the day. If you go someplace in the buggy with Ezekiel, they will think you are courting perhaps."

Courting? Becca glanced at Zeke and felt her cheeks burn. He too looked ill at ease and glanced down at his feet, then turned to pour more coffee into his cup.

Hattie's comment must have caused him distress. If his heart was still with Irene, he would want nothing to do with Becca.

And what about her life? Had she been courted? Did she have a husband? Was that who had chased her through the woods?

Tomorrow, when they searched the wooded area, they might find some new clue to her past. Going in daylight, even though it was dangerous, might provide the clues she needed to unlock her memory.

"Caleb said the crew will be filming in town tomorrow," Zeke told Hattie. "That is why he is stopping here to pick up the eggs and baked items."

After they ate and the dishes were washed and returned to the cupboard, she opened a chest in the corner of the living area and pulled out a lovely green dress. "Come here, Becca, I need to see about the hem."

"I'll hold it up. You place a straight pin, Hattie, where the hem should be. I'll do the sewing."

"Are you sure?" the Amish woman asked.

"Of course. I've been sewing for years."

Zeke stared at her.

She turned to look at him. "I remembered something."

He nodded. "You remembered sewing."

She smiled, and a surge of relief swept over her. "Maybe going to town and to the studio was good for me. Something must have triggered my memory."

"Time has passed," Hattie said with a nod. "The trauma to your head is healing. This is *gut*."

Becca took the dress and the needle and thread Hattie handed her. She settled into a chair near one of the oil lamps and turned up the hem, and then started to stitch it in place.

She glanced at Zeke and expectation stabbed her heart. If only this was how her life could be, sewing by the light of the oil lamp with Zeke nearby.

Zeke watched her sew, leaning into the ring of light around the side table, and thought of how his mother used to sew or read by the light of the oil lamp.

Everything about Becca that he had seen so far indicated she was Amish. Which meant the feelings he had for her weren't inappropriate.

He let out a breath and settled into a chair near the wood-burning stove, enjoying its warmth and the inner glow he felt from sitting close to Becca.

He glanced at Hattie's Bible on the bookshelf. She read from it nightly and had worn the pages thin. Reaching out, he touched the leather cover, thinking back to when his mother was alive and the family would gather together in the evening to play checkers. *Mamm* would pop corn and the house would be filled with laughter. Before bed, his *datt* would read from Scripture, the verses chosen with care to provide a fitting end to a day of hard work and family togetherness.

The long-forgotten memory brought warmth to his heart. Looking into the future, he thought of evenings shared in similar ways with Becca.

"You are thinking of Irene."

Becca's voice was almost a whisper.

He glanced at her and raised his brow. "Why do you say that?"

"The smile that tugged at your lips. Much was said about her today. Your mind is returning to what you both shared. It is a good thing, Ezekiel."

He did not understand nor appreciate Becca's comments. His thoughts had not been on Irene. The way her life had ended was tragic and not one that brought smiles. Two years and he was still weighed down with the guilt.

Frustrated by the past and not knowing what the future would hold, he rose from the chair. "You do not understand, Becca."

Her eyes widened and pain flashed from her gaze. "Did I say something wrong?"

Without explanation, he climbed the stairs and headed to his room. The unlit oil lamp stood on his dresser, but he remained in darkness and stared outside into the night. The problem was Zeke and the mixed-up emotions he felt when he was around Becca.

He needed to know more about her before he allowed

this newcomer into his life. Would he ever learn who she was and where she had come from?

Becca's heart was heavy when she climbed the stairs that night. She hung the hemmed green dress on a wall peg near the blue dress Hattie had washed and returned to Becca's room earlier in the day.

Sifting through the folds of blue material in the skirt, Becca found the large tear. Pulling out the swatch of fabric she had found on the path tonight, she held it up against the torn portion of the dress.

The fabric matched perfectly.

Becca's heart was heavy. The path she had taken that fateful night had been from the studio, along the trail and then into the deep brush they would explore tomorrow.

Zeke had acted strangely tonight, which troubled her and sapped her enthusiasm for uncovering any more clues to her past. What if her memory returned and brought with it the terrible reality of what had happened that night?

Becca wasn't ready to find out the truth about her past. Not now. Maybe tomorrow she would be stronger and able to handle whatever she would learn.

Tonight, she needed to sleep without dreaming about a Montcliff Studio logo and a stained carpet and bloody knife. Tonight she wanted to dream about Ezekiel holding her in his arms.

Chapter Fourteen

Becca rose early the next morning, eager for the day to advance. The small revelation that she enjoyed sewing made her optimistic. Hattie had said the blow to her head was getting better and more of her memory would soon return.

Excited about her progress, Becca slipped on the green dress, enjoying the feel of the crisp cotton. The color was a favorite.

After pulling her hair into a bun and settling her *kapp* in place with hairpins, she raced downstairs, almost tripping over her feet.

"Hattie," she called. "I'm remembering more things."

"Wunderbar." Hattie greeted her with open arms. The women hugged.

"I told you not to worry," the older woman assured Becca.

She glanced out the window and saw Zeke in the barnyard.

"Fetch the butter and milk," Hattie requested. "We will eat soon. Zeke said he wants to box up the baked goods early to be ready for Caleb's arrival."

"I'll hurry."

Becca ran outside and waved to Zeke. He finished adding water to the trough for the horses and then approached Becca.

"The dress suits you." He smiled, and his eyes twinkled.

"Guess what?" she said, finding it hard to hold back her excitement.

He shook his head. "What?"

"My memory is returning."

The smile left his face and worry flicked across his gaze. Evidently he didn't share her exuberance.

"What have you remembered?" he asked.

"You don't look happy for me."

"I am glad you have remembered some things, but I want to hear what you have learned."

She pointed at the dress. "Green is a favorite color."

He nodded. "And you've learned something else?"

"That I enjoy sewing."

"You said that last night. Is there something new?"

Her enthusiasm plummeted. "That's all, but it's exciting, Zeke."

He nodded. "*Yah*, of course, it is something *gut* to know about yourself. But I thought you had remembered more important things."

"I will," she said with a forced smile. "Everything will come back to me."

She grabbed the milk and butter from the bucket filled with cool water and hurried toward the house. She wouldn't let Zeke's indifference temper her optimism. They might be only two small memories, but they were a start. More would come.

At least she hoped they would.

Before she went inside, she heard the rumble of motor vehicles. The sound interrupted the peaceful stillness of the farm. Swallowing down the fear that grabbed her throat, Becca hurried into the kitchen. She stepped to the window and peered outside. A convoy of vehicles, all with the Montcliff Studio logo, drove past the farm and down the mountain.

She shivered. If her mind would stop playing tricks on her, she might uncover the reason for her upset.

After breakfast, Zeke boxed Hattie's baked goods and stacked them on the table. Becca washed the morning dishes and tidied the kitchen, then helped box the eggs so they wouldn't break on the drive to town.

"I want to meet Caleb," Becca told Zeke once all the eggs had been packed in the protective containers.

"Are you sure that is wise?" he asked.

"If Caleb recognizes me, then I will learn more about who I am. I need information, and Caleb might provide what I need."

"He has a good heart," Hattie said. "I do not think Caleb would do you harm."

"Then it's settled." Becca looked around the kitchen. "Do we have everything?"

"*Yah*, by packing the baked items in boxes, all of them should fit in Caleb's sports car." Zeke turned and smiled at his aunt. "The movie people will enjoy your baking, Hattie."

"This is my hope," Hattie said with a nod of her head. "If this first order pleases, I will make whatever more the cook needs."

"I can help you." Becca stepped closer.

"And I am glad for your help. After the *gut* job you

did hemming the green dress, I will pull out fabric. We can start quilting."

Quilting?

The word brought to mind a small lap covering pieced with various shades of green fabric. Instinctively, Becca knew it was her quilt, one she had made when she first learned how to sew. The realization brought another insight into her past.

"My grandmother taught me how to quilt," she shared. "I remember a small quilt that was my first attempt. It was made of pieced green fabric."

"Oh, Becca, you have remembered something new." Hattie patted her hand and smiled with satisfaction. "Your mind is working again."

"If only it would work harder." Grateful though Becca was to learn about the quilt, she wanted the cloud to lift from her memory completely so she knew everything about her life.

Hattie's eyes twinkled as she turned to Zeke. "Soon we will learn that Becca lives on a farm not far from the mountain. She has an Amish mother and father and brothers and sisters who love her."

Becca wanted to share Hattie's optimism, but four men had chased after her. There was more to her past than a loving family. Someone wanted to do her harm. If only she knew why.

Caleb pulled into the drive and stepped from his sports car as Zeke and Hattie hurried outside to greet him. Zeke stretched out his hand, and the two men shook.

"Do you have time for a cup of coffee?" Hattie asked.

"Not today. But thanks. I need to get to town."

"Everything is boxed and ready for you."

Zeke ushered Caleb into the kitchen and introduced Becca. "She is visiting Hattie and offered to help."

Caleb nodded a greeting, but did not seem to recognize Becca. Zeke noticed relief in her gaze.

"The cook will love getting all the baked items," Caleb said. "And the movie crew will enjoy them, as well."

Working together, they grabbed boxes and loaded the items in Caleb's car.

Once again, the sound of a vehicle driving at a high rate of speed caused them to glance at the road.

Not a car but a black limousine.

"That's the producer," Caleb said as the limo raced past the farm and down the mountain.

"The man who left to find the movie star?" Zeke asked.

"That's right." Caleb nodded. "He couldn't find her. Vanessa's husband is claiming something has happened to his wife."

"But they had been separated," Zeke said.

"That's what she told everyone here. I'm not sure the husband thought the separation was permanent. From what people have said, Vanessa Harrington was fickle and flighty. No telling where she is now."

Zeke glanced at Becca. Her face was drawn. Was she thinking of the bloodstained carpet?

She stepped toward Caleb. "From what Zeke has told me, the movie studio only has a few Amish men working in the carpentry department. What about housekeeping? Are Amish women employed in that capacity?"

"That's contracted through a cleaning service," Caleb said. "Are you looking for a job?"

"If I stay in the area. I can cook and clean."

"Housekeeping might have an opening. I'll find out who you can contact and let you know."

"Perhaps someone has not showed up for work recently," she said. "I could fill in. Will you let me know if a position becomes available or if there is need for a part-time replacement?"

"I'll be happy to ask in town today. If I find out anything, I'll stop by here on my way back to the studio tonight."

Zeke walked Caleb out to his car and watched as he turned onto the main road. Had Becca remembered something more last night than her ability to sew? Had she remembered cleaning the studio? If so, that could be the reason she was concerned about the trellis carpet. Knowing about the bloodstains on the carpet could be the reason she had been chased through the woods.

After Zeke had tended the animals and completed a number of the other chores he had neglected since Becca had come into his life, he hurried into the house for lunch. The kitchen smelled of apple pie and fresh baked bread.

"More food for the movie studio?" he asked.

Hattie smiled. "And some for my favorite nephew. Wash for lunch. Today we will have cold cuts and cheese with the warm bread."

"Das smeckt mir gut," he said with a laugh.

"You are easy to please. By the way, Becca helped me with the baking. She is a gem."

Zeke poured a cup of coffee and turned at the sound of her coming down the stairs. Her cheeks were rosy, and her eyes bright. His chest tightened, and he almost spilled the coffee as he focused his attention on her.

"You have worked hard this morning," she said, flitting across the kitchen. "I am sure you're hungry, Ezekiel."

He liked the way she said his name. In fact, he liked everything about Becca.

"You wanted to explore the trail we were on last night," he said. "The day is cold but clear. I checked the almanac and snow is forecast over the next few days."

"For this, I am not ready," Hattie said as she sliced bread and placed it on the table.

"I have chopped enough wood for the stove and there is food to carry us through the winter." Zeke glanced through the window to the woodshed. "Snow will not be a problem."

Hattie laughed. "Perhaps not for us but the *Englischers* at the movie studio might have trouble navigating the icy mountain roads, especially if they do not slow down."

Becca filled a glass with water and placed it where she was sitting, then slipped into the seat as Hattie and Zeke did the same. "Exploring the trail would please me, Zeke. Again, I am grateful for your help."

His face warmed, but not from the coffee. He bowed his head to give thanks for the food they were about to eat, but also for the lovely woman sitting across from him.

Keep her safe, Gott, he silently added before he glanced up and caught her staring at him. For the longest moment, she held his gaze. Then Hattie started talking about a quilting the following day at the widow Shrock's home.

She patted Becca's hand. "I want you to go with me, dear."

"Would that be wise, Hattie?"

"Sometimes information can be learned as the ladies sew. Besides, I do not think the ladies in my quilting circle are the people who searched for you. We are a senior group, mostly widows. But we will decide tomorrow. A lot can change in a day."

Zeke knew how quickly things could change. As much as he wanted Becca to stay on the farm where she would be safe, he knew the importance of finding out about her past. In some ways, she seemed impatient, which concerned him.

Rushing too quickly into a situation could be dangerous. A lesson Zeke had learned. When he had found Irene, he had insisted she return home with him. In hindsight, he should have given her more time. Patience had never been his strength.

"Did you say something?" Becca asked once lunch was over and they were in the buggy heading up the mountain.

He had been silent since they had left the farm. "I regret what happened last night at the studio, Becca. It was not wise of us to go there."

"No harm was done."

"Still, I am concerned about your safety," he said truthfully.

"We will not go to the studio today, Zeke. You do not need to worry."

"But we must be careful and stay together. If I say we leave, you must climb into the buggy. Do you understand?"

"*Yah*, I understand." She glanced at the clear sky.

"We saw the buzzards flying overhead that first day. What was the reason for them?"

He shrugged. "A dying animal perhaps. Buzzards clean debris. It could have been anything."

"My dress had blood on it the night I arrived."

"You had a large lump on your head that was bleeding."

"Is it my own blood that I dream about?" She shook her head. "I don't think so."

"What else do you dream about?"

He stared at her for a long moment. "You will not tell me?" he asked.

"I dream of running in the woods."

"There is something else."

"Blood on a carpet, as I mentioned last night."

The hesitancy in her voice told him there was something more. Something she had not revealed. Something that frightened her or even worse, something she was not willing to admit.

The turnoff to the back path appeared on the left. "We must not take any unnecessary risks."

"I'll do whatever you say, Zeke, if that's what you need to hear."

What did he need to hear?

He needed to hear that Becca was an Amish woman who had been chased, but not because of anything she had done.

What if she had committed a crime?

He would have to walk away from her. Would he be strong enough? He looked at her pretty face. The way he felt, walking away from Becca would be impossible.

Chapter Fifteen

Turning onto the path unsettled Becca. She had been fine earlier. Now she was nervous and on edge. A sense of claustrophobia washed over her as the branches of the trees closed in around the buggy. She leaned back, wanting to climb into the rear and hide.

Instead she clenched her jaw, determined to face whatever they would find.

"The spot where we discovered the blue cloth is just ahead," Zeke said. "From there on, we will leave the buggy and travel by foot. I will hold back the branches so you do not tear your dress."

"Hattie was so good to give me this dress. She made it for Irene, didn't she?"

He shrugged. "My aunt wanted to make certain Irene had Amish clothing to wear once she came back to the mountain."

"Like the blue wedding dress?"

"That was a long time ago."

"Two years is not long enough to get over losing someone you loved, Zeke."

He pulled the mare to a stop and turned to look at

her. His gaze was heavy with emotion, probably sorrow for his love lost.

Becca wondered about her own past. Had she loved and lost, as well?

"I fell in love with being in love, Becca. I was young and foolish. Irene made herself out to be someone she was not. She told me we would live Amish after she had a little time to experience the outside world. I should have known the plain life would never make her happy."

"Did you think about leaving the Amish way, as well?"

"My mind was filled with all sorts of thoughts. Irene was not a lost love. She was a fickle confusion that happens to young men at times, especially young men who do not think with the wisdom of years."

"Stopping by her home yesterday must have brought back memories that made it seem so real again."

"*Yah*, it was real, but twisted and manipulative on her part, and a mistake on mine." He pointed to the broken twigs and the place where they had found the swatch of fabric. "The day passes. We must explore this area and then get back to the safety of the farm."

He climbed from the buggy and helped her down. She pulled the bottom of her skirt up just a bit and held the extra material around her knees so it would not snag on the branches.

True to his word, Zeke pushed aside anything that could scrape her skin or pull at her dress.

He went first, forging the way. The forest was eerily still as they trampled through the underbrush.

"I see a path of broken twigs, Becca. You were running through such dense bramble. No wonder you were scraped and scratched."

The memory of that night returned full force. Her heart pounded as if it had just happened today. She grabbed Zeke's hand.

He turned, concern evident in his gaze. "Are you all right?"

"Maybe we should go back to the buggy."

"We are close to the ravine. There is not much farther to walk."

"Ravine?"

"Did you not know? There is a waterfall and a steep drop-off."

"I heard water before I fell. Sometime later, I wandered along the road, but that's all I remember until I woke at Hattie's house."

"You might have fallen over the eastern edge of the ravine that winds down to the roadway below. That's where I found you. Had you gone farther up the mountain and more to the west, you would have come to the waterfall. There is a road that winds to the top, but also a path not far from here. The drop-off is dangerously steep. An *Englisch* boy fell from there some years ago. His body was never found."

She shivered, thinking of the dark night and not knowing which direction to turn.

"Perhaps the man who chased me was trying to warn me," she mused.

"Why do you say that?"

"I believe he told me to stop, Zeke. If he knew of the steep drop-off, he could have been trying to protect me instead of doing me harm."

"It is a possibility, yet something caused you to run in the first place."

He was right. She had run to get away from something or someone, no matter why the man had chased after her.

Zeke squeezed her hand and ushered her forward. She sensed his support and concern. Her fear, while still in the back of her mind, became more manageable.

Although thankful to have returned in daylight, she shivered again, thinking of her plight during the dark night.

"Here, Becca." Zeke pointed to a twisted branch. "Another piece of fabric, low to the ground. You came this way."

She reached down to retrieve the small piece of blue cloth and heard the distant sound of falling water.

Her mouth went dry, and she clutched Zeke's hand all the more tightly.

He shoved aside a large branch and pointed. "We are near the edge. Be careful."

She stepped into the partial clearing and peered down, seeing the sloping mountain and the large ravine down which she must have fallen.

"Stay back while I check the edge," Zeke said.

Releasing his hand, she struggled to control the fear that threatened to overtake her again. In her mind, she heard the man chasing after her and felt herself running toward the edge of the drop-off and then tumbling down.

Zeke approached the edge. Glancing down, he narrowed his gaze.

"What do you see?" she asked.

"What appears to be a roll of carpet that has lodged against one of the boulders far below."

Her gut tightened. "What color carpet?"

"It is hard to say. The backing is beige."

Could it be the carpet she saw in her dreams? If so, why was it on the side of the mountain where she had fallen? Had she seen the carpet that night? Was that the reason it kept playing over and over in her mind?

Instead of answering questions about who she was, the search through the woods was making her more confused.

She turned, holding her dress, ready to run back the way they had come.

"Becca," Zeke called after her.

Just like the night in the woods. She was running from someone again. This time she was running away from Zeke.

Zeke raced after Becca and grabbed her arm. "Everything is okay. You do not need to run from me."

She pulled in a deep breath, her eyes wide as she gazed up at him and then looked back to the edge of the ravine. "I'm scared."

"It is only rolled carpet. I have rope in the buggy. Stay here and I will be back in a few minutes."

"What do you plan to do?"

"I will go down the side of the hill to look at the carpet."

"It's too dangerous. You could slip and fall."

"I rappelled down the mountain often as a boy and called it sport. Besides you tumbled down that same hill as far as we know."

"I survived, but now I have no memory. This is not what you want."

She peered at the ledge again. "I walked out of this area somehow because you found me on the roadway.

Let's go back to the road and see if we can find a path that leads to the lower outcrop."

"I could lower myself without problem, Becca."

"And how would you get up here again? I could not pull you up, and I cannot drive the buggy. You would have to hike to the road and then climb up the way we came."

Realizing she was right, he guided her back to the overhang, and together, they studied the terrain below. "What you said is true, Becca. It looks like a deer trail leads toward the road. We might be able to come to that area without much searching."

They retraced their steps. The path Zeke had cleared earlier provided an easier way out, but they both sighed with relief when they arrived at the buggy.

The ride to the main road did not take long, and they soon found a turnoff and small clearing.

"I will cut a path for you, Becca. Unless you want to stay with Sophie."

She rolled her eyes. "You know I want to go with you."

He smiled. "I thought that is what you would say."

After tethering Sophie to one of the trees and satisfied that the buggy would not be seen by anyone passing on the road, they began their ascent up the mountain.

"There," he said, pointing ahead. "Do you see the trail through the forest?"

"A deer trail?" she asked.

"Probably. It is what I saw from above. The walk will be easier now. We will not have to worry about the bramble and branches."

Sounds of a car on the roadway caused them to turn.

Through the break in the trees, they saw the limousine racing up the mountain.

"It looks like the producer is returning to the studio."

"His chauffeur is driving too fast," Becca warned.

Zeke turned back to the path. "We must hurry. Some of the other movie personnel might follow the producer to the studio."

The deer path eased their climb and before long they approached the area Zeke had spied from above.

"Where's the carpet?" Becca asked, glancing around them. "It's not here."

"We cannot see it from this angle, yet we spied it from above. It must be close by." He headed toward a cluster of rocks. "Perhaps it is hidden behind some of those boulders."

She pulled at his arm and glanced up. "I can see the waterfall."

"It is positioned a little to the west, but you can hear the falling water. Someone stumbling along at night could easily have gone the wrong direction and headed toward the falls."

"You mean *Gott* was with me, directing my steps so I went to the best part of the mountain from which to topple?"

He nodded and smiled. "That is exactly what I am saying. It was *Gott*'s will that you survived that fall for which I am glad."

She squeezed his hand. "I am, as well."

"Now let us look for the roll of carpet."

They searched behind the nearby boulders and found nothing. Zeke was disheartened and looked up again at the rim of the ravine where they had stood just a short time ago. The carpet could not have disappeared.

"Zeke, what's that?" Becca pointed toward a stand of trees where the path continued to weave through the undergrowth.

"It looks like a continuation of the deer trail." He smiled and pulled her along after him. "You have discovered the problem. This first clearing is not the one where the carpet was laying. We must travel farther along the path."

They hurried through the dense trees until Becca gasped for breath. "You're going too fast. I need to rest."

He slowed down. "Sorry. I was not thinking."

"You were thinking of finding what we came to see." She pulled in a series of deep breaths. "Okay, I'm ready. But let's go a bit more slowly."

He kept her in mind as he led the way through the forest and was relieved when they exited into the daylight. He looked up, realizing this was directly below the place where they had stood.

"The carpet should be behind those boulders."

Hurrying forward, he nodded as he spied the rolled rug.

Bending down, he pulled on the stiff backing. "Is this what you've been seeing in your dreams, Becca?"

She gasped. "The green trellis design. The exact pattern I see in my dreams. If we unroll it, we should find a large bloodstain."

He tugged at the rope holding the carpet, released the knot and did the same with a second cord that held it bound.

Once the two ropes were free, he pulled back on the edge of the carpet.

Becca stepped closer.

"I don't understand."

They both looked down at the large spot. Not a dark black bloodstain. Instead, an area of the carpet was void of color.

"It looks like someone tried to clean the carpet with bleach that took out the color."

"The bleach took something else out," she whispered.

He leaned closer.

Becca's eyes widened. "It took out the bloodstain."

Chapter Sixteen

Becca's dreams about the carpet had been real, but without the bloodstain, there was no evidence to provide the sheriff should he become involved.

"Someone hurled the carpet over the edge of the ravine in the same area where they thought I had fallen." She tried to fit the pieces together. "Did they want my body to be found along with the rug or were they convinced no one would find either me or the rug?"

Zeke shook his head. "Maybe they hoped the sheriff would think you had fallen while throwing the rug over the edge."

"How could I have moved the carpet?"

"It is not that large of a rug." He glanced at the roll of carpet. "Probably six feet by eight feet in size. You could carry it, but it would have been a struggle. Or perhaps someone helped you?"

"The man chasing me?"

"It does not make sense," Zeke agreed.

"Nothing makes sense." She worried her fingers. "Now I'm even more convinced that something very,

very bad happened to cause me to run scared that night. But what?"

"You were at the movie studio. You must know someone there or you worked there."

"Perhaps Caleb will learn of someone from housekeeping who has not showed up for work these last few days."

A sound came from above. Zeke grabbed her hand and pulled her under the overarching ledge.

"What are you—" she started to object.

He covered her mouth with his hand, making her pulse race. She wrinkled her brow and pulled free of his hold.

He held his finger to his lips. "Shhh."

She shrugged and mouthed, *What?*

He pointed to the ledge above them.

Listen, he said silently.

She read his lips and turned her ear, struggling to comprehend what she was hearing. Voices?

A pebble fell from above, followed by a few more stones. Someone was standing on the ledge.

Zeke held up two fingers.

Two men? she mouthed.

He nodded, then pulled her back even farther.

"The carpet's still there," one man said. "Looks like the ropes binding the rug came undone."

"Which probably happened when we tossed it over the ledge."

"I told you not to worry. The cops will find it only when we want them to. First we need to stage the scene."

"I've got everything we need."

"Good. We can't have any mistakes."

The voices faded as the men left the ledge.

Zeke grabbed Becca's hand. "We have to hurry back to the buggy. Follow me, but don't make any noise."

She nodded and started after him. When they were almost to the forested area, she accidently stepped on a brittle branch that broke with a loud snap.

Her heart stopped. She turned and glanced up. A man ran back to the ledge. Tall, with disheveled hair that hung around his neck. His eyes widened when he saw her.

Becca remained frozen in place for half a second before she ran after Zeke and disappeared in the dense forest.

"Stop! I'll find you. You can't hide from me."

Hearing the man shout, Zeke guided Becca through the underbrush, his pulse racing. "We need to hurry."

The man on the ledge had seen Becca and would come looking for her. Could they get to the buggy and down the mountain in time?

They ran along the path, then slowed as they came into the initial clearing. Zeke glanced up and nodded before he motioned her forward.

Becca kept her eyes on the path as if she was worried about tripping and falling. Zeke did not need to tell her that sound carried in the forest. Any man-made noise would alert the men to their exact location.

Relieved when they arrived at the buggy, Zeke tied one of the carpet ropes around a tree set back about a yard from the roadway.

"The rope will alert us to the turn-off when we return." He helped Becca into the buggy.

"We're coming back?"

"If we need to retrieve the carpet for any reason."

He grabbed the reins and encouraged Sophie forward. Before guiding her onto the roadway, Zeke glanced up the mountain, searching for any sign of the two men.

Once they were on the pavement, he urged Sophie to increase her pace. He glanced back, relieved that no one was following them.

"I will tell Caleb about the carpet, in case the studio realizes something criminal has happened," he said as his focus turned back to the road. "The Amish do not usually get involved with the sheriff's office unless law enforcement questions them, but if the sheriff starts an investigation, they will need to know what we found."

"Law enforcement worries me, Zeke. If they are told, they might come looking for me."

"I will not mention your involvement to Caleb, so there will be no reason for anyone to draw you into the investigation."

"Do you think I am involved?"

"I know nothing at this point, Becca, and neither do you unless you have remembered something more."

She dropped her head and rubbed her hand over her brow. "If only I could remember."

"Caleb thinks you are visiting Hattie, which you are. He did not recognize you. He probably stays in the food service area of the studio lot and does not mix with those involved in filming except when they take their meals."

"Did I take my meals there?"

"An Amish woman might bring her own food, perhaps a bit of bread and some cheese or apple butter." He glanced back again to ensure the men had not followed them. "If you were cleaning the studio at night, you might have stumbled onto something they did not want you to see."

"The bloody carpet, but I don't understand why it was thrown in the same area where I was last seen."

"The men thought you had fallen to your death. Perhaps they planned to connect you to whatever happened."

"But how? And what about the scene the men mentioned? What do they plan to stage?"

"You remembered liking the color green and enjoying sewing. More memories will return before long. It will all unfold in *Gott*'s time."

"*Gott* does not listen to me. He listens to others, perhaps to you and Hattie, but he has turned his back on me."

Zeke nodded. "I feel the same at times. *Gott* listens to my father's prayers, but he turns a deaf ear to mine. Hattie has tried to convince me differently, yet I am still not sure. Perhaps *Gott* is not willing to help an Amish man who has made so many mistakes in his life. My *datt* said I would pay for my transgressions."

"Surely, he didn't mean that."

"He was hoping I would ask for forgiveness, but I am not ready to confess wrongdoing."

"You tried to save Irene's life. How can that be wrong?"

"I ran after her in my father's opinion. She was not Amish. Amish men only marry Amish women."

"But she had planned to return to the Amish faith."

"My mistake was believing her."

"Perhaps if your father knew what really happened?"

"He has ears to hear and eyes to read the news reports, yet he believes what he wants to believe."

"Like Mr. Gingerich."

Zeke nodded. "It is true about both men, although they are different in so many ways. One is a bishop of the Amish faith, the other left the faith and made his own way being *Englisch*, yet they suffer from the same stubbornness and hardness of heart."

A sound filtered up the mountain.

"Shhh." Zeke held his finger to his lips.

He and Becca both tilted their heads to listen.

"Motor vehicles are headed this way," he said.

"What else is located this high up on the mountain?"

"Only the studio, but there is a turn-off just ahead, before the bend in the road. We will hide there." He flicked the reins. Sophie increased her speed.

Zeke's gut tightened. They needed to turn off onto the narrow road before the convoy came around the bend.

"Get going, girl," he encouraged the mare.

The sound of the approaching vehicles grew louder.

The turn-off appeared on the right. He pulled back ever so slightly on the reins and guided Sophie into the turn at a higher speed than he would have done normally. One of the buggy's back wheels raised off the ground for a second, tilting the rig at a precarious angle.

"Please, *Gott*," he prayed, fearing the buggy might topple over on its side.

The wheel dropped back to the dirt roadway. Relieved, he reined Sophie to a stop behind a thicket of heavy brush and tall trees. Peering from their hiding place, Zeke watched a van bearing the Montcliff Studio logo and two large trucks with the same markings pass by on the main road.

"We made it just in time," Becca gasped.

Zeke nodded. "They are returning early today."

Becky clasped his hand. "I'm glad we were on the path before they passed. Something about the logo unsettles me."

"You will know more as soon as your memory returns."

"Oh, Zeke." Becca stared at him, her eyes filled with worry. "What if my memory never comes back?"

Chapter Seventeen

After returning to Hattie's farm, Zeke settled Sophie in the barn and was walking back to the house when Caleb pulled his sports car into the drive.

"Can I offer you a cup of coffee?" Zeke asked as the younger man climbed from his car.

"I had one before I left town, but thanks." Caleb waved to Becca who hurried from the house.

"Did you learn the name of the housekeeping contact for me?" she asked as she joined the men.

"Susan Mast is her name, but no one filming in town knew her address. I called the housekeeping department and left a message. I'm hoping they'll call me back. If not, I can ask tomorrow at the studio office."

"Don't tell them who wants to know. I would rather find out more about the job first."

"Then I won't mention your name. If you decide you're interested, you can fill out an application at the studio office. Nicholas Walker is the producer. His trailer is in the executive circle, not far from the commissary. The main office is located in the trailer next to his."

"From what I saw last night," Zeke said, "it appears that the studio plans to stay on the mountain for a period of time."

Caleb nodded. "At least one more film is scheduled. Although with all the structures they've built, I don't think they'll leave anytime soon."

"Have they talked about buying the land from your father?" Becca asked.

"I doubt he would sell. He may have left the Amish faith, but he is still Amish at heart, and the land means everything to him. That is part of his upset. He had hoped Irene would settle on the farm, marry and raise her family here. He planned to grow old surrounded by his grandchildren and cared for by his daughter and son-in-law."

Zeke saw the cantankerous old man in a new light. The plans he had for his senior years had been destroyed when Irene died.

"And what of you?" Zeke asked. "Did he not plan for you to farm the land?"

Caleb shook his head. "He has never seen me as a farmer and never taught me the farming ways for whatever reason. Probably because I was an awkward kid who made a lot of mistakes. My father lost patience with me and then became overly lenient and allowed me to do whatever I pleased. I needed a little tough love, but perhaps he was tired of trying to mold me into someone I was not. Some say I was a spoiled kid."

Zeke smiled, remembering Hattie had said that very thing just last night.

"You find that funny?" Caleb asked.

"My father claimed I was spoiled, as well," Zeke

shared. "He said everyone in our generation is focused on worldly pleasure instead of faith and family."

"Perhaps our fathers do not remember when they were young. I understand both of them had more freedom than they needed. My uncle has told me stories about their escapades."

"Our fathers?" Zeke was surprised by Caleb's statement. "I did not know they were friends."

"In their youth, they were close. I am not sure what happened to drive them apart. Ask your father, Zeke. He might share more with you than my father does with me."

Zeke shook his head with regret. "You do not know my father if you say this, Caleb. Ever since he became bishop, he knows what is best for his youngest son. Perhaps he wears a mask of goodness, if what you say about his youth is true, to make up for the mistakes in his past."

"My father is the opposite. He wears a gruff mask, when inside he has a soft heart that has been wounded." Caleb stepped toward his car. "He's getting so forgetful these days."

"Before you go, I need to tell you what Becca and I found today near the waterfall."

"Something to do with my dad?"

Zeke shook his head. "Not your dad, but it may be tied to the studio. A piece of carpet discarded at the foot of the ravine. It appears to have been thrown from the overhanging ledge. A large area of the rug is void of color as if bleach had spilled on it. Do you know if carpet has been replaced in any of the studio buildings recently?"

Caleb thought for a moment before he shook his

head. "I can't think of any furnishings or carpets that have been redone. Everything is fairly new so there would be no reason for any changes."

"It looks like someone tried to clean the rug," Zeke said, "and used the wrong product."

Caleb narrowed his brow. "I'm confused as to why it was discarded."

"I am, as well. That is why I wanted someone at the studio to be aware of what we found."

"You mean because of Vanessa Harrington?"

Zeke shrugged. "That came to mind, although as you mentioned, she is probably being temperamental and left to get her own way. Still—"

Caleb nodded. "Still it is a concern."

"Do not use my name, Caleb. After what happened with Irene, I do not want to get pulled into another investigation."

"I'll tell one of the managers and see what they think, but I will not mention your name. From what I've heard, they want to keep Vanessa's disappearance quiet."

"Yet they notified the sheriff's office," Zeke said. "I talked to a deputy when I was in town. Remember Mike Frazier? We knew him growing up."

"I saw Mike not too long ago. He's a good guy."

"He knew about the missing movie star but said no one filled out a missing person report."

"The studio wants to keep the information from the media. Larry Landers planned to distribute flyers once he got the go-ahead from the producer. Thankfully he still had them in his office. Mr. Walker returned to Montcliff this morning and wasn't happy from what I heard. He thought the flyers would have been bad publicity for the studio."

Becca tilted her head. "I don't understand what the problem would be."

"News travels fast, and a huge amount of money is needed to produce a film. The backers will be angry and rescind their financial commitment if they learn Vanessa has disappeared. It causes a number of head-aches for the producer."

"Did Landers not realize what he was doing when he created the flyers?" Zeke asked.

Caleb shrugged. "He's a bit of a free spirit. I'm not sure how long he's been with the studio. I've overheard a couple comments about him having ties to someone with money outside of Montcliff, but I couldn't tell you who that would be."

"If you hear anything, let us know. We will deliver more of Hattie's baked goods in a few days."

"I should have mentioned sooner that the cook was thrilled with what she had baked and asked for a similar delivery day after tomorrow, if that gives her enough time. He put her check in the mail."

The kitchen door opened, and Hattie stuck her head outside and waved. Caleb repeated what he had told Zeke about the baked goods.

Hattie smiled broadly. "I am glad the items were well received. Thank you for delivering them today, Caleb."

"Not a problem, Hattie. Your check is in the mail."

"*Yah?* This is *gut*." She returned to the kitchen and closed the door.

Zeke extended his hand. "We must stay in touch even though our fathers have not kept their friendship going."

"I told you yesterday, I know you had nothing to do with Irene's death. I read the reports. You pulled her from the cabin and tried to resuscitate her. For which I am grateful."

"Perhaps someday your father will realize I am not to blame."

"I'll tell him again what really happened, although he may not listen. As we talked about earlier, it is a hard realization, but one he must face if he is to regain some sense of peace. Right now he is a bitter man with a broken heart."

Caleb patted Zeke on the shoulder. "You know about broken hearts yourself, but you have healed." Caleb glanced at Becca. "Life goes on, *yah?*"

"What you say is true. Life does goes on."

Caleb climbed into his sports car and nodded his farewell before he headed to the main road.

Zeke thought of Irene, musing how things would have been different if she had not died, but then he would not know Becca. Pulling in a cleansing breath, he felt a release of something he had held on to for so long.

He smiled at Becca. The past was over. It had ended the day of the explosion when the cabin caught on fire. Now he was ready to embrace the future whatever it held.

The afternoon and evening passed quickly, filled with work that needed to be done. Later that night after the meal had been eaten and the dishes washed and put away, Zeke struggled with a restlessness that confused him even more than everything that was happening at Montcliff Studios.

Becca and Hattie had retired early, claiming to be tired. Eventually Zeke followed them upstairs, but soon thereafter, he returned to the kitchen and then stepped outside to check the horses in the barn and gaze at the pastures and surrounding farmland.

"You seem anxious about something?"

He turned to see Becca standing in the open doorway to the kitchen. "I heard your footsteps on the stairs, Zeke, and expected you to return to your bed in a short time. When I didn't hear you, I got worried."

She stepped onto the porch. The moon was hidden behind the clouds, yet the stars provided enough light to see the remnants of the bruise on her forehead and her scraped cheek.

"Are you feeling all right?" he asked, still concerned about the blows she had sustained just a few nights ago.

"My health is fine."

"Perhaps you should have seen a doctor."

She held up her hand. "A doctor would have notified the sheriff. That is not what I wanted."

"You did nothing wrong, Becca."

"How can you be certain?"

"Because I know you. I know who you are."

She shook her head as if dismissing his comment. "You know who you want me to be. I don't even know myself."

Glancing up at the mountain, she shrugged. "Sometimes I stop and stare into the emptiness of my mind, trying to remember, yet it continues to fail me. I fear there is a reason I cannot remember, a reason that is so vile and heinous that my subconscious will not allow me to remember it again."

He stepped closer. "But that does not mean you were the one doing the vile act, Becca."

She stared up at him. "How can you be sure, Ezekiel? You are seeing me through the eyes of a man who has shut himself off from life. I stumbled into your solitude and awakened a part of you that you probably thought was dead. You have feelings for me. I can see it in your gaze. But your feelings are for a life that you are ready to embrace again. You are eager to leave your reclusive existence here. That is a good thing, Zeke, but it has nothing to do with me."

"Oh, Becca, you are so wrong. It has everything to do with you. You say that I was reclusive, but I went to town and interacted with the store owners and shop-keepers there. I bought and sold grain and livestock. I took Hattie's produce to market. I was not holed up here like a hermit."

"Yet your heart was closed, Zeke. You built a wall around your emotions, and although you may have in-teracted with people, you did not let them into your world, the private inner world you built for yourself."

She moved closer. "Did you ever read books about the knights of old? They lived in castles and went out to defend the king's land and protect the royal family. After the battles, they returned to the castle on the hill with the fortification, the moat and the stone walls that cut off those inside the castle from the rest of the world."

"I am not a knight, Becca."

"You are, Zeke. You're a good man who wants to pro-tect those you love. You take care of Hattie. You reached out to an old man who thought you were a killer. You did not try to change his mind because doing so would make him realize the failings of his only daughter. That is heroic, Zeke."

"You are looking at me through a fog and seeing what you want to see. You do not know me."

"I know you better than you know me."

"Becca—" He reached out and touched her hair that fell around her shoulders. "I do not need to know the Becca of the past when I know the Becca of this moment."

His hand circled her neck and everything within him wanted to pull her even closer. She had talked about the wall to his heart. If he had built that wall, he wanted Becca to step through it and to be with him no matter how isolated he was from the outside world.

"Do you know how beautiful you are?"

She shook her head. "That is not so."

"Of course it is."

"An Amish man does not talk of such things, and an Amish woman does not listen. Pride could swell within me, Zeke, which is not good."

"Not pride, Becca, but admission of the truth. You are beautiful. In every way. Not only your expressive green eyes and silky chestnut hair, but the warmth of your smile and the concern you have for others. There is so much about you that I want to explore."

The moon broke through the clouds and light played over her face. Her lips parted as if she wanted to say something, but then she stopped and everything in her gaze told him that she too felt the desire to draw closer.

Slowly and ever so patiently, he leaned in, his lips close enough to hers that he could feel the warmth of her mouth as if it had already joined with his.

Her eyes widened, she stepped back, leaving him empty and chilled by her rejection. She turned and fled back into the house, running away from him, just as she had done before.

Irene had left him for another man. Becca would

leave him because of her fear of the past. She could not accept today when she did not know who she was.

Was there someone else in her past who pulled her from him? Would he find her fleeing him again and running into the arms of a man she had loved before?

Where would that leave Zeke? Alone again. Broken. He would go back into the castle Becca had mentioned, but he would never again be able to venture outside the walls he had built to protect his heart. Not if he lost Becca.

Becca entered her bedroom, still surrounded by the nervous glow she had felt standing in the moonlight with Zeke. He had almost kissed her. The memory of his closeness warmed her from head to toe but also frightened her. What if she loved another man? Could that be?

She clutched her hands to her heart. Did the past matter when the present offered such promise?

Even if her memory never returned, she had today and tomorrow and the days going forward.

With her spirits bolstered, she almost laughed. Sleep would be hard tonight due to the promise of what life *could* be, no, *would* be in the days ahead.

Zeke had loved Irene, but he had told her more than once that Irene was in the past. Becca was here and now.

She twirled around the room, her full skirt billowing out. In her mind's eye, she imagined herself dancing with Zeke.

She stopped. Did Amish people dance?

Why didn't she know the answer?

There was so much she had forgotten and so much she needed to learn again. Surely with Hattie's and Zeke's help, she could master the nuances of the Amish faith. Not knowing if she had been baptized, she would have to talk to Zeke's father. She hoped that would not be a problem, especially if she wanted to be fully Amish.

Again she smiled, thinking of Zeke's words. *Amish men only marry Amish women.* Was he assuring her of what the future could hold for both of them?

Her euphoria was short-lived as her mind started firing other thoughts so fast her head spun. The bloody carpet, the knife, running through the woods, and being chased again the next day and later in town.

How could she be dreaming of Zeke when such confusion surrounded her? She needed to think through everything she had learned so far.

If she had worked with the housekeeping department, she might have stumbled upon the bloody carpet. Someone could have walked in on her when she was cleaning that night and then chased after her because of what she had seen.

What about the actor in town who had grabbed her arm at the cattle auction? Was he somehow involved with what had happened?

If Vanessa Harrington had been kidnapped, a ransom would be demanded from her husband or perhaps from the studio, which could be the reason they wanted her disappearance to be kept quiet.

The men on the ledge by the waterfall had talked about the scene they planned to set. A movie scene or the scene of the crime?

She sighed and rubbed her hand over her forehead. If only her memory would return.

Chapter Eighteen

Becca slept fitfully. The next morning she woke before dawn and hurriedly dressed and descended to the kitchen to help Hattie with breakfast.

"What is wrong, dear? You look like you did not sleep last night."

"I... I had a lot on my mind."

"Of course. Pour a cup of coffee. Caffeine will perk you up."

Becca feared she would need more than caffeine to brighten the day, but she dutifully retrieved a cup from the cabinet and filled it to the brim.

The first sip was bitter, but she forced another sip and then another as if the coffee had medicinal properties. Thankfully, some of the tension she had felt through the night eased.

"I'll get the butter and milk."

"Make sure you put on a wrap. The temperature has dropped."

Becca pulled a sweater from the peg by the door and hurried outside. Zeke approached carrying an armload of wood.

"Winter has arrived along with snow." His expression gave no hint that he had struggled through the night.

Becca smiled seeing the falling flakes. "I'll tell Hattie."

"I am going to town after I do the chores. I want to talk to the deputy about what we found."

"Yesterday you said law enforcement didn't need to know about the carpet unless an investigation was opened."

"According to the almanac, the snowfall will be heavy. I need to tell Mike Frazier what we found while we can still find the rug."

"But—"

"I will not mention your name, Becca."

"You wouldn't have been searching for the carpet if not for me. How will you explain that to the deputy?"

"Mike and I climbed the mountain in our youth. Exploring the cliffs and boulders was a favorite pastime. He will not think it strange that I found something on the ledge."

"If you're sure he won't want to talk to me."

"I am not sure of anything, but I will discuss the carpet with him and not the woman staying at my aunt's house."

"I'll stay here with Hattie."

"Do not forget the quilting she mentioned. I know it is important to her."

"She can go alone."

"Which is not wise. There is safety in numbers, *yah*?"

"Two women would not be much of a match for a couple of muscular guys."

"That is the reason I want you to go to the quilting.

The widow Shrock lives some distance from town. No one will look for you there."

Zeke took the wood into the house while Becca grabbed the butter and milk from the ice-cold water.

She glanced at the falling snowflakes and tried to imagine her childhood. She closed her eyes. For a split second, a scene flashed through her mind. She had come inside on a snowy day to get warm. Her grandmother had hot cocoa and homemade sugar cookies waiting for her.

The memory buoyed her spirits.

"I remember my grandmother," she announced as she hurried inside.

Zeke turned to look at her. "Just now?"

She recounted what she had seen.

"Such good news," Hattie enthused.

"I could see *Mammi* and felt her loving gaze. She had gray hair pulled into a bun and her *kapp* sat on her round face."

"Her *kapp*?" he asked. "Your grandmother was Amish?"

"Of course. Didn't you know I was Amish?"

"I thought this, *yah*, because of the clothing you wore when you arrived, but there were so many things you did not remember about the Amish way."

"The amnesia blocked it all from my memory, but it's coming back, Zeke. It's all coming back."

"You look relieved," he said.

"Relieved to have learned something new."

Hattie smiled. "Soon we will find that house where your grandmother lives."

"I was a young teen. A lot could have happened over the years. My grandmother could live far from here. My parents and I could have been visiting."

"Did you see your parents, as well?" Zeke asked.

She shook her head. "Not yet."

"The next memory. It will come." Hattie's eyes twinkled. "In the meantime, we are family here, Becca, and you are included, as well."

Becca warmed at the comment about family. It was true, she felt part of this household. If only she could truly be family. Standing in the large inviting kitchen gave her a sense of home and acceptance. She was drawn to Hattie's faith and her love for the Amish way and the plain life. Her habits of hard work and concern for others were rubbing off on Becca. She had started to feel that same sense of commitment to provide nourishing food and a clean and tidy house. After the vision of her grandmother, Becca felt even more at home in this Amish farmhouse filled with love.

She blushed at the thought of having her heart filled with love, as well. Love for Hattie, but also—was it love?—for Zeke. Such a good man who was concerned about her and her well-being. The best part was knowing she was Amish. Sharing that faith made all the difference.

"I knew you would start to remember," Hattie enthused. "*Gott* has brought you here to us for a reason, a very joyous reason."

Becca hoped the reason had something to do with Zeke.

Although nervous about meeting the older Amish ladies at the quilting, Becca was even more nervous about Zeke talking to the sheriff.

"Please don't tell Mike Frazier anything more than is necessary," she pleaded as Zeke pulled the buggy into the widow Shrock's drive. Zeke hurried around the buggy to help Becca and Hattie down.

"And be careful," Becca whispered to him, not wanting to frighten Hattie. "If the men on the ledge saw you with me, you might be a target, as well."

"I was well hidden in the woods. Besides, the *Englisch* think all the Amish look alike, with our matching clothing and black hats. No one will recognize me."

Still she was worried and stood watching as he rode out of sight.

"Come, dear." Oblivious to Becca's concern for Zeke's safety, Hattie motioned her toward the house. "With the snow, we are a small group today. You will enjoy the ladies and they will enjoy meeting you."

Hattie's comment proved true. The four ladies were delightful and made Becca feel instantly at home.

She enjoyed the sewing as well as the chatter that flowed all the while the women quilted. Little bits of news were spiced with laughter and shared along with the stitches.

"Mattie King has taken to her bed," Annie Shrock said. "Her daughter fears it is the flu."

"So many are sick now," another lady added. "Have any of you learned what happened to Susan Mast?"

Becca glanced up at the name Caleb had mentioned, the woman in housekeeping.

"Her husband says only that she is infirmed, but her daughter told my granddaughter that she had an accident coming home from work."

"At the movie studio?" another asked.

"*Yah*. She works at night. The roads are dark. It is not good for a woman to be alone on the mountain."

"We did not have problems before the movie studio arrived," Hattie said. Her four friends nodded.

"Did someone run her off the road?" came the question.

"This is what I heard." The hostess pulled her needle through the cotton. "Susan's buggy ran into a ditch and turned over. Evidently she was left for dead."

"How terrible."

"*Yah*. Her husband was worried and went looking for her, which probably saved Susan's life."

"*Gott* provides," an older lady intoned. Heads bowed in agreement.

Annie Shrock frowned. "I do not understand why her husband would not talk about the accident."

"He is a man of few words. Perhaps that is the reason."

"Perhaps."

Becca kept sewing and tried to keep her voice on an even keel. "Does Susan live close by?"

"Hers is the house that sits back from the road, just around the first bend when you travel up the mountain from here. You will pass the Mast farm as you and Hattie return home, Becca. You cannot miss their red barn with two silos."

The conversation switched to other people who were sick and to a woman who had given birth to twins.

Becca nodded at the news but kept thinking of Susan Mast and the buggy accident. Had she been run off the road as the quilter surmised and if so, why?

If the housekeeper had witnessed something she should not have seen, Becca wanted to talk to her. Perhaps she and Susan had something in common.

Chapter Nineteen

Mike Frazier listened attentively to Zeke's mention of the stained carpet.

"Usually I wouldn't take the time to look at a discarded rug, Zeke, but you and I go back a long way. If you're concerned, I'm willing to check it out."

Zeke headed back to the mountain turnoff and waited until the deputy arrived. They parked on the road and hurried along the path he and Becca had taken yesterday.

Once they stepped into the second clearing, Zeke was relieved that Mike had agreed to come with him today. A heavy dusting of snow covered the boulders and ledge, and from the low cloud cover, it appeared the flurries would continue throughout the day, eventually obscuring the roll of carpet.

Leading the way around the boulder, Zeke stopped short.

"Where's the carpet?" the deputy asked.

Zeke shook his head. "It was here yesterday. Someone must have taken it."

"Who would want discarded carpet?"

"The person or persons who poured bleach on the

bloodstain and did not want the carpet found, Mike. It has something to do with the movie studio."

"How can you be so sure?"

"Because I saw the same trellis-patterned carpet in one of the movie trailers."

"I'm not going to ask what you were doing spying on the trailers. At least not now. I'll stop by the studio and have a look around."

Mike's cell rang.

He raised the phone to his ear and narrowed his gaze. "Yeah? Do you have a name? Larry who?" He nodded. "Landers worked at the studio?"

Zeke stepped closer.

"Did you contact the coroner?" The deputy paused as someone on the other end spoke. "I'm headed there now."

Mike pocketed his phone. "I'll talk to you later, Zeke. Go home and stay put."

"What happened?"

"That was one of the security officers at Montcliff Studio. There's been a death on the property."

Zeke's breath hitched. "Who?"

"Larry Landers. I talked to Vanessa Harrington's husband yesterday. He hired Landers to keep an eye on his wife. Evidently the job was too much for him. Landers hung himself and left a suicide note."

"Which could have been written by someone else," Zeke said. "If the movie star is missing and Landers was hired to watch out for her, maybe someone wanted Landers out of the picture."

The deputy tugged on his jaw. "You don't think his death was suicide?"

"That is something you need to determine, Mike, but if not suicide, then it has to be murder."

* * *

Becca and Hattie said goodbye to Annie Shrock and the other ladies at the quilting and hurried outside when they saw Zeke approaching in the buggy. Becca crawled into the second seat so Hattie could sit next to her nephew.

As soon as Zeke turned the buggy onto the main road, he told them about Larry Landers's death and that he had been working for the movie star's husband.

"The same man who chased after me in town?" Becca asked.

"The man who stopped by our house and wanted to film on our land?" Hattie added.

Zeke nodded. "Yes to both of your questions. He may have also been one of the men on the ledge when Becca and I found the carpet."

Hattie tapped Zeke's arm and then glanced back at Becca. "There is something neither of you have told me."

Becca explained finding the carpet and the two men talking above them on the ledge before adding, "As Zeke said, one of the men could have been Landers, although it is doubtful if he was working for Vanessa's husband."

"He was supposed to watch out for Vanessa," Zeke added. "Perhaps he became despondent when she went missing and took his own life."

Becca shook her head. "It does not make sense."

Noting the approaching bend in the road, she spied the red barn and double silos and tapped Zeke's shoulder. "Would you mind stopping at the farm. Susan Mast lives here, and I want to talk to her. The ladies at the quilting said she was recently in a buggy accident."

"The Susan Mast who works at the studio?" he asked.

"That's right. I want to find out if the buggy crash could have been something other than an accident."

Zeke pulled Sophie to a stop near the farmhouse. He helped Becca and Hattie from the buggy, and the three of them hurried to the door.

"Susan's husband is probably putting out corn and hay for the livestock because of this snow," Zeke said. "Perhaps we will find her alone."

No one answered their first knock. Hattie rapped on the door and raised her voice. "Susan, I need to talk to you. It is important."

A woman appeared at the window. Hattie smiled a greeting and pointed to the door.

Slowly it opened.

"I heard you were sick." Hattie pushed past the woman and stepped inside. "You know Ezekiel Hochstetler." She introduced Becca as a family friend.

Susan seemed unsettled and clutched her hands nervously. "I must ask you to leave, Hattie. I have not been well."

Becca stepped closer. "I worked in housekeeping at the studio."

Susan straightened her spine. "I know the people I hire, and you are not part of the housekeeping department."

Becca was taken aback by the answer. "You have not seen me before?"

"Never. Why do you ask?"

"Because your buggy was run off the road and someone left you to die."

Susan drew her hand to her mouth. "How did you know?"

"Something happened at the studio," Becca continued. "Vanessa Harrington is missing, and you have information that ties in with her disappearance, which is why you were attacked. They wanted to scare you. Or kill you."

Susan's shoulders slumped, and she nodded. "*Yah*, I fear you are right."

"Can you tell us what happened the night of your accident?" Zeke asked.

"I saw a light on in the office trailer. Earlier, I had received a note saying the office did not need to be cleaned, but I wanted to make certain everything was tidy. Just because someone did not want cleaning does not mean I could forsake my obligation."

She looked at each person as if waiting for their agreement.

"This is true," Hattie confirmed with a nod.

"Go on," Zeke encouraged.

"I had the master key and opened the side door, never expecting to see anyone."

"Who was there?" Becca asked.

"Two men. They were Hispanic and didn't speak English. They used hand gestures and signaled for me to go away and close the door."

"Why?"

"They were laying new carpet in the entryway."

Becca's stomach tightened. "What did the carpet look like?"

"It was the same carpet that is in each of the other trailers and the same as the rug that had been in the office previously. The rug had a beige background with a green trellis design."

The carpet Becca had seen in her dreams and on the ledge near the waterfall.

"I left work that night never thinking anything would happen. A black car ran me off the road. I was thrown to the ground and must have hit my head. The driver got out of his car and stood near me. I was too stunned to move. He called someone on his phone and said the problem was solved and that he had taken care of me."

Her eyes were somber as she added, "I believe the man thought I was dead."

"Hopefully we will soon learn who did this to you," Becca told the distraught woman. Hattie gave Susan a supportive hug before they left the house.

"Who wanted to keep the new carpet installation a secret?" Zeke asked Becca and Hattie as they headed home in the buggy.

"Probably the same men who are chasing after me," Becca said. "Only I managed to escape serious harm. To keep Susan quiet, they tried to kill her."

Hattie shook her head in amazement. "And Susan is fearful, so she holes up in her house, claiming to be sick."

"It's called intimidation and is against the law," Becca said. "At least, it should be against the law."

Zeke flicked the reins, encouraging Sophie. "Mike Frazier is at the studio now. He plans to stop by the house on his way back to town. Maybe he will have more information."

"What if Landers killed Vanessa and then someone killed him?" Becca mused.

"Or he could have taken his own life," Hattie said with a sigh.

Zeke nodded. "We will know something soon. Very, very soon."

Chapter Twenty

True to his word, the deputy stopped by later that day. Not wanting to be seen, Becca hurried upstairs when his knock sounded at the door.

Hattie invited Mike in and poured him a cup of coffee.

He sat at the table with Zeke while Hattie busied herself in the kitchen. "Care for a piece of pie, Mike?"

"Thanks but no, Miss Hattie, although the coffee hits the spot."

As Mike took a long draw of the hot brew, Zeke told him about Susan Mast and her buggy accident. "Perhaps you should stop there on your way back to town." Zeke provided the address.

"I appreciate the information."

"What about Larry Landers's death?" Zeke asked. "Are you still calling it a suicide?"

"We're investigating, that's all I can tell you now. I did find some information in his trailer that was interesting."

The deputy opened the notebook he had placed on

the table. "Landers was onto something that no one else has mentioned at the studio."

Zeke leaned closer.

"Landers thought a second person had gone missing, although when I questioned the human resources department, they claimed the person had given her notice and had planned to stop working within the week, which might be the reason no one seemed concerned about another missing woman."

Zeke glanced at Hattie and then turned his attention back to the deputy.

"Landers compiled some information on the woman. The gal comes from a dysfunctional home. Her mother has a record and is currently serving time."

"Her mother is in jail?" Hattie asked.

"That's right. The woman doesn't have a record, but my guess is she's probably been involved in some shady deals if her mother was in so much trouble."

"Which might no : prove true," Zeke noted.

"I see a lot in this job, Zeke. It's hard to find a good apple on a rotten tree, if you get my drift."

"What are you saying?" Hattie asked.

"I'm saying we've got another missing woman who may have something to do with Vanessa Harrington's disappearance. Landers printed a missing person flyer on the movie star and then made a second flyer on the other missing person."

His phone rang.

"Excuse me while I take this." Mike scooted back from the table and stepped toward the stairwell.

Hattie's eyes were wide as she stared at Zeke. He shook his head ever so slightly. Neither of them needed to say anything to the deputy about the woman upstairs. Not yet. Not until they knew more about what had happened.

"Yeah, did you find anything?" Mike nodded. "Good fortune was on our side for a change. Run the prints through the database." He glanced up the stairwell and nodded again. "I'll meet you at the office."

Frazier returned to the table. "Thanks for the coffee, Hattie. I need to get back to town. Looks like everything is falling into place."

He pocketed his phone. "A couple of guys spotted a body in the river south of town. Evidently it was hung up on a downed tree."

"Vanessa Harrington?" Zeke asked.

"Appears to be her. She'd been stabbed multiple times." He picked up his notebook. "We found what we think is a murder weapon in one of the dorm rooms at the studio. A hefty letter opener covered with what looks like dried blood. The forensic guys will check it out. It's got the studio logo on the handle. One of the deputies lifted prints, then found what appear to be similar prints on the furnishings in the room."

Zeke rose from the table. "Are you saying someone at the studio killed Vanessa?"

"It looks that way. Funny to leave the murder weapon behind. But then, she left her belongings, although she didn't have much. We found the letter opener wrapped in a small green lap quilt. Looks old. Maybe something from her youth."

Hattie gasped.

The deputy glanced out the window. "That snow's piling up. I need to get going."

He started for the door and then turned back. "I almost forgot. I wanted to give you folks a copy of the missing person flyer Landers created on the second woman. Not too many people live this high on the mountain. Doubt you'll come to town soon with the bad weather. I wanted you to be on the lookout in case she appears in this area."

Zeke's pulse raced as he took the paper from Mike's outstretched hand.

"I'll let myself out. You folks have a good night and be careful if you see this woman. When I first learned of her disappearance, I thought it was coincidental, but finding the letter opener in her room makes her a person of interest in a murder investigation. She could be a killer. Pretty as she is, but, we all know, looks don't mean a thing."

He opened the door, and a blast of cold air swirled into the kitchen. Zeke glanced at Hattie, who bit her lip and shook her head. He lifted the paper and glanced at the picture in the center of the page.

His world rocked.

Without saying a word, he placed the paper on the table and then grabbed his coat and hat and headed to the door. "I'll be in the barn, Hattie. Don't hold dinner. I've lost my appetite."

Becca stood at the top of the stairs and heard portions of the conversation below. Closing her bedroom door behind her, she ran to the window and saw the deputy drive off, then watched as Zeke hurried to the barn.

Hattie climbed the stairs. The look on her face scared Becca when she pulled the door open.

"You heard?" the older woman asked.

"I heard enough."

"You need to see what the deputy gave Zeke. He is upset. I must check on him."

Tears burned Becca's eyes. She took the paper from Hattie's outstretched hand.

"No matter what Zeke says, dear, you can stay here until all this blows over."

Hattie left the room and hurried down the stairs.

A lump filled Becca's throat. How could a movie star's murder and a man's suicide blow over? Did Hattie really want her to stay?

Becca's heart hitched. Ezekiel had left the house. No doubt, he did not want to see her again.

Her mouth went dry. She glanced at the paper and homed in on the photo.

Her world came to an abrupt halt.

She studied the likeness of the woman in the picture—chestnut hair, green eyes, a slender nose, high cheekbones, full lips—then searched for a mirror, knowing full well she would not find one in this Amish house.

Stepping to the window, she stared into the glass, seeing the faint outline of her reflection. If only she could see her own face more clearly…chestnut hair, green eyes, slender nose and full lips.

A tearful lament issued from deep within her, gut-wrenching in its intensity as she realized the truth the flyer revealed.

Raising her hand, she touched the glass. The photo was identical to the woman staring back at her from the windowpane.

Becky Taylor was the name printed under the photo. She wasn't Becca Troyer, an Amish woman. She was Becky Taylor, an *Englischer* who had gone missing.

How could she have been so mistaken? Everything she had felt over the last few days since coming into this home had proved she was Amish, yet it was all a lie.

An Amish man can only marry an Amish woman.

Zeke couldn't marry her. He couldn't marry anyone who was *Englisch*. Plus Mike Frazier considered her a murder suspect because the letter opener, which she had thought was a bloody knife, had been found wrapped in her green quilt.

Who was Becky Taylor? The daughter of a convict, an *Englischer*, according to what the sheriff's deputy had said. Becca had wanted her memory to return, but now she was glad she couldn't remember all the terrible details of her past life.

No matter what Hattie said, Becca needed to leave the area. Staying on the farm would only cause Zeke and Hattie more upset, which she never wanted to do. Leaving Amish Mountain would be hard, but the hardest part would be leaving Zeke. Never seeing Zeke again would break her heart.

Zeke closed his ears to Hattie, but the sweet woman continued to defend Becca and encouraged Zeke to talk to her. "Things can be worked out," his aunt insisted. "Becca is not a killer."

Which was what Zeke wanted to believe. The initial shock of learning Becca was a missing *Englisch* woman and a possible murder suspect had made him unable to think clearly. Hattie's calm assurance that Becca was the same woman whether her name was Troyer or Taylor had brought him back to his senses.

Surely the murder weapon had been planted in her

dorm room at the studio. Was that the scene the men on the ledge had mentioned they needed to create?

"She was upstairs earlier, Zeke. Becca needs to know that everything is all right."

Hattie's words played over in his mind as he and his aunt entered the kitchen.

"Becca?" Hattie called from the foot of the stairs.

Failing to hear a reply, Hattie glanced at Zeke, concern covering her round face.

"I'll check on her," he said, climbing the stairs two at a time.

If Becca had overheard his conversation with the deputy, she would be frightened. He had to reassure her.

"Becca?" He stopped at the top of the stairs, seeing her closed bedroom door.

Needing to ensure she was okay, he tapped on the door. "Becca, it is Zeke. Are you all right?"

He tapped again.

His heart pounded. All sorts of scenarios played through his mind about why she was not responding. None of them were good.

He pushed open the door, then peered inside, prepared to see her strewn across the bed with tearful eyes.

What he found sent a jolt of fear into his heart.

Her black bonnet and cape were gone. So was Becca.

The missing person flyer Mike Frazier had provided lay crumpled on the floor.

He picked it up. His gut tightened seeing Becca's photo. How could she be involved in a movie star's murder?

The name printed under the photo was Becky Taylor, but the woman in the picture was Becca Troyer, a beautiful Amish woman who had worked her way into his heart.

He had lost Irene. He could not lose Becca.

He ran back downstairs and hurried out the front door, knowing he or Hattie would have seen Becca if she had left through the kitchen.

"Becca," he screamed.

He turned to glance in all directions, studying the winter terrain, hoping to catch sight of an Amish woman in a green dress and black cape. He saw nothing, and his heart nearly stopped when his gaze fell on the path into the woods. She had run away like she had done the night he had found her in the woods. Was her amnesia merely a way to hide the truth about who she was?

He did not care about her past. All he cared about was her present.

"Becca," he shouted as he ran into the woods.

He had to find her. He had to find her before someone from the studio found her first. She was running away again, running from her past. Only this time, she was running away from Ezekiel and that cut his heart in two.

Chapter Twenty-One

Becca fought back tears until she could hold them in no longer. They spilled down her cheeks and clouded her vision so that she couldn't see the trail. Struggling to control her emotions and needing to keep moving forward, she pulled a handkerchief from the waistband of her dress where she had tucked it this morning and wiped her cheeks.

Imagining footsteps, she looked back. The forest seemed to be closing in around her, like that terrible night when she had run scared.

She was running scared again, but for another reason. Her mind was playing tricks on her. She envisioned Mike Frazier at Hattie's house, climbing the stairs and pounding on the bedroom door, demanding to arrest Becca.

Would he call her Becky? Was that truly her name?

She had to get off Amish Mountain and this rural area and make her way to another place where no one would find her. But she had no money and no way to leave. She tugged at her bonnet with frustration and wanted to cry all the more.

Yesterday, she had returned to Hattie's farm and had found it filled with love. That was the reason she had to leave. She couldn't let anything happen to Hattie and Zeke. They were both so special to her and such good people with loving hearts.

So different from who she must be.

She hated amnesia, hated that she had tumbled down a steep incline and hurt her head. Sometime that night she had lost her memory.

Her life had changed just as it had changed when she had overheard the deputy telling Zeke about the letter opener wrapped in her quilt. Mike Frazier's revelation about the murder weapon only compounded the pain she had felt when she learned the truth of who she really was.

Her head throbbed thinking of what she had found out about herself. She was an *Englisch* woman who somehow was associated with the death—the murder—of a movie star.

Becca shivered. The temperature was dropping. She pulled the cape around her arms and ducked her chin into the neck of her cape. She had to think of her own safety and where she could hunker down out of the wind and snow.

"Oh God, or *Gott* as Zeke says, I'm lost and alone and frightened. Help me, Lord. Please. Help me."

All too soon, Zeke realized searching for Becca was like trying to find a grain of sand in a bed of gravel. He retraced his steps back to the barn and harnessed Sophie to the buggy.

Hattie hurried out of the house. "What happened? Did you find her?"

He shook his head. "She could be anywhere, although most likely, she took the path that leads up the mountain. If she left by the front door and rounded the outbuildings, the path would be the logical direction to go to ensure we did not see her."

"Why, Zeke? Why did she run away?"

"She heard us talking to Mike Frazier. Learning she was *Englisch* and a person of interest in a murder case had to be upsetting. Perhaps she feared we would reveal her presence to Mike."

"I feel responsible," Hattie said with a moan. "I gave her the missing person flyer."

"And I did not offer her support. Instead I ran to the barn to sort through my own thoughts."

"Where could she go?" Hattie lamented. "She does not know the mountain and so few folks live in this area."

"She is not thinking clearly and instead is reacting out of fear."

"The temperature is dropping. Tonight will be bitterly cold, especially for a woman wearing only a wool cape. You have to find her, Zeke."

"Pray that *Gott* leads me to her."

"I have been praying." Hattie grabbed his arm. "You need to pray too."

"*Gott* does not listen to me."

"You feel that way because of what happened to Irene. *Gott* heard your prayer, but Irene had closed the Lord out of her life. The problem was not you, Zeke. The problem was Irene." Hattie rubbed her hand over his shoulder. "You did everything right."

"Except I could not save her. In fact, I am responsible for her death, just as her father insists."

"*Ach.* Do not say such foolish things."

"It is true, Hattie. I went to the cabin to convince her to come back to Amish Mountain, but what I saw sickened me. She was burning scented candles, but the smell of acetone and other chemicals soured my stomach. Irene was high on drugs and threatened to ignite some chemicals used in making meth. I told her she had her own life to live, but what I needed and wanted was living Amish with or without her. I walked away never expecting her to act on her threat. She screamed for me to stay with her, but I did not look back...until the explosion and subsequent fire that quickly engulfed the cabin. I was still nearby but could not save her in time."

"You cannot carry such guilt, Ezekiel, when Irene was the problem."

"Do you not understand, Hattie, why I am to blame? I left Irene that day. She could not take the rejection. Whether she purposely caused the explosion, I will never know, but it was a reaction to my rejection."

"Oh, Zeke, you have blamed yourself all this time. Irene made her choice when she left Amish Mountain and took up with the drug dealer. She rejected you and the Amish way. Seeing you walk out of her life meant she was not getting what she really wanted. Irene's death was due to the choices she made not to anything you said or did."

Hattie gazed lovingly into his eyes. "Do you understand, Zeke?"

"Right now, I cannot dwell on the past. I have to save Becca. If anything happens to her—"

He could not finish the statement, but he was sure Hattie could read the dread that filled his heart. If anything happened to Becca, he could not go on.

"You will find her, Zeke. *Gott* will lead you to Becca."

If only Hattie's words would prove true.

He climbed into the buggy and flicked the reins, then flicked them again, hurrying Sophie along the drive.

"Find Becca," Hattie called out to him as he turned onto the main road. "And bring her home."

Chapter Twenty-Two

Becca ran until she could run no longer. Her side ached, and she gasped for air. Slowing to a walk, she rubbed the stitch in her side and kept moving along the trail, not sure where she was headed.

Thinking back to the time in the buggy with Zeke, she tried to remember seeing other Amish homes that might provide food and water and someplace safe to stay for the night. She needed time to decide where she would go and how she would get there.

On the trip to town, they had passed homes, but none were close to Hattie's farm. Plus, the path she was on lead up the mountain, not toward town.

She rubbed the back of her neck, realizing her own foolishness. Much as she didn't want to be alone on the mountain, she couldn't stay at Hattie's farm. The deputy would have found her. He would have arrested her and taken her to jail for the murder of Vanessa Harrington.

She shivered at the thought of being hauled away to jail and imagined looking back to see Ezekiel and Hattie standing in front of the house as the deputy's sedan disappeared from sight with her handcuffed in the rear.

Instead of being hauled away, she had made a decision to save herself and thus save Hattie and Zeke. They would not understand, but she couldn't stay there on the farm and draw shame on them. Still, she wished she was anywhere but on this lonely path not knowing where she was headed.

The sound of voices startled her. Her heart lurched, and she stopped to listen, trying to get some sense of where the sound was coming from. She scurried farther along the path and up a small rise to a clearing. Hunching down, she peered over the rise and studied the surrounding countryside.

Suddenly she grimaced. She knew where she was and it wasn't good, but at least, she had stumbled upon another house. Just not one that might offer sanctuary.

Peering over the rise again, she saw Mr. Gingerich standing forlorn on his driveway, talking to himself.

"What are you doing out here, Dad?" Caleb raced out of the house. "You'll catch a cold."

"I'm thinking about the studio. Those folks think they can push me around, but they can't. I own the land and I'm not about to let them buy even one square foot of property. They can continue to rent, as long as they give me what I need. A sizable monthly rent check and access to the property."

"The only place you've gone recently is to the doctor in town, Dad. You don't need access to the movie studio."

"Maybe not, but I want to make sure they're not hurting my land."

Caleb shook his head. "Come on, Dad. Let's head back to the house. I have to return to the studio and talk to one of the managers. Promise me you'll stay inside until I get back."

"All right, but I'm not about to let anyone tell me what to do."

"Have I ever told you what to do?" Caleb asked.

"Reckon you haven't. Fact is, you've been a good son, although I've failed to tell you that too many times. I like having you with me. If your sister were still alive I would be a happy man."

"You can choose to be happy even though Irene is gone. People survive. It's painful and hurts, but you're strong, Dad. You can go on."

"Maybe I can survive, but some days I don't want to make the effort."

"I need you, Dad. Don't leave me."

The old man put his hand on his son's shoulder and the two of them walked toward the house.

Although she was glad the father and son had reconciled, Becca needed to find shelter. The barn door stood open. Once the men were inside the house, she entered the barn.

The stalls were empty, but the wooden structure still smelled of horses and feed. A tractor sat near the door. No doubt, when Mr. Gingerich turned *Englisch*, he had forsaken the horse for the engine.

Becca touched the cold steel tractor, thinking of the difference between living plain and fancy. Wherever she ended up, she wanted it to be an Amish community where she could focus on the simple pleasures of life. *Gott* had answered her prayer in the woods and had brought her to this protective hideaway.

Thanks to Hattie's deep faith, Becca was beginning to see that her problems had nothing to do with *Gott*'s lack of concern and understanding, but more her own lack of faith. Over time, she hoped—no, she prayed— her faith in *Gott* would grow stronger. No matter what had happened to her in the past, she needed the Lord now.

In the rear of the barn, she found bales of hay that would provide a place for her to rest and a horse blanket in the tack room that would keep her warm.

Peering out at the house, she saw no one and scooted through a back door to the empty paddock. Ignoring the chickens who perched in the nearby henhouse, she pumped water into a tin cup, rinsed it clean, then re-filled it and drank deeply.

Just as before, *Gott* had provided.

If only both Gingerich men would stay inside and not come to the barn. The possibility of not being in-terrupted over the next few hours until she could form a plan gave Becca hope.

She grabbed the blanket and wrapped it around her head and shoulders, appreciating the warmth, and stretched out on the hay bale. The smell of the dried grass was strong and made her drowsy. Closing her eyes, she wondered about her roots, whether they were agricultural and rural, or urban. What had she done in her former life? Probably not found shelter in a barn cuddled up on a bale of hay.

She drifted to sleep and woke with a start sometime later to the sound of raised voices.

Thoughts of the deputy who had stopped at Hattie's farm came to mind, but when she threw the covering aside and peered through a small crack in the barn door, she was more confused than ever.

Caleb's car was gone, and Mr. Gingerich stood in

the driveway arguing with someone whose back was to Becca. He wore a dark-colored hoodie pulled over his head, along with jeans and work boots.

The roar of her pulse sounded in her ears, making it difficult to hear what the two men were saying. She strained to see what was happening, then turned her ear toward the opening in the barn, hoping to pick up at least a portion of the heated discussion.

The sound of a fistfight made her stomach tighten. She leaned closer to the opening and spied Mr. Gingerich stagger back, his hand raised to his jaw.

The man who had struck him appeared in view and leveled a second blow, then another. With each punch, Becca grimaced, feeling the pain as the attacker continued to pummel the older man with his fists.

"Tell me what you know," the attacker demanded.

"I won't tell you anything." The older man struggled to maintain his balance. He raised his fists and refused to back down.

Becca searched the barn and found a pitchfork.

Peering from the barn, she saw Mr. Gingerich lay sprawled on the ground. The attacker knelt over the old man, his fist raised to strike again.

She slipped out the door, ran full steam toward the assailant and jabbed the pitchfork into his right thigh.

He screamed with pain, grabbed the handle and ripped it from her hands. With a fierce growl, he struck her with the back of the heavy steel tines.

She fell to the ground.

He kicked her side. She gasped.

The guy grabbed her arm and jerked her upright.

She struggled to free herself from his hold. "Let me go."

"Becky?" His eyes narrowed. "How'd you get here?"

Becky? She blinked, seeing the man who had chased her into the bull pasture. Shaggy beard, beady eyes and unkempt hair pulled into a man bun.

"I'm protecting an old man from you. You're despicable. Pick on someone your own age."

He looked confused. "Don't you recognize me? It's Kevin Adams." His voice softened ever so slightly as if he was trying to either assuage her anger or his. "The movie star. We're friends. Remember?"

The only thing she remembered was they weren't friends.

He smirked. "Everything will work out, hon, the way I said it would. Vanessa's gone so you can take her part in the next movie."

Her stomach soured. "I'm not your hon," she insisted. "I'm Becca Troyer."

"You're taking this Amish role too far. Cut it out, Becky. You made the costume and told me you felt Amish when you put it on, but you've got to end this foolish notion to actually become Amish."

"I don't know what you're talking about."

"Nicholas Walker—the producer—planned to fire Vanessa and give you a part in the film."

"I don't remember."

"Of course, you do. That's why you went to the trailer. He wanted to see you dressed Amish. You worked in the costume department and made the outfit. You told Nick it was totally authentic."

Kevin pushed her toward the car. "Let's go back to the studio. We can talk there."

She balked. "I'm not going anywhere with you."

"You're taking this too far, Becky." His tone hardened along with the glare in his eyes.

She jerked her hand from his hold. Snippets of conversation and flashes from the past played through her mind.

"You're wrong, Kevin." She steeled her gaze as she started to remember. "I didn't want anything to do with you or the movie business. I made the Amish costume and agreed to model it for the producer, but I had put in my notice and was leaving Montcliff Studio."

"You wanted to be a movie star."

She shook her head. "You wanted me in the film because you were tired of Vanessa and needed a new girlfriend, but I was never interested in you. Nor did I want to be a movie star."

"I'm tired of your foolishness." He grabbed her arm with one hand and shoved her forward. "You made me look like a fool to Mr. Walker."

"What about Vanessa Harrington, Kevin? You killed her. I went to Mr. Walker's office that night because you told me to. It was her blood on the rug."

He opened the van door and pushed Becca onto the passenger seat. She fought back. He fisted his hand and punched her stomach. She doubled over in the seat, the air whizzing from her lungs. She gasped, unable to breathe.

He lifted the bottom edge of his sweatshirt and pointed to the weapon stuck in his waistband. "Don't try to cross me, Becky."

Still struggling to breathe, she turned to glance at Mr. Gingerich's limp body. "Help…the old man," she gasped. "He's hurt…could freeze…to death."

"Which is exactly what I want." He slipped behind the wheel, turned the key, and the engine roared to life.

Despondent, she cowered away from him and glanced back, seeing Mr. Gingerich. *Protect him, Lord. Send help.*

On the opposite side of the entrance road, movement caught her eye. Someone in a buggy. He jumped to the ground and ran toward the van just as it pulled out of the drive.

Zeke!

Once again, snow started to fall. Zeke ran all the faster, his arms reaching for her.

Kevin pushed down on the accelerator. The van fishtailed onto the road heading up the mountain.

She looked back, her heart breaking seeing Zeke as he continued to run after her.

Tears streamed down her face. She wasn't Amish, which meant she couldn't be with him. If she couldn't be with Zeke, nothing else mattered.

"Becca!" Zeke screamed as he ran after the van, his boots slipping in the snow. The van accelerated even more and disappeared around the bend.

The man who had chased Becca had found her.

Although frantic to save her, Zeke had to ensure Levi Gingerich was all right. He ran back to the older man, relieved to find him sitting up and wiping his head.

The cut on his forehead had stopped bleeding. Zeke put his hand under the man's shoulders. "Mr. Gingerich, let me take you someplace safe."

"Zeke, you've got to get that guy. Name's Kevin Adams. He claims to be a movie star. He wanted to find Caleb. He'll come back. You've got to warn my son."

"We can call him."

The old man shook his head. "My home phone's not working, and I refuse to get a cell."

Zeke sighed with frustration. "It is not safe for you to stay here, sir."

"It's my house. I'm not leaving."

"I'll take you to my aunt's house."

"You mean Hattie's place?

"*Yah*. She will tend the cut on your forehead and give you something warm to eat."

Working quickly, Zeke eased Gingerich into the buggy and covered him with a blanket. Then he hurried Sophie down the hill. All the while, his heart was torn in two, thinking of Becca. Where had the guy taken her and what would he do to her?

Hattie heard their approach and was on the porch as they neared.

"What has happened?" she said, hurrying to help Levi down from the buggy.

Zeke filled her in. "Take care of Mr. Gingerich. I'll head up the mountain. I have to find Becca."

"Be careful, Zeke. The roads are icy."

"If Mike Frazier stops by, tell him I could use his help."

Once assured Levi and Hattie were safely inside with the doors locked, Zeke flicked the reins, encouraging Sophie onto the main road.

The low cloud cover and falling snow added to his concern about Becca, not knowing where she was and what the man planned to do with her.

"Giddyap, Sophie. We have to find, Becca."

Gray sunlight filtered through the dense clouds and barren trees. Glancing up, Zeke saw the waterfall in the distance. A flash of chrome from a vehicle appeared on the winding access road that led to the falls. His gut wrenched thinking of the boy who had fallen to his death, his body washed downstream and into the river, never to be found again.

"Gott," Zeke said, not knowing if his prayer would be heard. "Protect Becca and stop Kevin Adams. Forgive me for the mistakes in my past and let no harm come to Becca."

He clucked his tongue. Sophie increased her speed.

A fierce wind blew and the snow fell harder as they climbed in elevation. Zeke pulled his hat down farther on his head and blew into his hands to warm them. He had to get to the top of the mountain, but would he get there in time to save Becca?

Chapter Twenty-Three

Kevin was driving like a madman. Becca clutched the dash with one hand and the console with the other and gasped as they rounded each curve in the road. She looked out the passenger window at the sheer drop-off that rimmed the outside edge of the narrow roadway. Her stomach roiled, and she glanced away, unwilling to be frightened by the steep cliffs and river far below. She had enough to worry about with a crazed lunatic at the wheel.

"Slow down," she screamed. "You're going to kill us."

Kevin laughed. "That's the plan."

"What?"

"I'll make it look like you drove off the road. You took the van once you realized everyone knew you had killed Vanessa."

"I couldn't and wouldn't kill anyone."

"I'll tell people you wanted the lead role in the next movie. You made the Amish costume so Mr. Walker would give you the part. You had an Amish grandmother who taught you how to sew."

"So I truly am Amish." Relieved to confirm her ancestry, she was terrified of what might happened next.

"You lived with your grandparents more than a year, Becky, after your mother went to jail."

She wanted to cover her ears and drown out his voice. As much as she needed to remember her past, the fact that her mother was a criminal was too painful to bear.

"Once your grandparents died, you had no one. That's how you ended up working for the studio in the costume department. I was tired of Vanessa and wanted someone new. You weren't interested in me so I convinced Nick Walker to give you an acting role, hoping your feelings for me would soften."

"You tried to manipulate me, Kevin, but I wanted nothing to do with acting or with you."

"Vanessa got wind of my plan to convince Nick to give you an acting part. You know Vanessa. She had a temper and knew how to throw her weight around if someone tried to cross her."

Becca could see the carpet and the bloody weapon in her mind's eye. "You killed her, Kevin."

"I didn't kill her, but everything points to you being the killer."

"That's crazy."

"Maybe, except your fingerprints are on the letter opener."

"The letter opener with the Montcliff Studio logo on the shaft," she said, having a clearer vision of the murder weapon.

Kevin smiled. "You do remember."

"You killed Vanessa with the letter opener on the beige carpet with a lime green trellis design."

"Sounds like a kid's board game." He chuckled. "Vanessa tried to attack you."

"What?"

"She was in the office and overheard me and Nick talking about giving you a part in the next film. Vanessa thought Nick was going to give you *her* part. You stepped inside, never realizing Vanessa was there. She grabbed a marble statue off the bookcase and knocked you out. Then she found the letter opener and raised it to strike you."

Becca shivered. "But you killed her first."

"Actually, the producer killed her in self-defense. Vanessa turned on him. She knew Nick was no longer willing to put up with her tantrums."

"The sheriff will arrest both of you."

"We wiped the letter opener clean and then placed it in your hands so your fingerprints would be on it."

"Then you tried to clean the bloodstained carpet with bleach."

"I grabbed the wrong product. Instead of removing the bloodstain, it removed all the color. That's why we threw the rug over the ledge where you had fallen. I tried to catch up to you that night and saw you slip and fall. I thought you had died."

"No wonder you looked surprised when you saw me in town."

"You mean at the Cattle Auction?"

"You were the Amish man who chased me."

He nodded. "I was in costume for the filming of the trailer for the next movie. I had seen you walking along the road that first day and chased you into the pasture. Once I realized you were alive. I kept trying to find you. After Nick got back to the studio, we decided to make it look like you committed the murder. We were on the ledge soon after you and that Amish guy must have found the carpet."

"A rug won't prove I killed anyone."

"No, but the murder weapon will. We took the small quilt from your bedroom at the studio and wrapped the letter opener in it."

The green patched quilt she had made with her grandmother.

"The weapon bears your prints, Becky, which will prove you murdered Vanessa. The motive is clear. You wanted Vanessa's part in the next movie. We've thought of everything."

"What if Nick accuses you of being the killer?" she posed, hoping to burst his euphoria.

Kevin snickered, like a child, and patted his shirt pocket. "I videotaped Nick with my phone. He was in a rage and stabbed Vanessa over and over. He never saw me, but the video is proof in case he shifts the blame to me."

Knowing she was running out of time, Becca scooted closer to the door. As they rounded a curve, a gust of wind hit the van. Kevin struggled to keep the vehicle on the road.

Becca raised her leg and jammed her foot into Kevin's injured thigh where she had stabbed him with the pitchfork.

He groaned and lost control of the wheel. The car skidded across the icy roadway.

She screamed, fearing they would plummet over the edge.

Just in time, he turned the wheel toward the mountain. The van went into another skid.

Her heart stopped.

A giant boulder came up to greet them as they crashed into the side of the mountain.

Becca's head slammed against the dashboard. She moaned and glanced at the gauge on the console. Someone had inactivated both airbags.

Kevin lay slumped over the steering wheel.

She groped for the knob and pushed open the door. She had to get away.

The wind whipped around her head, tearing at her bonnet and sending it flying. Her outer cape billowed as the wind caught in its folds. She slipped and slid down the incline, needing to escape the man who had run after her that night in the woods.

She tripped. Her hands caught her fall, the ice on the roadway as cold as her chilling fear. She stumbled to her feet and continued on.

The car door opened. Footsteps sounded behind her.

"No," she screamed. Kevin grabbed her and threw her to the ground.

"You can't run from me, Becky. I've got to teach you a lesson. People will be upset when they learn you killed Vanessa and tossed her over the ledge. They'll also be upset when they find your body at the bottom of the waterfall. Or maybe they'll never find you."

"Kevin, please. I didn't do anything to hurt you."

"That's not true. You rejected me. You weren't interested in what I offered you. Sometimes I can't keep things straight, but I know one thing. You rejected me so you need to die."

Zeke saw the studio van that had crashed into a boulder on the side of the mountain. His breath caught in his throat.

Where is she? Where is Becca?

Peering down from the buggy, he looked through the open van door to the empty interior and flicked the reins. Sophie forged on. Her pace slow but steady as she labored along the narrow roadway.

Rounding the next bend, Zeke's heart stopped. He recognized the movie star from the photo Caleb had shown him. Kevin was standing near the top of the ledge, holding a gun to Becca's head.

Behind him, water spewed over the falls. Ice had formed on the edge of the rock, making it all appear surreal.

"Let her go." Zeke pulled back on the reins. "She has done nothing wrong."

Kevin laughed. "She rejected me to sew costumes. She wasn't even interested when I offered her a part in the next movie."

Fear flashed from Becca's eyes.

Zeke raised his voice over the roar of the falling water. "Take me as your hostage instead of her."

The man sneered. "Don't be a fool, Amish. Both of you are my hostages. Bring your buggy closer to the edge."

"Becca, move toward the mountain and away from the ledge." Zeke's voice was firm.

Kevin pushed her aside. "Do what he says, Becky. You'll be with your Amish boyfriend soon enough."

He motioned Zeke forward. "Bring the buggy closer."

Sophie pinned her ears back. She pawed the snow.

"Go on, girl," Zeke encouraged under his breath. "We will show this city slicker how smart you are."

Zeke encouraged her closer.

The movie star grabbed the harness. "Nice horse."

"Easy, Sophie," Zeke soothed.

Kevin pulled his phone from his pocket and motioned to Becca. "Get in the buggy with your boyfriend. I want to take your picture."

She shook her head. "I'm not moving."

"Do what I say, Becky. Now."

A car sounded behind them. Zeke let out a breath of relief and turned to welcome the new arrival, expecting to see Mike Frazier or one of the other sheriff's deputies. His gut tightened when he saw the Montcliff Studio logo on the side of the van.

Nick Walker, the producer, climbed from the vehicle, gun in hand. "What's going on, Kevin?"

"Just getting rid of our murderer and her boyfriend."

Nick pointed to Zeke. "Why'd you include him?"

"We'll say they were working together. It only makes our story better. We found Becky and tried to talk her into giving herself up, but she and her boyfriend headed to the waterfall. We'll call it Lover's Leap, just like in the movies. They couldn't face going to jail and a future without one another."

The producer scowled. "You're a fool, Kevin."

"What?" Anger flashed from the leading man's eyes. "I'm the one who stayed behind to clean up the mess you made."

"And ruined the carpet."

"I got rid of the rug and recarpeted the entryway. That kid from food services is our only problem."

Nick laughed. "I took care of Landers and the kid from food services won't make it down the mountain. I tampered with his car. Both of them knew too much. Their deaths are unfortunate but will not be tied to either of us." He pointed to Becca and Zeke. "Now we need to get rid of these two."

Zeke had expected law enforcement to come to their aid. Time was running out. Zeke could not rely on the sheriff or his men. He had to find a way to save Becca, even if it cost him his life.

Chapter Twenty-Four

Chilled to the core, Becca rubbed her hands over her arms and tried to think. She had to do something, but what?

Nick Walker glared at her.

"You killed Vanessa," she stated, hoping to throw him off guard.

He narrowed his gaze.

"You killed her," she continued. "Kevin told me."

Nick laughed nervously and glanced at the leading man. "You talk too much."

"We'll take care of them, Nick. I promise."

"You can't do anything right." The producer grabbed Becca's arm and shoved her toward the buggy.

"No!" She tried to jerk free.

Zeke leaped down to protect her.

The producer jammed his gun against her head. "Stay back, Mr. Amish, or she dies."

"Let her go," Zeke demanded, his hands fisted.

The producer laughed. "I thought the Amish were nonviolent. Read my lips. You breathe, and she dies."

He dragged Becca to the buggy still holding the gun

against her temple. "Get in. Now. Or I'll kill your boy-friend."

"You'll kill him anyway."

Kevin stood in front of the mare and jerked forward on the harness. "Come on. Nice horse."

"Back," Zeke commanded under his breath.

Sophie pinned her ears. She whooshed her tail and took a step back.

Nick twisted Becca's right arm behind her. "Climb in. Now."

Her left hand was numb from the cold as she tried to grab the metal arm rail. She raised her foot, but her shoe slipped on the icy step and she fell against So-phie's flank.

The mare reared up. Her front hooves nearly hit Kevin. He dropped the harness and jumped back. His feet slipped. He tried to right himself and flailed his arms. Zeke lunged around the buggy and reached for him, but not in time.

Kevin's eyes widened. His splayed fingers clawed at the icy ledge, unable to grab hold.

"No!" he screamed as he slipped over the edge.

Becca gasped and covered her mouth with her hand, fearing she would be sick.

Zeke seized the reins and backed Sophie away from the ledge. "Good, girl. Easy now."

The producer sneered. "I planned to kill Kevin. You saved me the trouble. We'll forget the buggy. Both of you can jump off the ledge. Kevin was right. We'll call this Lover's Leap."

Unable to comprehend his callous disregard for life, Becca moved toward him. Out of the corner of her eye, she saw Zeke rounding the far side of the buggy.

"You're evil," she shouted at the producer, flailing her arms as a distraction. "You killed Vanessa and Larry Landers and now you caused another person to die, but you won't get away with any of the crimes."

He laughed. "You're amusing, Becky, and much too righteous, especially since the police will learn you killed Vanessa as well as Kevin."

She took another step toward him. "Do you know what *righteousness* means, Mr. Walker?" She accentuated his name as if he were scum. "It means God-fearing and virtuous. A righteous person is decent and honorable, not like you."

"My, my, you might have an acting ability after all. What a shame you won't star in our next movie. Now get back with your Amish boyfriend."

He glanced toward the buggy and hesitated for half a second. Long enough for Zeke, who had inched around the rear of the buggy, to tackle him. The producer crashed to the icy ground with a thud. The gun flew from his hand.

A siren sounded. Zeke turned as Mike Frazier pulled his cruiser to a stop. The deputy jumped from the sedan, gun raised and at the ready.

Zeke quickly filled him in.

Mike cuffed the producer, read him his Miranda rights and then shoved him into the rear of his squad car. He secured the producer's weapon while Becca explained what Kevin Adams had revealed.

"Nicholas Walker killed Vanessa," she said. "They wiped the letter opener clean and put it in my hand so my prints would be on the shaft. Kevin tried to clean the rug and then threw it over the ledge."

"Our guys found the rug about an hour ago. They

used bleach on the main stain, but blood spatter was also found on other areas of the rug. We'll have the forensic guys check it out."

"Kevin's phone," Becca suddenly remembered. "He made a video that shows the producer stabbing Vanessa."

Mike Frazier glanced around. "So where's the actor and his phone?"

Zeke peered over the edge. "Lying on a ledge about twenty feet down. I have rope in the back of the buggy."

"You'd be crazy to go down the mountain in this weather," Mike said.

Zeke looked at the deputy and smiled. "Like old times, Mike, when we were kids."

"Don't do it," Becca pleaded. "It's too dangerous."

"The storm will only get worse. The wind's increasing. Our only chance to save Kevin is for me to go down now."

Zeke guided Sophie into a turn so the mare and the buggy were faced away from the cliff. He gave the reins to Becca, and then tossed his hat into the buggy and slipped on his heavy work gloves.

"Give me a hand, Mike. We did this when we were kids. We can do it again today. I can make a Swiss seat out of extra rope and use snaplinks to secure Kevin so we can haul him up."

Mike nodded. "It's worth a try, if you're willing to take the risk."

Working quickly, they anchored two ropes to the buggy. Mike helped Zeke thread another rope between his legs and around his waist to make a seat. Together they attached the rappelling ropes to the seat with a snaplink.

Once satisfied with the position of the ropes, Mike nodded.

Zeke glanced at Becca, then walked backward. He crouched low and disappeared over the edge.

Her heart nearly stopped, and she trembled, not only from cold but also from fear.

Gott, help Zeke. Protect him, she prayed silently.

She stood next to the buggy, holding Sophie's reins. "Steady, girl."

"He made it to the lower ledge," Mike shouted back to her.

"I found something else," Zeke called, his voice barely audible over the howling wind and the waterfall.

After what seemed like an eternity, she heard his voice again.

"Pull up."

"Let's go, Sophie," Becca said to the mare. "Come on, girl. Nice and slow."

Sophie shook her mane then took a step forward, then another and another.

The deputy worked the rope at the edge of the ledge.

Kevin's man bun came into view. Mike grabbed his shoulder and the rope that secured his arms and pulled him over the edge. The movie star appeared unconscious but still alive. Mike disconnected the ropes and threw them back to Zeke.

Becca held her breath.

"Pull." Zeke's voice.

She encouraged Sophie forward.

A face appeared, then a man's body.

Zeke!

Relief swept over her, and she blinked back tears of joy.

* * *

"He needs medical attention," Zeke shouted over the wind after assessing Kevin's injury. "We must get him down the mountain." Working quickly, Zeke and the deputy bundled the movie star into the squad car.

Zeke handed the deputy the cell phone. "This is what I also found on the ledge. Play the video, Mike. You will find out the truth about Vanessa Harrington's murder."

"I need the judge to okay a warrant, Zeke. Besides, it's too cold for a cell phone to work out here."

"The producer mentioned tampering with Caleb Gingerich's car. Do you know anything about him?"

Mike nodded. "His car was stalled on the side of the mountain. One of my deputies picked him up, along with his father from your aunt's house. Both of them were taken to the hospital for evaluation. As far as I know, they're both doing well."

Zeke nodded his thanks, then headed to his buggy.

Becca sat wrapped in blankets in the front seat, waiting for Zeke.

"You should go with the deputy," he said as he climbed in next to her. "His squad car has a heater."

She shook her head. "I'll stay with you."

Mike Frazier waved as he started down the mountain. Zeke flicked the reins and encouraged Sophie. More than anything, he wanted to pull Becca into his arms and hold her close, yet she looked tired and cold and probably still in shock after everything that had happened.

The initial blow to her head had been severe enough to block her memory. He feared more damage had been done today. When he glanced at her pretty face, his gut twisted, seeing the new bruises and scrapes, feeling responsible. If only he had worked harder to keep her safe.

"Thank you for all you did, Zeke," she said, her voice little more than a whisper. "I never wanted to be a bother."

He smiled weakly. "You bring joy to my life, Becca. You could never be a bother."

She rubbed her forehead. "I still don't remember everything from my past."

"Whatever happened in the past remains there. Today starts now. Who you are is who you are at this moment." He took her hand. "Much has happened today. You need some of Hattie's good cooking and a sound night's sleep. Tomorrow will be a new day."

As usual, Hattie saw them coming and stepped onto the porch as the buggy came to a stop.

"Oh, Becca, it is so good to see you. Come, dear, you need to sit near the stove. There's coffee and a pot of hot soup to warm you."

Zeke helped Becca down from the buggy. She was so light in his arms. He wanted to hold on to her forever and never let her go.

She glanced up at him questioningly.

"Go inside and get warm," he encouraged. "I'll take care of Sophie."

"Give her an extra treat for working so hard to get us down the mountain."

Zeke nodded, grateful to have heard the first spark of lightness in Becca's tone.

"Oh, Hattie." Becca glanced down at the green dress, as if seeing the smudged dirt and tears in the fabric for the first time today. "Look what I have done to this beautiful dress."

Hattie rubbed her hand over Becca's shoulder as if to soothe her worry. "We can always make more dresses, dear, as long as you are with us."

Becca smiled and followed Hattie into the house.

Zeke looked at the falling snow, feeling cold and alone and fearful of what Becca would decide to do with her life.

She was *Englisch*.

Amish men only marry Amish women. Zeke had some soul-searching to do tonight.

After feeding Sophie and ensuring the mare was warm and dry, he hurried inside. Becca had gone upstairs, claiming she was too exhausted to eat.

He missed her already. What would he do if she left him for good? The thought cut to his heart.

Chapter Twenty-Five

Zeke sat by the woodstove in the rocking chair after Hattie had gone to bed, reading from her Bible. The house was quiet, the only sound the crackling fire. Using the end iron, he rearranged the burning wood and threw another log into the stove, watching as the bright embers danced around the flames.

He shut the cast-iron load door and settled back in the rocker, turning again to Hattie's Bible, the worn pages bringing comfort.

Glancing up, he saw Becca standing in the open entryway to the kitchen. He placed the Bible on the side table and stood. "I did not hear you come downstairs."

"Hattie told me you were still up."

Becca's hair hung free around her shoulders. Her green eyes were filled with question.

"Hattie also told me that which I'm searching for may be right before me." She stepped closer.

"Decisions take time, Becca. Do not rush yourself."

"I wanted to know about my past so I would understand my future, but what I found confused me more."

"Your past is not important."

"Perhaps not, but you still need to know some of what I've remembered. I was born in Birmingham and my grandparents came from Ethridge, Tennessee."

"An Amish community is located there."

She straightened her spine and pulled in a deep breath. "I never knew my father. My mother was imprisoned in Montgomery for a drug offense and released last year."

"What about you, Becca?"

"I've held a number of jobs—waitress, supermarket cashier, retail clerk—before I took the seamstress job with Montcliff. When I put in my notice to leave the studio, my supervisor said she was pleased with my work and was ready to increase my pay."

"Then you plan to stay?"

"Not at Montcliff. Hattie said she enjoys my presence here."

He stepped closer. "There is someone else who enjoys your presence and everything else about you."

She tilted her head.

"You don't know much about me, Zeke."

"I know how you make me feel, Becca." He touched her hair and ran his fingers down her cheek. The confusion he had read earlier in her green eyes softened.

"I want to talk to your father."

He waited, not knowing what she else would say.

"I need to know if his district would welcome me."

"You wish to be baptized?" he asked.

She nodded. "Why would I look elsewhere when everything I've ever wanted is right in front of me?"

He smiled, his heart nearly bursting with joy. "I plan to talk to my *datt*, as well."

"Baptism?" she asked.

He nodded.

She touched her hand to his chest. "You will bring joy to your father's heart."

"And to my own. My only hesitation was not knowing what you would do."

"And now you know. Does that change anything?"

"It only makes me a very happy man." He gazed into her eyes and found them filled with longing. "If we are both to be Amish, we will have time for courting. Perhaps you would allow me to take you on a buggy ride?"

She laughed. "Only if you promise no trips to Lover's Leap. I want to stay away from waterfalls and icy roads."

"But Amish Mountain? You could live there?"

"*Yah*, I will stay with Hattie for now if her invitation stands."

He took her hand. "That is the near future, Becca, but I am looking far ahead."

She stepped closer. "What do you see?"

"I see my life as an Amish farmer, with children to bring laughter to my home, land to work, a faith to sustain me. Most important, I see a beautiful woman to walk with me into the future."

"Tell me more about the woman you see."

He touched her cheek and trailed his fingers around her neck. "I see chestnut hair and green eyes, high cheekbones and full lips that are meant for kissing."

"Are you sure?"

He nodded, then lowered his lips to hers. All the love that filled his heart burst forth like the bright embers in the fire.

He pulled her closer and kissed her again, deeply,

and again and again, never wanting anything to pull them apart.

Finally, she eased back. Her lips were swollen, her eyes soft and inviting, her cheeks flushed.

"I love you, Becca Troyer or Becky Taylor."

"You're sure?"

"Cross my heart."

Then he pulled her deeper into his embrace and continued to kiss her. The fire crackled and warmed the house all the while the snow fell outside and covered the world with a blanket of white. No matter what would come in the future, they would always be secure with *Gott*'s love and their love for one another.

"Marry me, Becca. I want to be with you for as long as *Gott* gives us."

"Oh, Zeke, that's what I want. To be with you always. The past is over and the only thing that matters is today and tomorrow and what we make of the future."

"A future together," he whispered before he kissed her again.

Epilogue

Sunshine poured through the bedroom window as Becca finished whipping the hem on the wedding dress, pleased with the blue-green fabric she and Hattie had found in town.

"It accents your eyes," Hattie had said, then insisted on paying for the material. "Plus, the wedding will be held at my house. It is the least I can do. You and Zeke have brought much joy to my life."

Warmed by Hattie's generosity, Becca held the dress up and smiled with approval at her own workmanship. Not taking pride but appreciating all her grandmother had taught her. She thought again of her loving *mammi* who had been that source of refuge in Becca's early life.

Over the last few months, her memory had slowly returned with a clear picture of the dysfunction that had surrounded her early years. Some memories had been hard to accept, yet with Hattie's and Zeke's help and with prayer, she had come to understand her wayward mother better and had forgiven her for the havoc she had created in Becca's younger days. If not for the firm foundation provided by her Amish grandparents, Becca's life would have turned out so differently.

"I am grateful," she said aloud, thinking of how the Lord had protected her and brought her to Amish Mountain. She hoped someday she and her mother would reconnect, if it was *Gott*'s will.

Stepping to the window, she saw Zeke hauling lumber toward the new house next door. As if sensing her gaze, he glanced up and smiled. She waved, her heart nearly bursting with gladness.

She hung the dress on the wall peg and hurried downstairs. The smell of fresh baked pastry filled the house with an aroma that made her mouth water.

"I finished the wedding dress," she announced as she entered the kitchen. Hattie pulled a pie from the oven, and Becca raced to place the cooling rack on the counter.

"Zeke and I can never thank you enough, Hattie, for all you've done and for insisting we have the wedding here."

"It gives me a reason to cook, *yah*? Less than a week away, and there is much to do. So many people will be here. Old friends, relatives. Everyone wants to take part in the celebration." Her eyes twinkled. "But I like a full house. Zeke's father is coming for lunch today. You can talk more about the wedding with him. I invited Annie Shrock."

"The widow who hosted the quilting I attended?"

"*Yah.* Her husband died last year. She is lonely. So is Zeke's father. He has mourned for my sister too long."

"And what about you, Hattie? Levi Gingerich seems to be stopping by more often these days since he asked forgiveness and returned to the faith."

Hattie blushed and turned back to the stove. "We were friends in our youth. I am glad to have him as a friend again."

"He seems like a new man."

Hattie nodded. "Thanks to Caleb's insistence that he go to a cardiologist. The medicine for his heart helped. He feels better and is able to do more."

"He is also happy about the way Zeke and Caleb repaired his home and the fences on his farm."

"*Yah*, and Caleb is helping him more and more. The young man remains *Englisch*, but we will see what the future will hold. At least he got rid of his sports car."

The future. Becca smiled, thinking of sharing her life with Zeke. "Do you need any help, Hattie?"

The woman made a shooing motion. "The midday meal is almost ready. Tell Zeke his father will be here soon."

Becca hugged Hattie, then raced outside to where Zeke was sanding a piece of wood. She stopped a few steps away to once again take in the house that would be their new home after the wedding.

Sensing her presence, he turned, dropped the sandpaper and opened his arms. She ran into his embrace, smelling the fresh cut wood and newly plowed Georgia soil in the distance.

"I did not know my future husband would be such an accomplished carpenter. You can do everything, Zeke. I have heard the townspeople talk. You climb mountains, you turn struggling acreage into a productive farm. You help your neighbors and have brought joy back to your father's heart. They also talk about how you and your dad worked with the new producer at Montcliff to ensure the studio provides wholesome films and a good working environment for its employees."

"Are you listening to town gossip, Becca?" His lips twitched playfully.

"I listen only to the truth, Ezekiel Hochstetler."

"Soon my time will be taken up with other endeavors," he teased.

She raised a brow. "What are you talking about?"

He winked. "A new husband must ensure his wife is well loved."

Her cheeks warmed and her heart skittered in her chest. "You are making me blush. What would your father say?"

"He would encourage me all the more. As he told me after church last Sunday, he is eager for grandchildren."

She snuggled into his arms. "Children will come in *Gott*'s perfect time. You told me to take each day as it comes, although I must admit our wedding cannot come soon enough."

"Another few days," he said. "The house will be finished just in time."

"Do Amish husbands carry their new brides over the threshold as the *Englisch* do?"

He laughed. "If this is something you want, I would be happy to carry you anywhere."

"The only place I want to be is with you, Zeke. As confused as my early life was, everything worked together to bring me to Amish Mountain. Looking back, I am able to accept my past because I know *Gott* was leading me to you and to this moment."

He looked down at her, his eyes filled with love that she knew would last forever. "And you are the reason I returned to the mountain, Becca. I knew in my deepest core that I would find you someday. You told me I had built a wall around my heart. You were right. You broke down that wall and saved me from becoming a bitter man. I was dying, but you brought me back to life."

"Just as you and Hattie gave me shelter and saved me when I didn't even know my name."

"We no longer need to look back, Becca, but only enjoy today and tomorrow and all the days ahead."

He gazed for a long moment into her eyes. The world stood still, and all she could see was the righteous man she loved. Then ever so slowly, he lowered his lips to hers.

A weaker woman would have died from the burst of love that exploded in her heart, but Becca had been strengthened by adversity and was strong in her commitment to make a wonderful life for her soon-to-be husband and the children *Gott* would provide.

Then she stopped thinking of anything except the warmth of Zeke's embrace and his kisses that, she knew, would continue to thrill her for the rest of her life.

* * * * *

Get 4 FREE REWARDS!

We'll send you 2 FREE Books plus <u>2</u> FREE Mystery Gifts.

FREE Value Over **$20**

Both the **Love Inspired®** and **Love Inspired® Suspense** series feature compelling novels filled with inspirational romance, faith, forgiveness, and hope.

YES! Please send me 2 FREE novels from the Love Inspired or Love Inspired Suspense series and my 2 FREE gifts (gifts are worth about $10 retail). After receiving them, if I don't wish to receive any more books, I can return the shipping statement marked "cancel." If I don't cancel, I will receive 6 brand-new Love Inspired Larger-Print books or Love Inspired Suspense Larger-Print books every month and be billed just $6.24 each in the U.S. or $6.49 each in Canada. That is a savings of at least 17% off the cover price. It's quite a bargain! Shipping and handling is just 50¢ per book in the U.S. and $1.25 per book in Canada.* I understand that accepting the 2 free books and gifts places me under no obligation to buy anything. I can always return a shipment and cancel at any time by calling the number below. The free books and gifts are mine to keep no matter what I decide.

Choose one: ☐ **Love Inspired**
Larger-Print
(122/322 IDN GRDF)

☐ **Love Inspired Suspense**
Larger-Print
(107/307 IDN GRDF)

Name (please print)

Address   Apt. #

City   State/Province   Zip/Postal Code

Email: Please check this box ☐ if you would like to receive newsletters and promotional emails from Harlequin Enterprises ULC and its affiliates. You can unsubscribe anytime.

Mail to the Harlequin Reader Service:
IN U.S.A.: P.O. Box 1341, Buffalo, NY 14240-8531
IN CANADA: P.O. Box 603, Fort Erie, Ontario L2A 5X3

Want to try 2 free books from another series! Call 1-800-873-8635 or visit www.ReaderService.com.

---

*Terms and prices subject to change without notice. Prices do not include sales taxes, which will be charged (if applicable) based on your state or country of residence. Canadian residents will be charged applicable taxes. Offer not valid in Quebec. This offer is limited to one order per household. Books received may not be as shown. Not valid for current subscribers to the Love Inspired or Love Inspired Suspense series. All orders subject to approval. Credit or debit balances in a customer's account(s) may be offset by any other outstanding balance owed by or to the customer. Please allow 4 to 6 weeks for delivery. Offer available while quantities last.

Your Privacy—Your information is being collected by Harlequin Enterprises ULC, operating as Harlequin Reader Service. For a complete summary of the information we collect, how we use this information and to whom it is disclosed, please visit our privacy notice located at corporate.harlequin.com/privacy-notice. From time to time we may also exchange your personal information with reputable third parties. If you wish to opt out of this sharing of your personal information, please visit readerservice.com/consumerschoice or call 1-800-873-8635. **Notice to California Residents**—Under California law, you have specific rights to control and access your data. For more information on these rights and how to exercise them, visit corporate.harlequin.com/california-privacy.

LIRLIS22R2

HARLEQUIN
PLUS

Announcing a **BRAND-NEW** multimedia subscription service for romance fans like you!

Read, Watch and Play.

Experience the easiest way to get the romance content you crave.

Start your **FREE 7 DAY TRIAL** at www.harlequinplus.com/freetrial.

HARPLUS0822

WE HOPE YOU ENJOYED
THIS BOOK FROM

LOVE INSPIRED
INSPIRATIONAL ROMANCE

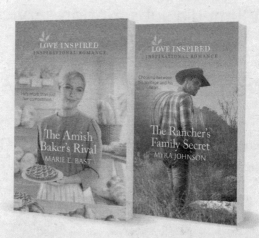

Uplifting stories of faith, forgiveness and hope.

Fall in love with stories where faith helps
guide you through life's challenges, and discover
the promise of a new beginning.

6 NEW BOOKS AVAILABLE EVERY MONTH!

LIHALO2021